BREATH LIKE WATER

Books by Anna Jarzab
available from Harlequin TEEN/Inkyard Press

Red Dirt
Breath Like Water

BREATH LIKE WATER

ANNA JARZAB

inkyard
press

Recycling programs
for this product may
not exist in your area.

ISBN-13: 978-1-335-05023-6

Breath Like Water

This edition published by arrangement with Harlequin Books S.A.

For questions and comments about the quality of this book, please contact us at CustomerService@Harlequin.com.

Inkyard Press
22 Adelaide St. West, 40th Floor
Toronto, Ontario M5H 4E3, Canada
www.InkyardPress.com

Printed in U.S.A.

For all the beautiful dreamers.

"Does the tide hurry, seeking something,
and never give up? O I the same."

—WALT WHITMAN

PROLOGUE

FINA World Aquatics Championships
Budapest, Hungary
Women's 200m Intermediate Medley Finals

The water is breathing. At least, that's how it seems. I've always imagined it as a living thing, benevolent and obedient and faithful. A gentle beast at first, like a pony, but over time something faster. A thoroughbred, maybe. A cheetah sprinting across a flat, grassy plain.

But, of course, the water isn't breathing—it's rippling, with the echoing wakes of eight elite swimmers as they poured themselves into one last swim, one final chance to grab the golden ring. Now they're gone, and in half a minute, I'll be right where they were, reaching for my own shot at glory.

This is my first international competition. I turned fourteen in May, so I'm the youngest member of Team USA. In January, nobody knew who I was, but by my birthday I'd broken the women's 200 IM record in my age group twice and finished first in the same event—my best—at World Championship Trials. My summer of speed earned me a lane here in Budapest. All I have to do now is not screw it up.

Earlier, in the semifinals, I clocked my fastest time ever in this event, and I'm coming into finals seeded third overall. I have to beat that by almost a second if I want to win.

The announcer introduces me over the loudspeaker. I wave to the crowd but my mind is far away, already in the pool, charting out my swim. I shake out my limbs and jump to get my blood pumping, then climb onto the block. I adjust my goggles, my cap, my shoulders. These little rituals feel solid and reliable. The rest is as insubstantial as a dream you're aware of while you're dreaming it.

"Take your mark—"

The signal sounds and I'm in the pool. My mind lags half a second behind my body, registering every breath, stroke and turn only after it happens.

First: butterfly, arms soaring over the water, fingertips skimming the surface.

Then: backstroke, concentrating on the lines in the ceiling while waves boil around me.

After that: breaststroke, stretching, pulling, kicking, gliding.

And finally: freestyle, bursting off the wall like a racehorse released from a starting gate.

I go six strokes without taking a breath and snap into my highest gear for a mad-dash last push, coasting along the razor's edge of my perfectly timed taper. No thinking, just doing. No drag, only flight.

My hand touches the wall, and my eyes begin to burn. It's over. Instinctively, I look for my coach. Dave's on the sidelines, frowning, and I think: *I blew it.*

He notices me watching and breaks into a rare grin. Hopeful, I turn to the board. I can't find my name, so I force myself to look at the top spot. There it is: *RAMOS*. Number freaking one.

I whoop and blow kisses at the people in the stands. They're on their feet, chanting, "USA! USA!" American flags billow like sheets.

It cost my parents a fortune to fly themselves and my sister all the way to Europe on such short notice, credit cards stretched to their limits. I can't even see them in the crowd, but I know they're somewhere in that jubilant crush of people. My heart feels so full it's like a balloon about to pop.

As soon as I'm out of the water, Dave wraps me in a bear hug.

"How do you feel?" he asks.

"Great!" I sigh and shake out my arms. "Tired."

"Gold, Susannah," he says. His voice is tight with something like awe.

Gold. It doesn't feel real yet—won't, until that medal hangs around my neck, until I can hold it in my hands while the national anthem blooms through the natatorium speakers with patriotic brio. Maybe not even then. I could have more wins here, but right now, this seems like more than enough.

"You're a world champion," Dave says. "Next, I'm going to make you an Olympian."

*Freshman Phenom Flops Flat into Sophomore Slump:
What Happened to Susannah Ramos?*

By Kris McNamara
Posted July 25

It's a familiar story: a kid with some talent breaks out for a split second way too early in their career, then disappears from the rosters, never to be heard of again. Sometimes it's an injury, sometimes they can't handle the pressure and sometimes it is plain old biology dragging them down by the heels, which is what seems to have happened to Susannah Ramos.

You remember her. The fourteen-year-old wunderkind who came out of nowhere two years ago and hopped from one national competition to the next, tearing up the pool in the 200 IM, then took home a gold from Budapest?

Well, it looks like all the up-and-comers who were quaking in their flip-flops over Ramos's meteoric rise can rest easy. The Illinois swimmer, who enters her sophomore year next month, hasn't placed in a single national competition since her world championship win, and though she's got a full schedule of events at the upcoming GAC Invitational, she seems unlikely to fare any better on her home turf. If she has any hopes of triumph at next year's US Olympic team trials in Omaha, she's got a long way to go.

You have only to look at a recent picture of her to figure out why. A growth spurt during this year's long-course season transformed Ramos from a petite powerhouse into a broad-shouldered Amazon, and her new build seems to be weighing her down in the water. It's a sad fact of the sport that some swimmers peak young and never find their way off the time plateau. Surely Ramos, who competes with the Gilcrest Aqualions Club, hopes she won't be one of them, but the statistics aren't on her side.

For the sake of her college prospects, here's hoping she can beat the odds.

CHAPTER ONE

330 days until US Olympic Team Trials

THERE'S NOTHING LIKE THE MOMENT A RACE BEGINS. IT'S THE highest height of the roller coaster, the top of the drop, all potential energy and anticipation.

That powerful feeling of launching off the block is my favorite thing about swimming, the weightlessness of flight before slipping neatly into the water. Despite all the disappointment of the past eighteen months, that excitement right before the start never left me. Today is no exception.

The simple act of climbing onto the block floods my body with adrenaline. My vision narrows, and all the noises of the pool—the slap of waves against the gutters, the shouting from the stands, the voice of the announcer as he calls out the names and positions of the swimmers already in the water— recede like a tide until I can hear nothing but the sound of my own breathing.

The 400 IM relay starts with the backstroke, and the breast-stroke comes next. The third leg of this race—the butterfly—belongs to me. Jessa's behind me, hands on her hips, dripping wet and still panting; she started us off strong, touching the wall first with one of her best backstroke splits to date. Casey, our anchor, stands to the side, watching and waiting for her turn. Amber's in the pool now, holding on to Jessa's lead with her high-velocity whip kick, coming at me full speed.

My skin starts to tingle, not from anticipation but from a sudden sizzling lightning bolt of fear, the fear of screwing up that blossoms inside me like an infinitely expanding fractal. That fear is an old enemy, and yet sometimes startlingly new. Even now, when I should know what to expect, it sneaks up behind me and leaps on my back, knocking the air from my lungs and wrapping its arms around my chest so tightly that I can barely breathe.

But there's nothing I can do about it—I'm already on the block. As Amber closes in on the wall, I make the calcula-tion, that inexplicable formula learned through what seems like a million years of racing. I give it *one Mississippi, two Mis-sissippi, three*—then I jump.

The moment I hit the water, instinct tells me something's off, but everything *feels* okay. I'm an arrow beneath the sur-face; the momentum from my dive, my painstakingly per-fected streamline and my powerful dolphin kick are enough to get me to the fifteen-meter mark before my head breaks the waterline.

Arms back, then out, and then I'm flying.

My muscles are tense, and the first few strokes are a strug-gle while I search for my rhythm. Once I find it, my body melts into the swim so naturally that it comes as more of a surprise than a relief. I haven't felt this good, this capable, in months. Even my left shoulder, which sometimes bugs me, isn't a problem today. Fear loosens its grip, and a rush of water carries it away.

By the first turn, I'm feeling cautiously optimistic, and by the second I'm almost hopeful, though I can tell from quick spot checks that my creakiness off the start has lost me some of Jessa and Amber's lead. I'll make it up. I've done it before; I can do it again. Otherwise, what has all of this been for?

The surge of confidence pushes me harder into each stroke, and by the final lap I've caught up to the swimmer on my left, who passed me at the midpoint of the race. I put everything I have into that final sprint and slam into the wall like it's done something to me. Like I'm punishing it.

Casey explodes off the block, soaring over my head. I heave myself out of the water, limbs shaking with the aftershocks of enormous effort. It's a familiar, gratifying feeling, one that reminds me that, whatever happens, I worked my ass off. *No hay peor lucha que la que no se hace*, my abuela always says. There's no worse struggle than the one that never begins.

I may be struggling, but there's no denying I began a long time ago. And still, here I am.

The first thing I usually do after a race is look for Dave, but this time I'm too busy cheering for Casey as she tears up the pool, scraping out a lead of half a body length. Everything happens so fast; it's not until she jams the heel of her palm into the timing pad that I realize we're winning. That we've *won*.

I turn toward Dave, beaming with a mixture of shock and

pride, expecting to see a look of, if not joy, then certainly approval on his big, ruddy face.

But he isn't smiling, he's glaring—at me.

What? I mouth.

He holds up his left hand and creates a circle with his pointer finger and thumb. At first, I think he's telling me everything is OK, but then he turns his hand over, giving me the same gesture except upside down, and I realize he's literally spelling it out for me: *d. q.*

I shake my head and exchange a bewildered look with Jessa and Amber. Casey's still in the water, accepting tepid congratulations from the girls we beat.

Over the PA, the announcer broadcasts our first-place finish. Dave must be wrong. I replay the race in my head, searching for any mistake I might've made, and come up empty. My times have taken a hit, but I'm impeccably trained, and I know the rules.

Except…there's that weird feeling I had when I entered the water, that something was wrong. It hits me again and this time I can't shake it. I feel suddenly exposed, like in one of those dreams where you look down to realize you're naked. I've always stood out on a pool deck, even before I shot up six inches, because I'm one of the few brown kids on a mostly white team. But this is different; it feels like everyone knows something I don't, and they're all waiting to see the truth crash down on me.

It's excruciating.

Dave points at one of the officials who was assigned to watch our lane for infractions as he scurries over to the judges' table. They huddle, whispering, then break apart. Dave turns his finger to the ceiling and, as if on cue, the announcer gets back on the PA.

"Ladies and gentlemen, the judges have disqualified the Gilcrest Aqualions for a false start by Susannah Ramos on the butterfly leg of the 400-meter intermediate medley relay. The first-place finish in that race has been awarded…"

I stop listening as a wave of hot shame pours over me. Amber puts a gentle hand on my shoulder.

"Don't beat yourself up," she says. "It happens."

"Yeah, I know," I say with forced lightness. Sometimes I wish she weren't so nice. I don't deserve her comfort, or anybody else's. I failed them. I *failed*, yet again.

My muscles are shaking from exertion and I feel kind of faint. I need to warm down, drink some water, scarf an energy bar. But I can't move. My gaze locks on Dave.

He's looming over the judges' table, arguing against the DQ the way he would for anyone else—wild gestures, flying spittle, red-faced bluster, the whole pageant drama. But I can tell his heart's not in it. It's not the judges he's angry with; it's me.

After the judges have calmly and firmly told him to get over it and go away, Dave stalks over to me. I wrap my goggles around my hand, tight enough to hurt, and stand my ground with my chin up and my mouth clamped shut. There's nothing Dave has say to me that I'm not already thinking. He can't make me feel worse than I already do.

"Disqualified!" he shouts, swinging his clipboard like he's about to hit me with it, though he doesn't. "At our own *fucking* meet!"

I take a deep breath. "I know. I'm so sorry."

"What the *hell* was that?" he asks, loud enough for everyone around us to hear. Amber, Jessa and Casey wisely make themselves scarce.

"It was an accident," I tell him. "I made a mistake."

"A false start isn't a *mistake*—it's a fuckup," Dave hisses. "You're too old for this shit!"

My jaw is clenched so tightly that my head starts to ache. "I didn't do it on purpose. It won't happen again."

Dave folds his arms across his chest. The tattoo on his bicep peeks out from under his sleeve: Olympic rings. His medals, two bronzes and a silver, hang in frames on the wall of his office, not twenty feet from where we're standing. Every time I wonder why I put up with this sort of treatment, I tell myself: *He's an Olympian. He makes Olympians. That is why I'm here.*

He scowls at me like I'm a speck of dirt on his shoe. I've grown a lot in the last year, but I'll never be as tall as him. No matter how old I am, he'll always look down at me.

"It will happen again," he snaps. "Or something else will. For the past year it's been one problem after the next, except this time, it's not just you—your teammates are suffering because of what you did. That win was theirs, and you lost it."

"The win was ours," I remind him. "And so was the loss. I swam that race, too."

"You might as well not have. I could've put one of those plastic duck toys in the pool in your place and it probably would've had better splits!"

I'm used to getting dressed down by Dave. It happens all the time. But the insult hits me so hard that I take a step back, reeling like he's smacked me.

"I had a good swim," I protest.

"You had an average swim," Dave sneers. "Which was worthless because it didn't count. Most of the time, you can't even manage that. You'd better figure out if you really want this, Susannah, because it doesn't seem like it. And even if you do, I'm starting to wonder if you have what it takes. I really don't think I can help you."

Dave points at me with his clipboard. "You," he says, "are becoming a waste of my time."

Then he turns and walks away. I feel flattened, but I can't just stand here—I have to get out, *now*.

I head for the locker rooms with my gaze locked on the tile, determined not to look at anyone, afraid they might be looking back, that they might see how upset I am. How ashamed. There's a sign in Dave's office that says *Feel your feelings all you want, just don't feel them in front of anybody else.* It's an unofficial GAC rule: on the pool deck, only triumph is welcome. You deal with failure alone.

Of course, that applies only to swimmers. Dave can feel and do and say whatever he wants, whenever he wants, *wherever* he wants, and we're supposed to take it. Rage at the injustice of it tears at my throat as I hurry to get someplace I can be alone. I'm barely watching where I'm going and I almost slam into someone outside the girls' locker room.

Large hands wrap themselves around my shoulders to prevent impact. I glance up reflexively to see who they belong to, then wish I hadn't.

The guy is a stranger, mostly. I don't know his name, but all the swimmers my age in this region tend to look familiar after so many years in the endless wash, rinse, repeat cycle of elite competition. And he *is* a swimmer; if the racing suit didn't tip me off, his body would have. He's tall and lean, long-limbed and broad-shouldered, sleekly muscled in the way of those who are born for the water.

Okay, so he's hot; a lot of swimmers are. I'm not oblivious, but I don't spend seven hours a day, six days a week in the pool for the eye candy. I don't need another distraction. There's enough getting in the way of my swimming as it is.

Right now, this particular swimmer is getting in the way of my escape.

"Sorry," I mumble, avoiding his eyes. I step back, and he releases me. "If I could just—"

I gesture toward the entrance to the locker room.

"Sure," he says, stepping aside to let me pass.

His voice is so rich and deep it surprises me. Curiosity momentarily supersedes embarrassment and I take a good look at him.

Despite the voice and the body, which make him seem older than he can be if he's competing in this invitational, there's something endearingly boyish about his face. His cheekbones are so high they have summits, but there's a soft roundness to his jaw, and his blue eyes are wide and expressive. His hair is a gorgeous red–gold color that flares under the natatorium's bright fluorescents.

He's more than hot—he's handsome. Which, for some dumb reason, makes the fact that he's caught me at such a low moment so much worse.

"Hey, are you o—"

I brush past him and dart into the locker room before he can finish his sentence. In an empty bathroom stall, I sit and cover my face with my hands. The air is heavy with the scent of chlorine and the smell of towels left to molder on a bath-room floor. It makes me gag, but I force myself to take long, ragged breaths through my nose. Tears threaten, but they don't fall. I refuse to cry about this.

When I went through puberty and started slowing down, I decided the only way I was going to get back on top was by becoming a machine: ruthlessly efficient, tireless, relentless.

Machines don't cry. They just tick on, ever forward. So that's what I'm going to do.

CHAPTER TWO

330 days until US Olympic Team Trials

MY PARENTS HAVE NEVER SEEN DAVE GO OFF ON ME BEFORE, and they're furious. They're all fired up to call and give him hell as soon as we get home from the invitational.

"He can't talk to you like that!" Dad fumes, crashing around our kitchen in search of the GAC phone book. Our eight-year-old mutt, Lulu, follows at his heels, confused by all the excitement. She barks and whines until Dad snaps, "¡Cállate!"

I grab Lulu and bury my face in the long, caramel-colored fur of her neck. Not much has the power to cheer me up when I'm feeling bad, but my animals always do.

"I think you need a bath, Lu," I whisper in her ear. She kind of stinks. I'll wash her tomorrow, even though it's Nina's turn.

Lulu licks my hand and turns to look at me, and I swear to God she smiles. I love dogs.

Dad mutters something to himself in Spanish, then shouts, "You're just a kid! I could kill him!"

And he's my levelheaded parent. Mom looks like she's about to punch someone.

"It's not a big deal," I insist. It hurt, and it was embarrassing, but if I crumble after every setback I'll never make it through the season, let alone to the Olympics.

"It's a big deal to us," Mom snaps, so sharply that I wince. Her expression softens and she puts a gentle hand on my wrist. "We're trying to protect you, mija."

"I don't need protection," I say. Lulu whines and rests her head on my knee. "Dave's right. I keep screwing up. It's like I'm not good anymore."

It costs me a lot to admit that to them. My parents have always been supportive of my swimming, but wary of it, too. They think it demands way more than someone my age should be expected to give.

They'd never say it, but I know there's a part of them, deep down, that wishes I'd quit.

"You're still good, Susannah," Dad assures me, but I can tell he's only half listening. He's too busy digging around in the bottom of a junk drawer.

"You're one of the best swimmers on that team," Mom says.

"Not anymore," I say.

"Who's better than you?"

"Sarah. Casey. Lauren. *Jessa.*"

"You're at their same level," Mom argues. "And you don't compete in the same events."

"Doesn't matter. They're going to Nationals and I'm not."

"There's still time to qualify," Mom reminds me. "And you

could've gone to Juniors if you wanted. We would've found a way to swing it."

"What's the point? I can't make the team." I stroke Lulu's head. "It wasn't worth the expense."

Because I've competed in an individual Olympic event at World Championships, even though it was two years ago, I'm not eligible for the US Junior Nationals team. One of the many ways in which that stupid gold medal has ruined my life.

Not that I want to be on the Junior Nationals team. It's Nationals or nothing. But I don't have the times right now to qualify for the meet, let alone be one of the top six in an event to make the roster.

Dad yanks the battered GAC handbook out of a cabinet and waves it triumphantly.

"I'm calling Dave *right now*," he says. "Where's my phone?"

"Charger in the living room, I think," says Mom. Traitor.

"Dad, please don't," I beg. "It's over now; it doesn't matter anymore."

What I don't tell them, because it'll only make them angrier, is that if Dad goes off on Dave, Dave will take it out on me. If I'm lucky, I'll just get Punishment—extra laps at the beginning and end of every practice until he figures I've learned my lesson.

But he'll probably find a better way to penalize me, something more psychological and insidious. He's been known to freeze out swimmers he's not happy with, neglect them in practice and ignore them in competition. Just one look from him has the power to make me wither inside. My life goal is to make it to the Olympics; my daily goal is to stay on Dave's good side.

"What kind of parent would I be if I let a grown man yell at my daughter in front of hundreds of people and said nothing?" Dad asks.

"A swim parent," my older sister says, appearing in the doorway with a dog-eared copy of *The Glass Menagerie* in her hand. Nina wasn't at the pool today because she had play practice, and anyway, she doesn't come to my meets anymore.

"Most of the kids on that team, their parents would be the ones yelling," Nina says. "If you rush to Susannah's defense, she'll look weak."

Mom and Dad stare at Nina, appalled, but they know she's not wrong. We've all seen the way certain people—my friend Jessa, for example—get treated by their winning-obsessed parents. As if they have more riding on their son or daughter's performance in the pool than their kid does. That kind of unreasonable preoccupation has never made sense to Mom and Dad.

"That's ridiculous," Dad says. "Susannah's not weak, she's *sixteen*. He can't beat her up because she made a mistake. She's not his employee. *We* pay *him* to train her, and that team's not cheap."

"Hector," Mom says in warning. She squeezes my hand. "It's not about the money."

Dad sighs. "Of course it's not. I didn't mean it like that."

"We want to do what's right for you, Susannah. Can you let us do that, please?"

"No," I say. Nina chuckles, and Dad shoots her a *you're not helping* look.

"Overruled," Mom says.

Dad disappears into the living room to find his phone. I

want to scream, but I know how that would go over. I rest my forehead on the table. Nina gives me a condescending pat on the shoulder. Mom swats her away and rubs my back. Lulu curls up at my feet and rests her chin on my toes.

"It's going to be okay," Mom says. "Dad's only trying to help. We love you, mija. All we want is for you to be happy."

"I would be *happy* if you and Dad would back off and let me make my own decisions."

"You make a lot of your own decisions," Mom says. "Maybe too many."

"What's that supposed to mean?"

"It means that you're our child and we get a say in what goes on in your life," Mom says. "And don't you dare speak to me like that—I'm your mother. You were raised better. Both of you."

"What did I do?" Nina asks.

"You inserted yourself in something that wasn't your business," Mom tells her. "Now go to your room, please. Susannah and I need to talk."

"I'm not in the mood to talk," I say.

"It sounds like you're in the mood to be grounded," Mom says. "Is that what you want?"

I roll my eyes. "Ground me, I don't care. I'm going to take a shower."

"Dinner in half an hour," Mom says firmly as I trudge up the stairs.

I toss my swim bag on my bedroom floor and kick it into the closet. We get a break between the GAC Invitational and the start of school, so I won't be needing my equipment for two weeks. Shutting it all away, if only for a little while, feels more satisfying than I expected.

As I close the closet door, I catch a glimpse of myself in the full-length mirror I put away when I started to hate the sight of my reflection. When I won gold in Budapest, I was slim and hydrodynamic. I slipped through the water like a minnow, a flash of quicksilver between the lane lines.

Then I got older and everything changed. I grew everywhere, shooting up to five-eleven, widening at the hips and shoulders, filling out in the chest—the genes that made my mother's beautiful curves and gave my dad his height finally expressing themselves.

You'd think I'd be grateful for the increased wingspan and the size-ten feet and the boobs Nina would kill for, but I didn't know how to handle my big new body in the water. It won't move like it did before. It's slow and cumbersome and useless. I thought once I got used to it, I'd get back to where I was, but it's been over a year and that hasn't happened. I'm starting to give up hope that it ever will.

A high-pitched *mew* draws my attention to the two gray cats sitting in the window. Frick and Frack are brothers, a pair of Russian blues that we rescued when a family in the neighborhood moved abroad. They're the gentlest cats we've ever owned, so docile you can pet their teeth, and they don't mind being held, which is good because I could use a cat hug right now.

I pick up Frick and cuddle him for a second, then carry him to the corner of the room to check on Frida and Horace. Frida is my cockatiel; she's a rescue, too, in a way. The senior community where my abuela lives now doesn't allow pets, so we took her when Bela moved. I tried to train Frida to speak, but the only thing she says is "Hola, Bela." She whistles "Yankee Doodle Dandy," too; Bela taught her that. Horace is the only animal in the house I raised up from a baby. He's a box turtle.

Not counting family, there's nothing I care about more than swimming, but animals come a close second. If I'm lucky, my career will last into my twenties, but once it's over I think I'd like to be a vet.

Instead of heading to the shower, I lie down on my bed, shut my eyes and let the exhaustion I've been holding at bay wash over me. Everything that happened today—the false start, Dave's insults, that boy who tried to comfort me—pushes its way into my head.

I bury my face in a pillow. Frack joins Frick and me on the bed. The two of them crawl on top of me and paw at my hair like they're trying to braid it.

How are you doing? Amber texts. I tell her I'm fine and put my phone on silent.

Fighting with Mom and Dad is the worst. I can't seem to find a way to make my parents understand how badly my slowdown has broken my heart. For years, the Olympics has been the one thing I've wanted, the one thing I'd give anything to have. I've worked hard for it. I've made sacrifices.

But so have my family. What Dad said about paying for the team sits under my skin like a splinter. Swimming is an expensive sport, and we're not poor, but we're not rich. Dad teaches history at a local college, but when I started getting good, he took a second job waiting tables at his cousin's restaurant. He said it was to help Miguel, but I'm not stupid.

His tips go straight into a checking account reserved for my swimming expenses.

It's one thing to suffer for my sport and another thing altogether to watch my family suffer, too. Nina skipped the junior class ski trip last year because it cost too much. Dad's car is super old, the house could use a new roof and we've never taken the trip to Mexico that Mom keeps talking about. I travel around the country to compete, but most of the time my family stays home, because we can't afford airfare or accommodations for more than one person, and Mom and Dad can't miss work.

There are days when giving up seems like the only reasonable solution. But if I do that, I'd be throwing away all the opportunities Mom and Dad have scrimped and saved to give me.

And worse, if I quit, I don't know what I'd have left. Who I'd *be*.

How do you even begin to mourn the death of a dream?

I don't come down for dinner. Maybe I'm sulking, but I'm also trying to avoid hearing how Dave reacted when Dad read him the riot act. I know I'm in for it when I return to practice, but I'd rather not confirm that right now.

I burn five thousand calories a day, though—I can't skip meals. When the house is quiet, and I'm sure everyone else has gone to bed, I sneak downstairs to raid the refrigerator.

There's a plate of chicken with beans and rice covered in cling wrap waiting for me. The sight of it puts a lump in my throat. I know my parents want what's best for me. If it's swimming, if it's the Olympics, that's great. But if it's not, if it's something else, that's fine by them, too. For better or worse, swimming doesn't affect how they see me. They would love me the same no matter what.

But swimming is a part of me—the biggest part of me—and the fact that it's irrelevant to them makes me wonder: Who is it they think they love?

While I'm heating up my dinner, I notice a light on in the living room. Mom's a paralegal, and last year she started going to law school in the evenings and on weekends. She spends every night she's not in class studying, often until very late. More than once I've come downstairs before morning practice to find her passed out on the coffee table, dark curly hair fanned out over her books.

I put the kettle on, then sit down to eat while the water boils. Frick and Frack tumble into the kitchen. They circle my ankles under the table, waiting for something to drop.

"You have food in your bowls," I tell them. They've learned bad habits from Lulu. The three of them eat their own food only after we've all gone to bed, when all hope of scraps is gone.

When I'm finished, I enter my dinner into my calorie counting app, then slip the dirty plate into the dishwasher and start the cycle. The whoosh of water as it swirls around the machine is soothing.

Before the kettle can screech, I grab it and pour hot water into two mugs. Mine says *I love the smell of chlorine in the morning*. It was a team gift from the GAC Boosters a couple of years ago.

Mom's sitting on the floor in front of the coffee table, hunched over her books. I set a mug down in front of her.

She looks up, blinking at me like she just wandered out of a dark tunnel into the sun.

"Oh, hi," she says, rubbing her eyes. "Is that for me?"

"It's energy tea. Figured you could use it."

I sit on the couch. Frick and Frack tussle briefly for the spot in my lap. Frack, who's slightly larger and way bossier, wins as always.

"Gracias, mi amor." Mom grabs her tea and comes to sit next to me. Frick wastes no time curling up into a ball on her thighs.

"De nada."

I wish I knew more Spanish. Mom and Dad are both second-generation Mexican American, and they grew up in a primarily Latino neighborhood where it was the language you used with your family and community. They raised Nina and me in the suburbs, and we speak mostly English at home. I've been taking Spanish in school, but no amount of studying can give me the confidence to engage in entire conversations. Nina, contrarian that she is, takes French.

Mom nods at my mug. "That's not energy tea, is it? You need sleep. You're very cranky."

I shake my head. "Chamomile."

"Good girl." She takes a big sip. "Ah. I can feel the neurons firing already."

I laugh. "I don't think I'll need tea to get to sleep tonight."

"It was a long day." Mom puts an arm around me. I let my head fall against her shoulder. "You have a lot of those, kiddo."

"I know it's not easy on you guys, either," I say. "Between practices and competitions and travel and equipment and membership fees and Boosters meetings—"

"And the bake sales!" Mom says. "All those freaking bake sales."

"I know it's not just me who's giving everything up for this silly dream," I say.

"Oh, mija." Mom hugs me, jostling the dozing cats, who glare at her resentfully. "It's not silly. It's a beautiful dream. And we're not giving *everything* up. It's our pleasure as your parents to be able to provide you with what you need. It's all worth it, a million times over, as long as you're happy."

"Thanks for not asking me if I'm happy right now." If she did, I don't know what I'd say.

"I know sometimes it can be hard to tell. There are nights I sit down to my homework at the end of a miserable day and I think: *Why am I doing this? Is this really what I want?* But the next day, the sun rises, I go to work and I remember how much I want to be a lawyer—so much I was willing to return to school at my age and take weekend classes for the next eight years and go into debt that will take eight hundred more years to pay back." Mom kisses the top of my head. "I know you think we can't understand, but I imagine that's kind of how you feel."

"Pretty much." Except my debt isn't just financial, and it'll take my whole life to pay back. But there is one way I can start to make a dent in everything I owe them.

I shift so that I can look at Mom. "You know it's not just about the Olympics. If I can swim well enough over the next few years, I'll get a scholarship. Swimming could pay for college."

After all the money my parents have spent on my swimming, I can't bear the thought of them taking out loans to finance my education. I'm not their only child.

"I wish you didn't have to worry about that," Mom says, but she doesn't tell me not to worry.

Mom gives my shoulder one last squeeze. It hurts a bit actually; I never warmed down my muscles after my last race, and I'm feeling sore.

"Time for me to go back to work," she says. "And you need to go to bed. Did you eat?"

I nod.

"Then get some sleep," she says. "Tomorrow the sun will rise, and you need to be ready for it."

CHAPTER THREE

314 days until US Olympic Team Trials

DAVE BANGS HIS CLIPBOARD WITH THE HEEL OF HIS HAND TO get our attention.

"Hey! Quiet down!" he shouts. "I have an announcement to make."

I'm sitting in the pool mezzanine, surrounded by my teammates. The mezzanine is a huge balcony with carpeted bleachers that are as wide as couches, and it stretches the entire length of the natatorium, but we're all clumped together in our usual spot overlooking the diving well, which is as still as a millpond. It's the first GAC meeting of the fall; school started today, and everyone is amped for the new season. We're supposed to be stretching, but most people are gathered in small groups, chatting animatedly and pretty much ignoring Dave.

Jessa and Amber are beside me, talking in low voices. I think they're debating the relative attractiveness level of the handful of swimmers who just joined GAC, but I'm not really listening—unlike everyone else on the team, I'm watching Dave.

It's been two weeks since the invitational, since Dave dressed me down on the pool deck over my false start—two weeks since Dad called and yelled at him for berating me in front of the entire Chicagoland swimming community.

Dad and I haven't discussed it since—his vain attempt to protect me, I guess—and I didn't hear anything from my coach over the break. The suspense is killing me. I half expected Dave to tell me not to return to GAC.

That didn't happen, but I'm afraid it still could. I keep trying to catch his eye, but every time it seems like I might, his gaze slides over me like I'm not even here.

When people don't pipe down, Dave grabs a bullhorn from the floor near his feet. There's an unfamiliar white woman standing next to him. She's tall and slender, with long mousy brown hair tied back into a severe ponytail and a pair of glasses in electric blue frames sitting on the bridge of her nose. They're too big for her face, but somehow, they suit her.

She stands with her hip resting against the glass railing and her back to the aqua expanse of the pool below. I barely have time to wonder who she is and why she's here before Dave starts shouting into the bullhorn.

"Everybody settle down and SHUT. UP!"

I cover my ears—that bullhorn packs a wallop. It does the job, though. We all shut up.

"Finally." He sets the bullhorn on the ground and tucks his clipboard under his arm. "Okay, so first of all, welcome to the first GAC practice of the season."

A cheer goes up and someone lets out a sharp whistle. Dave smiles.

"I hope you guys got some rest during the break, because today's sets are going to crush you. But before we get to the good stuff, I've got an important announcement to make."

Dave points to the woman standing next to him. "This is Beth Ramsay. As most of you know, Mills accepted a job as head coach of the Beaumont Bruins—"

People boo at the mention of our local rivals, but Mike Mills was a Dave clone, just ten years younger—a fratty-looking white bro who strutted around the pool deck in Vineyard Vines polos and Sperrys like he was God's gift to swimming, barking orders and treating us like babies. Jessa thinks I'm being sensitive, but I swear he was especially dismissive of people who didn't look like him—i.e., the team's small handful of swimmers of color, and the girls. I'm not sorry to see him go.

"—and Beth will be taking over his spot as assistant head coach," Dave continues. "I expect you to treat her with respect and listen to everything she tells you. You monsters go easy on her. Got it?"

He turns to her. "Beth, any last words?"

She laughs. "Nothing special. I'm happy to be here, and excited to work with you guys. I hope you'll enjoy working with me, too."

Dave nods and dismisses us with a wave of his hand. "Hit the deck, and don't let me catch any of you slacking. Break's over, time to get back to work. See you down there."

I try once more to catch Dave's eye, but he turns to talk to Beth. I make my way up the bleachers behind Jessa and

Amber, swept up in the flood of swimmers streaming through the door at the top of the mezzanine. A tall guy I don't know waits patiently as people push past. Even though it's his turn, he holds the door open for my friends and me.

I don't recognize him at first, but when I do I almost trip right out of my flip-flops. It's the boy I ran into at the GAC Invitational. The one who asked if I was okay as I was fleeing the scene.

My face gets hot. He's the last person I ever wanted to see again, and now here he is, at *my* club. We're teammates. The thought of having to swim every day with the stranger who witnessed one of the lowest moments of my year makes my stomach drop.

"Hey," he says. "Good to see you again. How's it going?"

"Um, good." I hurry through the door.

When he's out of earshot, Jessa whispers, "Do you *know* him?"

"No." Technically, it's not even a lie.

Jessa and Amber aren't going to let me get away that easily. They follow me into the locker room, waiting impatiently while I strip off my warm-up clothes to the suit underneath and then rummage around in my swim bag for my new Swedish goggles.

"You're sure you don't know him? It seemed like he knew you," Jessa insists. "Come on! Tell us tell us tell us. He's so cute. I heard he used to swim for the Bruins. How did you meet him?"

"Leave her alone," Amber says, snapping her towel at Jessa.

I want to hug her. Jessa won't give up when she thinks you're holding out on her, but Amber respects things like privacy and other people's wishes. You know, as any decent human being would.

"Know who?" asks Casey as she pulls another suit over the one she's already wearing. Most of us wear more than one swimsuit to practice; the second suit is usually an old baggy one that's lost all its elasticity from too much chlorine. It creates extra drag, which helps you go faster in actual races when you've got on only one thin layer of tight Lycra.

Swimmers will do just about anything to get an edge in competition, myself included. The only thing I refuse to do is grow out my leg hair for the ritual shave before big meets. When I was twelve, Sarah Weller teased me about how dark my body hair was—in front of *everyone*—and I've been self-conscious about it ever since.

"That redhead guy, the one who was holding the door for everyone," Jessa tells her.

"Oh, yeah, he *is* cute," Casey says. "Harry something. I heard him introducing himself to Avik and Nash in the mezzanine."

"Harry Something," Jessa murmurs. "Hmm. Hot name, too."

"I've always wanted to be Mrs. Something." Casey giggles. "You know him, Susannah?"

"She doesn't," Amber says so I don't have to, bless her, then changes the subject. "What do you guys think about Beth?"

"What's there to think?" Jessa asks with a shrug. "We don't know anything about her."

"A female head coach," Casey says. "We've never had one of those before. Why are all swim coaches old white dudes?"

"The patriarchy," Amber says in disgust.

"Sing it," I say, high-fiving her. I love Amber. We both joined GAC when we were seven, and instantly gravitated toward each other; because she's Black and I'm Latina, we shared the feeling of being outsiders in a sport where almost no one looked like us. One of my favorite things about Amber is that she says things out loud that I feel all the time but can't put into words.

"She's an *assistant* head coach," Jessa says dismissively. "She's not replacing Dave."

But there's got to be a reason Dave brought on a female assistant. He never has before. Female coaches are common enough at the developmental levels, but they're infuriatingly rare in elite swimming, and if the misogyny of the sport had a mascot it would be Dave.

Under any other circumstances, I'd be thrilled to have a female coach, but I'm worried that Dave's hiring of Beth has something to do with what happened at the invitational. What if he tries to foist me and every other swimmer he's gotten bored with on her?

I make myself a promise: I'm never, ever swimming for anyone except Dave. GAC is one of the best swim clubs in the country, and he is the reason. I might not like it, but he's an Olympian. He *makes* Olympians. And I'm not going to settle for second best. My career is too important to risk it.

The Lions Natatorium is no ordinary pool. It's the nicest and most professional high school natatorium in the state. The pool is eight lanes and fifty meters long, with movable bulkheads that allow it to be reconfigured for all three types of races—short-course yards, short-course meters and long-course meters—plus a fourteen-foot diving well, three diving boards and a hot tub on the north end. The mezzanine can hold one thousand people, and on the south end there's a viewing area behind an enormous picture window that can accommodate five hundred more; during the school day, students study and eat lunch there. I've seen facilities at NCAA Division I schools that were far inferior.

For almost a decade, this place has been my home, but since my slowdown it feels like a prison. I still love the water—I don't think that will ever leave me—but the pool where I rose through the ranks, where I put in the daily work that propelled me to the top of a world championship podium, is not a place I want to be anymore.

Of all the disappointments my body's changes brought into my life, losing that feeling of safety and peace my pool used to give me is one of the worst. And yet, tonight after practice, when everyone's gone home, I stay late to work on my start.

I didn't think Dave would let me. He can't leave me here alone, and I figure he's not going to skip dinner with his family to stay with me of all people. But when I ask, he nods and calls to Beth, who's helping a younger swimmer wrap an ice pack on her shoulder. My chest tightens with hope. Does he forgive me for the false start? That doesn't sound like Dave, but he can be kind when he feels like it.

"Ramos wants an extra hour in the pool tonight," Dave tells her. "You free to supervise and lock up when she's done?"

"Sure," Beth says. She smiles at me. "Do you need help with something, because I could—"

"No, I'm fine, there's just something I want to work on by myself," I say.

This isn't a normal request, but she rolls with it. "I'll be in the office if you need me," she says.

The coaches' office has windows that look out onto the deck, so I'm sure Beth's watching me, but I pretend she's not there. It's a relief to have the place to myself. Without all the noise and chaos of sixty swimmers practicing, the pool is like glass. The soft slap of water hitting the gutters relaxes me.

"Take your mark," I whisper, tightening my grip on the block.

I do probably thirty starts, and each time my body unfolds neatly in flight, assembling itself into a streamlined arrow before plunging into the water. This is stupid. My disqualification had nothing to do with the power or technique of my start. It was fear—of being late off the block and losing our lead, of freezing up and not jumping at all—that did it.

There are no do-overs. A hundred good starts now won't erase the one that I flubbed.

But I keep going, taking comfort in the rhythm of it, in the feeling of doing something well, until I happen to glance at the clock. It's been an hour, which is as long as I can reasonably expect Beth to give me. I toss my goggles onto the deck and hoist myself out of the pool.

"It's probably none of my business, but I don't think there's anything wrong with your start."

The sound of another person's voice takes me by surprise. My foot slips on the slick metal gutter and I almost topple into the water. I grab the block to catch myself.

Harry Something is standing near the entrance to the men's locker room, staring at me with those big, super-chromatic eyes, carelessly leaning against the wall like he's holding it up instead of the other way around.

A pang of jealousy hits me square in the chest. An athlete's job is to understand his or her body and what it can do. It gives you a special kind of confidence, which Harry seems to have. I used to have it, too, but now my body is so foreign to me I'd need the Rosetta Stone to puzzle it out.

"I know there's nothing wrong my start," I tell him. I wrench my swim cap off with a wince. It seems to take half my curls along with it. "You scared the crap out of me."

"Sorry about that." He strolls toward me, shoulders thrown back, hands in the pockets of his jeans, all arrogance and ease. As he gets closer I realize he's chomping on a Red Vine.

"I thought I was the only one here," I tell him. "Except Beth."

"That's her in there?" He mimes wiping sweat from his brow. "I was afraid it was Dave."

I wrap a towel around my waist, feeling exposed and a little embarrassed, as if Harry's caught me giving myself a pep talk in the mirror. Why is he suddenly always around at times like these?

"How long have you been watching me?" I ask.

He crams the last of the Red Vine into his mouth and swallows hard. "Don't say it like that! I wasn't *watching* you, like in a creepy way. I saw you through the glass on the way to my car."

I glance over my shoulder at the windows that look into East Commons. It's empty, all the tables and chairs put away for the night. I wonder if we're the only people on campus.

"Why are you still here?" I ask Harry.

"I forgot a couple books in my locker and I need them to-night. Don't teachers know they're not supposed to give this much homework the first week? That was the unspoken rule at my old school."

"Not here." I feel so awkward. I don't know what to say, or what to do with my hands. Why couldn't he have walked on by and left me alone?

Harry sits down on a nearby bench and pats the spot next to him. I hesitate, then collapse beside him, feeling the full weight of my exhaustion. I sigh.

"Yeah, same," Harry says. "Dave wasn't kidding. That practice was grueling."

"I feel like I've been fed through a meat grinder," I tell him. He nods in sympathy.

"Which reminds me—why are *you* still here?" he asks.

I lift an eyebrow. "I know you saw that false start at the invitational."

He scrubs his fingers against his scalp. The bright fluorescent overhead lights pick up the gold in his hair. We're sitting so close to each other that I'm practically dripping on him.

"I saw," he admits. "Dave completely overreacted. I almost decided not to join GAC because of it. I'm not about working my ass off for someone like that."

"So why did you join?"

Harry looks around the natatorium. "This place, for a start. The pool I swam in with the Bruins looks like a backwoods watering hole next to this one."

I laugh. "It is nice."

"Plus, we moved to Gilcrest over the summer and I trans-ferred schools. Seemed stupid to drive all the way to Beaumont for practice every day when there's a perfectly good club here," Harry explains.

He pauses, then says, "Dave was wrong to treat you like that. This sport demands a lot, and it's not like you false-started to spite him. I'm sure you felt bad enough as it was."

My throat tightens. "I deserved it," I say. "I screwed up."

"So? It happens. Shouldn't mean you get a beat-down."

"Yeah, well, I let him down. I let my teammates down." I swallow hard. "I let myself down."

I'm not getting into my history with this guy—I mean, I hardly know him—but he's looking at me in a way that makes me think he might understand. Like there have been times he felt the same way.

My heart is beating so hard that it feels like it's going to punch its way right out of my chest. I can't even remember the last time I was alone like this with a guy. Maybe never.

I twist my towel in my hands and stare at Harry's knee, which is bouncing up and down like he's got so much energy he can't contain it. We might be sitting *too* close. I can smell him over the omnipresent fug of chlorine in the air: Irish Spring soap and clean cotton, with a hint of red licorice.

Harry radiates warmth, with his hundred-watt smile and inability to keep still. Every time he looks at me, it's like I'm sitting in a spotlight.

"I get it," Harry says. He points to the water. "But *that's* not going to help."

"What, practicing?"

"Come on. You know how to dive off the block. That's like Competitive Swimming 101, you've done it a million times. So—were you practicing, or were you punishing yourself?"

"Punishing myself?"

"Throwing yourself at the water like that. Reminding yourself how awful it felt to screw up, so you never do it again."

I gaze at the cap and goggles in my hand. "What else can I do?"

"I read up on GAC before I chose to swim here," Harry says. "I know Dave's whole schtick is using data and analysis and massive yardage to bludgeon people into perfect swimmers, but a) half of that is junk science, and b) we're not machines."

"But we can be. That's the whole point."

"No, we can't."

"Why not?"

"Because we want stuff. Desire is one of the defining characteristics of our species. Machines don't want things. They just obey their programming."

"I guess." I can't deny that I want things. I want to win, and maybe more than that, I want not to lose.

"You seem disappointed," he says. Looking at him, I finally understand the expression *His eyes were laughing.* I never thought much about eyes before, but Harry's really are expressive. You can see his thoughts swimming in them, like fish flashing silver beneath the clear surface of a pond.

Right now, I'm pretty sure he's thinking I'm ridiculous.

"Sometimes I think I'd be happier if I didn't want things," I tell him. I keep forgetting we're strangers. It feels nice, right now, to have someone to say this stuff to, though I might regret it later.

Harry shrugs. "Probably."

"And I don't see what's so great about being human. We're ruining our planet. Do you know how many species go extinct a day? Two hundred! With all our technology and resources, people don't have potable water, children are going hungry, polar ice caps are melting, refugees are being turned away at our border and—"

I cut myself off. I'm sure he doesn't want to hear any of this. I chance a look at him. His eyes aren't laughing anymore, but he does seem to be listening.

"And?"

"Forget it," I say. "All I'm saying is, humanity isn't all it's cracked up to be."

He lifts his hands in surrender. "No arguments here. But I still think it's better than being a flawless, unfeeling automaton, which is what Dave wants us to be. Don't you think?"

I shrug.

"The trade-off is that sometimes you don't get the gold star."

"At this point, I'd settle for not getting DQ-ed," I tell him.

He laughs, and then so do I. Harry nudges me with his elbow as if to say: *See? It's not so bad.*

"But you're a great swimmer," he says.

"What makes you so sure?"

He smirks. "Um, aren't you a world champion?"

"How do you know that?"

"I told you, I read up," Harry says. "You're on the list of team accomplishments in the website's About Us section. That's another reason I decided GAC was worth it. Dave might be a jerk, but his swimmers win medals."

"I tell myself the same thing," I admit. "But I'm not a world champion anymore."

"You'll always be a world champion. That's how it works. Can't fool me."

I smile. When I arrived at the pool for early practice this morning, I didn't think anything could make me feel better, but somehow Harry has. Maybe the fact that we're strangers helps him see what I need more clearly than my friends or family or even I can.

"Some people, when things don't come easy, they give up. But you clearly don't. You could be licking your wounds at home, but you're here *doing* something about it. I respect that. I think it's cool."

Am I imagining things, or is he blushing? It's probably just the heat. It's like a sauna in here.

"Anyway, *that* is why I came in here," he says. "To tell you that."

He's looking across the wide blue ribbon of the pool, deliberately avoiding my gaze. If I didn't know any better, I'd think he was nervous. But that would be silly.

I stare at my feet. The nail polish on my toes is chipped. "Tell that to Dave."

"You know the saying that nobody can make you feel inferior without your consent?"

I nod. "Honestly, I think it's kind of bullshit."

"Same. I mean, no offense to Eleanor Roosevelt, but of course people can make you feel inferior without your consent. Nobody wants to be treated like garbage. And if you're not a total narcissist, self-doubt always manages to creep in. I guess the trick is to not let it stop you."

"How?"

"If I figure it out, you'll be the first to know. But you're going to be all right," he says. "I promise. That's the nice thing about swimming: the water is new every day."

"Why are you doing this?" I ask. He frowns, looking confused. I gesture between the two of us. "This. Saying these things? You don't even know me."

He rubs the back of his neck and turns away from me. I feel bad. I think I've embarrassed him.

"I thought you could use some cheering up," he says, standing. "Sorry if I bothered you."

"You're not bothering me," I insist. "I appreciate what you said."

Harry relaxes. "We're teammates now. I've got your back." He offers me his hand to shake. "Harry Matthews."

"Susannah Ramos."

"Nice to meet you, Susie."

"Actually, it's—" I stop myself. Nobody's ever called me Susie. I think I like it. "Nice to meet you, too."

Harry grins. "And now I know you."

CHAPTER FOUR

313 days until US Olympic Team Trials

HARRY'S NOT THE ONLY PERSON WHO'S EVER WARNED ME not to be so hard on myself. My parents do it all the time. But they don't know, like Harry does, the pressures of the clock.

It's such a relief to be told that failure isn't a permanent state. Our conversation plays on repeat in my head all night. *We're not machines. You're human.* I carry it with me like a lucky penny. But the more removed from it I get, the less real it feels, like a vivid dream that fades before you fully wake.

By the time Dad and I hop into the car at five a.m., it's hard to be sure what happened. I spend the whole ride trying to figure out how to act around him. One pep talk doesn't mean we're friends. The potential for awkwardness is high.

In the locker room, there's more laughter and chatter than normal for predawn practice. Amber blows past me on the way to her locker and starts rifling through her stuff.

"What are you looking for?" I ask.

"My phone. I want a picture before Dave makes us clean it all up." She brandishes her phone in triumph. "You've got to see this. It'll make your day."

I trail after her, tucking my swim cap and goggles under the strap of my suit. "What's going on?"

Amber opens her arms in a flourish as we step out of the locker room. "Ta-da!"

It takes me a second to realize what she's talking about: someone has filled the pool with soapsuds and rubber ducks.

At first, I just stare. Then the sight of those little yellow ducks bobbing around like deranged buoys triggers something inside of me, and suddenly I'm laughing so hard my ab muscles start to ache. The pool that for so many years has represented both promise and misery has been transformed into a giant bathtub. For some dumb reason, it's the funniest thing I've ever seen.

Amber and Jessa are near the diving well, taking pictures and swapping theories with a group of our teammates about who might've done this. How anyone managed to get their hands on that many rubber ducks—there are hundreds—and sneak them all in before morning practice is a total mystery.

Dave is red-faced with anger and disgust. He hates pranks, and the ducks are one thing, but all that soap can be bad for the filters. Whoever did this is going to be in a lot of trouble.

Harry catches my eye and comes over to stand next to me, leaning that effortless lean.

"Fun fact," he says. "Bath toys are cheap when you buy them in bulk off the internet."

"That *is* a fun fact," I reply. "You did this?"

He shrugs. "Maybe. Maybe not."

"Don't worry, I won't tell," I promise. He shrugs again, but his grin ruins the charade. "Wait—there's no way you were able to get this many rubber ducks off the internet overnight."

He steps back to admire his handiwork. Dave has a group of freshmen attacking the ducks with skimmers, but it's slow-going. There are just so many of them.

"I didn't actually buy them. My friend Tucker's uncle manages Wacky Waves, that water park up in Hartbrook. These are from their annual rubber ducky derby. He said I could borrow them as long as I returned them."

"How are you going to get them back without Dave finding out it was you?"

"I'll confess," he says. "Getting away with it wasn't the point."

"What *was* the point?"

"Maybe I'm just a lord of misrule," he says. I roll my eyes and smile. "Or maybe I figured there's someone on this team who could use a laugh. And a little revenge."

"Revenge?" Then I remember what Dave said to me at the invitational: *I could've put one of those plastic duck toys in the pool in your place and it probably would've had better splits!*

"But you'll get in trouble!"

"I can't have him thinking it was you," he says. "Although, honestly, I'd be surprised if he remembers all the shitty things he says. He probably won't make the connection, which is a bummer."

"You didn't have to do this," I tell him.

"Obviously. If I *had* to do it, it wouldn't be half as charming."

God, he's so arrogant. And yet, when he smiles at me, I feel light-headed. Clearly, I'm suffering from low blood sugar. I should've eaten more than the granola bar I scarfed on the car ride over.

"The fact that you know it's charming makes it half as charming," I say.

"That's what my stepdad's always telling me. He says my antics would come off more lovable if I didn't act so pleased with myself all the time."

"You do stuff like this a lot?" I can't imagine having that kind of time or energy to devote to anything besides swimming.

"I dabble." He touches my arm and leans in close, lowering his voice. My skin tingles under his fingertips. "Hey, my friend Tucker—"

"Heir to the rubber duck fortune?"

He laughs. "His mom's out of town, so he's having a party on Saturday. You should come."

I stiffen. Harry is nice, and I like him, but no guy has ever paid me this much attention and I don't know what to do with it. Part of me wants to spend more time with him, but another part—a much stronger, more familiar part—panics at the thought of him figuring out I'm not as interesting as he thinks and wants to stay far, far away so he never gets the chance.

"You can bring friends if you want," he says. "Invite whoever."

"I'm not much of a party girl," I tell him. "But I'll think about it."

Harry beams at me. "Cool."

"Hey!" Dave shouts.

Harry jumps. Sixty heads swivel in Dave's direction. Amber hides her phone behind her back.

"Stop gawking and start helping! I want this pool cleared in fifteen minutes!"

"You heard the man, Susie," Harry says, kicking off his deck shoes. "Let's go duck hunting."

Later that week, after evening practice, I knock on the door to the coaches' office with a tin of cookies in my hand. Beth smiles when she spots me through the glass. She waves me in.

"Hi," I say, feeling silly now that I'm here. Beth has been nothing but friendly, but it's always weird with new coaches. I thrust the tin at her. "I brought you some of my mom's Mexican wedding cookies. We made them last night, so they're fresh."

"Ooh," she says, lifting the lid off the tin. Powdered sugar gets all over the fleece she's wearing.

"I should've warned you. They can be messy," I say.

She swipes at a white spot on her jacket before giving up with a shrug. "No worries. I was going to wash this, anyway."

"There are nuts in them," I warn her as she picks up one of the cookies and pops it into her mouth. "Sorry, I didn't even ask if you were allergic."

"I'm not," she says around the cookie. She swallows hard. "These are delicious. I'm going to have to ration them."

"We make them for every GAC bake sale, so there'll be opportunities to have more."

"You guys do have a lot of bake sales, I've noticed," she says, glancing at the GAC events calendar hanging on the wall.

"Those cookies are a popular item. They always sell out."

"You'll have to give me the recipe. They're called wedding cookies?"

"That's what we've always called them. They have other names. My family is Mexican, but my mom is part Polish, too," I tell her. "She says her babcia used to make them, but she called them Russian teacakes. They're an international cookie."

Beth makes me so nervous I'm reduced to babbling about baked goods. She comes off so cool and collected. There's a part of me that wishes I could be more like that and less like…well, me: anxious and worried and too tightly wound.

"Thank you, Susannah," Beth says, replacing the lid on the tin.

"You're welcome. I just wanted to say I appreciate that you stayed late the other day so I could spend more time in the pool. That was nice of you."

"It was no problem. But if you ever want help with anything— if you need extra coaching or you want to talk about stuff—you can always come to me. I'm here for you guys. And I know what it feels like to struggle with your training."

I frown. "That's not— I don't— I'm fine. I don't need anyone's help."

"Not true," Beth says. "Every swimmer needs help. That's what coaches are for."

"I mean, I don't need help from *you*."

Guilt hits me before the words are even out of my mouth. She's trying to be nice, and I'm acting ungrateful. But I'm not her swimmer, and the sooner I make that clear, the better.

"Dave is my coach," I say, more gently this time.

"It's not unusual to have multiple coaches, Susannah. Most swimmers do."

"Yeah, but I *don't*."

Beth holds up her hands in surrender. "I get it. I had the

same coach for most of my career, too. Sometimes people get attached."

I'm not attached to Dave; I just know I can't win without him. But there's no point in trying to explain that to Beth. I've made enough of an ass of myself already. This is not how I wanted this conversation to go. I wanted to thank her, and I've messed it all up.

"Anyway. Yeah. So… I hope you enjoy the cookies," I say, heading for the door. "If you're going to keep them here, hide them. They're Dave's favorites. He'll eat them all when you're not here."

"Noted," Beth says. "Thanks again, Susannah."

I nod, then book it right the hell out of there before I make an even bigger fool out of myself.

On my way to the locker room, I see Harry at the south end of the pool, helping a few of the younger swimmers clean up the equipment we used during practice. It's part of his punishment for the whole rubber duck thing.

Well, in theory he's helping—in actuality, he's teaching the boys how to punt the kickboards into the wire bins where they're stored. They're not great at it, so there's a lot of hard foam flying through the air, then skittering across the deck.

Harry manages to get one in the bin and the group erupts in a cheer. He's pumping his fists in triumph when he looks up and sees me watching. His arms come down and he gives me a more dignified but no less enthusiastic wave.

He cups his hands over his mouth and shouts, "You're coming to the party tomorrow, right?"

The boys have abandoned the kickboards and are now

beating each other with pull buoys, but they break to laugh at Harry.

"Is she your *girlfriend*?" one of them teases him. Harry gives him a light shove.

"Maybe!" I call back to Harry. "I guess you'll have to wait and see."

Harry presses his hand against his chest like he's been shot in the heart. The boys fall on him like wolves on a wounded deer, using the foam pull buoys like mallets to hit him all over his back and shoulders. He grins at me, then does a graceful dive into the water to escape them. I duck into the locker room before he can surface.

Under the hot needlepoint spray of the shower, I play what just happened with Harry over in my mind. Did I *flirt* with him? I never flirt. I didn't even think I knew how to flirt. But with Harry it came so easily, like floating in water, like breathing. And it felt *great*.

I am in so much freaking trouble.

CHAPTER FIVE

309 days until US Olympic Team Trials

What do you mean you're NOT GOING?

IT'S SATURDAY, AND AMBER AND JESSA HAVE BEEN TEXTING me all afternoon, asking if I'm going to the party at Harry's friend's house and if they can come with me and if I've thought about what I'm going to wear and if I want help applying "some actual makeup for once in your life" (Jessa). I kept putting them off, because I honestly could not make up my mind, but around six p.m. I decided: I'm skipping it.

That did not go over well.

I'm finishing up the last of my homework when my phone rings. It's Jessa. I put her on speaker.

"Did you hit your head?" she asks.

"I don't think so. Maybe I did and it erased my memory, like in a telenovela. Why?"

"Then what possible reason do you have for not going to this boy's party?"

"It's too much pressure. He's too cute, and too nice, and too…just too *too*, okay?"

"Wow, that's a lot of *toos*. You're spiraling."

I sigh. "Yeah."

"Okay, so, counterpoint: you don't have to marry the guy. It's just a party. A little flirting, a little kissing, maybe, then you go home and enjoy the fact that a boy you like likes you back for a couple of days. Plus, I bet he's not even that nice. They never are in the end."

"What happens after a couple of days?" I ask, ignoring that last part. Jessa has always had a take-no-prisoners approach to love. She treats it the way she treats everything else: like a battlefield.

"You move on to another boy. At least, that's what I do."

"I know. The pool deck is littered with the shards of your exes' broken hearts."

"Don't be melodramatic. They can't be exes because they were never boyfriends. They were crushes. There's no harm in a crush, but no boyfriends till next August."

For Jessa, boys are a healthy distraction from the rigors of training, but only in a noncommittal sort of way. She has this superstition that being in a relationship would compromise her chances at making it to the Olympics.

As superstitions go, it's not that unreasonable, but this is the first time I've given it much thought. I'm no casual dater—I'm no casual anything—and I've never liked a guy enough to consider something more serious.

With my slowdown putting my career in jeopardy, right
now doesn't seem like the time to start.

"Note that she didn't say anything about girlfriends,"
Amber chimes in. "I can have as many girlfriends as I want.
Not that I have any, but in theory."

"No girlfriends, either," Jessa says.

"Damn," Amber says with mock-disappointment. She's always telling me not to take what Jessa says so seriously.

"Hey, Amber. I didn't realize you guys were together. What
are you doing?"

"Going on a mission," Amber says in a low voice that I
guess is supposed to be mysterious.

"What kind of mission?" I ask. This is suspicious.

"You'll find out very, *very* soon," Jessa replies. Then she hangs
up.

A second later, my bedroom door flies open and Jessa and
Amber storm in. Frick and Frack, who were napping on my
bed, startle and streak out of the room. Frida whistles from
where she's perched on top of her cage. She loves visitors.
"Hola, Bela!" she chirps.

Jessa, who hates birds, shoots Frida a dirty look, but Amber
points to herself and says, "Frida, say Amber. *Am-ber.*"

"Hola, Bela!" Frida says, then launches into a few bars of
"Yankee Doodle Dandy."

"You're hopeless," Amber tells Frida with a disappointed
eye roll.

"You didn't pick the lock on the front door, I hope," I say.

"Nina let us in," Jessa said, gesturing over her shoulder.
Nina's standing in the doorway, with Frick cradled in her
arms like a baby, smirking at me.

"*Et tu*, sister?"

"Go to a party, Susannah," she says. "It'll be good for you."
Then she leaves.

I almost call after her to stay—we hardly ever see each
other, and I miss her sometimes. We used to have fun together. We were close once. We joined GAC together, a long
time ago now. But she wouldn't want to hang out with me
and my friends, except maybe Amber, who she's always liked.

"Listen to your sister. She's older than you, and therefore
very wise," Amber says. "You are going to this party, missy,
and we are going to help you get ready."

She has a massive bag in her hands that clatters as she flings
herself across my bed.

"Jessa's going to dress you, and I'm going to do your
makeup," she tells me. "Nothing outrageous, don't give me
that look. You have foundation, right? Mine won't match you."

"What do *you* think?" I rarely wear makeup, and even
when I do, it's just mascara, maybe blush if I'm feeling sassy.
I spend half of each day in the water, so what's the point?

She rolls off the bed. "I'll ask Nina. She'll have something
we can borrow."

Jessa puts her hands on my shoulders and stares into my eyes.

"Are you going to this party, Ramos?" she asks.

"Are you guys going to make me miserable until I do?"

"*Susannah*, we're your friends." For a second, Jessa sounds
genuinely hurt, but then she grins. "Of course we will."

"Yeah," I say with a sigh as she drags me over to my closet.
"I'm going."

Harry texted me the address of the party earlier in the
week, but I don't map it until the three of us are piling into

Jessa's car. I assume we'll have to drive to Beaumont, since that's where Harry lived before he transferred. But the party isn't far from my house, which means Tucker goes to our school. I wonder if we've ever had a class together. Gilcrest has about four thousand students, so I doubt it.

My parents think we're getting dinner and going to a movie. I feel bad about lying, but they'd never agree to let me go to a party at the house of someone I don't know. They're barely comfortable with Jessa driving. Dad wanted to drop us off instead; it took twenty minutes to talk him out of it.

"What'd you say this guy's name was?" Jessa asks, backing into the street. "Trevor?"

"Tucker," I reply.

"I don't know any Tuckers, do you?"

Amber and I shake our heads. The swim life is all-consuming. We pretty much don't know anybody who's not on the team.

Tucker's house is even smaller than mine, one of the squat three-bedroom ranch houses in the older part of town, but it's hard to miss with all the cars crammed in the driveway and lining the street. Jessa double-parks in front of the house—the girl has, like, a hundred tickets; I don't know how she still has her license—and we make our way to the door.

My palms are so sweaty I have to wipe them off on the hem of my dress. I think my makeup looks good, thanks to Amber, who stuck to her promise of not going overboard, but Jessa made me borrow the dress from Nina after she deemed my entire wardrobe "unacceptable for social occasions of any kind," and it's too short. I keep tugging the back to make sure it's covering all my important parts.

Getting dressed up for a guy feels weird. I've never done that before. I want Harry to think I'm pretty, but if he likes how I look tonight, in Nina's clothes with Amber's makeup on my face, will that mean he doesn't like how I look without them? I'll never be able to do this every day, and I don't want to. But if he doesn't like it, I'll feel dumb and desperate.

My mind spins out further with ever more apocalyptic scenarios: What if Harry isn't here and then we're stuck at some stranger's party? Or worse, what if he *is* here and I make a fool of myself in front of him? The possibilities of self-humiliation are endless, really. I should go home.

Amber grabs my arm. "I can see what's going through your head *all* over your face. Cut it out. We're going in."

Tucker's house is even more cramped on the inside than it looks on the outside—the rooms are tiny, the hallway is narrow and the dark, oversize furniture is worn. An enormous TV takes up most of one entire wall in the living room, and the floor in front of it is littered with gaming consoles and controllers. Hip-hop blares from a giant subwoofer near the window. Harry mentioned Tucker's mom, but there's no sign that anyone but a teenage boy lives here. Even with a party going on, the place seems kind of lonely.

There's hardly any room to stand; people are stuffed in every corner of the place. Most of them have red Solo cups in their hands, which I'm sure do not contain soda. I don't recognize anybody.

"Kitchen," Jessa says, pulling me by the hand through the front room.

The closet-size kitchen is at capacity, but Jessa manages to thread us through the crowd. She bounces off to fetch us all something to drink, and Amber starts introducing herself to people she doesn't know, as is her way. My shoes stick to the old-fashioned linoleum; someone must've spilled something. There's a black trash bag slumped at my feet, overflowing with cups and cans.

I scan the room for Harry, but he doesn't seem to be here. I consider texting him, but will that make me seem overeager and clingy?

"Susie! Susie, hey!"

I turn to see Harry slipping through a knot of people near the doorway. When our eyes meet, I light up like a Fourth of July sparkler—I can't help it. He's beaming that megawatt smile at me, and I feel the electricity all the way down to my toes. I've never been like this around a guy before. It's exciting. And terrifying.

He looks great in a pair of dark jeans and a Pearl Jam T-shirt that seems soft and shows off his swimmer's physique to maximum effect. If she were here, my mom would one hundred percent say he was "hunky," after which I would die of embarrassment, but it's true. His red-gold hair is shorter than it was yesterday, like maybe he got it cut this afternoon, and the lighter strands glow like the filaments in an antique light bulb.

As he approaches, I admire the color of his eyes, which are the loveliest part of him; the blue of his shirt makes them look like pools of indigo ink.

"You came!" he shouts over the music.

He moves closer to me, like he's going for a bear hug, but it turns into one of those awkward one-armed sideways hugs. Does he think a real hug would give me the wrong impression, or is there just not enough room to use both arms? Maybe Jessa and Amber are wrong about him liking me as more than a friend. It would make way more sense if he didn't. Why won't my hands stop *sweating?*

"It's great to see you," he says.

"You saw me yesterday!"

Harry looks down at his shoes, a pair of battered old Chucks, but his smile doesn't waver.

"Yeah, well, it's still nice. I wasn't sure you'd make it."

"Amber and Jessa brought me here," I confess. I nearly said *dragged*, but I didn't want him to take it the wrong way.

He grins. "What do I owe them?"

"A hundred and seventy-five dollars, before tax, and don't forget to tip your kidnapper," Jessa says, appearing at my elbow with three drinks balanced precariously in her hands—a beer, a bottle of water and a soda.

"Worth every penny," Harry says, taking the two cups. He hands me the beer.

I shake my head. "I don't drink."

"Me neither," he says, switching my beer out for the soda.

"Suit yourselves. I'm DD, so none for me, either." Jessa cracks open her water.

"I'll just hold this for Amber," Harry says. I smile at him.

"I'm here, I'm here," Amber says, emerging as if by magic out of a clump of strangers. She takes the beer from Harry. "Thank you, sir. That was very gallant of you."

"That's me," Harry says, bowing at the waist and flourishing his hand theatrically. *"Gallant."*

Amber taps her forehead. "It's never too early to start studying for those SATs."

"Gallant is not an SAT word," Jessa says with a sniff. She's

very intense about standardized testing. Her parents started enrolling her in prep classes back in eighth grade.

"You look really nice," Harry tells me. My chest cramps, and I realize I'm holding my breath. "But then, you always do."

"Right answer," Amber says, punching his arm in a friendly way. She winces and shakes out her fist. "What are you made of, dude? Rocks?"

"Petrified Red Vines, mostly," I say. Harry laughs and pats his back pocket; there's a half-empty pack of licorice sticking out of it.

My friends look at each other like they're about to abandon me.

"We should—" Amber begins, but she's cut off midsentence by the arrival of a white boy I don't recognize. He flings his arm around Harry's shoulders and sort of joggles him.

"Hey, man, I lost you," the boy says.

"Well, now you've found me," Harry replies with a good-natured roll of his eyes. The boy seems a bit buzzed. Harry shoots him a wary look, like he's afraid his friend might say something to embarrass him. "Guys, this is Tucker. He goes to Gilcrest, too. His house, his party. Say hi, Tuck."

"Hi," Tucker says. Harry introduces us, but Tucker barely feigns interest. He came over here for a reason, and he's laser focused on that.

"Harry, the people are demanding a show," Tucker tells him, punching his arm repeatedly. Okay, maybe he's more than buzzed. Tucker's a skinny guy with a medium build, so I doubt it hurts, but Harry pulls away and holds up a hand to fend him off.

"Not tonight, man," he says. He gives me an apologetic smile.

Tucker grabs Harry by both shoulders. "But the people, Matthews. Think of *the people*."

Harry laughs. I can tell he's uncomfortable, maybe a little nervous. I want to pull him into a quiet corner, away from everyone, which is probably what a more confident girl would do, but I just stand there feeling self-conscious. What are they even talking about?

"The people are going to have to learn to deal with disappointment," he says.

"Really? I thought you'd do it just to impress this one." Tucker angles his head at me.

I narrow my eyes at him as my face grows hot. Between the temperature and the embarrassment, I bet I'm red as a stop sign right now.

Harry glares at Tucker. Something about the way they're interacting reminds me of me and Nina. Tucker's getting under Harry's skin in the way only siblings or longtime friends can. "More like horrify her. I'm not doing it."

"Doing what?" I ask.

"You'll see," Tucker says with a wink.

"No, she won't," Harry shoots back, giving Tucker a light shove. To me, he says, "It's stupid."

"I want to see it now, whatever it is," Jessa says, crossing her fingers. "Please be a strip show."

"Me too, me too!" Amber agrees. "Although I'm cool if you keep your clothes on."

Tucker turns to me. "What about you, Susanne? Don't you want to see the Flow?"

"It's Susannah," I say. How hard is it to remember a name

you heard three seconds ago? "And I don't know what the Flow is."

"Believe me, it's great," Tucker says, ignoring Harry's angry stare.

"Okay, sure. Let's see it." I give Harry an encouraging smile. Tucker's not giving up. Maybe if Harry does what he wants, he'll leave us alone.

"Fine," he says with a world-weary sigh. "Let's go prep the stage."

"The stage? What is happening right now?" I mutter as they walk away. Tucker throws his arm around Harry's shoulders again, but Harry shakes him off gently.

Amber shrugs, but Jessa's so preoccupied with a text she just got that I don't think she heard me.

"You. Guys." She looks up from her phone, wide-eyed. "Remember Kara Walker?"

"Sure," Amber says.

"What about her?" I ask.

Kara is a few years older than us, one of the best swimmers Dave's ever coached at GAC. She swims for Stanford, and last year at the NCAA Championships she placed first in all of her events except one. I've always looked up to her.

"She's *pregnant*. Apparently, it's a boy. Mazel tov, I guess," Jessa murmurs. She returns the text so fast I'm surprised she doesn't singe her fingertips. "Lucy says Kara met a guy at Stanford and they started going out and now, buh-buh-boom—bun in the oven."

"How?" I sputter.

"Don't make me explain where babies come from. My version does not involve storks."

"I mean, she's supposed to go to the Olympics. Everyone had her pegged for a multigold contender! She can't train if she's pregnant, and she can't go to the Olympics if she doesn't train."

"She could train pregnant—Dara Torres did," Amber says.

"Not everybody is Dara Torres," Jessa argues. "Her body's going to majorly change. It could throw everything off. She might never get back to where she was competitively."

The mention of changing bodies strikes a nerve. Of the three of us, I know best how that can affect your entire career. Maybe even end it.

I want to keep talking about this—I cannot wrap my mind around the fact that Kara Walker won't be going to the Olympics—but the squeal of a microphone distracts me.

On the other end of the room, Tucker is standing in front of the kitchen island, which is now entirely cleared of chip bowls and abandoned drinks and other party debris. He's holding a portable karaoke machine in one hand and a wireless mike in the other. Everyone quiets. Tucker clears his throat.

"Ladies and gentlemen," he says, his voice reverberating through the tiny speaker. "I give you...the Flow."

A familiar hip-hop song starts playing on the stereo and Harry takes a flying leap off a chair positioned in the corner, landing in a crouch on the island. His momentum carries him a bit too far and one of his feet slips, but he rights himself. I suspect he's practiced this.

Tucker tosses the mike at him and Harry snatches it out of midair. Then he stands up, closes his eyes and starts to rap. The room erupts in applause and cheers. Most of them seem to have been expecting this.

"This is his party trick," Tucker says, wedging himself in beside me. "People love it."

That's clearly true, but the best part is that, despite how reluctant he seemed earlier, *Harry* loves it, too. It's obvious how happy it makes him to get the lyrics right, how good he feels slicing the air with his hands in time to the beat. He's holding the mike like a beloved thing, rolling his shoulders and swaying his hips and dropping rhymes. He looks ridiculous.

Except, because he doesn't seem to care what he looks like, or what anybody thinks, he careens right past the threshold of ridiculous and loops back to awesome.

I feel weightless, like the floor has suddenly vanished from under my feet. Harry is way too cool for me. I don't know why I thought, for even a second, that we could make sense together. Or that, with my career in such a fragile state, I had any business messing around with a guy.

No boyfriends until next August, like Jessa said. One mistake can hurt your entire career. Kara Walker is living proof of that.

"I want to go home," I tell Amber. Coming here was a terrible idea. All it did was make me hope for something I can't have right now.

Amber takes one look at the agony on my face and snaps into mama bear mode. She taps Jessa on the shoulder and says, "We're leaving now."

Jessa, who seems to find the Flow annoying, doesn't put up a fight. My friends give me a hard time, but when push comes to shove they're on my side.

It's easy to make our way out of the house while everyone's preoccupied with the Flow. They move when we try to pass, then close back up behind us like a curtain. From his perch on the island, Harry must notice us leaving. He invited me here, and now I'm bailing without even saying goodbye. If it were the other way around, I would feel awful. I turn back, but Harry's completely absorbed by his performance; he's not even looking at me.

Jessa grabs my arm and says, "You wanted to leave, so let's go."

I hesitate, then follow her out the door.

"What happened back there, Susannah?" Amber asks, turning around in the passenger seat to look at me. "Are you okay?"

"I don't know!" I tell her. "It was, like, a moment of fight or flight. Whatever that is, or could be, with him—it's not a good idea. But I shouldn't have left like that."

"Probably not," Amber agrees. "I could see how upset you were, though. It seemed wrong to try to force you to stay."

I press my forehead against the cool glass of the car window and close my eyes against the memory of what just happened. A wrecking ball of self-loathing slams into me. When I sense a threat to my swimming career, it's like being poked in an open wound—I flinch, and I panic, and I run. Harry probably thinks I don't like him. What a shitty thing to do to someone who's been so nice to me.

"Was it that awful lip dub? Because that would turn me off, too." Jessa snorts. "The Flow. LOL."

"What have we told you about using text speak in polite company?" Amber scolds her. To me, she says, "It was that Kara Walker thing, wasn't it? It scared you."

I nod. Of course Amber gets it. She's always been the most emotionally intuitive of the three of us. But I can tell from her frown that even though she understands, she's frustrated with me, too. All she was trying to do was get me to have some fun, and I ruined it. And Amber would never treat someone the way I treated Harry tonight.

"There are ways to avoid getting pregnant, you know," Jessa says. "We shouldn't have pressured you into going to that party. You take everything so seriously."

"*I* take things seriously?" That's pretty rich, coming from the girl who made her parents build a lap pool in her backyard because the one they had was too small to work out in.

"I take *swimming* seriously," Jessa says. "Who cares what boys think?"

"Jess, just this once, will you please shut up?" Amber begs. "You're not helping."

Jessa glances at me in the rearview mirror. "I know it sucks," she says. "But it's worth it."

"Yeah," I say softly. "It's worth it."

I've always known that earning the right to wear Olympic rings, to have a tattoo and medals like Dave's, would mean making sacrifices. I've made plenty already, and most days I'd be happy to make more, if it meant I could even come close to getting the thing I want most.

I just never banked on meeting Harry or imagined that he would be one of them.

CHAPTER SIX

307 days until US Olympic Team Trials

THE MONDAY AFTER TUCKER'S PARTY, I ARRIVE AT MORNING practice to find Sarah Weller and Nash Grol, the GAC co-captains, standing sentry outside the boys' and girls' locker rooms, which never happens. I'm already dreading having to face Harry after ditching him at the party, so all I can think is, *What fresh hell is this?*

"Team meeting," Sarah tells me as I pass her. "Suit up if you're not already, then head upstairs."

Weird. We have most team meetings before evening practice; Dave knows we'd be half-asleep and miss most of what he's saying if he held them in the mornings. I put my suit on at home, so I shove my swim bag into my locker and proceed to the mezzanine.

My body feels like it's made of lead; I practically have to drag myself up the stairs. I spent all of yesterday in my room, beating myself up and writing dozens of apology texts to Harry that I couldn't find the courage to send. When Bela came over for Sunday dinner, she took one look at me and asked if I was sick. *Not sick*, I thought. *Just frustrated with myself.*

I don't see Harry in the mezzanine, which is a relief, but Jessa's here already—no surprise there. She's doing ab work while she waits. I sink down near her and start my daily prescribed dose of crunches, but I can't focus.

"What do you think is going on?" I ask Jessa in a low voice. Something about it being just past dawn, and the mezzanine being almost deserted, makes me feel like I should whisper.

"No idea," she says, adding a Russian twist to her sit-up. "But I haven't seen Dave."

Dave likes to prowl the pool deck before practice, like a lion surveying his territory. He told me once that he visualizes the entire day's sets in fast motion, trying to predict how everyone's going to perform, and then adjusts based on what he sees. It's unheard of for him not to be here. Something's definitely up.

I've switched from crunches to full sit-ups when Amber arrives. She waves at us but doesn't speak, only yawns and stretches. She's no lark of the morning, our Amber. She swims on autopilot in the a.m. and you can't get a word out of her until eight o'clock.

When I come up for my last rep, I notice Harry near the door. He looks at me and our eyes meet. I panic, thinking he might try to talk to me about the party in front of everyone. But he turns his back to me, and I realize he never meant to speak to me at all.

Right. Of course. I wouldn't want to talk to me, either, if I were him.

At five-thirty on the dot, Beth calls the meeting to order. Still no Dave.

"Hey, guys, I'm going to make this quick," she says. "Dave was doing some repairs at his house this weekend and he twisted his back. He's in a lot of pain and he can't really walk, so he's not going to be at practice for a while."

"How long is a while?" Jessa asks.

Amber mouths at me, Not "Is he okay?" But that was my first thought, too.

"Probably just this week," Beth says. She assures us that she'll work us as hard as Dave would, then dismisses us.

"This isn't good," Jessa says as we wriggle out of our sweatpants and T-shirts in the locker room.

"Why not? I like Beth," Amber says. "Don't you?"

"I like her fine, but she hasn't coached world champions and Olympic athletes, and we're at the point where every practice counts. Don't you care about qualifying for Trials?"

"Not really," Amber replies.

Jessa and I exchange a surprised look. Every elite swimmer in GAC cares about that. This is the first I've heard Amber say she doesn't.

"Don't be ridiculous," Jessa scoffs. "Anyway, Susannah knows what I mean."

Amber looks deflated. I don't want her to think we're ganging up on her, and I'm not sure how comfortable I am being lumped in with Jessa.

"It'll be fine," I say. "Dave's so controlling I bet he's still planning the sets. Beth's just here to make sure we're doing them."

"Actually," Amber says, "we don't know who Beth's coached. I couldn't find any information about her at all, could you?"

Jessa and I shrug and turn back to our lockers.

"Come on, I know you both Googled her," Amber says. She glares at us with her hands on her hips. "I'm not the only cyber stalker here. Confess."

"Okay, I did," I admit. "But I didn't find anything."

"Me neither," Jessa says. "Not even any social media. Isn't that weird?"

Sarah pokes her head into the locker room and shouts at everyone to get moving. Beth smiles at me as I pass her on the way to my assigned lane.

I smile back, but I can't stop wondering: *Who* are *you?*

I was wrong about one thing: Dave's not planning workouts—or, if he is, Beth's not using them. Dave's a traditionalist; he believes that the more you swim, the faster you'll go. Beth doesn't subscribe to that philosophy. Starting that first morning, she reduces our yardage from eight thousand to five thousand yards per workout.

That's not to say the practices are easy. True to her word, Beth works us as hard as Dave—maybe harder—but instead of forcing us to swim endless sets at larger intervals, she has us practicing less at higher speeds that are more like race conditions.

"You'll never have to swim like that in competition, so why do it in practice?" she says with a shrug when a group of sprinters and middistance swimmers balk at the change. Only the long-distance swimmers get workouts that look like Dave's.

Beth's regimen also puts a lot of emphasis on the mental aspects of the sport, which Dave never bothered much with before, apart from the occasional criticism for "not thinking like a winner." She makes sure we understand why we're doing certain things and asks for our input so we don't feel like we're just blindly following instructions.

On the more woo-woo end of the spectrum, she forces us to do affirmations, which are like silent pep talks: *I'm going to win this race; I'm going to break 2:10 on my 200 IM; I'm going to ace this test.* Beth believes in putting positive energy into the universe.

Focusing on the good does not come naturally, so while I can't say affirmations do much for my swimming, they do make me feel better sometimes.

In my years of competitive swimming, I've never been treated like a partner in my own coaching. It both energizes and unsettles me. How can I possibly know what's best? But the really wild part—the part I tell myself isn't true for as long as I possibly can—is that I'm improving. Because we're practicing at closer to race speeds, I can see my progress in every workout.

I'm getting stronger, and what's weirder is that I'm getting *faster.*

We have a meet most Saturdays, and this week it's a dual with Harry's old club. The Beaumont Bruins are only a few towns away, so we swim against them pretty frequently, but our old assistant coach runs the show over there now and the whole team is writhing with excitement to beat him. For most people, it's good-natured competitive spirit, but I can't stand the thought of falling to one of Mike's new swimmers in my best event. I have to do well.

It's a home meet for the Bruins, so we have to travel to Beaumont. A pipe broke in our kitchen this morning while

Mom was at study group and Dad was at the vet with Lulu; the chaos that ensued makes me late to meet the rest of the team in the school parking lot. When I finally board the bus, Beth gives me a stern look.

"We waited for you," she says.

"I know, thank you, sorry," I pant. Dad was late, too, for a shift at the restaurant, so he dropped me off at the front entrance of the school and I had to run across campus to get to the bus.

"Take a seat, Susannah, so we can get going," Beth says, checking me off the attendance list.

I make my way gingerly down the aisle, trying not to smack people with my overstuffed swim bag, when I discover a problem—there's only one empty seat on this bus. The one next to Harry.

My chest tightens and my legs go numb as my nerves kick into overdrive at the prospect of having to face him. My friends are sitting together in the back, and Amber catches my wide-eyed stare. *Do you want me to move?* she mouths. I shake my head. I can see Harry looking at me out of the corner of my eye, and I don't want him to think that I don't want to sit next to him.

Harry gives me a polite smile and pats the empty space next to him. It reminds me of that night at the pool when he invited me to sit next to him on the bench.

"All yours," he says.

"Thanks." I shove my swim bag under my seat and slump against the headrest. I'm in good shape, but running is not my sport. I'm still catching my breath.

Harry turns to look out the window as we pull onto the

street that leads to the highway, ignoring me completely. I don't blame him, but I can't sit here in silence for half an hour, imagining what he must think. I can't explain about Saturday, either; that's a private conversation, and there are too many people around who could hear. The bus is so quiet I can hear Jessa snoring in the back.

Think of something to say! I command myself. My stomach is churning. This is torture.

I clear my throat. "So, uh...are you excited to be back in your old pool?"

I figure that topic has to be safe, but Harry says, "Not really," without turning away from the window. The dismissal stings, but I expected it. I need to keep trying.

"Why not?"

Harry sighs, like I'm annoying him, but he does look at me this time. "Because," he says, "I didn't love swimming there. The people weren't very friendly."

"I've noticed that." I lower my voice. "Around here, we call them the Beaumont Bastards."

He struggles not to smile. "Yeah, well, we called you guys the Gilcrest Asshole Club."

I laugh. "Not entirely inaccurate."

Harry looks me in the eye. "No?" he asks with feigned casualness. I don't think we're talking about swim clubs anymore.

I shake my head. "We act like assholes sometimes," I say. "But we don't mean to. And we're sorry when we do."

Things are silent between us for a beat or two while Harry ponders this. Finally, he says, "Good to know." Then he settles back against the window and closes his eyes.

I take a deep breath and let it out slowly. Clearly, this conver-

sation is finished. And I don't know if it changes anything between us. Maybe he's still angry with me. But at least it's a start.

Duals with the Bruins aren't very exciting. We're a much
better team than they are, and we often outscore them by one
hundred points or more. This meet is no different. The only
wild card is Beth, and the effect she has on the team. Dave
is a shouter, a shit talker and a hothead—he thinks it's mo-
tivational. Beth, on the other hand, is calm and supportive,
so the anxiety we feel when Dave's running the show is ee-
rily absent today. I like it, but I don't trust it. If my body isn't
thrumming with nerves and fear, what's going to fuel my race?

While I'm swimming it, I don't think my 200 IM is going
particularly well. I feel stiff and slow at first, and only sink com-
fortably into the swim halfway through the breaststroke—too
late, by my calculations, to touch the wall with a good result.

But when the race is over and I raise my head to look at
the scoreboard, what I see floors me: not only did I win my
heat, I shaved two seconds off my most recent personal best.

It's off from where I was two years ago, and not enough to
qualify for Trials, but it's still a monumental accomplishment.
More important, it's progress. As I climb out of the pool, I
start to wonder: What if Dave's not the coach who will get
me to the Olympics? What if *Beth* is?

CHAPTER SEVEN

298 days until US Olympic Team Trials

"WHAT ARE YOU WORKING ON?"

I glance up from my math textbook to see Harry standing over me. He gives me a tentative smile, nothing like his usual cocky grin, and suddenly my tongue feels too big for my mouth.

It's almost nine o'clock. I'm sitting on the floor in the natatorium lobby, doing homework while I wait for Mom. Everyone has already gone home. Dad picked up a last-minute shift at the restaurant, Mom has class and Nina doesn't have her own car so she can't come to get me. I wish I'd known earlier so I could have caught a ride with Amber or Jessa, but I didn't see Dad's text until they had both left. I was annoyed by it at the time, but now I'm grateful. Who knows if Harry would've ever talked to me again if he didn't find me sitting here?

This is the first time he's intentionally struck up a conversation with me since Tucker's party. The bus doesn't count, because I talked to him. I'd hoped that might change things, but it didn't. I've been focusing on swimming and trying not to think about it, but every time I look at him I feel the bruising ache of regret. Why did I have to ruin things? Why can't I ever get out of my own way?

"Hi," I say, giving him my brightest smile. *Speak more words, Ramos!* But my lungs feel like those uninflated oxygen bags in airplane safety videos. They say air is flowing, but how is that possible? I can't seem to get enough to choke out a sentence. Not that I'd know what to say if I could.

It's stupid, but it doesn't occur to me to answer his question. I'm so happy he's talking to me I can't even remember what it was.

"Can I sit?" Harry asks, slinging his swim bag over his shoulder.

"Sure!" Okay, that was way too much enthusiasm.

He flops down next to me and flips the cover of my textbook over so he can read the title.

"Advanced Algebra II. So you're one of those dumb jock types, huh?"

"Guess so." Oh my God, my chest is on fire. My body is exhausted from today's workout, but I feel like I've been electrocuted, sparks flying through my veins.

My traitorous stomach picks that exact moment to complain. I haven't eaten since lunch. Harry digs through his bag until he unearths a couple of energy bars.

"Want one?" he offers. "Gotta feed the beast."

"God, yes, thank you!"

Harry gives me an energy bar, then taps his against the one in my hand. "Cheers."

I laugh. "Cheers." Then I tear open the thin foil wrapper and take the daintiest bite I can manage given how ravenous I am. Harry finishes his in two swallows.

"I know these things have a ton of calories, but I always feel hungrier after I eat one." He peers at my notebook. "208."

I stare at him.

"The answer to the problem you're doing," he says. "It's 208."

I close the textbook and shove it in my bag. "How did you figure that out so quickly?"

Harry shrugs. "I'm good with numbers."

"One of those dumb jock types?"

"Exactly. Why are you still here? Practicing starts again?"

I shake my head. "My mom's picking me up, but she's running late."

"If you want, I can drive you." He dangles his keys from his finger, making them jingle. "Unless you'd rather sit here working on differential equations."

From his tone, I sense he means something like, *Unless you don't want to spend time with me*, but he's too proud to say it. I wonder if he feels as weightless and fizzy with nerves as I do.

"Nope," I say, getting to my feet. "Let's go."

I tell myself it's the ride home I'm excited about, but I've never been a very good liar.

As we walk to his car, Harry keeps squinting at me. I'm not sure why, but I follow his line of sight straight to my chest.

"Eyes up here," I joke, pointing to my face, then regret it.

He's being polite, offering to drive me, and here I am making it awkward. I'm hopeless.

But I don't want him to look at what I'm wearing. I found this ratty old GAC sweatshirt in my locker, and that's what he's staring at. I remember with horror what I usually look like after practice.

"I was just thinking," he says. "What the *hell* is an aqualion, anyway?"

"Something Dave made up. You should ask him."

"I would," Harry says. "I'm honestly so curious, but he's not a big fan of mine right now."

"The rubber ducks still?"

"You'd think he'd be over it, but no."

Harry's car is nicer than any car my family has ever owned. Our school district is huge, covering several towns of varying socioeconomic statuses. We Ramoses are solidly middle class. Harry, I realize, might be well-off. I climb into the passenger seat and take a quick look around, expecting to see a lot of garbage strewn about the floor, due to: boy. But it's tidy.

"He made me stay late so we could have a 'talk' about my 'dedication to the sport,'" Harry says. He tosses our swim bags and my school backpack onto the empty backseat, and then hands me his phone so that I can plug my address into his GPS app.

"What's that supposed to mean?" I ask. I shoot Mom a quick text to tell her I'm getting a ride home. The last thing I need is for her to show up, find me missing and assume that I've been kidnapped.

"Basically, he thinks I goof off too much and don't take

swimming seriously enough *'given my enormous potential,'"*
Harry says with sarcastic air quotes.

He backs out of his parking space and sets off across the
empty lot with no regard for the lines on the asphalt.

"That does sound like Dave," I say.

"He said that unless I can get my head out of my ass and
start working harder, I should reconsider whether I belong
at GAC."

"He's kicking you off the team?"

"More like putting me on probation. He's just trying to
scare me."

"It's kind of true, you know," I say. Harry gives me a sharp
look. "I wouldn't put it the way Dave did, but… I watch you
at practice sometimes and you're fast, but it doesn't seem like
you care that much about swimming, or the team. Why do
you stay if you don't like it?"

Harry smirks. "You watch me at practice sometimes?"

"Not…in that—you know what I mean," I sputter. "I watch
a lot of people at practice."

"Sure, sure. Well, I do like the team," he says. "It's the whole
swimming industry that I hate, and people like Dave, who
think winning races is the only thing that matters. Let's face
it—most of us aren't going to the Olympics. If we're going to
work like dogs, don't you think we should have fun doing it?"

"To be honest, swimming's not something I do for fun."

"You can't be doing it for the money—not much of that
in this sport. Glory, then?"

"Maybe. Is there something wrong with that?"

"No. And for the record, I care about swimming," Harry
says. "I just try not to care too much because if I do it'll make

me miserable. I know that from experience. But I don't want to get kicked off the team."

"Good. That would suck."

"Why?"

"You're a great swimmer," I tell him. "It would be a real waste of talent if you did."

He stares out the windshield at the road, frowning. "Can I ask why you left the party, or would that be a real waste, too?"

I release the breath I'm holding. "I've been waiting for you to ask about that."

"Sorry, I assumed you'd *tell* me," he says, his voice tight with irritation. "Like, explain or something. I figured you had a good reason. But now I'm thinking maybe you don't? Or, I guess, not liking me enough to stick around is a good reason. Is that why?"

I can't say I don't like him because I do. But I can't say that, either. So I don't say anything at all, which is probably the worst of the options, but I honestly don't know what to do.

"Got it." His shoulders stiffen and he grips the steering wheel so hard the leather squeaks.

For a few minutes, the only person speaking is the woman who narrates the GPS app. My head starts to ache, and my chest feels hollow and empty. I can't let him think what he's thinking. It's not true, and it's not fair, and I don't want to hurt his feelings. But how do I explain what I felt at that party, what that story about Kara Walker dredged up in me? How do I make him understand all the fear I carry around on my back?

It seems like too much to share with a boy I barely know.

"That rubber duck thing—you know I did that for you, right?" Harry says.

"You pretty much told me you did. Was I not sufficiently grateful?" I ask. He can't possibly think that one grand gesture I never asked for entitles him to something from me.

"No, that's not—I didn't mean it like that. You don't owe me any gratitude."

I stare out the window at the night-drenched road, avoiding my reflection in the glass. My shoulders are sore from practice, and the left one throbs like a warning: *Stop embarrassing yourself.*

"I'm saying this all wrong." He takes a deep breath. "I'm not mad about the party. I know the Flow is super dumb, and I get that I can be...a lot. Not everyone's all in for this."

He gestures to himself, and I almost say, *I think plenty of girls are all in for that,* but I don't.

"It's hard being the new kid," he continues. "You have no idea where you fit in. But when I was around you before, I felt like—this is going to sound so weird, but when I saw you practicing your start, working so hard after a long practice just to get it perfect, I understood that complete and total fear of having fucked up and never wanting to do it again. I feel like that, too. All of the time. It's not about swimming. It's other things, with me."

"What other things?"

He shakes his head. "It's hard to explain. I guess my point is, I liked that about you. Your relentlessness. I thought we might have something more in common than favorite bands and TV shows and swimming. Maybe I'm wrong. But I'd like to find out. I'd like to be friends."

"You have arrived at your destination," the GPS woman says.

Harry pulls into my driveway and kills the engine. I know I should say something, but I feel like I'm being dragged out to sea by a strong current—completely overwhelmed and incapable of finding my way back to shore. *Thank you* won't cut it. *I'd like to be friends, too* is only part true. So I act on pure, mindless impulse and hug him.

I. *Hug.* Him.

After a small hesitation, Harry hugs me back, and then we're holding each other awkwardly, like children. The gearshift is jabbing me in the ribs and my seat belt is cutting into my neck, but when I try to tear myself away, it's like separating two pieces of Velcro. Neither of us seems eager to let go.

"This is a surprise," Harry says into my hair. His voice is muffled by my curls.

"I should call my mom and let her know I'm home," I say, finally pulling away.

"Definitely, go do that," he says. And there it is: the Harry Matthews smile. Like the sun emerging from behind a cloud.

He sits back in his seat. He looks a bit thunderstruck, like he's not quite sure what just happened. I'm not, either, but I feel like the door that slammed shut inside of me when I left the party might be opening again. It's terrifying. But I don't want to close it again.

"See you tomorrow, Susie," he says.

I smile. "Bright and early."

I stand on the porch until Harry's taillights disappear around the corner. The door opens and Nina pokes her head out. Lulu wiggles through her legs and jumps on me, barking hello.

"Where's Mom?" Nina asks. "I thought she went to pick you up."

"I got a ride."

I pat Lulu on the head and slip into the house. There's a delicious smell wafting out of the kitchen. It's Nina's night to cook. She's pretty good at it; she went through a phase where she binge-watched YouTube cooking tutorials and experimented on us for months, with mostly positive results.

"Enchiladas?" I ask. They're her specialty, and my favorite.

She follows me into the kitchen. "Who drove you?"

"Someone from GAC," I say, like it's no big deal, when in fact it is the *biggest* deal. Nobody's ever told me they liked my *relentlessness* before. Usually, when someone uses a word like that to describe me, they don't mean it in a good way. I'm practically floating.

I dump my swim bag in the mudroom and shoot Mom a text saying I'm home. Then I grab plates to set the table for dinner.

"A *boy* someone?"

"Were you watching us?" I ask, glaring at her. Nina's always been such a snoop.

"Maybe. There's nothing good on TV right now."

Nina opens the oven to check on the food. She sets the timer and leans against the counter, staring at me as if it will make me spill. Lulu parks herself near the oven and whines until I pet her.

"What's the deal with the dude? Are you dating him?"

"*No.*"

"But you like him. I saw that hug."

I hate that she was watching. This thing with Harry is confusing enough without Nina squeezing me for details or, worse, telling me what to do about it. I know what she would say if she knew. She'd tell me to go for it; YOLO; I'm too careful; I worry too much. But it's not that easy to go against every instinct you have and dismantle the walls you built to keep yourself safe. You can't just decide to be a different person and pretend your fears don't exist.

"It's none of your business," I tell her. "Leave me alone."

"But none of my business is my favorite kind of business. You know, if you have questions about that sort of stuff, you can always ask me," Nina says. "I give great advice."

"Says who?"

"Trust me. I'm an expert on boys. I'm very experienced and wise."

Experienced, sure. Nina has a different boyfriend, like, every other week. We can tell there's a new guy by reading the changes in her. If he's goth, she wears all black and talks about getting a tattoo; if he's into football, she commandeers the TV every time the Bears play. If he's got a sweet tooth, she bakes; if he's vegetarian, she gives up meat. She has no idea what she wants yet, or who she wants to be. And if that's the way she likes it, great, but it's not for me.

"Let's not forget humble," I say.

"Come *on*," Nina whines. "You never talk to me about stuff like this. Let me help you."

Nina doesn't want to hear about my life. She and I joined GAC together back when we were kids, and when she was still swimming, we talked all the time. After she quit, lured away by new high school friends and activities, it was like she stopped caring about me.

She doesn't care about this, either. She's just bored. And much as I'd love her to take an interest in my life, I'm not going to girl-talk for her entertainment.

"I don't need help," I tell her.

"You never do," she says.

"What's that supposed to mean?"

"It's not *supposed* to mean anything. It actually means that you expect everyone in this house to build their lives around you and your sport and your dream, but God forbid any of us ask a question or have an opinion."

Nina shakes her head. "You were such a sweet kid, Susannah. When did you get so selfish?"

CHAPTER EIGHT

297 days until US Olympic Team Trials

"THIS IS GOING TO BE SUPER WEIRD, ISN'T IT?" I ASK.

Amber, Jessa and I are standing at the locker room entrance as our teammates stream through the doorway, suited up and yawning into their hands. I'm afraid to step onto the pool deck, certain that now he's had time to think through the awkwardness of last night's conversation, Harry won't want anything to do with me. And I can't get what Nina said out of my head. If I'm selfish, it's because I've had to be. No one else is going to fight for my dream. But I don't want to hurt people, and I can't figure out how to protect them while still protecting myself.

"It'll only be weird if you make it weird," Jessa says. Sarah Weller bumps her as she pushes past us. Jessa scowls at her back, then adds, "So, probably."

Amber smacks her. "It's going to be fine. He said he wants to be friends, right?"

"Yeah." I twist my goggles in my hands. "But I bet he thinks I'm so strange."

"You're not strange," Jessa says. "In the scheme of things, what's one guy? Someday, when you've got Olympic gold hanging around your neck, you won't even remember his name."

Amber groans. "The two of you, I swear. How did I end up with the most unromantic friends on earth? If a girl I was into liked me back, I'd quit GAC *tomorrow.* And not because relationships and swimming don't mix, just because I'd finally have something better to do."

"Shut up, you wouldn't quit," I say with a laugh.

"Maybe I would," Amber grumbles.

"I barely have enough hours in the day to sleep. There's no time for boys," I say without conviction.

"Nobody has time for a boyfriend," Jessa says in that all-knowing tone she sometimes puts on with me. "Until they've got one. Then they don't have time for anything else."

"You know what's going to affect your future?" Amber snaps. "*Not going to practice.* You can't hide in the locker room all day, so take a breath, put your big-girl pants on and get out there."

I didn't need to worry about what to say to Harry after last night, because I don't get to talk to him during practice. Dave has returned to GAC, but his back must still be bothering him because he's in a fouler mood than normal.

In an unusual move, he and Beth split the elites between them, each coaching two lanes of swimmers with entirely different workouts. I don't realize how badly I want to train with Beth today until Dave assigns me to one of his lanes.

It doesn't escape my notice that Dave's group is mostly

boys, and Beth has only girls. A few weeks ago, I'd have been beaming with pride at being one of the few female swimmers Dave selected for himself, but now I feel disappointed.

Predictably, the workout Dave puts us through is merciless. I love a hard practice—the more challenging, the better—and I throw myself into it. I tell myself I'm trying to impress Dave, to remind him why I'm still worth training, but halfway through a particularly difficult set I find myself searching the next lane for Harry, to see if he's watching me, and I realize my efforts are more for him than my coach.

Dave gave up on me a long time ago. He hardly looks at me and doesn't speak to me much during the three hours I'm in the pool. I wonder why he even chose to have me in his lanes today.

Beth does talk to me—once—during a long, brutal IM set in the second half of practice. She says, "Your backstroke needs work."

I glare at her, panting hard. This drill allows for very little rest, and I'm irritated she's wasting my precious break with feedback I didn't ask for when she didn't even bother to put me in her lanes.

"You can't distinguish yourself in the IM with a weak backstroke," she adds.

I turn away from Beth and push off from the wall, pouring my frustration into my swim. If she wanted to coach me, she should've fought to have me in her group, but she didn't. She can save her criticism for someone else, as far as I'm concerned. I get enough from Dave as it is.

A couple days later, I wait outside the boys' locker room after practice. I dressed quicker than I ever have before to make it out ahead of Harry, so I could grab him before he takes off for the night. I need to ask him for a favor.

My pulse drums in my throat. We haven't talked much since he drove me home, just a few quick chats in the water between sets. Which isn't to say people haven't noticed.

Tonight, Dave put us through a grueling set of lung-busters—one full pool length underwater and a freestyle sprint back on a near-impossible interval, over and over until you're worn out. Harry's always trying to get out of lungbusters. They're his least favorite set. I know that because we were in adjacent lanes during practice again, and he flat out told me so.

"Why?" I panted. My chest heaved as I tried to catch my breath. I was so relieved things weren't weird between us. Everything seemed normal, like that awkward hug never happened.

Harry grimaced. "Being underwater that long makes me feel like I've been buried alive. I don't think I'd like to drown."

"I don't think anybody would like to drown," I said.

"Yeah, but I mean, of all the ways to go..."

"It's a good thing you can swim, then," I said.

"Even strong swimmers can drown," he replied.

"Ramos! Matthews! What the hell are you doing over there?" Dave loomed over us. "Is the workout getting in the way of your conversation?"

"No, sorry," I said at the same time Harry muttered, "Kinda."

Dave scowled at Harry and pointed to the pace clock. "You missed your interval."

I still had a few precious seconds on mine, and Dave took the opportunity, with Harry kicking along the length of the pool, to lecture me.

"You've been hanging out with that Matthews kid," he said.

"Not really." I shook my head to clear some water out of my ears. Maybe if I ignored him, he'd find someone else to lecture.

"I don't like his attitude," Dave said. "And the last thing you need is something to draw your focus away. I'm looking out for you."

"Uh-huh," I said, getting ready to push off from the wall.

"You'll thank me," he said, right before I went underwater.

Dave controls a huge part of my life; he doesn't get to choose my friends, too. But I'm not here, waiting for Harry, out of some childish attempt to defy him. This is about my swimming.

When Harry emerges from the locker room, he's with Avik Kapali, another sophomore who started GAC the same season as me and Nina. They're laughing and shoving each other playfully as they walk through the doorway. I have half a mind to bolt, but when Harry notices me, I freeze. His smile fades for a second, then returns even brighter than before.

"Susie," he says. "What's up? Do you need a ride?"

"No, um…"

On cue, every word in my brain disintegrates. What did I want again? Harry and Avik stare at me.

"I had something I wanted to ask you," I mumble.

Harry claps Avik on the back. "See you tomorrow, man."

"Later," Avik says, taking off.

"So…what was it you wanted to ask me?" Harry asks after we stand there for a few silent seconds, smiling at each other.

"Oh! Yeah." I take a deep breath and gather my courage. It's never been easy for me to ask for help. "I want your advice on my backstroke. It needs work."

Harry nudges my shoulder with his. "That's not a question."

My face falls. "You think so, too?"

"No, I mean, you said you had something to ask me but 'I need your advice on my backstroke' is a statement," Harry says with a laugh. "Questions sound more like this? Usually people's voices get higher at the end?"

I punch his arm. He rubs his shoulder and chuckles. I wish he wouldn't laugh. Can't he see how hard this is for me?

"I need to work on my backstroke, and it's your specialty, so I was wondering if you would consider watching me after practice one day and giving me some pointers. I bet Beth wouldn't mind staying late again considering she's the one who said I needed some help, so—"

I cut myself off to catch my breath. My lung capacity is pretty good, but not when he's looking at me like he wants to kiss me.

He does not *want to kiss you*, I scold myself savagely. *He probably thinks you're ridiculous.*

"Not sure there was a question in there, either," Harry says. "But I'm happy to give you some pointers on your backstroke."

"Thank you," I say, taking a much-needed sip from my water bottle.

"Let's not do it after practice, though. We'll both be too tired. How about Sunday?"

"This Sunday?" Harry nods. "You want to spend your day off from swimming in the pool?"

"I want to spend my day off from swimming with you. If that has to happen in a pool, let's just say I'm not surprised," Harry says.

I look down at my shoes, too flustered to meet his eyes.

"Besides, I doubt it'll take the whole day. You're not a guppy who needs lessons."

"Sometimes I feel like I am," I tell him. Now that Dave's returned and I've stopped training with Beth, I'm back to feeling heavy and slow in the water.

"You're not," Harry insists. "Are you sure you don't need a ride home?"

I shake my head. "My dad's waiting for me in the parking lot."

"Cool. See you Sunday, Susie," he says, walking backward down the hallway so he can continue to grin at me as he leaves.

On Sunday, Harry shows up at my house a little before six-thirty a.m. He texted last night to warn me he'd be here early, but I thought he was exaggerating. When I answer the door, I'm still in my pajama pants and a GAC T-shirt from a couple of years ago, though I did have the good sense to put on a bra.

"Suit up," Harry says cheerfully, like it's not the butt-crack of dawn on our one day off. "We've got work to do."

He's not dressed like we're going to work out. He's wearing a pair of dark jeans and a black fleece, a blue buffalo plaid shirt that brings out his eyes, and a Cubs hat with a frayed bill and sweat stains along the rim. The sight of him does funny things to my nether regions. I guess when you spend most of your time in a bathing suit, seeing people with clothes *on* can sometimes be sexier.

"What's that?" I ask, squinting at the plastic bag he's carrying through bleary eyes.

"Energy bars and Gatorade," he tells me. "Go get ready,
Susie. I'll wait in the car."

"Um," I say hesitantly. "No, you won't. My parents want
to meet you. They have this policy of not letting me get into
a car with someone they don't know."

Mom and Dad were not pleased when they found out Harry
drove me home from practice the other day. When I told them
we were going out this morning, they insisted he come in
and sit down for Dad's patented "responsible driver" lecture.

Harry checks his phone. "It's almost six-thirty," he says.
"I don't think they have time to get to know me. That could
take months."

I roll my eyes and grab his hand, pulling him into the
house.

"This'll only take a second," I promise, relishing the feeling of his skin against mine. He doesn't pull away, so it's almost like we're holding hands for real. I really need to stop
thinking like this.

Mom and Dad are both early risers, even on weekends;
years of driving me to morning practice seem to have permanently reset their circadian rhythms. They're at the kitchen
table, nursing cups of lukewarm coffee and reading the newspaper. I love that they sit together and pass the sections back
and forth, even though they could obviously get all the same
articles on their phones. It's a bonding thing, one of the small
rituals of their marriage, and the dependability of it makes me
feel as though, no matter what those pages have to say about
things going on in the world, everything's going to be okay.

My parents may have glimpsed Harry at meets before, but I haven't talked about him much at home. Dad questions him sternly about how long he's had his license and what kind of car he drives, how well he maintains it and does Harry know that when I'm in the passenger seat he's ferrying some of the most precious cargo on earth? It's so embarrassing. Harry passes the exam, charming them both without breaking a sweat, a feat few of my and Nina's friends have managed to achieve.

"Where are we going?" I ask ten minutes later when he takes the wrong turn out of my subdivision. "School's the other way."

"There's a Masters team that uses the pool every Sunday morning," he explains. "They're total lane hogs. But the JCC pool has free swim every morning five to nine. It'll be fine."

"I didn't know you were Jewish," I say, adding that little nugget to the pile of Harry Facts I've been collecting. He's also left-handed, lactose intolerant and—apparently—a Cubs fan.

"I'm not," he says. "Bruce is—my stepdad. But you don't need to be Jewish to have a JCC membership. It's open to everybody."

"Oh, got it," I say, eyeing the baseball cap. I've never seen him wear one before. It makes him look younger somehow, or maybe it reminds me that despite how grown up he looks, he's still a boy.

"What? You don't like the hat?" He tugs on it self-consciously. I turn away, embarrassed to be caught staring, and at the same time pleased that he cares what I think.

"Might be time for a new one," I say gently. The thing is clearly falling to pieces.

"I love this hat," he whimpers.

"Yes, but do you wash it?"

He shakes his head in dismay. "I can't believe this. My stepdad gave me this hat. It's a family heirloom, passed down through generations of Matthewses. Well, two generations, but still. It's perfectly worn in."

"Sure looks like it."

Harry yanks the cap off with a growl and plops it on my head.

"There," he says. "Maybe you need to wear it to understand the magic."

"How *dare* you," I say, tossing it back at him with a theatrical gasp. "I am a *White Sox fan*."

"What?" Harry shouts. *"Why?"*

I shrug. "My parents are from the South Side. They grew up next door to each other in South Lawndale. Loyalties die hard."

Harry smiles. "Then I guess I can forgive this atrocious lapse in judgment. Nobody's perfect, but your mom and dad seem pretty great."

"They do?" I thought he might find Dad's overprotectiveness annoying.

"Yeah. You said they were neighbors growing up? How long have they been together?"

"Since they were in high school," I tell him. There's something about how my parents act around each other, the seamless way they move through spaces together and finish each other's thoughts midsentence, that gives you the sense they've been partners for a very long time.

"And they say young love can't last," Harry says.

"My parents would tell you it wasn't easy. They made a lot of sacrifices to stay together."

"Well, I'm glad they did."

I laugh. "Me too. Obviously."

★ ★ ★

The pool at the Jewish community center is designed to look like a Roman bath, with fluted columns and elaborate mosaics of mythological sea creatures decorating the walls. Harry shows them off like he made them himself, and I realize this isn't his first time swimming here.

Aside from a few old folks doing a leisurely crawl in the outer lanes, Harry and I have the place to ourselves. Harry has me swim a few laps of backstroke for observation.

"Okay, I see what's happening," he says, crouching near the lip of the pool. "Your head's a little too far forward and it's messing up your streamline. And when you get tired, your left arm drifts and it increases your stroke per minute. Each pull becomes less powerful. That's your sore shoulder, right?"

I nod. It's been giving me trouble for almost a year. I'm surprised he's noticed, but I guess I shouldn't be. I spend a lot of time in the pool watching him. Maybe he's been watching me, too.

Sometimes it's difficult to concentrate on much except how badly I want to touch him. I love his body as much as I hate my own—his shoulders and his arms, the broad expanse of his back and the way the muscles of his lower abdomen cut a V-shape that disappears below the waist of his suit. He's beautiful, really, and I can't get enough of the sight of him. I always want to be near him. It makes me feel out of control. And I shouldn't be lusting after my friend when I know he wants more, but I don't know how to stop feeling it.

The first step is probably to stop staring at him so much.

I lower my eyes and fiddle with my swim cap to have something to concentrate on.

"How come you always wear jammers to practice?" I ask him. It never struck me as odd that Harry practices in the long, formfitting suits most guys use only in competition, the ones that look more like bike shorts than Speedos. Then I heard Nash snickering about it the other day and I started to wonder. He's wearing them again today.

I expect him to laugh the question off, but he tenses up, his expression darkening.

"I guess I just prefer them," he says in a tone that tells me I shouldn't press him further. "Concentrate on making your bicep brush your ear during recovery. That should help."

I worry I've upset him, but during the time it takes for me to get down the pool and back, his sunny mood returns and it's like I never asked. After about an hour spent on adjusting my form and doing short drills, we drive to a nearby diner for breakfast. I insist on paying as a thank-you to Harry.

"All right," he says, attacking his omelet with a fork. "But I'm still not sure why you thought you needed my help."

"Clearly I did or you wouldn't have found so much to correct."

I heap scrambled eggs onto a piece of wheat toast and take a careful bite. It's chilly outside, so Harry lent me his fleece to wear. I don't want to dump food down the front of it.

"Yeah, sure, but why the extra practice? Why the backstroke?"

"Beth told me mine needed work," I say. "She thinks I suck."

Harry laughs. "She can't think you suck, because you don't suck."

"Says you," I reply.

"Do you trust her? Does she seem to know what she's doing?"

"When she gives me advice, it usually pays off," I admit. I hesitate, then say, "I think I'd be better off swimming for her instead of Dave."

"I was wondering why you weren't in her training group," Harry says. "When she was subbing for Dave, you seemed to get a lot out of it. You seemed happier."

I consider this for a moment. "I guess I was. It's been a long time since swimming made me happy."

Harry gazes at me in silence. I consider not telling him what I said to Beth when she first started—what if he thinks it was petty? But the idea of confessing brings a wave of anticipatory relief.

"I told her I didn't want to train with her," I say, feeling ashamed. I always say I'll do anything for my swimming, make any sacrifice, and yet here I am, clinging desperately to the last tattered remnants of my pride. It's pathetic.

"That explains it," he says. "But why?"

"Because I thought it would mean something if I switched coaches. Like I'm not good enough to swim for Dave anymore. That's what people would think."

"But don't you care more about your swimming than what people might think?" Harry asks. I nod. "And how much does what other people think matter, anyway?"

"What some people think matters. I care what college scouts think. I care what USA Swimming thinks. What potential sponsors might think, if I ever get that far," I say. "But I get your point."

"What if you ask to train with Beth?" Harry suggests.

I chew my bottom lip. "She might say no. Or Dave might, to spite me."

"Or they might agree to it. Only one way to find out," he says.

On the way home, I snuggle up inside Harry's fleece and start scheming of a way to keep it. It's soft and comfortable and smells like him, like chlorine and whatever shampoo he uses after practice, and also a little like baby-powder-scented dryer sheets.

We're both tired and full, so we don't say much, but I'm comfortable here with Harry, sitting so close to him our shoulders almost touch, with the faint sound of the Top 40 radio station spilling cheesy love songs we can only half hear.

Harry pulls into my driveway. "Hey, Susie?"

"Yeah?"

"Don't you dare try to steal that fleece."

Swimming together on Sundays becomes our weekly ritual. We fall into an easy pattern of Harry picking me up at six-thirty, then spending an hour or two in the pool working on form—my backstroke, his breaststroke, which *he* asks *me* for help with—and finishing at the diner for breakfast.

I feel at ease with Harry, much more relaxed when it's just us in the pool. He gives me a lot of feedback, but I never feel like he's trying to tear me down. Our time at the diner is even better, because we talk about things besides swimming— family, school, books, music. We become friends on those Sunday mornings. If I'm honest, it feels like we're becoming something more, but I try not to think about that too much.

Then one Sunday, with no notice, he doesn't show up.

CHAPTER NINE

261 days until US Olympic Team Trials

"I'M GOING TO TALK TO BETH TONIGHT," I TELL HARRY AS I help him clean up the deck after evening practice. It's incredible, the mess a bunch of teenage swimmers can make.

"Finally done putting it off?" Harry teases, punting a kickboard into one of the metal bins. He can't even perform minor bits of drudgery without turning them into a game. I drop an armful of pool buoys into a bin and take a deep breath, steeling myself.

"Harry, what happened on Sunday?" I ask. "Is everything okay?"

I've been trying to work up the courage to confront him about this all week, going back and forth between being mad that he blew me off and telling myself it's nothing—people have lives; plans change last minute. If he'd canceled, I'd have been disappointed, but it wouldn't have bothered me so much.

What bugs me is that he didn't tell me, he didn't respond for hours when I texted him to check in and then he didn't show up for school or practice on Monday or Tuesday. I went from hurt to concerned, and when he did come back, he was tired and subdued. Distant. He never gave me a real explanation, so I'm still worried. But he keeps pretending everything's fine.

He turns away from me to fidget with a pile of tangled bungees. "I told you, something came up," he says. He yanks at the knotted bungees until one of them snaps back and hits him in the chest.

He presses his hand to his collarbone. "Shit, that stings."

"Here, let me help you."

I take the bungees from him and undo them easily. He wasn't really struggling with them, he was using them as an excuse not to look at me. He's embarrassed. I can tell by the way his neck flushes. He won't turn around.

Something came up. That's what he said when he finally responded to my texts. I know he's not my boyfriend, and he doesn't owe me explanations. Technically, *I'm* the one who wants to be friends.

There's no denying how I much I like him, though. I know it, and I'm sure he does, too. Despite years of swimming for Dave, I'm no good at hiding my feelings, especially ones I've never felt before. I've had crushes—I've even been kissed a few times, by a boy at swim camp a few summers ago—but nothing close to Harry. I hate myself for not being able to get these feelings under control. But as always, my body is the ultimate traitor.

Harry takes the bungees back from me and coils them up before placing them in the plastic container at his feet.

"You don't need to help me with this, Susie," he says. "Talk to Beth. I'll finish up out here."

Then he walks away. Whatever's bothering him, he's not going to talk to me about it. Maybe I was stupid to think that he would.

On my way to the coaches' office, I stop by the coolers to heap a spoonful of ground ice into a plastic bag and fix it to my left shoulder. It takes me a few tries to wrap it properly, but it's necessary. Every day, it hurts a little more. I've got to take better care of it.

In the coaches' office, Beth is sitting at her desk, scribbling in a warped spiral-bound notebook.

"Designing tomorrow's torture?" I ask.

She looks up, startled, like she didn't hear my knock, then smiles when she sees it's me.

"Hi, Susannah," she says, setting the notebook aside. "What's up? Do you want to sit?"

I take a seat across from her. I feel nervous, like I'm in trouble. I know there's a real chance she'll turn me down.

Beth eyes the ice pack on my shoulder. "What's going on there?"

"Nothing. Just some soreness."

She nods. "So how can I help you?"

"Well..." I take a deep breath and let it out in a big rush: "Here'sthethingIwanttotrainwithyou."

Beth squints at me. "Repeat that?"

"I want to train with you. I know I said—"

"I thought you only wanted to train with Dave," she says.

"That's what you told me. It's why I asked Dave to put you in his group instead of mine."

"I know that's what I said, but I was being stupid. I was afraid of what it might mean if I stopped training with Dave. Like I wasn't good enough for him or something. I thought everyone would think I was a failure."

"What's changed?"

"When Dave was out with his back thing and you took over practice, I wasn't sure what to expect," I explain. "But I felt so much better in the water with you coaching me. I got faster. And when he came back, and I got put in his group, all that progress stopped. My dream is more important to me than my pride. So..." I spread my hands. "So that's why I'm here."

"You're here because you've decided I'm worth the risk," Beth says. It's not a question. And I don't think there's any judgment in it, either. "You've decided to trust me with your career."

"Yup. Bad backstroke and all."

"I didn't say your backstroke was bad," she says. "I said it needed work."

"Will you help me improve it?"

Beth frowns. "That depends."

"On what?"

"Can I ask you a few questions before I answer that one?"

"Uh, sure."

She turns away from the desk and faces me straight-on. "How long have you been in the sport?"

"Since I was seven, so about nine years."

"And your specialty is..."

She knows this already. Dave must've told her, and even

if he didn't, he keeps files on all his elite swimmers. I'm sure she's gone through them. But I owe her an apology, and I think playing along with this interview is my way of doing it.

"Sprint freestyle and butterfly. The 200 IM is my best event."

"Dave has you lead off on the 400 free relay, too."

I nod. "And I swim fly in the 400 IM relay a lot."

"Do you like it?"

"The relay? Or the 200 IM?"

"Both. Either. I'm trying to get a sense for what you enjoy swimming."

She follows this line of questioning with several more: Is there an event I hate? One I wish I could swim but Dave won't support me? She wants to know times, favorite workouts, how I feel about morning versus evening practices, what I think of my teammates.

Finally, we come to the inevitable: my slowdown. I never want to talk about it, but I think about it all the time.

"I understand," she says after I explain. "You got older, your body changed, it got harder. It happens to a lot of female swimmers. Did you ever talk to a therapist about it?"

I laugh. "No."

She cocks her head. "What's so funny?"

"I'm trying to imagine asking my parents to pay for me to complain to some stranger about how getting boobs ruined my life. They spend enough on me as it is."

"That's not the point of therapy. You were poised for something special, and in a few months, that all changed," Beth says. "You lost something important to you. Don't you think you should talk to somebody about that? Figure out how to cope with the loss?"

"I can get back to where I was if I work hard enough," I insist.

If you'll train me is what I really want to say, but after what I told her before, it wouldn't be right for me to put this on her. It's on me.

"You're certainly working hard."

Beth takes out her notebook and flips to a page with my name on it. My heart lifts. She's been taking notes on me, paying attention. She wouldn't do that if she wasn't still thinking about training me.

"You kill yourself in practice," Beth continues, "but you're making only modest improvements. Given how much you're in the water, you should be progressing much faster."

She puts her hands on her knees and looks me straight in the eyes.

"I'm going to level with you. You're never going to be the exact same swimmer you were when you won that gold medal at Worlds. You have a different body, and there's nothing we can do to change that. But we can take the body you have and make it work in a better, more efficient way."

"That's what I want."

"I've been watching you," she says. "I've been watching everyone. What I'm looking for are swimmers who have a natural feel for the water and haven't harnessed their full potential for whatever reason. I think you might be one, and it's possible I can help you get back to where you were, speedwise. In fact, I think I can make you faster than that."

"Really?" Back to where I was would be a monumental achievement. Faster seems like too much to even dream about. But that's where I need to be if I'm going to have any shot at the Olympics.

Beth smiles. "Really."

Maybe Beth's wrong. Maybe she can't fix me. But there's a voice inside my head that says, *Maybe she can*. It's tiny, but it's stubborn, an unmovable barnacle of hope on the hull of my sunken career. And anyway, what have I got to lose?

"Do you think Dave will let me switch training groups?" I ask. I can't imagine him caring whether he coaches me or not, but he won't like that I'm asking to be moved. The man's ego could fill a football stadium.

"Let me handle Dave."

"Then I'm in," I tell her. "I'm one hundred percent in."

"Take the night to think about it. Because I'm not like Dave at all. You got a glimpse into the way I train my swimmers when I was subbing for him, but that's just the beginning. I'm going to push you way outside your comfort zone, and you strike me as the sort of person who likes what they know."

"I want to go to the Olympics. I don't care how I get there."

"Do you know what I mean when I say you have a feel for the water?" Beth asks.

"Not exactly," I admit. People throw that phrase around a lot in this sport, but it's always been an abstract concept to me.

"Some swimmers want to dominate the water, like it's something that can be tamed, or beat into submission," Beth says. "But when you get out of the pool, the water remains. It *always* wins. The trick is to work with it instead of against it. To free yourself from all the forces inside the pool that want to beat you back. To read the water and figure out the best way to move through it. It requires making small adjustments to increase efficiency without having to think about it. Does that make sense?"

"Perfect sense." I have no idea what she's talking about, but I want so badly to learn. Nobody has ever talked to me like this about swimming before. With Dave, it's all about yardage, how far you can push yourself daily in the pool.

Beth squares her shoulders. "My dad is Grady Watson. Do you know who that is?"

"Of course." Grady Watson is a legendary coach. It seems like half the best swimmers in the country train at his Southern California club. "But I thought your last name is Ramsay."

"It's my mother's maiden name. They're divorced," Beth says. "Grady was my coach until I was eighteen, and even when I was in college, I went back to his pool every summer. During the school year he still had a big hand in my training. He's a traditionalist, like Dave. Maybe he was extra hard on me because I'm his daughter. I don't know. But by the time I was a senior, I was so burned out on swimming that I quit. I changed my name and we haven't spoken since."

I squint to bring Beth into sharper focus. It's easy to forget coaches have lives outside of swimming, that anyone does. But this explains why, despite endless Googling, I haven't been able to find any information on her.

Beth smooths her long hair back into a ponytail and tugs it self-consciously.

"I'm convinced that the way I was brought up in the sport was fundamentally flawed," she says. "It's not about how many yards you can swim per day, or how many times a week you practice. It's about technique and understanding the best way to move through the water.

"You're not getting any faster because you force your way through races instead of listening to your body and doing what feels natural," she continues. "You're trying to swim the same way you did when you were smaller, using the same style and mechanics Dave taught you when you were a guppy. But when I tell you to change something, you adjust without hesitation. That's not easy. If you do train with me, we'll need to break down your old habits and build up new ones. I want to change the way you move, the way you think, the way you interact with the water on a material level. I want to redefine the physics of your swim. But I can only do that if I have your full cooperation and trust."

"You do," I assure her.

"Anyone can be a machine," Beth tells me. "I want you to be an animal. Because that's what you are. Animals don't overthink—they react, and they adapt. But you have to be present. You have to be willing to forget everything you know and come at this with a beginner's eyes."

What Beth is talking about, it's the sort of thing Dave would call "touchy-feely bullshit." He's all about pushing us past our limits in order to establish a foundation of endurance and stamina that's supposed to help us go faster. He'd balk at Beth's theory that skill is more important than power.

"Does Dave know about any of this?" I ask.

"Dave agreed to give me a certain amount of leeway," Beth says. "I think he sees the value of experimentation. He might be less rigid than you give him credit for."

"I doubt that," I say, but I feel lighter already, and even

though I've had some hard practices today, I wish I could get back in the water.

"You'll find my methods unorthodox," Beth warns me, but I know that already. Amber's in her training group, and she's told me all about Beth's training regimen. It's pretty bizarre, but it worked for me before.

"I want to go faster," I tell her. "I don't care how it happens. I'm sick of feeling like a loser."

"It would be irresponsible for me to promise you anything," Beth says. "But there's no reason you can't have what you want if you're willing to do what it takes to get it. You're not a loser, Susannah. Don't ever let anyone convince you that you are—especially yourself."

CHAPTER TEN

241 days until US Olympic Team Trials

BETH WASN'T KIDDING WHEN SHE SAID HER METHODS WERE unorthodox. Aside from the dramatic reduction in yardage, which I expected, and the return of affirmations—not my favorite thing in the world, but harmless—once Beth is in charge of my workouts, the rhythm of my life in the pool completely changes.

At my first practice with her squad, Beth warned us her entire focus for the next few weeks will be breaking down our preconceived notions of how we should conduct our lives as swimmers, in and out of the water. That included cutting our practice time...*in half.* When I told Beth she couldn't dismiss us early or tell us not to show up because we'd get kicked out of GAC, she gave me a look of such deep disappointment I felt like a fairy-tale character who'd failed a test of faith.

But she didn't yell at me, like Dave would if I dared to disagree with him. She told me to do what I wanted, but she'd be training me in the water five times a week. If I wanted to swim more than that, I could do it for Dave. I skipped the practices she told us to skip and Dave didn't say a word. In fact, he hasn't spoken to me at all since I changed coaches. Harry thinks I should be relieved, but I don't know. It feels ominous, like threatening storm clouds on the edge of the horizon.

Thankfully, the shake-up didn't last long, but when we resume our twice-daily workout schedule at the end of October, I do feel more energized and well rested.

We aren't idle outside of the pool, either. Beth increases our dry-land work and weight training and enrolls us in Pilates classes. We even take a few boxing classes to spice things up. It's all in service, Beth says, of strengthening our cores and teaching us to think more deliberately about how we hold our bodies, how we maintain balance. Then she applies those same ideas to our swims.

Practice becomes less arduous, because Beth believes in variety, always keeping things fresh. One day, she empties a jar full of pennies into the diving well and makes us compete to see who can collect the most coins in the least amount of time—a game that doubles as a hypoxic exercise. Beth's all about increasing our lung capacity and training our bodies to breathe only when necessary.

"*Wanting* air is not the same thing as *needing* it," she tells us.

It's embarrassing how long it takes me to understand what she's trying to do, how she's trying to free us from the net of accepted swim theory we've been trapped in since we were guppies. At first, all I feel is frustration and fear, and my performance in competition reflects that. But after a particularly lackluster invitational swim, Beth is quick to reassure me.

"When you make such big changes, it's like hitting a reset button. You'll get faster once you adapt," she says.

As much as I like swimming for her, and as hopeful as I am about her methods, I'm worried I've ruined everything by taking this risk. If my big Beth gambit fails, what will I even have left?

"You're getting stronger," Harry says as we leave the JCC. After that weekend where he bailed on me, we resumed our routine like nothing happened, and he hasn't done it again.

On the other hand, he doesn't flirt with me anymore, either. The October air is chilly, and even though I'm wearing a heavy sweatshirt, my wet hair is making me shiver, but he doesn't offer me his fleece. I guess now that I've locked myself away in the friend zone, Harry's decided to take the chivalry down a notch.

I know I should be relieved by this, but I'm not. Why can't I ever be grateful for what I have? Why do I always want more?

"You think so?" I ask, hating how desperate I am for this morsel of praise. Harry takes his role as my unofficial stroke coach seriously and he's full of critiques, most of which are helpful but still. I want him to think well of me.

"Oh, yeah, I can tell the difference," he says. "Your form is so much better. Not that it was bad before, you know, it's just been...optimized. Maybe I should look into Pilates."

"Can't hurt," I reply with a smile. He doesn't return it.

"Hey, so..." he says when we reach his car. He spins his

keys around on his finger. "I can't get breakfast with you today. I've got to go home to shower and change."

"Oh. Okay, no worries," I say. He unlocks the car doors and I slide into the passenger seat, tossing my bag over my shoulder into the back.

"Big plans today?" I ask, hoping the question sounds casual.

"Just hanging with Tucker. I haven't been around much and I think he's feeling neglected."

"What are you guys going to do?" I ask as he pulls out of the JCC parking lot. It's not far from here to my house. I can feel my time with him slipping away. I wish he would ask me to join them.

Harry shrugs. "Video games, probably. Nothing major."

"Sounds fun."

My phone chimes with a text from Jessa on our group chain with Amber: We're going to Deer Park this afternoon. Not that I think you'll say yes but do you wanna come?

"I've got plans this afternoon, too," I inform Harry.

Ugh. It sounds like I'm lying to save face, which I sort of am, or like this is some sort of competition over who's busier and more popular. I'm an idiot.

But he's barely even paying attention. We're at a stoplight and he's looking at a text he just got.

"Cool," he says, but I doubt he heard me.

We reach my house a few minutes later. I climb out of the car and wave goodbye to Harry.

"Have a good one, Susannah," he calls through his open window as I trudge toward the house.

I text Jessa that I'm in. Amber sends a bunch of balloons

and party hat emojis in response. I get a fainting goat GIF from Jessa.

It's not until I'm halfway to my room that I realize: he called me Susannah.

"This place is a hellmouth," I say as a group of moms nearly plow into us with their giant strollers. "How is this better than the real mall?"

Deer Park is our town's huge new outdoor shopping complex. Parking was practically impossible, and the sidewalks are so crowded that we're forced to walk together in a single file line. The day is bright and sunny, but a cold wind slices through our down jackets. We have to keep walking and shopping just to stay warm.

"It's outside!" Jessa sips her giant white mocha and swings the shopping bags she's accumulated in a wide arc that knocks Amber's Cubs cap off her head. "Spending money is so much fun."

"Hey!" Amber cries, righting her cap. "Careful."

"Spending money is fun for *you*," I say. The only thing I've bought is a box of ear dry drops at CVS because I ran out and the last thing I need is an infection. I never forget how much wealthier Jessa's and Amber's families are than mine, but it's less conspicuous when we're in the pool.

"Hey, that's right, you hate public places," Amber says. "Not that we don't love all your adorable grumbling and whatever, but how come you decided to come with us?"

The truth is embarrassing, but I'm in a confessing mood.

"Harry had plans after our workout today and I didn't want

him to think I was a friendless loser so I told him I did, too. And I didn't want to lie, so..."

"Gee, I'm so honored," Jessa says. "The elusive Susannah Ramos *deigns* to hang out with us to fake out her fake boyfriend."

"Don't be mean," Amber says. "Can't you see she's heartsick?"

"I'm not— Oh my God, guys, don't look but it's Harry."

Jessa grabs my arm. "He's with Tucker. Did you know we're in the same English class? I didn't even realize that till after the party. Let's say hi."

"Let's not," I beg. The last thing I need is for Jessa to insinuate something about my feelings for Harry because she thinks it's funny to watch me squirm, which she would totally do.

Harry and Tucker are sitting on the edge of a nearby fountain, and by the looks of it they're trying to push each other into the empty pool. Tucker notices us and shouts Jessa's name.

"Yo! Hey! Come over," he calls. Jessa drags me toward them by the elbow. Amber shoots me an *I'm so sorry* look, but it's too late for her to rescue me.

I smile at Harry, who looks pleased to see me, but wary, too. It becomes clear why a minute later, when three girls I don't recognize join them at the fountain. One of them throws her arm around Harry's shoulders and gives him a squeeze.

I plaster that smile on my face and don't let it waver, but inside I'm dying. He's here with a *girl*.

Tucker gives Jessa a hug and I shoot Amber a questioning look. She shrugs, but she doesn't look surprised. Are Tucker and Jessa friends now? If so, she hasn't told me. Or maybe I just wasn't paying attention.

"Hey, Susannah," Tucker says. He glances at Amber. "You were at the party, right?"

She nods and tells him her name, which he seems to have forgotten, then Tucker introduces us to the other girls.

"This is Val, Hallie and Fiona," he says, pointing to each one in turn. Fiona is the girl who's got her arm around Harry. *My* Harry.

No, not your *Harry, Susannah—get it together.* I smile at them, but Harry gives me a weird look.

"Fee," the girl says, pointing to herself. "Have you guys met Harry?"

Jessa finally gets what's going on here. She narrows her eyes at Fee.

"Yeah, we're on the same swim team," she says in a tone that implies she thinks Fee is kind of stupid. Fee brightens.

"Oh, that's awesome," Fee says. "Harry's a great swimmer, but we've never met any of his friends from the team." She gives Harry a light smack. "Always keeping secrets."

"The team is not a secret," Harry mutters.

"He refuses to tell us when any of the meets are," Fee confides to me in a fake whisper. "We were together for *months* and he never let me see him swim."

"Then how do you know he's a great swimmer?" Jessa asks.

"Look at him," Fee says. "Plus, there's all those medals he's got in his room."

We were together for months. We were together for months. I guess I should've assumed Harry wasn't always single, but he never mentioned any girlfriends to me.

Were, were, were, I force myself to remember. As in, *not together anymore.* Right?

But also: *She's been in his room.* What did they do in there? Not homework, I'll bet.

Harry seems mortified.

"The meet schedule is on the GAC website," I tell Fee. "They're open to the public. You could come whenever you want."

Fee grins at Harry. "Maybe I will."

"Thanks," Harry says, glaring at me.

"No problem."

"What'd you buy?" he asks me, nodding at my CVS bag.

"Just some Swim-EAR," I say. This is ridiculous. I need to leave. Harry looks like he's thinking the same thing.

"Oh, do you have swimmer's ear? Harry gets that all the time," Fee says, pinching his earlobe. It's an unbearably intimate gesture. He closes his eyes for a second but doesn't wince or pull away.

"No." I pretend I've received a text. I am so uncomfortable I want to crawl out of my skin. "My mom wants me home. Nice to meet you guys. See you in the pool, Harry."

I walk away without caring if my friends are behind me. I'll hide out in a store and meet up with them later. I can't be around Harry and his...girlfriend? Ex-girlfriend? Not for one second longer. But there's a part of me that thinks, *You did it again. You freaked and you bailed. What a coward.*

I feel a hand drop on my good shoulder.

"Susannah," Harry says.

My breath catches in my throat and all the muscles in my back tighten. I turn, steeling myself. If I can pretend I don't care about this, it'll be over soon. Everything ends eventually, even pain. If nothing else, swimming has taught me that.

"Hi!" I say. The sun is in my eyes, and I can't see his expression. "So, Fee is nice. How come you don't want her at meets?"

"We're friends," he says. "We went out for a while, but I haven't seen her in months. Tuck invited them. I didn't even know they'd be here until they showed up. I didn't blow you off for her."

"I didn't think you did," I tell him, nervously zipping and unzipping my coat. "Besides, we're just friends, too."

He stiffens. "That's right."

"So it doesn't matter who you hang out with."

"Back there it seemed like it did a little."

"It doesn't. But you should let her see you swim," I say, because I really am so proud of him, of how good he is when he lets himself be. "Everyone who loves you should see you in the water."

"Okay," he says, looking sort of confused. "Maybe."

I pat his arm in a friendly way. "See you later, Harry."

"Bye, Susannah."

My heart falls out of my chest and splatters onto the sidewalk like a water balloon. I wish he would go back to calling me Susie. But the thing that really breaks me is the realization that he touched my right shoulder, not my left, because the left is the one that always gives me trouble.

Harry would never knowingly hurt me, not even to stop me from walking away.

CHAPTER ELEVEN

225 days until US Olympic Team Trials

"WHAT DID I *TELL* YOU, SUSANNAH?" BETH SHOUTS HAPPILY, reeling me in for a hug.

"That was incredible," she tells me, rocking me back and forth. "You did such a great job."

When I pull back, we're both grinning. I'm panting and dripping, too. I've just climbed out of the pool after winning my first 200 IM in competition since Beth took over my training.

Coming in first is amazing, but we're celebrating my *time*, which was good enough to put me on the roster for Winter Nationals. If I can hit the qualifying mark in the same event at that competition, I'm going to Trials. The California sky is bright blue and cloudless, and I feel like I could float right up into it.

"Go warm down," Beth says.

I wait until I'm out of her sight range to massage my left shoulder. I didn't feel any pain during the race—too much adrenaline and distraction—but now that it's over, the damned thing is throbbing.

No big deal, I think as I hop into the warm-down pool. When I get out of here, I'll ice it and take some ibuprofen. Nothing so insignificant as a little discomfort is going to bring me down from this high.

When I get back to my hotel room, I text Harry about my race results. He's supposed to be here with the rest of us in California, but at the last minute he got sick—a bad flu, Dave said, but Harry never mentioned it to me. He's been so distant since we ran into each other at Deer Park.

Still, I send him my time, knowing he'll get what I'm trying to tell him, then check my phone every five seconds hoping he's messaged back.

Finally, those three wavering dots pop up…then they subside. Then they pop up again…and disappear. I groan and fling myself across the bed. The high is gone. I might as well go to sleep.

Finally, my phone chimes. I fumble for it, but when I pull up his message, all it says is: !

"A *single exclamation point*?" I shout.

I'm sharing a room with Amber, who chooses this moment to walk in.

"Whoa, what did that phone do to you?" she asks.

I shove it at her. When she sees Harry's message, her eyes widen.

"What a chump," she says, letting the phone drop to the

bed. "Don't let it bother you. You're going to Nationals. If he's not happy for you, sucks for him."

"He's one exclamation point's worth of happy for me," I mutter, covering my face with a pillow.

"That time is worth two exclamation points *at least*," she concurs. "I would've sent you three."

"That's very generous of you, friend."

She slaps my hip. "Get up. We're celebrating. Dinner's on me. You can even order dessert."

"The team is paying for dinner," I remind her.

"Well, in that case, order two desserts."

By the time we get back from California, Harry has recovered enough to return to practice, but he looks run-down. I feel terrible for him. The one time I had the flu, it flattened me for a week. We swim in adjacent lanes, but he's clearly not up for our normal chatty banter. Maybe his minimal response to the text about my time means nothing, but I'm afraid that he might be mad at me.

I dress in a hurry after practice, forgoing a shower, and hustle out to the hallway to wait for him outside the men's locker room. It takes him a long time to appear—it seems like every single member of GAC has left by the time he emerges—and I realize too late that he was probably trying to avoid me.

"Hey," he says. He looks uncomfortable. "What's up? Do you need a ride?"

I gather up all my confidence and say: "That depends."

"On what?"

"On whether you're upset with me or not."

"Oh." He shifts his bag from one shoulder to the other and

leans against the doorjamb, staring over my shoulder at the wall behind me. "I'm not."

"Come on. I know something's up. Just talk to me."

There's a horrible feeling in the pit of my stomach, like I've swallowed a diving brick and it's dragging me under. That awkward encounter at the shopping center was not my finest moment. Every time we seem to be on solid ground, I panic and run away. If he's mad about that, I can't blame him. If I keep doing it, how can he trust me?

"I'll drive you home," he says, pushing off the wall. "We can talk in the car."

But once we're on the road, he doesn't explain, or even bring the topic back up. I have to do it.

"So…?"

He drags his hand down the side of his face. "Sorry, I haven't been feeling well. It's hard to text when you're puking your guts out."

"That bad, huh?"

Harry shoots me a look. "I was *sick*. Thanks for the Get Well Soon card, by the way."

Shit, he's right. I didn't even bother to check in and ask how he was feeling. I just threw a number at him over text and expected him to shower me with praise on cue. I am such an asshole.

"I'm so sorry," I say. "I was thinking about you the whole time. I missed you in California."

"You did?"

"Of *course*. I miss you all the time when you're not around… sometimes even when you are."

It strikes me only after the fact that this is a dangerous thing to say. I feel as if my heart has fallen out of my body, like it's dangling from my chest like a puppet on strings. All it would take is one smack from Harry to send it flying right out the open window to be crushed under his tires like roadkill.

"You do?" he asks, concentrating on the road. His whole body is tense and he's gripping the steering wheel like he's trying to choke it to death.

He's so nervous, and all I want is to comfort him. I put a hand on his knee. He flinches.

"Please don't touch me," he says—not meanly, but with great force.

I snatch my hand back. "Okay. I'm sorry."

We used to touch each other all the time—correcting each other's form, helping each other wrap ice around aching joints, fixing each other's caps—and he never seemed to mind. Something really has changed between us, and I'm worried there's no going back.

He sighs. "I can't fake this 'just friends' thing anymore. It's too hard. I'm a mess."

"You're not a mess," I insist.

"You don't know what I am," he snaps. He makes a frustrated noise in the back of his throat. "Uncertainty makes me uncomfortable. I can't live my life in a middle zone where I don't know what's going on day to day and I feel a million different ways about the same fucking thing all at once. I work hard to keep my life balanced and manageable and I can't seem to do that with you."

"What does that mean?" I ask.

"It means that I like you, and I think you like me—in fact I'm absolutely fucking positive you like me, but some days it's obvious you do and other days it's not, and you keep telling me we can't be anything more than friends but in so many ways I feel like we're *a lot* more than friends and I don't know what to do with pretty much any of that, ever. I *hate* it, Susannah. I fucking hate it."

"Shit," I say, more to myself than to him.

What he's describing is exactly how I feel, too. Being around Harry brings joy to what is, most days, an otherwise hard slog of a life. I don't want that to go away. But I don't want to hurt him, either.

We're getting closer to my house, to the end of this ride, maybe the last one we'll ever have. I don't want it to end. What if I get out of Harry's car without explaining myself, without giving him, at the very least, some peace of mind? Will we lapse back into our pattern, the one that makes Harry miserable? Or will we become strangers to each other again?

Neither option seems bearable. I can't hide my feelings, but I've learned over years of relentless training to compartmentalize them, shove all the bad stuff down in some forgotten corner in the basement of my soul, so I can keep going—so I can swim. But what I feel for Harry, what's growing between us—whatever it is—is too big to shut away.

Harry turns down my street. He slows the car, creeping toward my house, waiting for me to reply. Finally, he pulls over a few houses down from mine and puts the car in Park.

"Say something, Susie, please," he begs.

"I don't know how to care about anything but swimming," I whisper. "It's my whole life."

Harry presses his forehead against the steering wheel. "Yeah, I know."

"I thought I could live that way forever," I continue, grasping at thoughts as they streak through my brain like fireworks across an open sky, letting them tumble out of my mouth before they can explode and fizzle into nothing. "I got by for so long all by myself. Then I met you and you were so kind to me, you tried to understand me, and I liked that—I like *you*. And it scared me—you scare me."

"I would never—" he says.

"I don't mean it like that," I tell him. "It scares me to think something else could matter to me like swimming does. That I could get distracted from the one thing I've ever wanted, the one thing I've spent all this time and energy fighting for. That for even one second, I could stop thinking about swimming, and in that moment, I could do something or something could happen that would rip it out of my hands forever.

"It's not about the glory," I continue. "It's not even just the Olympics. Practically every extra penny my family has goes to my swimming, and if I screw it up now, I throw all that away. I can't pay for college without this sport. One way or another, *my future depends on this sport*. I'm sorry you feel jerked around, I never meant to do that. I don't want to hurt you. But I'm very, very afraid."

"Okay," he says, turning to look at me. "But I care about your swimming, too, more than I care about my own. I would never do anything that would jeopardize your career."

"I know. But there's no separation between my swimming and me. Letting someone get close feels like putting it at risk and I don't know if I'm brave enough to do that."

Harry swallows hard, nodding, then says, "Well, I'm not going to bully you into it. I can take rejection—"

I open my mouth to object.

"Let me get this out," he says. "I can take rejection. But I can't take not being clear on what we are. I can't take saying we're friends but acting like something more, tying myself into knots hoping it'll happen but not knowing when. You know what I want. Decide what you want."

"How long do I have?" I ask.

"I'm not going to give you a deadline. This isn't a college application. It's not a race. There's not a mark you can come in under to qualify."

He shrugs wearily. "Just be a person. And remember that I'm a person, too."

CHAPTER TWELVE

207 days until US Olympic Team Trials

I MAY BE A PERSON, BUT I HAVE MORE PRACTICE AT BEING A machine. I need a deadline. So, I set one for myself: Nationals. By then, I'll have figured out what I want and how much I'm willing to risk.

What I try to ignore, but keeps creeping up on me in weak moments, is the sad fact that if I flame out at Nationals, it's probably the end of my Olympic dream, anyway, for this cycle if not forever. Maybe, after this meet, I won't even have to choose.

I don't tell Harry any of this, but he must sense it, because he keeps his distance in the weeks leading up to the big competition. He has his own races to focus on; he qualified earlier in the fall, but he hasn't been taking it seriously—something Jessa comments on every chance she gets.

"God, they're losers," she says one day near the end of practice as she watches Harry and Avik trying to shove each other underwater. "Don't they care about this at all? Susannah?"

I defog my goggles, pretending not to hear her. I'm trying not to think or talk about Harry right now, but my friends are making it difficult. They're full of questions after what happened at Deer Park, and the fact that I refuse to answer them just makes them more curious.

"The fact that he's even going to Nationals is a fluke," Jessa continues. "He got lucky with that height and that wingspan and those big feet. He's not a real swimmer."

"He's a real swimmer," I snap. "You have no idea what you're talking about."

I feel guilty for jumping down her throat, because in some ways she's kind of right. Harry swims the 100- and 200-meter back, the 100-meter fly and occasionally the 200-meter individual medley, which is the only event we have in common. And he's *fast*, naturally so in a way that would consume me with envy if we had to compete against each other, and still does a bit even though we never will.

But he's lazy in the water, undisciplined and often disinterested, like swimming is one big goof to him. Most of the time in competition he just gives up and lets whatever's going to happen, happen. Sometimes it works and sometimes it doesn't, but it never seems to affect him one way or the other. It makes me wonder about what he said when we first met, how he picked GAC because Dave coaches champions. If he doesn't care about winning, why would that matter to him?

Part of me envies his indifference, and part of me is annoyed by it. Either way, it makes me want to work harder. It's been a hard, lonely road back to where I used to be, but sometimes

I still believe I'm capable of great things. I want to show everyone what I'm made of, but especially—embarrassingly—I want to prove myself to Harry. Maybe even inspire him a bit.

And I'm not going to just stand here while Jessa insults him.

"I don't know why you even care," I say to her. "You don't know him."

"Oh, and you do?" Jessa raises an eyebrow at me. Amber floats over from the next lane, her attention drawn by Jessa's raised voice. "You're some kind of Harry Matthews expert, huh? His girlfriend might be interested to learn that."

"She's not his girlfriend," I say, surprised and wounded by her obvious desire to hurt me. Jessa's always been flinty—there's a fine line between sarcastic and mean, and she was born on it—but she's not usually vindictive.

I tell myself it's the pressure. It's getting to all of us. Once Nationals is over...but that's not really true. If we make it through with the marks we need, this meet is only the beginning.

"I'm sure that's what he told you." Jessa adjusts her cap and pulls her goggles down over her eyes. "But Tucker says they've been hanging out a lot, Harry and that girl. He thinks they're getting back together."

"Who cares what Tucker thinks?"

"He's Harry's best and oldest friend. He knows things about Harry, things he'd never tell *you*."

"What things?" I ask, suddenly worried. I've always sensed that Harry keeps secrets, but never found the nerve to press him on it.

Jessa shrugs in a bored sort of way, but does not elaborate. It's infuriating.

"Are you kidding me?" I say, but she's already pushed off the wall for her next set.

"Do *not* listen to her," Amber says. "She's making stuff up. Jessa told me Tucker's a vault when it comes to Harry."

"Why is she even asking about him in the first place?"

"Because she knows he's important to you, and she's looking for a way to get into your head."

"I can't believe that. We're supposed to be friends."

"Haven't you noticed? She's jealous of all the progress you've made with Beth and she's feeling threatened. You know if she doesn't do well at Nationals, her dad will, like, disown her."

She's exaggerating, but Jessa's parents put a lot of pressure on her. My family is so different, sometimes I forget what it must be like for her, but Jessa's experience is not uncommon. The sport is full of swimmers chasing after more than their own dream.

I lean back against the pool wall. "I don't know what to do with that."

Amber shakes her head. "Don't think about it. Eyes on the prize."

"You don't know Ramos like I know her," Dave says to Beth. They don't know that I'm listening. "She's a good kid, but ever since that win at Worlds she cracks under pressure. You watch—she'll blow it at Nationals, and there goes what's left of her confidence. She's already a mess as it is."

I'm standing in the coaches' office, outside the half-open door to the tiny interior room where Beth and I meet every few days to discuss my progress and strategize for upcoming races. We're supposed to be having one of those meetings now; looks like Dave beat me to her.

I didn't come here intending to eavesdrop, but Dave's so loud I'd be surprised if everyone on the pool deck couldn't hear him.

It's not like I don't agree with Dave. I am a mess—disassembled, then put together wrong. Or, at least, I was before. I don't know what I am now. Not as good as I once was, better than I have been...whatever it is, for the first time in a long time, there's hope singing in my veins.

But with only a few words from Dave, I can feel it bleeding out of me. No matter how much Beth encourages me, no matter how hard I work, his voice is still the one I hear in my weakest, most vulnerable moments, saying over and over again: *You're not good enough.*

"You gave up on her too easily," Beth tells Dave. "There's a lot of talent there. She's proving that right now! You've seen her times."

"Her chance to distinguish herself in this sport has passed," Dave insists. "At this point, she's just another fast swimmer."

The door swings open, and suddenly I'm face-to-face with Dave. If he's afraid I might've overheard him, it doesn't register on his face.

"Hey, kid," he says, giving my bad shoulder a hard pat as he pushes past me. I wince, glaring at his retreating back in disgust. Beth appears at the door. She sighs.

"I assume you heard that?" she asks. I nod. "I'm sorry. Come on in, let's chat."

"It's fine," I tell Beth as we sit down. "Honestly, he's said way worse things to my face."

"That's awful. You shouldn't listen to him. You're doing great. With more time and effort, you can do better."

"But…" I hate to ask this, but I have to. "What if he's right?"

Beth doesn't rush to reassure me. She considers the question thoughtfully before saying, "I'll admit you got sidetracked for a while, Susannah, but that doesn't have to mean your career is over. Not everybody can come back from that, but I really think you can. Look how well you're doing already. Can't you feel how different things are now, even compared to a few months ago?"

I can't deny that I do.

"I'm excited about Nationals," I tell her. "It feels like a turning point, an opportunity to show people I'm still in the game."

To show Dave that, with some elbow grease, messes can be cleaned up.

"You should be excited," Beth says. "I want you to take it easy on the butterfly at Nationals—that shoulder's not doing you any favors right now, and I don't want you running down your engine on that first fifty. By the time you come out of the breaststroke turn, you'll start flagging.

"Instead, I want you to coast through the fly and start ramping when you hit the backstroke. It's improved so much, you can get a lot of speed off it. Head back, arms close to your ears. Make your breaststroke powerful, but precise. And when it's time for the freestyle, that's when you take it to your highest gear."

"I'm nervous about pacing," I admit. It's one of the IM's biggest challenges. When you're only doing one stroke in an event, it's easier to sink into a groove. You can read the race better. When you're alternating, like in the IM, you need a different strategy for each fifty.

Ever since I slowed down, I've struggled with that. Beth made it one of her priorities, but that kind of body consciousness takes time, and I'm not used to mine yet.

"Let's break down Santa Clara tonight," she suggests. "There's something I want you to see."

Every Thursday, Beth and I go over my recent swims, flipping through the challenges and triumphs of that week's practices like a well-thumbed scrapbook. Tonight, we watch the video of my 200 IM at the Santa Clara meet, the race where I qualified for Nationals.

At first, I have no idea what Beth thinks is special or reassuring about that race. It was a high point, sure, but my swimming looks the same as always.

On the second butterfly turn, though, I notice something: there are no jagged edges or slight hesitations in my transition to backstroke. Every movement shows a grace and fluidity I know wasn't there six months ago...or even two years ago, when I was at my best.

It looks natural. Organic. Not practiced or staged. For the first time, I see it, the animal in me Beth always promised was there.

Watching myself swim through the objective lens of a camera makes me think about how many versions of ourselves we each contain. I feel like I'm one person in the water, and another on dry land. Me on land is still hesitant and uncertain; having faith is hard for her, and so is letting go.

But me in the water, the girl Beth found beneath the rubble? She's elegant and powerful and fast.

She's also not an accident. I've never worked so hard in my life. Beth pushes me past my limits. She has me in the Pilates studio on weekends and the weight room every other day. There are painful, stinging ice baths and excruciating deep tissue massages, yoga twice a week. My body has morphed, shedding fat, gaining muscle, breaking down and building up again. I run my hands over it every night in the shower, mapping its new contours. The curves are still there, but the way I feel about them has changed—it's like my body is no longer a suit I have to wear but, finally, a skin that belongs to me.

"Your pacing will be fine," Beth tells me. "I want you to feel your way through this next race. Your body knows the rhythms—trust it to find them, and don't let your head interfere. Got it?"

I assure her I do, but I can't help wondering where—between my body that's an animal and my head that gets in the way—my unruly heart fits in.

The 200 IM is my only event at Nationals, and in the prelims my nerves almost bury me. I ignore Beth's race plan and blitz through the butterfly way too fast, then start to crumble when I turn into the breaststroke.

I can sense rather than see the swimmers on my left and right closing in, so I dig into my stroke, ignore the lactic acid eating away at my muscles and claw my way to the finish. I feel like crap, but I clock in with a time fast enough to get seeded last in the finals heat—barely.

Beth catches up with me after my warm-down. She sees the agony on my face and says, "I know that race was hard. But it was gutsy. If it was hard, then it had to be hard. I want you to remember that you're a world champion in this event, Susannah."

"That was a long time ago," I remind her.

I bend over at the waist, hands on my knees, chest heaving as I suck in air. My racing suit is so tight I can barely breathe. The straps dig angry red lines into my flesh; my bad left shoulder aches. Why does everything in this sport have to be so painful?

"It wasn't that long ago." Beth rests a gentle hand on the center of my back and squats to speak into my ear. "You're a champion, so swim like a champion. I don't care if you win. There will be other opportunities for you to win. I just want you to have a race you can be proud of."

As I step up to the block before the finals heat the next day, my stomach turns over like a motor. I'm in major trouble over in lane eight. The way races are structured makes it difficult for someone from the exterior lanes to surge in the lead. You're coming in with a slower time, plus you've got to deal with wake from the swimmers on the inside lanes, which pours over you with each stroke. And nothing creates more waves than the butterfly.

My family is somewhere in the upper deck, and so is Harry—in the sea of onlookers, I pick him out easily. His swims are done for this meet, and his performance was adequate at best. Dave is almost certainly pissed at him for once again squandering his physical talents, but knowing Harry, it was on purpose. Whatever he's here for, it's not a first-place finish.

I'm grateful that he stuck around to watch me swim when he could've flown home. He leans forward on his elbows and gazes at the pool with deep concentration, as if he's willing me to victory.

Our eyes meet and he waves. Then he mouths something, but I can't make it out.

"Take your mark."

I bend and curl my fingertips around the edge of the block. I tense my muscles, imagine them compressing like springs. Less than a second after the signal sounds, I hit the surface with the force of a torpedo. Water courses over my shoulders and back, and I force my head down, keeping a near-perfect streamline position as I kick to the fifteen-meter mark before powering into my first stroke.

The ghost of Beth's voice echoes in my head: *You're a champion, so swim like a champion.*

This is how the butterfly works: the arms come out to the side like wings as the head dips and the body undulates like a wave. Then the arms enter the water together, and your hands make a keyhole shape, pushing forward with another kick and gaining momentum for the next stroke.

Dave taught me to breathe every few strokes, and thanks to Beth's hypoxic sets it's easier to fight the urge to lift my head up. I turn my brain off and let my body lead me through the butterfly. I don't strain or panic when it feels like I'm not going fast enough, and my goggles are fogging, so I can't see my competition, anyway.

It's just me and the water, the truest love story I have ever known.

As I turn into the backstroke, Beth's advice comes back to me in pieces, soft and flimsy like tissue paper. I've always liked the backstroke because you never have to stop breathing. But in lane eight, with the wake of the other swimmers crashing over the lane line and ricocheting off the gutter, controlling my breaths is the only way to prevent water from going up my nose.

I concentrate on my technique, everything she and Harry taught me, getting the most out of my arms and centering myself in the lane. The backstroke is over before I realize, and I'm into the next fifty.

The breaststroke feels like the natural way to move through the water, but it is slow, so swimming it in competition takes concentration and endurance. Of all the strokes, it requires the most technical precision. If your form is off, you can end up practically swimming in place.

I have to focus. When I get to this point in a race, I sometimes start to founder, like a ship that can't be righted. I'm not tired, but Harry's face flashes through my mind as I try to puzzle out what he said to me up there in the bleachers, the words I couldn't make out. I need to know what they were.

I also need to tell him things—what I feel, what I want. I'm done hiding it, done running from it. I can swim and be happy at the same time, or at the very least I'm willing to try.

I bulldoze through the breaststroke in a way that really feels like flying, then I turn into the freestyle leg and let myself go.

I've managed to conserve some energy and I'm ready to sprint hard. I charge through the first twenty-five and know that I've clocked one of the fastest splits in my career so far. With my goggles so fogged up, I can't see anything but the thick black line along the bottom of the pool. I swim harder in the last twenty-five meters of that IM than I ever have in my life and slam into the finish, punching the touchpad so there's no doubt about when I hit the wall.

I stay underwater, eyes closed, afraid to surface and look at the scoreboard. If I've come in eighth, I'll die. If my time is higher than the Trials cut, it'll all be over.

Panting, I strip off my goggles and rise out of the water. Before I see the board, I see Harry jumping up and down in the stands, and I know I've done something good.

I force myself to look at the board: *2. Ramos*—with a time that's five seconds faster than my qualifying time, and two seconds faster than I swam in the prelims.

"Oh my God," I gasp, sinking back into the water. I'm going to the Olympic Trials.

I'm in Beth's arms as soon as I hoist myself, sopping, onto the deck.

"That was *fantastic*, Susannah!" she cries. "Look at that *time*. You should be so proud."

She shakes her head in amazement. My time is way better than either of us dared to hope for. Something intense and almost magical happened in that pool, but I'm afraid to believe it was me.

"I am proud," I say, but I'm so dazed that nothing seems real right now. I tug off my cap and crumple it in my fist.

"Susie!" Harry shouts from upper deck. My head snaps up at the sound of his voice. He points at the door that leads from the bleachers to the pool level and disappears through it.

"Susannah, go warm down," Beth instructs me. Instead, I take off toward the locker rooms.

I sprint through the labyrinth of lockers and benches and emerge into a hallway where people—lots of fully clothed, dry people—are milling around waiting for their swimmers or searching for the stairs to the upper deck. I whirl around, searching for Harry. Someone calls my name.

Startled bystanders scatter to make a path for Harry as he runs toward me. He's going so fast he slams into me and knocks what little breath I have left right out of my lungs.

"You were incredible," he says, breathing hard. "Total outside smoke."

So that's what he mouthed to me from the bleachers: *Outside smoke*. It's the term for a swimmer in an exterior lane who, even though they're seeded to lose, comes up from behind and wins the race.

I didn't win, but I feel like I did.

"Come here, you dumb jock," Harry says, pulling me closer. I laugh. "I'm so proud of you."

"Thanks," I say, suddenly shy. The intensity of his gaze makes me feel naked. The warmth of his skin is so acute it's almost painful.

Harry presses his forehead against mine. "How do you feel?"

"Amazing," I whisper. "Thank you."

"For what?" Harry leans closer and I think—I know—he's going to kiss me. But then a hand settles on his shoulder and pulls him back.

I blink and look up to see Beth standing there. We're making a spectacle of ourselves, but the part of my brain that registers embarrassment is malfunctioning. I couldn't care less.

"I know you're excited, but this is not the place," Beth says. "Susannah, you've got to warm down or you'll be sore as hell tomorrow. Harry, back up in the stands."

"Okay, okay," Harry says. He doesn't take his eyes off me. "I'm so, so proud of you, Susie."

After my warm-down, back in the locker room, I sit on a bench and bury my face in my hands. My eyes burn, and there's a lump in my throat the size of a tennis ball, but I hold it all in, savoring the sense of accomplishment and pushing away the fear that comes with having something and knowing how easily it can be lost.

Once I'm changed, I hurry out of the locker room and find Harry leaning his signature lean, doing something on his phone. The hallway is deserted now. I drop my bag and walk toward him with my heart pounding hard and fast in my chest. I call his name. He lifts his head and smiles. "Hey—"

Before he can say anything else, I bracket his face with my hands and press my lips to his lips in a long, hard kiss that leaves my head spinning. *You can have this, and swimming, too,* I assure myself. *It's not a choice, it's a decision.*

My mind is half a second behind my body, and even though it was *my* move, it takes me a second to realize what's happening—I kissed Harry. We're *kissing.* He buries his fingers in my wet, tangled hair and my hands drift down his neck, where his pulse quickens under my thumbs.

When we separate, his eyes meet mine and he smiles again. "Yeah?"

I nod, speechless and surprised by myself for a whole bunch of reasons. Proud of myself, too. Harry lifts my chin with his fingers and takes my lips with his, easing them apart. His palm comes to rest on my jaw and his other hand drifts to my hip, drawing me in by the waist.

Before one kiss is even done, I want another, and another, and I feel this uncomfortable tightness in my chest at the thought of not kissing him anymore, but I have to pull away to catch my breath. I grip his shoulders and command the world to stop spinning, which it stubbornly refuses to do.

I don't know where to look, so I fix my eyes on his nose and laugh. "What's so funny?" he asks.

"You have freckles," I say, drawing the pad of my thumb across the bridge of his nose.

"Oh, yeah. Curse o' the ginger." Concern flits across Harry's face. "You okay?"

I feel like I might faint, but I can't tell if it's because of that kiss or everything that happened in the pool, all the adrenaline sluicing through my veins. My limbs feel loose and heavy. Blood pounds in my temples to the steady rhythm of distant chanting: another race.

The world is marching on, but out here, in the quiet, empty corridor, it feels like Harry and I are the only ones in it.

*Susannah Ramos's Surprising Surge to the Finish
at National Championships*

By Kris McNamara
Posted December 10

Don't call it a comeback! We love it when someone we'd written off a long time ago as a one-hit wonder comes out of nowhere and proves they're not dead yet.

That's exactly what happened at Nationals today in Greensboro, North Carolina, where Susannah Ramos of the Gilcrest Aqualions Club came out of nowhere after limping into the A Final of the 200 IM seeded eighth to grab a second-place finish and an Olympic Trials qualifying time.

Ramos still has a way to go if she wants to wear rings this summer, but it hasn't escaped our attention that the former phenom has a new coach and an updated training routine. It seems to be working, but Ramos can't rest on her laurels. There's a hard season ahead with big meets lined up like dominos through the spring, and this summer's Trials are shaping up to be one of the most competitive to date.

Here's hoping she can pull it out in the end. We'll be keeping a close eye on Susannah Ramos, and we know you will be, too. Because none of us can resist an underdog story.

CHAPTER THIRTEEN

189 days until US Olympic Team Trials

ELEVEN MONTHS OUT OF THE YEAR, I'M THE ONLY SERIOUS athlete in my house, but my parents feel about Christmas the way NASCAR fans feel about the Indy 500, and when the clock strikes 12:01 on the day after Thanksgiving, they turn into Dale Earnhardt, Jr., and Danica Patrick, with Nina and me as their pit crew. Nationals was my excuse for wriggling out of the more time-consuming tasks—like hanging the lights on the front of the house, a chore I loathe—but when it comes to the Ramos family annual tamalada, it's all hands on deck, school and swim practice and boyfriends be damned.

Harry is my *boyfriend*. It's so new it still feels completely unreal, but I have a feeling that introducing him to my whole family at the tamalada will give it a sudden, juddering actuality. We're something different now, and the Ramos and Ramirez clans can't wait to put their fingerprints all over it.

I avoid inviting Harry to the tamalada for as long as I can, but when Mom threatens to call him herself, I give in. One way or another, Harry is going to meet my parents for longer than ten minutes...and my sister...and about fifty or so assorted grandparents, aunts, uncles and cousins. It's a lot, and I wouldn't blame him if the mere thought of it made him want to take off running, but when I tell him about it, he seems less than thrilled, and I feel strangely disappointed.

"What is it exactly?" Harry asks, snatching a hash brown off my plate. It's Sunday morning and we're doing our homework at the diner postswim. I menace him with my fork.

"Hands off my potatoes," I warn him. "I need those carbs for energy."

"So do I!" He pouts and strokes my calf under the table with his foot, as if that's going to convince me to sacrifice my breakfast to his bottomless appetite—not a chance.

Still, the flirty gesture makes my chest feel tight and warm. We touch each other now for no reason except that we want to. It's almost too good to believe. I don't think I've ever been so happy in my entire life.

"Then order your own. A tamalada," I explain, "is a tamale-making party. My parents throw one every year before Christmas. People from both sides of my family come, plus neighbors and friends and Mom's and Dad's coworkers. I invited Jessa and Amber, too."

"Will I be expected to make tamales?" Harry asks. "Because I don't know how to do that."

He keeps doing that stroking thing with his foot on my leg. It's hard to concentrate, but concentration is overrated. He's got sneakers on, and I'm wearing jeans, and we're in public, but the image of his bare foot gently touching my bare leg as we lay wrapped around each other in bed keeps flashing through my mind. I feel a sudden, strong desire to speed through the next two and a half years until we're in college and can be together in private whenever we want.

I shake my head to clear it. We're supposed to be having a conversation here.

"Everybody pulls their weight. But everybody goes home with tamales, too, so it's worth it. And don't worry, my aunts will be lining up to show you how. Tía Lillia's going to insist you knead the mole into the masa, because you're 'un chico muy fuerte,'" I tell him, giving his bicep a playful squeeze.

"I'm going to assume that means 'a super-hot guy we totally approve of.'"

"You really should be taking Spanish," I say, turning back to my history notes. "It's the second most commonly spoken language in this country."

"I know, but look on the bright side—now you can teach me." He smiles at me. He's incorrigible, but it's hard to resist, that smile. "Are you fluent? I never thought to ask."

"Not fluent, no," I say. "My parents are, but we speak English at home. I understand it better than I read it, and I read it better than I speak it. There's something about languages that's...slippery. It's hard to hold on to the words. I try to talk to my abuela in Spanish sometimes, but a few sentences in it's like my brain and my tongue get all tangled, and we usually end up going back to English."

"I'm not very good at languages, either," Harry says.

"I wish I were better," I admit. "It feels like I'm not doing enough to hold on to my culture. I want to be fluent. I want to be able to write emails in Spanish to our cousins in Mexico, like my mom does, without having to put half my sentences through Google Translate. It's embarrassing. But to get better, I'd have to practice, and to practice, I'd have to mess up a lot, and you know I hate that."

"I do," Harry says fondly.

"Anyway," I say, "it's okay if you don't want to come." I love the idea of introducing Harry to my heritage, but that would mean putting him under the glaring spotlight of my family's attention. Part of me wants to keep him to myself a little bit longer.

Harry chews his lip, which means he's thinking something he doesn't know if he should say. If I press him, he'll back away from it, so I wait for him to answer.

"It's not that," he says. "It's just, you know, I'm nervous about meeting your family now that you're—that we are—"

"Yeah." Why am I so bummed about this? I didn't even want to invite him, for precisely this reason—I thought it might make him uncomfortable. But now I'm afraid that it means something that he doesn't want to come. Maybe he's second-guessing us. Maybe he's wondering if he's gotten himself in too deep. Meeting the family is, like, a *step*. Maybe he's not ready to take it with me.

Harry reaches across the table and takes my hand, turning it palm up and tracing my lifeline with his thumb. It tickles in a way I don't expect, and sends a pleasant shiver down my back.

"I'm afraid of being a curiosity," he says softly. "Don't ask me why, I just...am."

"No, I get it," I say, feeling relieved. This doesn't have anything to do with us. I give his hand an affectionate squeeze.

"Nina's brought guys she was going out with to the tamalada before, but my family has never seen me with anybody. All they'll want to talk about is Susannah's new gringo boyfriend."

"What if they don't like me?" he asks. "Will that make you like me less?"

"First of all, they'll love you," I assure him. "You're so handsome and charming, ugh, they'll want to trade me in for you. Actually, don't come, you'll only make me look bad."

Harry grins. "I like the sound of that. And second of all?"

"Second of all," I say, "nothing could make me like you less." He laughs. I shake my head. "No, wait, that came out wrong. What I mean is, nothing is going to diminish how I feel about you, Harry. Certainly not my abuela's review of you, which—and I would literally bet all the money I will ever have in my entire life on this—will be glowing."

"Well," he says. "Since you're promising me the undying love of all your female relatives *and* tamales, how can I refuse?"

I lean across the table and press a kiss to his cheek. "Thank you. But you have to work for those tamales. They don't make themselves."

"Noted," he says with mock-seriousness.

Harry returns to his math homework, and I go back to my history, but I keep sneaking glances at him, trying to puzzle him out. Harry's not shy, and I've seen him do the Flow in front of an entire party of captivated strangers, so I don't think he's unaware of his effect on people, either. He knows how magnetic he can be.

Maybe he's intimidated by meeting my family, but my gut

says there's something else going on here, too. I'm starting
to realize that a real relationship might be more complicated
than I imagined when I kissed him that day in the hallway
after my race.

We're on a short training break post-Nationals, which
works out well for Mom because I have no excuse to skip
morning preparations for the tamalada. The four of us are
up early to scrub the house top to bottom, then Mom drafts
Nina and me into kitchen duty and sends Dad out on multiple store runs to pick up last-minute groceries, liquor, and
other supplies. Mom's been planning this for weeks, but as
much as she loves entertaining, she's always nervous about
disappointing people. It's no mystery where I got that particular fixation from.

"We eat tamales all year-round, and yet somehow I forget
how much work they are to make," Nina grumbles as she
and I prepare the drinks and appetizers for the party. If you're
going to invite fifty people to your house on a Saturday and
put them to work, you have to feed them. A lot.

I'm not a foodie or anything, but I do enjoy cooking when
I get the chance. There's something so dependable about
recipes—you do this and this and this, then something delicious happens. Most days, food is just fuel to me; I don't have
time to enjoy it. But Nina let me help her plan the snacks for
the day, and we had fun together looking for recipes online
before settling on avocado bruschetta, creamy cauliflower
artichoke dip, spicy pineapple salsa and sheet-pan black bean
nachos. We've barely started and I'm already starving.

Nina has appointed herself bartender. She's mixing up

pitchers of Mom's signature cranberry agua fresca with mint and lime ice cubes, and a big bowl of pomegranate ginger apple cider punch for Dad to spike when he gets home. But I'm most looking forward to Bela's champurrado, which only she is allowed to make. The craving is so strong I can almost taste the chocolate on my tongue.

"Who's bringing Bela?" I ask Mom. My abuela still has her license, but she's not comfortable driving anymore. Whenever she needs to go somewhere, one of her kids or their spouses takes her.

"Lillia, I think," she says distractedly, fussing with the electric mixer. She gives it a hard smack and flips the switch, but nothing happens. Mom lets out a muffled scream. "I knew this thing was going to die today. I had a dream about it. How the hell are we going to mix the masa?"

"Aren't Tía Lillia and Bela bringing mixers?" You can buy masa ready-made, but Bela always made hers by hand and Mom insists on keeping that tradition alive.

"Yeah, but I was counting on having three." Mom sighs. "One of these days, I'm going to throw a party and *everything will go right*."

"Maybe it's a sign of good luck," I say. "Like rain on your wedding day."

Mom chuckles. "It did rain on my wedding day, and I guess that turned out all right."

"You *guess*?" Dad shouts in mock-outrage from the kitchen door.

"Hector, finally—how long does it take to pick up a few things from the store?" Mom grabs the grocery bags from his hands. "Can you go next door and ask Bridget if I can borrow her mixer? Tell her there's an extra dozen tamales in it for her."

Dad shakes his head. "The Levins aren't home, remember? They RVSP-ed no to the party."

"That's right, I forgot. Damn it!" she growls.

Mom spends the next twenty minutes trying to track down another mixer, but none of our neighbors have one that works, and all of the family members attending the party are already on their way. The goal is to make hundreds of tamales. Without enough mixers, that process is going to be *sloooow*. And painful for whoever gets stuck stirring masa by hand. Actually, Harry would be good at it, due to all those muscles.

That gives me an idea. "Harry said his mom likes to bake. I bet she's got a mixer, and they live close by. Do you want me to ask him to bring it?"

Mom's face lights up. "Yes! Please do that, Susannah, go do that right now. And make sure he invites his parents to come."

My stomach does a long, slow somersault at the thought of having Harry's parents at the party. It's not that I don't like them, I just don't know them very well. They're always working, so they hardly ever come to meets. I've only met them once, at a dual in October. Harry's stepdad, Bruce, was friendly and warm, but his mom...not so much. She wasn't rude to me or anything, but I could tell she wasn't impressed.

That was before Harry and I got together, though, so maybe she disapproved of our complicated friendship. When I asked Harry if I'd done something to make her dislike me, he said his mom could be skeptical of strangers and not to take it personally. But now she's my boyfriend's mother. If I still can't win her over, how else am I supposed to take it?

It doesn't help that Harry seems to be thinking along the same lines. He immediately responds to my text about the mixer with a promise to bring it, but when I say, You should bring your parents, too, it's a while before he responds. Finally, he asks, You sure that's okay?

I tell him it is, even though no, I'm not sure. The day is going to be chaotic enough without adding two people I want desperately to like me into the mix.

Too late now, though. They're coming.

"Mi vida," Bela says with a happy sigh, cupping my face in her hands. I have to bend so she can press a warm kiss against my cheek. "You're so tall! I think you grow an inch every time I see you."

"Maybe you're shrinking," I say. Bela pinches my chin in retaliation, but she smiles at me before turning to torment Nina about her grades.

"Buenas tardes, tía," I say, giving Tía Lillia, Mom's sister, a big hug.

"Buenas tardes, darling." She squeezes me tightly and rocks me back and forth, the way she always did when we were little, which makes me laugh. Tía Lillia has always been my favorite aunt, and not to flatter myself, but I think she likes me best of all her nieces and nephews.

We actually have a lot in common. These days, she's an accountant at a Big Four firm, but all through her teens and most of her twenties, Tía Lillia was a nationally ranked tennis player. Maybe that's why Mom's always been so cautious about my swimming career—she knew from watching Tía Lillia as they were growing up how much sacrifice being an elite athlete requires. But Tía Lillia's always encouraged me and my dreams.

Bela is saying to my sister, "You have to get good grades so you can go to college. No more messing around. You worry your parents to death."

"I know, Bela, I know," she says, then hastily adds, "Susannah's boyfriend is coming to the party. Can you believe she has a boyfriend now, our little Susanita?"

"You have a boyfriend, Susannah?" Bela coos, grabbing my hand. "How nice."

I shoot Nina a glare. "That was shameless," I tell her.

Nina beams at me and wiggles her fingers in the air. "Misdirection."

"What is his name?" Bela asks at the exact moment Tía Lillia asks, "How'd you meet him?"

"Harry," I tell them. "And he's a swimmer. We're on the same team."

"I mean, come on," Nina says. "Where else would *Susannah* meet a guy?"

Mom pops her head into the entryway. "Oh, hi! ¿Como esta, mami?"

"Bien, bien," Bela says. Mom embraces Bela and Lillia warmly.

"Nina told us your little one has a *boyfriend*, Maria," Tía Lillia teases, snaking an arm around my shoulders.

Bela asks, "Is he a good boy, this…?"

"Harry," I say, thinking about what he said the other day: *I don't want to be a curiosity.* My heart sinks. My relatives are going to eat him alive.

"Yes, we like him," Mom assures them, although she and

Dad have only met him once, that first time he picked me up for a Sunday swim.

Dad pops his head in and shouts, "Even though he's a Cubs fan!"

I laugh and shake my head.

"He's a nice young man," Mom says, giving Dad a little shove. He disappears back into the living room. "He's coming today with his parents, so you might as well wait till they get here to torture Susannah with embarrassment. There's a lot to do in the kitchen, and you're detaining my help. Did you bring the mixers and filling? Girls, go get the stuff from the car—Lillia, give them your keys."

"Older sisters, always so bossy," Tía Lillia scoffs, handing over the keys to her Prius as Mom disappears into the kitchen. She winks at me. "Does this Harry make you happy, Susannah?"

I smile. "Yeah, he does."

"Then I can't wait to meet him."

Tía Lillia does, in fact, have to wait to meet Harry. And wait. And wait some more. Because he doesn't show up on time. He's not even fashionably late, like Jessa and Amber—he's just fucking *late*.

It's not like I'm surprised. Harry has a casual relationship with time, which of course Dave is a huge fan of. But I keep thinking back to that Sunday when we were supposed to hang out and he didn't show up, with no real explanation. Is that what's happening now? Is Harry ditching me?

I can tell Mom is anxious about the mixer he promised to bring. We started making the tamales, because we couldn't wait, but it's going slower than Mom would like. The masa is the star of the show—you can't make tamales without it. Since we're down a mixer, I help by kneading the corn flour and lard by hand. It's killing my shoulder. I keep texting Harry, but he doesn't reply.

Nina called shotgun on filling the tamales and grabbed Amber to help her as soon as she walked through the door. The two of them are chatting at the dining room table, which we extended with two card tables so it could accommodate twenty people filling and folding in an assembly line Henry Ford would be proud of. It's nice to see how well Amber and Nina get along.

My sister *doesn't* like Jessa, though, so she's in the kitchen with Mom, Bela and me, soaking corn husks in hot water to soften and make them easier to fold.

"Where's your man?" she asks me, popping a tortilla chip in her mouth. "I thought he was com   ."

"He is," I insist.

"He'll be here soon," Mom says, even though I'm sure by now she has her doubts. She's not a huge fan of Jessa, either. She thinks she can be a little mean.

As if on cue, the doorbell rings, and my heart surges against my ribs. In my rush to answer it, I almost trip over my three-year-old cousin Gabriel, who's playing with a set of Matchbox cars Mom gave him in the hallway. Lulu is barking her head off upstairs—I put her and the cats in Mom and Dad's bedroom so they wouldn't be underfoot all day.

Gabe looks at me, wide-eyed, and asks, "Where's the doggy? I want to play with the doggy."

"You can play with her later, I promise," I say, scooping

him up. I deposit him in the living room, where Dad's holding court with my uncles and male cousins. They're supposed to be watching the younger kids, but they're mostly watching sports and eating the appetizers I made.

"Whoops," my cousin Luis—Gabe's dad—says. "Guess he got away from me."

I glance at the TV. "Yeah, wonder how that happened." He gives me a sheepish grin. I pat Gabe on the head, and steel myself to answer the door.

The thing about Harry is, my irritation melts away when I see him. I can't help it—I love the sight of him. And my sore shoulder loves the sight of the KitchenAid mixer he's got in his arms.

"You made it," I say. "I'll take that from you."

"No, I'll carry it into the kitchen," he insists, kissing my cheek. "Hey, Susie. Sorry we're late."

Oh, that's right—*we*. Bruce and his mom are standing behind him. Harry's mom looks confused. "We're late? Harry, what time were we supposed to be here?"

"No worries, it's kind of a come-whenever sort of thing for guests," I tell her. "Hi, Mrs. Matthews, Mr. Matthews. It's good to see you."

"It's good to see you, too, Susannah," Harry's mom says. "Thank you so much for inviting us. You can call us Bruce and Paula."

"Okay. Thanks for the mixer. Ours broke this morning, so we had to get creative."

"It's no trouble."

Bruce claps his hands together. He's a big man, tall and broad, with a full beard and a huge, booming voice. "This is exciting. We've never been to a tamale party before. How can we help?"

"The guys are in the living room, so you can head on in there if you want," I tell him. "There's a game on, and some food and drinks."

"I can watch the game at home," Bruce says. "I came to make some tamales. Give us jobs!"

I laugh and Harry grins. He worships Bruce. "Okay, then, let's find you something to do."

Once I've introduced Bruce and Paula to my parents and Bela, the four of us sit down at the dining room table to help put together the tamales.

"So, first you take a corn husk and spread a layer of masa, like this," I say, demonstrating. "Then you put filling in the center of the masa. It's about a tablespoon, but you can eyeball it. We've got four kinds of filling here: beef, red chili and pork, chicken, and vegetarian—bean, cheese, and potato."

"You made all of this today? You must've started around dawn," Paula says.

"We made the beef and veggie fillings yesterday. My grandmother and aunt brought the other two," I tell her. "So, after you fill the husk, you fold it like this, to make a little envelope that holds the tamale together, and then tie it off so it doesn't fall apart in the steamer. Some people use strips of corn husk, but we use string because who has the time?"

Paula laughs. "Indeed."

"And that's basically it," I say. "Depending on which filling you use, you put the finished tamale on one of these colored plates, and then we steam them."

"When do we eat them?" Harry asks, popping a piece of shredded chicken into his mouth.

"Hey, don't waste the filling," I scold him. "If you're hungry, there are nachos in the kitchen."

Harry pushes back from the table. "See ya," he says, bolting out of the room.

Paula shakes her head and smiles. Harry doesn't resemble her much—Paula is short and stocky, with a round face and green eyes and blond hair shot through with gray—but in that moment I realize: his smile is all hers. "That boy could eat every hour of every day and never be full."

"Swimming burns a lot of calories," I say with a smile. "We've got to get them from somewhere." Then I remember she's a nurse and probably knows how the human body works.

"That kid better change his mind about not swimming after high school, because by the time he graduates we'll have spent his entire college fund on Pizza Rolls and he'll need the scholarship," Bruce says, laughing.

"What do you mean?" I ask.

Paula jabs Bruce in the ribs with her elbow. "He's joking. Harry's college fund is fine."

My smile wavers. "No, I mean about Harry not swimming after high school?" I always assumed he would swim in college, like me.

"I—" Paula stops when she sees Harry come through the door carrying an entire tray of nachos. "You didn't want to leave some for anyone else, darling son that I raised to be polite and have good manners?"

"Susannah's mom told me to take the whole tray," he

mutters, only sort of embarrassed by his gluttony. "And her grandma basically shoved it into my hands!"

"Bela likes to make people eat," I say. "It's how she shows her love."

"If that's true," Harry says, shoving a big piece of nachos into his mouth, "then I think your abuela wants to marry me."

Even though he's talking with his mouth full and wiping his fingers on his jeans and clearly didn't brush his hair today and was super late, a lightning bolt of affection and attraction hits me squarely in the chest when I look at Harry. I can't believe I thought I could control my feelings for him, or resist them for even a second longer than I did. Harry and I, we were inevitable. And nothing feels more right to me than us here, together, surrounded by our families and outrageously in love.

Once all the tamales are filled and folded and steamed, Paula and Bruce help me, Mom and Tía Lillia wrap them in foil and pack them up for people to take home. The unanimous opinion was that Harry couldn't be trusted not to steal a few for immediate consumption, so he joins Dad and the rest of the guys in refilling ice chests, pouring drinks, and setting out snack platters and sides on the table.

Not all of the tamales leave with our guests. Some we eat right away, during the second half of the tamalada, and that's when the party really begins.

While the adults set to work getting tipsy off Dad's spiked punch, I take Lulu out to pee. Jessa, Amber and Nina join me, but my aunts and cousins have Harry and his parents in a conversational headlock and refuse to release him. Serves him right for being so late.

"How long are we going to be out here?" Jessa asks, shivering in her inadequate coat.

"I told you you'd be cold," Amber says, but she puts her arm around Jessa to warm her up. Nina raises her eyebrows at them, then pulls her gloves off with her teeth and scrolls around on her phone.

"This is all I have to wear," Jessa snaps. "And I wasn't going to let you guys leave without me."

"I owe Lulu a long walk for being cooped up all day," I say.

"Frick and Frack were cooped up, too, but I don't see you out here with two cats on a leash."

Amber laughs. I shake my head. Jessa can be a bit much sometimes. "You'll warm up," I tell her. I almost didn't invite her, after the way she's been acting toward me lately, but I know how much pressure we're all under, and anyway, it's Christmas.

Eventually, even Lulu seems cold—there's no snow on the ground right now, but the temperature is hovering around freezing—so we make our way back to the house. When we get inside, I look for Harry, but he's not with my aunts anymore, and I can't find him anywhere. I come across Bruce and Paula in the garage, talking to my dad about the elaborate organization and storage system he rigged up in there, but he's not with them.

Bela grabs me as I pass through the kitchen. "Have you eaten dinner?" she asks. She presses a plate into my hands. "Eat, mi vida. You can't do anything well if you're hungry."

Knowing it's better to do what she says than to argue with

her, I heap my plate with tamales, salad, rice and beans, then carry it upstairs with me while I check quickly for Harry. I don't really expect to find him up here—my new best bet is the basement, where some of my cousins are playing video games—but I open my bedroom door and there he is, sitting cross-legged on the floor near the bed.

The expression on his face sends an arrow through my heart. He looks so *sad*. What happened while I was on that walk?

I sit down next to him and put the plate on the floor.

"You hungry?" I ask. He shakes his head. "What's wrong?"

"Nothing." He rests his head against the mattress and points up at the wall. "This is nice."

"Thanks. My dad made it." He's talking about the custom shelves that hold all my trophies and ribbons and medals. They're so packed there's hardly any room for new stuff.

"Where's your World Championships gold medal?" he asks.

"In there somewhere." But I know right where it is. About a year ago, I covered it up with a bunch of personal-best ribbons from my earliest swimming days, from before GAC even, when Nina and I competed in a local in-house league. Sometimes, I feel like those mean more, because back then I wasn't trying to win, I was just trying to be as good as I could be.

"What's that empty hook for?" he asks. I raise my eyebrows. He nods and says, "Right. Duh."

"Mom and Dad probably wouldn't let me hang an Olympic medal, though. They'd insist I put it in a safe deposit box or something. The hook is more symbolic than anything." I push a lock of hair back from his forehead and kiss his temple. "Did something happen? You seem upset."

"I'm not. I mean, I don't know, I get this way sometimes. It's no big deal." I feel like he's holding back, but I don't push him. "I just needed to be by myself for a while."

"Do you want me to go?" I ask tentatively. I don't want to leave him like this, but I feel as though I've intruded on a private moment.

He shakes his head and wraps his arm around me. I hold him, feeling panicky, not knowing what to do. I figure if I wait, he'll tell me as much as he wants to share.

"I've been feeling this way all day," he admits. "It's why I was late. I didn't want to come. It's not you, or your family— they're great. I'm just...feeling lousy."

"Do you want to leave?" I watch as he wrestles with the answer. "If you do, that's okay. I know that being around this many people can be overwhelming sometimes."

"Yeah," he says. "You sure you won't be mad?"

"Of course not. But I'm worried. I thought you were having fun."

"I was. I am. That's the worst part. I feel both at the same time."

I hug him tighter. "It's been a long couple of months," I say, thinking that might be what's gotten him down—the exhaustion of the fall season. Harry's a junior, which is the hardest year academically. Finals leer at us from the other side of the holiday break. There will be more training, more meets, and he'll have to start thinking about applying to colleges, if he's not already.

The future is so daunting, and time is moving at an unfathomable velocity. I wonder if that's what's weighing on him. It's certainly weighing on me.

"It's been a long couple of years," he says with a deep sigh. I feel a flicker of concern, wondering what he means by that. We're discovering new things about each other every day—tastes, quirks, passions, history—but there's still so much unexplored terrain.

"Do you want to tell me about it?" I ask, stroking his cheeks with my fingertips. His skin is warm, and I wonder if he might be developing a fever. If there's a cold going around, Harry always seems to be the first person to catch it.

He shakes his head. "Not right now. I kind of just want to go home and crawl into bed."

"Okay," I say, pulling him to his feet. "Go find your parents and I'll get you a couple dozen tamales to take home."

He hesitates. "I don't want your family to see me leaving and think I'm rude."

"They won't mind," I assure him. "People have been in and out all day. But maybe it would make you feel better to leave through the garage. That's where your mom and dad are, anyway. Then you won't have to spend an hour saying goodbye to everybody."

"Thanks, Susie," he says, putting his arms around me again.

"Of course," I say, stroking his back. "Whatever you need."

CHAPTER FOURTEEN

170 days until US Olympic Team Trials

"I'M WORRIED ABOUT THIS SHOULDER," BETH SAYS AS AN ATH-letic trainer bends my arm behind my back and rotates it in a slow, painful circle. I bite down hard on my lip to keep from wincing. The last thing I need is Beth pulling back on my workouts to accommodate my shoulder.

"I've got a whole pool of swimmers with bad shoulders and bad knees and bad backs," Dave says. "Susannah's no worse off, and *they* manage to make it through two practices a day. I don't see why she should be different. She can swim through it."

I bristle at the suggestion that I'm using my shoulder as an excuse to slack, but the point of having Dave here is so he'll talk Beth out of making a big deal about this. She's not afraid of him, but she'll back down for a while. This is, after all, his club. I'll worry about what comes next tomorrow.

"Are we boring you, Susannah?" Dave asks me, snapping his fingers in front of my face.

I thought I was being sly about checking the time on my phone, but apparently not so much.

"No," I say, shoving my phone in my pocket. It's after seven on a Friday night. Harry is waiting for me but explaining that won't get me out of here any faster.

"I still think you should take it easy for a while," Beth tells me. "I'll take a look at your upcoming workouts—there are probably some places I can switch in some legs-only sets."

"I don't need any adjustments," I argue. "It doesn't hurt that bad. I'll be better about icing and resting, and I'll do more strength exercises, I promise. Don't change my workouts."

Beth looks uncertain.

"I'm getting so much faster. Please don't make me dial back, not now," I beg. *"Please."*

She sighs and I perk up, sensing I've won.

"Wipe that smile off your face," she says. Beth rarely snaps at me. I feel guilty, but I can't let her sideline me out of an overabundance of caution. I don't have a day to lose if I'm going to be good enough to dominate at Trials.

"I'm not giving in," Beth warns me. "We'll take it day by day. If at any point I think you're in danger of further injuring yourself, it's the diving well with a kickboard for you. And I want you in the weight room *with a trainer* twice a week to build up strength in that shoulder."

I groan. I have no time for Harry as it is. He's busy, too, with swimming and his other mysterious time commitments, but it's been less than a month since we got together. Two

extra weight room sessions a week will eat into the precious
few hours we have to ourselves. But it can't be helped.

Beth glances at her watch. "It's late. You can go, Susannah."

I thank her and hop off the exam table. As I'm pulling a
sweater over the tank top I wore for the assessment, I try to
reassure Beth, who still seems concerned.

"I'll be careful," I promise her. "I don't want to get hurt,
either. And if it gets worse I'll tell you."

She ditches the worried grimace and smiles at me.

"I know you will. Have a good night. Tell Harry I said
thanks for waiting."

At the mention of Harry's name, Dave shoots me a dark
look. He's made it clear he doesn't approve of our relationship. But I leave the training room without acknowledging
his glare or letting it bother me. I'm too excited to be done
with the pool for tonight.

Harry and I are going on our very first real official date.

I find Harry sitting on the floor of the lobby, studying for
finals. He jumps to his feet when he spots me walking toward him, gathering his books and notes, clearly as eager to
get going as I am.

He pulls me into a hug, taking care not to jostle my bad
shoulder.

"All good?" he whispers. His breath is warm against the
sensitive skin behind my ear. A shiver travels down my back.

"All good." I hold tight to him, pressing my face into his
neck. He smells like clean skin and chlorine. I smile against
the collar of his well-worn fleece. Being with him feels like
a reward for every hard moment in the pool. I don't want to

step outside the comforting circle of his arms. But we have somewhere to be.

I just don't know where that is.

"Let's get out of here," he says, keeping one arm around me as he picks up his swim bag.

"Where are we going?"

Harry insisted on planning the whole date himself. It's not that we haven't spent time together as a couple, but most of it has been at my house, with my parents in the room or somewhere nearby. Between school and swimming and family stuff, we didn't get a chance to properly celebrate Christmas. We're exchanging gifts tonight, but that's all I know.

"It's a surprise," he says. He shoots me a grin. "Relax, Susie. Don't you trust me?"

We bundle into the car. He looks at me, and I look at him, and a second later we're kissing, as if we've been apart a thousand years instead of one hour, like we'll shrivel to dust and disappear if we're ever separated. I seem to exist only in the places where he's touching me; the rest of me is as weightless as a feather on the water. Harry is a current that's bearing me away, far from the shore of everything I've ever known, into the heart of a boundless, long-forgotten sea.

I surrender to the feeling, believing in my bones that wherever he might take me is exactly where I want to be.

I'm dimly aware of the plastic console between the two front seats digging into my hip. A strange noise rumbles from the back of my throat; it's not a sound I ever thought I could make, that I would even admit came from me if I didn't feel the vibration of it in my chest. Frustrated, I climb into his lap and straddle his hips with my knees, tugging gently at the hair on the back of his head, a cue for him to lift his chin so I can press my lips against the underside of his jaw.

"Susannah," he breathes, cupping the back of my head. "Susie, don't stop."

I have no intention of stopping. This right here—touching Harry, kissing Harry, being held by him—feels like what my body was really made for. Not swimming, not beating ceaselessly against never-ending wakes, not trudging back and forth in some miniature, artificial ocean, fighting for every breath, but this magic, *us*, is my body's true and destined purpose. How had I not realized it sooner? It's as if I've drowned and been brought back to life.

Harry reaches down and suddenly the seat drops, pulling us with it.

"Oof." The impact clears the fog from my head just a little. We laugh.

He grabs me by my elbows and yanks me closer. My skin tingles as if it's waking up after falling asleep—what sensitive things, elbows; I never knew. His mouth meets mine, then opens. His tongue lightly skims the sensitive inner part of my bottom lip. I shiver, stroking the soft, downy skin at the nape of his neck. I think I could be perfectly happy kissing Harry forever. When his tongue grazes mine, my body lights up with pleasure.

He might be a distraction, but he's a very, very good one.

Harry groans. "We should probably get going."

"What? Why?"

I press my mouth to his and he kisses me back eagerly, but a minute later he pulls away again.

"I had a whole evening planned..." He trails off as I brush

my lips along his collarbone. "Come on, Susie, give me a break here. I'm trying to be romantic."

I kiss him, once, twice, three times, testing his will to resist. It's very weak.

"This is romantic," I murmur.

"Yeah, but our night..." he says, laughing. He puts his hands on my arms and holds me firmly at a distance. "I planned it all out. If we keep going like this, it'll never happen."

I smile down at him. "Okay. You're right. I want to see what you planned."

"Thank you," he says, releasing me. I take advantage of the opening to sneak another kiss. He laughs against my mouth. "Susie! You're relentless."

"You like it," I tease, climbing off him and dropping back into my seat.

"You know I do," he says. He pulls the seat back up and presses the ignition button.

"Has the car been off this whole time?" I ask. "It's so hot in here."

"Thank you," he says with a wink. I toss a glove at his head. I was wearing them when I got in the car—it's below freezing outside—but I don't quite recall taking them off.

As the high of him starts to fade, I realize how messy my hair must be. I finger-comb it into place as best I can. The silver lining of having thick, wild curls is that they pretty much look out of control no matter what.

Harry pulls out of the parking lot, winding his way through the back roads behind the high school before merging onto a highway that leads out of town. I snuggle into my down jacket as Harry blasts the heat. He drives with one hand on the steering wheel and threads his fingers through mine with the other. For the moment, I forget about my shoulder, forget all about the empty hook that's waiting for an Olympic medal. Right now, it's just this—him and me. It feels like the only thing I could ever want.

"Tell me about the evaluation," he says as we coast down the road.

"Oh, it's nothing," I say, kissing his knuckles. He smiles. "Same old garbage shoulder. It'll be fine. Beth's making me do extra weight room sessions with a trainer."

"That sucks," he says. I can tell by the way his smile flickers that he's doing the math on how much less time we'll have to spend together. "You sure it's going to be okay? I've seen you at practice. It bugs you a lot more than you let on."

"I can handle it." I squeeze his hand. "Let's talk about something else."

He's silent for a second, but then he says, "Okay. We're almost there, anyway."

We turn off the main highway onto a dark side road and I let out an undignified squeal.

"I haven't been here in forever! We used to come when I was a kid."

Harry looks relieved. "Oh, good. I was afraid you'd think this was stupid."

"I thought they took it down after Christmas."

"Christmas isn't technically over," Harry explains. "Twelve days, you know. They'll start dismantling the installments on Monday. I called to confirm."

"You really did plan this," I say.

"Why is that such a huge shock?" he asks with a laugh.

He turns onto a long driveway and pulls up to a gatehouse. The guard inside is wearing a heavy coat, gloves and a hat, and I can hear the sound of a space heater chugging away in some unseen corner, but he still looks like he's freezing. Harry hands him a twenty and collects his change. The gate opens.

"Tune your radio to 93.9 FM and go on in," the guard says. "Enjoy, and Merry Christmas."

I spin the radio dial to the correct station. Trans-Siberian Orchestra's "Carol of the Bells" spills through the speakers. Harry pulls the car through the gate, and immediately the lights come into view.

Marshall House is a local mansion built by some long-ago robber baron right around the outbreak of World War I. It sits on a huge estate with sprawling gardens and deep woods, and every year the mansion—now a museum—allows the city of Beaumont to set up an elaborate drive-through holiday light show on the grounds for Christmas.

When Nina and I were little, our parents would take us, but we haven't gone for years. I guess Mom and Dad figured we were too old to think it was cool, but I stare out the window at the decorations, thrilled that Harry thought to do this. I forgot it existed.

"That one was always my favorite." I point at an installation made to look like a peacock fanning its feathers. "We called it Mildred."

"You know peacocks are always male, right?"

"*Now* I do. But by the time Mom told me, it was too late. He was Mildred."

It takes about a half hour for us to complete the route.

There are literally hundreds of lighted installations and arches, so many that it's impossible to look at them all. Strands of Christmas lights wind up the trunks of trees and drip like icicles from their branches. Reindeer rise into the sky as if by magic, elves cartwheel across the lawn, and the mansion itself is covered with glittering flecks of light, decorated to give the impression of a gingerbread house with icing along the eaves and gumdrops in the windows. At the end of the road, a larger-than-life installation of Santa Claus waves goodbye.

Harry glances at me as he pulls back onto the main road. "So…you liked it?" he asks, almost shyly.

I smile. "I did."

"Would you say your heart is filled with holiday cheer?"

"I would say that, yes," I say, laughing.

"How would you like to fill your stomach with French fries?"

"Yes! I'm starving. Diner?"

Harry nods. I feel my phone buzz with a text message. It's from Mom.

Hope you're having fun, it reads. Be home by 11.

My parents are a bit wary of the whole *our baby girl is dating* thing, even though Nina's had several boyfriends in the past few years, so they should be used to it. Nina's the impulsive one, the type of kid to run into the street after a ball without looking, always pushing back against the rules and testing the limits of my parents' patience. Even so, they're much more protective of me.

Maybe it's because I'm younger, or because they think I'm more sensitive, but I think it's because I've spent most of my life under the bell jar of the natatorium's thick glass walls.

They have faith that I'm safe in it, and that I would never leave it. Now that I'm building something outside of it, they're not sure what to do.

They trust me, I know, but I can almost hear Mom's worry vibrating through the phone. I assure her I'll make curfew and put the phone away.

The diner is a lot more crowded than it usually is when we go on Sunday mornings, but by now we're friendly with the staff. Lucille, our favorite waitress, gives us a booth by the window.

We already know what we want to eat, so we order immediately, then sit across the table from each other with giant smiles on our faces. Harry and I see each other every single day in the pool, but that in no way diminishes the specialness of these rare moments when it's just us.

Harry takes my hand at the same time I nudge his feet under the table with my toes. He laughs.

"Presents?" I ask, fumbling in my backpack for his gift one-handed.

"Presents," Harry says.

He carried a gift bag overflowing with red and white tissue paper into the diner with him, and he hands it to me now. I slide his wrapped gift across the table. He gives it a funny look, but when I ask what's wrong, he tells me it's nothing.

"You go first," I say.

I'm nervous, wondering if he'll like what I got him or not. I found it via a social media ad, and when I initially saw it, I thought it was perfect, but now I'm second-guessing. He's never been as into swimming as me. Maybe I've committed the cardinal holiday sin of buying something for someone else because I wanted it for myself.

He tears the wrapping paper off and pulls out a black leather notebook. It has his initials embossed in gold across the front. He stares at it for a second in shock, then starts to laugh.

"It's a swim log," I say. "You use it to keep track of your times and splits and workouts… You don't like it? It's okay. I can…well, I don't think I can return it because it's customized, but I can get you something else—"

"No, no, Susie, I love it," Harry says. "That's not it—how about you open your gift now?"

The bag is huge, the type you'd get at a department store if you bought a lot of stuff, and it's crammed full of tissue paper, so I'm expecting his gift to me to be large, but I keep pulling out pieces of tissue. Just when I think this is a joke and the bag is actually empty, I see a flat, rectangular black object lying at the bottom.

It's a black leather notebook, with my initials embossed in gold across the front.

"We got each other the same thing," I say, flipping through the pages. I look up at him. "How did we manage to get each other the exact same Christmas gift?"

He smirks. "I'm going to go out on a limb and say we got served the same ad."

I laugh. "Way to take the magic out of it."

"Do you like it?" he asks. His expression softens, and I realize he was as nervous as I was about getting the right gift.

"Are you kidding? I love it. Do you like yours?"

Harry nods. "I do. But actually…"

He hands me the notebook I gave him and takes back the one he gave me.

"We should switch," he explains. "That way, I can track all your splits and times while you're in the pool, and you can track mine. We do it in our heads, anyway. Might as well have some place to write it down."

"Great idea," I say.

Suddenly, he gets up out of his seat and slides into my side of the booth.

"You know what's a great idea?" he whispers, tucking a curl behind my ear and brushing the tip of his nose against mine. I swallow hard. I feel like I'm dissolving. "This."

He takes my lips in a slow, luxurious kiss. I brace my hand on his chest and feel his heart beating hard and fast in the center of my palm. I don't even care that we're in public, that dozens of people could be watching. He's here, and so am I, and we're kissing—that's all that matters.

Thoughts fly out of my head like dandelion seeds in a strong breeze, coasting away gently until the only things I can focus on are physical: the warmth of his skin, the soft slip of his hair sifting through my fingers, the taste of his mouth—minty fresh, like he just popped an Altoid, which he probably did.

I love kissing Harry. He's the first boy I ever really kissed like this, and I wonder if every boy kisses like this, then think that's probably not the case, which is a shame. The best way I've come up with to describe how Harry kisses is that he does it with joy. Like every tug of his lips is a moment of happy discovery, every gentle slide of his tongue against mine a delightful surprise. The playfulness that Harry brings to most things in his life is on full display in his kisses.

I don't think I'll ever be able to get enough of this feeling. The closest I've come to it before was in the water, back when I was fast—that overpowering sense of rightness, of belonging to something bigger than myself. It's as overwhelming as it is exhilarating, but I throw caution out the window and let myself drown.

When we pull apart, I can hear the heavy sound of my own straining breath. It's kind of embarrassing. Harry notices, too, and grins. I punch him softly in the arm.

"Always so pleased with yourself," I scold him, laughing.

He leans back against the booth and puts his hands behind his head. "I don't know what you're talking about. I'm a delight."

"Oh. Harry. Hi."

Fee is standing at the edge of our table. She seems uncomfortable intruding on what was obviously a private moment, but she doesn't leave. If I were in a more cynical mood, I'd think she was trying to interrupt us.

"Hey, Fee," he says, sitting up straight and shifting a few inches away from me. He runs his fingers through his hair. "Are you here with Val and them?"

She nods and points to a table behind us. "They're over there."

"You remember Susannah, right?" He turns to me and widens his eyes in a silent plea. I smile at Fee and give her a small wave.

"Hi again," I say.

"Of course. Nice to see you. I hope your ears are okay? No more infection?"

She taps her own ear, like I might not know what they are. I almost tell her that I didn't have an infection—the drops were *preventative*—but I stop myself. It doesn't matter.

"All good," I say.

Fee forces a smile. "I'm glad. Anyway, I didn't mean to bother you. I was just surprised to see you, Harry. I hadn't heard from you in a while."

He shrugs all casual like, *What can you do?* "Swimming."

"Right. Okay, well, I guess I'll see you around. Maybe at Tuck's sometime soon?"

There's a painful note of hope in her voice. I feel bad for her. She clearly likes Harry a lot, and I know what that's like. Doesn't mean I want her to stick around, though. I slip my arm through Harry's, feeling suddenly possessive.

"Maybe," he says. His expression brightens as Lucille approaches the table. "Oh, hey, food!"

Fee disappears, or maybe we're so hungry we stop noticing her once Lucille puts our plates in front of us. Harry sits next to me while we eat, talking a mile a minute about the new superhero movie trailer that just dropped, the Gwar concert he and Tucker are going to next weekend, the books he's reading in his AP English class. Not even the shyest person in the world could have a meal with Harry and resist being drawn in. He's a conversational riptide, and I float happily along in his wake, enjoying the sound of his voice as he describes in detail the expanded Marvel universe between bites of his burger. We do not discuss Fee.

Harry insists on paying for dinner.

"It's our first official date, Susie," he says when I try to argue. "Let me take you out."

I agree with some reluctance, though secretly I'm pleased. Things have changed since Harry and I got together—there's one hundred percent more kissing, which I particularly enjoy—but in some ways our relationship isn't all that different than before.

Paying for a date, though: that's something significant others do. And if Harry is anything to me, it's significant. *Harry is my boyfriend.* The thought fills me with what can only be described as glee.

Before we leave, I use the restroom. When I come out of the stall, Fee is standing by the sinks. It's probably a coincidence, but it feels like she's been waiting for me.

"Oh. Hey." I wash my hands, pretending not to notice the way she's chewing her lip, as if she's trying to get up the courage to say something.

"So...you and Harry, huh?" she says. "I thought he liked you, but I couldn't tell for sure."

I don't know what to say to that, so I go with a highly articulate, "Yeah."

"That's great for him. For you both, I mean. Harry deserves to be happy."

"Thanks," I say.

Thanks? What am I thanking her for? Being nice about it, I guess, since it doesn't seem like the thought of Harry and me dating makes *her* very happy.

"It's just, that, like—has Harry told you about his, you know...issues?"

I keep washing my hands, though they're plenty clean by

now, determined not to act surprised. What does she mean by "issues"?

"I don't know what you're talking about," I say, snatching a few paper towels from a dispenser.

Fee looks at the ground. She seems a tiny bit ashamed, but she pushes forward.

"There are a lot of rumors about him. People told me things back when he and I were... I don't know how much is true and how much is made up. Lots of people don't like him."

"Are we talking about the same Harry?" I ask. Sure, maybe a few people—like Jessa, and of course Dave—find Harry's good-natured mischief-making annoying, but I wouldn't go so far as to say anyone actively dislikes him.

"I know he seems like this super-chill, cheerful guy," Fee says, "but you know that's all fake, right? Or at least some of it is. That's the side of him he wants everybody to see, but he's got others."

"Nobody is one thing all the time," I tell her. Like, I can be uptight and single-minded and stubborn, but when I'm around Harry, my heart feels lighter, and the oppressive force of my expectations for myself are much easier to bear.

With him, I'm discovering a part of myself that's hopeful and optimistic. The other day, Nina caught me singing to myself and insisted on checking me for a fever.

"Sure," Fee admits. "But with Harry, it's different. He hides stuff. Haven't you noticed? You will. He disappears for days and then lies about where he's been. He pulls away and won't say why. It's why I broke up with him in the first place. I didn't trust him."

"*You* broke up with *him*?" I ask. "But don't you want—"

I strangle the thought midsentence. It seems rude to imply she's still interested in him, though I'm certain she is. If she wants to get back together with Harry, she can't possibly mean any of this. Unless she's saying it to make me doubt him, hoping *I'll* break up with him. But, all evidence to the contrary, Fee doesn't strike me as a manipulative snake.

Fee sighs. "It's complicated. Anyway, I thought I should warn you."

"You haven't really told me anything," I point out.

I can feel my face getting red. I don't know why I'm the one who's mortified here, but I feel foolish, because I *have* noticed how secretive Harry is.

"I guess I feel like I don't have a right to tell you anything specific," she says. "Harry should do that. But he won't. Talk to Tuck. Maybe he will."

I don't respond to that, and I don't think she expects me to, because she leaves. I wait in the bathroom for several minutes, praying that by the time I come out, Fee will be gone.

Thankfully, I don't see her as I walk back through the diner on the way to our table, where Harry is doing something with his phone. Could he be texting another girl? Is he texting Fee *right now*?

Because that was her implication, as far as I could tell— that Harry isn't faithful. What other reason would there be for him to go radio silent and then lie about it?

Harry looks up at me with a grin. "There you are! I thought maybe you fell in."

There's not a nonembarrassing yet still plausible explanation for a prolonged bathroom break, so I roll my eyes and reach past him to grab my coat.

"Ready to go?" I ask.

"Everything okay?" he asks warily.

I smile and nod. For the first time since we started to become friends, all I want is to get away from him. I need some time by myself to think through what Fee said.

Maybe I should tell Harry what happened. He should know that someone he considers a friend is talking about him behind his back. But it would hurt him. And, much as I hate to admit it, while some of what she said seems ridiculous, some of it struck a chord.

As Harry takes my hand and tugs me toward the door, I decide not to say a word about it to him until I know how much of what Fee told me—if any of it—is true.

CHAPTER FIFTEEN

164 days until US Olympic Team Trials

"WHAT UP, STALKER?"

We're standing outside the room where Tucker has fourth period study hall. This is the third time I've tried to approach him one-on-one this week—the other two times, I chickened out. I didn't think he saw me, but I might've been wrong about that.

I don't know what to think about Tuck. The fact that he's Harry's friend makes me inclined to like him, but he's not super nice to me. I can't tell if it's because he resents that Harry spends more time with me than with him, or if he finds me annoying in general, but whatever the reason, I get a vibe he prefers it when I'm not around.

Which makes standing here with him now feel weird. I can't stop fidgeting with the strap of my bag. It occurs to me that he probably knows Jessa better than he knows me, since they have that class together and I guess they've been talking a lot.

Maybe I should've asked her to come along as a buffer, but I didn't want to tell her about my conversation with Fee. I only confided in Amber. She's way less judgmental about... well, pretty much everything, though she did discourage me from going behind Harry's back and interrogating his friends.

"Would you like it if he randomly came up to me, or God forbid *Jessa*, and started asking us all kinds of personal questions about you?" she asked.

I'd hate to think Harry wouldn't trust me enough to ask me something like that straight out. But this isn't about trust. This is about not hurting Harry. I don't want him to think I believe a single word Fee said about him—and I *don't*—but I'm a worrier. And Fee made me worry.

Because he *does* disappear without explanation. He *does* go out of his way to pretend everything's perfect, even when I know it isn't. He *does* hide behind grand gestures and flippant banter. What does all of that mean?

Tucker waves his hand in front of my eyes to get my attention.

"Susannah? Can I help you?"

My mouth is dry. I clear my throat and ask, "Do you want to have lunch?"

Tuck's eyebrows shoot up so far they're practically touching his hairline. "Just you and me?"

"Is that weird?" I ask, feeling stupid.

He shrugs. "Yeah, but I don't mind weird. Let's go. They've got nachos on the menu today."

Once we have our nachos, Tucker and I seek out an empty

table in the busy cafeteria. He nods at a small round one in a quiet corner and we sit down across from each other.

"So," Tuck says, spooning a heap of sour cream, guacamole and cheese into his mouth with a giant tortilla chip. "What did Harry do now?"

I take a deep breath, struck by the realization he's had conversations like this with other girls.

"Well, I guess that tells me a lot," I say.

"Eh, not really," Tucker replies around a mouthful of food. "It's not his fault. He's so friendly girls sometimes think he's into them when he's not. And once they figure that out, who do they come running to for advice?"

"You," I say.

Tucker bows without getting up from his chair, then shoves another chip into his mouth.

"He's into you, though," he says. "In case that's what this is about."

"I know Harry likes me," I tell him.

"Then why are you here?" He squints at me. "You don't want help breaking things off with him, do you? Because I'm not the guy for that."

"What? No!"

"Okay. That's happened before, too."

I feel the conversation turning in the direction I meant to take it myself, but part of me wishes it wouldn't. Amber was right. I should've talked to Harry. But now I'm curious.

"How come?" I ask.

"Why does anybody break up with anybody?" When I don't respond, he sighs. "I don't know. Harry can be too… much, for some people." Tucker narrows his eyes at me as I shift in my chair. Then he reaches across the table and flicks my untouched plate of nachos pointedly. "Why are we eating lunch together, Susannah?"

Unless I want to tell him to forget it and walk away without answers, I have no choice but to spill about what Fee said, so that's what I do. When I'm finished, I brace myself for some major revelation that will upend the way I think about Harry and all my hopes for our relationship.

Instead, Tuck snorts. "Well, that was a shitty thing for Fee to do."

"Obviously. Was she telling the truth, though?"

"What do you think?" he asks.

"Don't be obnoxious." I feel like he's toying with me. I want him to reassure me Fee was stirring up drama out of jealousy so I can go back to enjoying my life for the first time in years.

"You're asking me to betray my best friend and tell you his secrets so you don't have to ask him about it yourself," Tuck points out. "If I'm being obnoxious, that makes two of us."

"You're right." I push back from the table. "This was a bad idea. Sorry. I shouldn't have asked."

Tucker puts a hand on my arm to stop me. "Hey, wait. Look, just ask him. He'll answer you honestly. I don't even think he's trying to keep stuff from you, he's just careful. People can be cruel."

"Okay, I'll do that," I tell him. I wish I'd never spoken to Tucker about this. Now I'm even more confused and worried than before. I thought that Fee was trying to tell me Harry was a player. But that's not what Tuck seems to mean at all.

My mind spins with possible scenarios. What if Harry is

sick? Or…oh God, what if he has a kid? He's seventeen, it's far from impossible. That might explain the random disappearances and the general evasiveness. I have no idea what I'm going to do if I find out that Harry is a father.

It takes me a second to realize Tucker is still talking.

"—and if it makes you feel better," he says, "Fee doesn't know what she's talking about. She's just going off rumors and other people's guesses."

This surprises me. "You mean Harry never told her?"

Tucker shakes his head. "I know she acts like she's still all in love with him or whatever, but I don't think she ever really cared enough about him to work up the courage to ask."

It takes me a week to figure out how to talk to Harry about all of this. A week during which I try pretending that everything's fine, but Harry is tentative around me, like he knows something is wrong and isn't sure what it is.

I don't want to shatter the happiness we've found together, but I can't hide from this forever. If we're going to make things work between us, we can't have secrets.

That night, I tell him over text that I need to see him as soon as possible the next day. When he asks me why, all I can bring myself to say is: Can we meet tomorrow morning before practice?

CHAPTER SIXTEEN

157 days until US Olympic Team Trials

IT'S FIVE IN THE MORNING, AND HARRY IS WAITING FOR ME in the natatorium parking lot. It's deserted excerpt for Dave's junky old Ford Fiesta. The sky is dark as ink. I told Dad I needed to be dropped off early so that I could help organize equipment, which is not a thing, but he was half-asleep and didn't question it.

I climb into Harry's car and rub my hands together to generate some heat. It's cold today, and foggy. The world looks about as confused as I feel, covered by a smoky white veil.

Harry's expression is grim, and he seems exhausted, like he didn't sleep well last night. The skin under his eyes looks bruised and there's a giant coffee container in the cup holder.

After a couple agonizing minutes of total silence, during which I try to remember how I planned on starting this conversation, Harry blurts out, "Whatever you're thinking, say it.

This is torture. Do you want to break up? Is that what this is? If it is, get it over with. There's no point in drawing it out."

I try to take his hand, but he flinches and I pull away.

"Harry, no. I don't want to... I just want to talk to you."

"Does this have anything to do with what Fee told you that night at the diner?" he asks, balling his hands into fists in his lap.

"Wait—you know about that?"

Harry nods. "She texted a few nights ago to tell me. I guess she was feeling guilty. But Fee doesn't know anything about me. We didn't go out for that long, and I never told her—"

"Never told her what?" I ask.

He refuses to look at me. Embarrassment, or anger, or some combination, make bright red splotches bloom in his cheeks.

"It's not something I tell people about right away," he says.

"That's what Tucker said," I say without thinking.

"You talked to Tucker?" His voice is quiet, but I can tell from the way his jaw is clenched that he's seething. "You went behind my back to grill my friend instead of coming to me?"

"I thought Fee was warning me that you were going to cheat on me. That you'd done that to her, and other girls. I was afraid to tell you, because I didn't want you to think I believed it," I say.

He narrows his eyes at me. "*Did* you believe it?"

"No," I insist. He looks unconvinced. "It didn't make sense, not with what I know about you. But I'm new at this, and there's a part of me that wonders if I'm too naive about guys and relationships to be able to trust my own instincts."

Harry lets his head fall back against the seat. He sighs. "That's not what she was talking about. I'm not a cheater."

"I know that. And I'm sorry I ever doubted." I take a deep breath and pose the question I've been panicking over silently for days. "Harry, do you have a kid?"

A wave of silence washes over us. Then, to my surprise, he laughs. He *laughs*, while I sit there feeling humiliated and ridiculous.

"What's so funny?" I snap.

He's laughing so hard there are tears gathering in his eyes. He wipes them away and splutters, "A kid? You think I'm hiding an actual *child*? Oh, Susie, I'm sorry. If I thought for one second that was what you were imagining, I never would've—no, that's not it *at all*."

I sit back in my seat, relieved. "Then what is it?"

He stares at the roof of the car. "Man, compared to a secret love child, the reality seems almost boring."

"Harry," I say.

"Okay, I'm sorry. I'll be serious." He takes a deep breath, then says, "The unvarnished, absolute, one hundred percent truth is that I'm bipolar."

I don't say anything for a few seconds, and neither does Harry. He darts a glance at me. He's not laughing anymore.

"Susie?" He pauses. "What are you thinking?"

"Bipolar?"

"Yes," he replies.

"I don't know much about that. I mean, I've heard of it, but I'm not sure...what it is."

"It's a mood disorder. Sometimes people call it manic depression, but that's an imprecise term. Bipolar disorder is characterized by emotional highs that alternate with extreme lows."

Harry's whole demeanor has changed. The smiling, mischievous charmer has fallen away and his whole body is rigid, as if he's bracing himself for a punch. His voice has lost its teasing quality, and in its place is something I've never heard from him before—the clipped, antiseptic speech of a medical professional. I wonder if he's repeating things he's been told before.

"I'm not crazy," he insists. "I hate that word. I'm living with a chronic illness, and I manage it with my psychiatrist, therapy, drugs, exercise...that's why I started swimming actually. My doctor thought it would be an outlet for my energy and a good confidence builder.

"There are different kinds of bipolar disorder," he continues. "I'm bipolar II, which means I've never had a manic episode. With me it's mostly depression with a few hypomanic episodes over the course of my life. I'm not psychotic, I'm not dangerous and I'm *not* crazy. Okay? I'm not crazy."

"Okay, I hear you." I think about all the times I've casually said the word *crazy*, especially around Harry, and feel ill. I'm never going to use that word again.

He closes his eyes. "I know it bugs you when I don't answer my phone or show up where I'm supposed to be. When that happens, I'm usually in therapy, or need to be by myself. Sometimes, it feels too hard to face the world. My meds work, but they're not a cure. I still get depressed, and when I'm feeling bad, I don't always want to be around people, even people I care about."

I put a hand on his arm. I'm shocked, not by what he said, but by the sudden flood of new information to absorb. My mind is like a capsized boat, and I struggle to reorient myself. The night of the tamalada, what he told me up in my room, makes sense now. I thought he was coming down with something, or finally feeling the impact of four solid months of hard swimming with no breaks. It didn't occur to me that what he was going through was part of his everyday life.

"I'm sorry if I ever made you feel guilty," I finally say, "or like you were doing the wrong thing by taking care of yourself. But if you want to tell me when you're feeling that way, I'm happy to listen."

He shakes his head. "It's not that easy. I know there's nothing shameful about being bipolar—it's how I was born—but most people only know what they've seen on TV and in movies. They jump to conclusions about who I am and what I'm like and how I think, all because of a label, and then I feel like I have to do all this extra...performing, to get them to see me for me. But then I think, is it really me if I amp it up just to prove their assumptions wrong? At some point it became easier to not tell anyone. Not until I know we can have an honest and open conversation about it."

"Do you feel like you can do that with me?" I ask. I feel a sharp pain in my chest, like I've been stuck with a needle, at the thought that he doesn't, that I ever made him feel like he couldn't trust me. But I get that this isn't really about me, and never was.

"I do," he says. "But I wasn't sure when to bring it up. It's not something you can casually drop into a conversation, at least I've never been able to, but sitting someone down specifically to talk about it overdramatizes the whole situation."

He drops his head back and sighs. "I don't want to have to 'come out' as bipolar to every person I know. Everybody's got hard stuff in their life. How come I always have to feel like

I'm doing something wrong by not laying all my challenges out on the table from day one?"

"You don't owe that to anyone," I say. "It should be your decision what to share, and who to share it with. I'm sorry I pressured you into it. I didn't know that's what I was doing."

"Yeah?" He sounds so hopeful it breaks my heart. I'm worried that he thinks this will change how I feel about him, but it doesn't. I'm as in love with him as I've ever been.

Because of course I'm in love with Harry. I've been falling in love with him ever since we met. But I've never been in love with someone before. It's the best feeling in the world, but I know that, in handing over my heart to him, I've given him the power to break it.

"I totally get it," I tell him. "I know it's not even remotely the same thing, but I don't tell people about the things that I struggle with, either. All the setbacks and the fear and the disappointment. I don't even talk about it with my friends that much, or with my family most of the time. I don't want people to know I'm not as resilient as I pretend to be."

"You talk to me about that stuff," Harry says.

"I might never have told you," I admit. "But you saw it. From the first day, you saw what I was trying to hide, and you made me feel like it was okay to be honest about it. It was such a relief."

Harry rubs his eyes and sniffs. "Well, shit, Susie," he says with a wobbly laugh. "That's a really nice thing to say."

"Get out of the car," I say. He shoots me a worried look. "Trust me."

We climb out, then I open the back door on the passenger side. He does the same, and we slide into the backseat, meeting in the middle. Harry stares at me.

"What are we doing?" he asks softly.

I wrap my arms around Harry and pull him close, hugging him so hard he gasps in surprise.

"Man, Susie, I knew you were strong but this is ridiculous," he says. He slides his fingers into my hair, closing his fist around a handful of curls.

I stroke his back, brushing my hands up and down his spine in what I hope is a soothing rhythm. His heart pounds against my chest. I can feel each heavy beat of it in my own throat.

At first, he's stiff in my arms, guarded and careful not to let himself go. But then he softens, his breathing steadies and his heartbeat shifts from a wild gallop to a soft, tranquil trot.

I don't really know what I'm doing here—if I'm saying the right things, or asking the right questions, or if I should be asking any questions at all. All I know is what I feel, which is that I want him to know I'm here to listen, that I want only what's good for him and to make him feel safe with me. That I'm not going anywhere, and I love him for exactly who he is.

But what Nina said months ago keeps cycling through my head. *When did you get so selfish?* I've been focused almost exclusively on myself for so long, because I was convinced that was the only way to make my dreams a reality. When Harry needs me, if he needs me, will I know how to help him? What if I constantly, always let him down?

I do my best to push those worries away and just hold him, because what I think might help Harry, more than anything I could say right now, is being made to feel like he deserves to be held. That someone wants him close, that he can relax against me, put his head on my shoulder, feel the warmth of my skin against his. That I can be his relief, too.

"Is there anything I can do to help?" I ask softly.

"This is helping," he whispers. His cheeks are wet. I wipe the tears from his face. "Do you have any questions? Is there anything you want to know?"

I loosen my grip on him; he pulls back and looks at me. He brushes the hair out of my eyes and gives me a small smile. "A few," I tell him. "If that's okay."

"Go for it," he says.

"How long have you known that you're bipolar?" I ask.

"About six years. When I was eleven, Bruce and my mom went through a rough patch. I was convinced they were going to get divorced. They were arguing all the time. It was stressful and I was already bipolar—I mean, I was born with it. But I hadn't been diagnosed yet. And I didn't know how to control my emotions or understand what was going on with me, so I started stealing vodka from Bruce's liquor cabinet and getting drunk in my room whenever my parents fought.

"It was getting harder and harder to concentrate in class, because I had all these racing and cluttered thoughts. This one time I decided to drink before school, thinking it would make me feel better, and one of my teachers noticed. They called my parents and suspended me. It was the first time anyone realized something was wrong."

My heart feels like someone took it in two hands and twisted. It *hurts* for Harry, physically hurts, as if the actual muscle is torn. That must have been so scary for him.

Harry's expression hardens. "Don't look at me like that."

"Like what?"

"Like you pity me. I'm not an invalid. I hate those condescending poor-little-sick-boy frowns," he says. "Or worse, the way people's eyes get wide when they find out you have a mental illness, how they step away from you like you're contagious or a bomb about to go off."

"I promise, that's not what I'm thinking," I say. He makes a frustrated noise, and I pause to wonder if maybe I am looking at him that way, even though I don't mean to. I rearrange my expression into something more neutral.

"Before I was diagnosed and went into treatment, I was destructive and angry and sad. I was so fucking sad," he says.

I run the pad of my thumb over his knuckles. His shoulders deflate, like he's forcing himself to relax, but he doesn't seem so much calm as tired.

"I did stupid stuff. Defaced a public building, got into fights with other kids. I was drinking and taking pills, and I..." He hesitates. "I cut myself, sometimes. Here," he says, patting his inner thighs. "Where no one else can see."

"That's why you wear jammers," I say. The competition suits are long enough to cover any scars.

"I don't do it anymore. It was a shitty, shitty time. I knew something was wrong, but I didn't have the words to tell people. I tried everything I could to make it all *go away*.

"I got stuck in anger management for vandalism," he says. "I spray painted one of the walls of my school with some, uh...pretty saucy language. They agreed not to press charges if my parents put me in a juvenile counseling program. That's where I met Tuck."

"Why—"

"Nope. That's Tuck's story. It's not my place to tell it."

"He said the same thing about you."

"Tuck's a good friend."

I knock his shoulder gently with mine. "So are you."

Harry frowns and lapses into silence.

"I told my first girlfriend," he says. He glances at me tentatively. "Not Fee, before her. We were freshmen and it wasn't serious, but she never spoke to me again. I didn't tell anyone after that but she must have, because people found out. They were...not nice about it."

"That's awful," I say. "And completely unfair."

I understand why he might worry about sharing this part of his life with people, after an experience like that. I'm careful with people, too. Don't get too close, don't let my guard down, don't put the most important thing in my life at risk. In my case, it's swimming, which I know is not the same, but it's the first thing that comes to mind when I try to imagine what he must be feeling. Swimming is my heart, the thing that feels like it's keeping me alive.

But in not that much time, Harry has staked out some prime real estate in my heart, too. I didn't think I had space in me to love more than a handful of family and friends on top of the dream that has defined me since I was a kid. It's taken me longer than it should have to realize the obvious: I have to *make* space. If we're going to be together, swimming can't be the only thing I care about. It can't be all about me anymore.

Harry's been trying so hard not to take up more room than necessary. Make it easy, demand no sacrifices, create no conflict. Looking back at the time since we met, I can see him struggling, desperate to keep himself small enough to clear the imaginary height bar hanging over the entrance to my life, and it makes me feel heavy with sadness, like my body is filled with sand. It's not just *his* imagination that put that barrier there—it's mine, too. I can't expect him to wedge himself around what *I* need and what matters to *me*. What he needs is just as important.

"I'm not breaking up with you," I say. He looks like he doesn't believe me.

"You should think about things before you say that."

"I've thought about it, and it turns out you're my favorite person in the whole world."

Harry's signature sunny grin appears for the first time in this conversation, and I'm so happy to see it I'm not even bothered by the certain knowledge he's about to make fun of me.

"*I'm* your favorite person? *Why?*" he asks, incredulous.

"Shut up, you know why. You're sweet and you're smart and you're hot and you're a *really* good swimmer, and—"

"Wait, wait, wait." His smile turns sly. "You think I'm hot?"

I bury my face in my hands. Harry has a vain streak. There'll be no living with him after this.

"I take it back!" I mutter. "You're hideous. An ogre. I can't bear to be seen with you in public."

"Nope, no take-backs." He chuckles. "You said it, Susie. I always suspected, but now you've confirmed it. I'm hot. So this is what it feels like."

I laugh. There's no *way* he doesn't know how attractive he is, and if he didn't before, surely the fact that I can't keep my hands off him must've offered up some hint. But Harry's nothing if not hyperaware of what other people think of him. He's only teasing me.

Silence creeps over us as the moment fades, the joke dissipating like the fog of warm breath in the cold morning air. I can see his mood rapidly disintegrating. He needs more reassurance than I've given him. But I'm afraid to say something that makes his discomfort, his fear, any worse.

"You're my favorite person in the whole world, too," he says. "But I'm a mess."

His eyes are wet. If he were jealous, or angry, or anxious, I think I'd know how to calm him. But this despair is beyond me.

"You're not a mess," I say. "It kills me to think you believe that."

"I swear I wasn't going to keep this from you forever," he says. "But I was hoping to, I don't know, ease you into it? It's kind of a long story."

"I like long stories," I tell him. "I read the entire Harry Potter series every year."

Harry laughs. "Yes, my life is exactly like Harry Potter, except with less magic and more meds. Although I guess that's its own kind of magic."

"What kind of meds? Is that too personal a question?"

"It's fine." He ticks them off his fingers. "I'm on a mood stabilizer, and Prozac, which you've probably heard of—it's an antidepressant. I also take Xanax for anxiety, and Ambien to help me sleep when I need it. Oh, and fish oil and vitamin B complex—my mom makes me take those. I don't drink at all, but you know that. Alcohol negates the effects of the medication. Everything except the vitamins comes with some nasty side effects, but it's worth it to me."

"What kind of side effects?" I ask.

"Migraines," he says. "Awful, brain-splitting headaches—that's the Prozac, so I've been talking to my doctor about a possible alternative. Hair loss, insomnia, dizziness, nausea, chronic thirst...the whole fun pack. I didn't skip the Santa Clara meet because I had the flu. I stayed home because my doctor adjusted my doses and my body didn't react well. I was vomiting, like, a lot. Felt like the flu."

"Who else knows?" I ask.

"My parents and Tucker," he says. "The school, because some of my medication needs to be administered during the day. Oh, and Dave. When I joined GAC, I had to fill out all these health forms, and tell them what medication I'm taking. I started swimming because my therapist said the exercise could help calm and focus me. And it *has* helped. When I'm swimming, all the thoughts that spin through my mind quiet down for a while. But I try not to get too intense about it because I tend to fixate on stuff. I need to be able to tell the difference between a hypomanic episode and an amazing week in the pool."

"Is that why you don't push yourself in races?" I ask.

He nods. "My doctor thinks that's unnecessary. But I don't know. Hypomania is sort of a trickster. It can feel great. You have lots of energy and feel really productive and excited, but you also feel sort of invincible, which can lead to poor choices. I want to stay on the safe side. But Dr. Porter doesn't think I should hold myself back from excelling at something I'm good at."

"I'm not a doctor," I say, "but it's obvious you could be swimming so much faster than you do."

"I know. Dave hates it. He's constantly lecturing me about it, as you know."

"You said it wasn't a cure, the medication. How do you feel on it?"

"Better than I felt without it. I don't know what it's like

to not need medication, so I can't say how it compares, but nothing has ever been a perfect fit. I still experience periods of depression, but they're shorter and less severe when I'm on the medication.

"My parents and I worked for months with my doctors to figure out what worked for me. I tried so many drugs and doses. Some stuff wasn't great. In the beginning, I was on an antidepressant that made me feel tired and separated from the world, like I was underwater. I don't take it anymore, obviously. We found something else that was better.

"I'd never be able to function in the world the way I want to without those drugs," he says. "They save my life, every day. I don't know why Jeremy doesn't take them." At my confused look, he adds, "My bio dad."

"Is he bipolar, too?"

Harry scrubs his fingers through his hair. "Yeah. My mom met him when she was super young and she's always saying things like, 'If I knew then what we know now, maybe I could've helped him.' But she didn't know, and he didn't, either. By the time they figured it out, they'd split up.

"Jeremy's the reason she realized what was going on with me, though," he continues. "Otherwise, I probably would've been diagnosed with ADHD or something. The longer bipolar disorder goes untreated, the worse it gets. Mom and Bruce fought to get me the help I needed."

"Do you still see Jeremy?" I ask.

"No," Harry says. "He lives with his parents, so I used to see him when I visited them, but he's inconsistent with his medication and doesn't take care of his mental health. It got to the point where my mom didn't feel comfortable sending me over there when he was around. Now if I want to see my grandparents I meet them somewhere, or they come over to our house."

"Does that bother you?"

"It used to. When I was young, before my mom met Bruce, I missed Jeremy. I didn't understand what was going on. My dad was around all the time and then he wasn't. I just wanted him to come home. Most of my memories of him from that time are great actually. He was such a fun dad. But then I got older and my mom could explain things to me, or I saw them for myself, and I stopped wishing for that. Bruce isn't a replacement for Jeremy, but he's been a real father to me. It's why I took his last name."

He takes a deep breath, then lets it out slowly.

"I think about Jeremy all the time. I know what he's going through, what it's like to be born bipolar and not know why you're feeling a certain way. It's luck that I was diagnosed young and he wasn't. It makes a big difference. But he has options and he doesn't use them. It's hard for me to relate to that. And he was shitty to my mom, and he's shitty to my grandparents, and he's been shitty to me, and there's no way for me to know if that's the bipolar, which is not his fault, or if he's a shitty guy who happens to *be* bipolar."

Harry smiles at me, but it's a sad smile, nothing like one of his lightning-bolt grins.

"I'm not ashamed of having bipolar," he says. "But every time I consider telling someone, I remember that, once someone knows, I'll have to keep convincing them that I'm okay. Any time I'm upset or unhappy or angry, I'm afraid people will assume it's a symptom instead of what I happen to be feeling. You're always going to worry about me now. I liked it so much better when you didn't."

"I can't promise I won't worry," I tell him. "It feels like I worry about everything, all the time."

"Yeah, I know," Harry says with a sigh.

"But nothing will change how I feel about you," I say.

"Don't treat me any differently, okay? I'm the same person I was the day you met me. You just know me a little bit better now."

He glances at the clock. "Oh, shit! We're late. Why are you not worried about *this*?"

"Because you're more important," I tell him. "How are you feeling?"

"I'm okay," he says with conviction. He takes my hand. "Are *we* okay, though?"

"More than okay," I tell him. "I'm really glad you told me, Harry."

Harry seems relieved. "I feel better now that you know." Then he hesitates, like he wants to say something else, but he seems to decide against it.

"Whatever it is, you can tell me," I say, giving his hand an encouraging squeeze.

"It's nothing," he says, opening the door. "We have to go— Dave's going to kill us."

"Come on. You have literally never cared about being late before. You can say it."

He laughs. "No!"

"Say it," I command in a low, stern voice.

"You do not give up, do you?" He shakes his head. "This is going to sound so cheesy. What you said before, about how I saw all the stuff you were trying to hide? I don't think I *saw* it so much as I recognized it. Which I guess is kind of the same thing, but it feels different to me."

"You've said that before. But I don't really know what you mean."

"I work so hard in therapy and with my medication and swimming and sobriety and, you know, *life*, to keep my brain in check," Harry continues. "It's sort of like what you do with your training. You bust your ass to succeed even with the odds stacked against you and I admire that. I *feel* that. Because that's what I'm trying to do, too. Every day. I think that's why I liked you so much, right from the beginning. I mean, it's one of the reasons. I also thought you were hot."

A smile tugs at my lips. It's nice to hear that Harry admires me—I don't think I've ever wanted someone's approval so badly. And the thought of someone seeing my drive, my ambition, and not dismissing it or being repulsed by it is intoxicating.

But more than that, it's good to hear him say out loud what I know in my bones is true: we're fighting very different battles, but at the core we're the same. Boats against the current, beating on in spite of it all.

"What?" Harry asks. "Did I say something funny?"

I press closer to him. I'm pretty much in his lap at this point, which is not a bad place to be. I kiss him behind his earlobe, which sends a shiver down his spine.

"You really think I'm hot?" I joke.

Harry laughs—an explosive, full-bodied, genuinely happy laugh—and for the moment I feel like we actually *are* going to be okay.

CHAPTER SEVENTEEN

114 days until US Olympic Team Trials

"YOU GUYS ARE SUCH CHICKENS," JESSA SAYS. "HOW MANY times have you done this? A thousand? Someone get in the damn tub."

"But it's so cold!" Amber complains. She's already shivering, even though she's wearing a sweatshirt and the thermostat in our room is dialed up to about eighty.

"Go on, Soos, get in," Jessa says, pushing me toward the bathtub.

I hang back. "How come I have to go first? If you're so brave, you go."

"I get to go last because I got the ice," Jessa says.

We could argue about this forever, but Jessa's not budging, and Amber refuses to take off her hoodie. I'm not even sure she's wearing a suit under there.

I sigh. "All right. You win, Jess."

"That's what I like to hear," Jessa says with a grin, swatting me on the butt as I wriggle out of my leggings and drop my T-shirt on the floor. I look at the tub full of ice water and shudder. The swimsuit I'm wearing will do precisely nothing to keep me warm.

But there's not much you can do to make an ice bath not suck. The only way out is through—eight minutes if you can stand it.

I lower myself into the water quickly. The cold hits hard, like a punch to the stomach, knocking the air right out of my lungs. The whole point of an ice bath is to speed recovery after hard training sessions, but when you're in one, it's pure torture.

My teeth are chattering so hard it feels like they might break, and after a few minutes I can't feel my toes. Amber and Jessa try to distract me with cat videos and gossip, but every second in the tub feels like an eternity. I look at the timer on my phone. It's only been three minutes. I make a low, keening noise—half sob, half groan—but it doesn't help.

"Susie? Are you okay? The door was propped, and I heard you—"

Harry pokes his head through the bathroom door. When he sees what's happening, he laughs.

"I wondered what that noise was," he says. "I thought you were crying. Or maybe giving birth."

He leans against the doorjamb and snaps a photo of me on his phone.

"Put that on the internet and I will end you," I say.

"But you're making such a great face!"

He turns his phone to show me the picture. I look constipated.

"Delete it," I growl. "Or I will never speak to you again."

Harry pouts. "Fine. But it'd make a great new profile pic if you ask me."

"You want to get in here?" I ask. My legs feel like they're on *fire*.

"Is that an invitation?" he asks with a wink.

"Gross," Jessa says, pretending to gag. "Keep it in your pants, dude."

"You want to go down to the beach when you're done tormenting yourself?" Harry asks me.

He's practically bouncing he's so happy—it's the end of February, but we're in Corpus Christi for GAC training camp, and sun-loving Harry is effervescent with joy at escaping the cruel Midwestern winter at home for the warmth of a Texas spring. There's a beach two blocks from our hotel, and he's been dying to go since we got here yesterday, but there hasn't been time until now.

I'm not a beach person. I like my water contained, where I can keep an eye on it at all times, not infinite and wild and full of hidden riptides that can carry you away from the shore in a blink.

I'll do anything to get out of this ice bath, though.

"Yes! Give me three minutes to change," I say, lifting myself out of the water at the exact moment my timer goes off. My legs are so numb that I stumble as I get out of the tub. Jessa catches me.

"You're shaking," Amber says. "You stayed in there too long."

I rub my thighs to wake them up. "I'm c–c–*cold*!"

"Maybe you should sit down," she suggests.

Harry takes off his fleece and spreads it open.

"Come here, Susie," he says.

I step in close and he wraps me up in his jacket. It's warm from his body and smells like him. I let myself be held until the shivers subside.

"There you go," he says in my ear. I smile against his shoulder. "All good?"

I nod. "Three minutes," I say, running out into the room to grab a set of dry clothes.

"I'm starting the timer!" he calls after me.

When I'm dressed, we head over to Beth's hotel room to check out. This trip is unlike any I've ever been on. When I was at my best, there was always someone watching me, guiding me, protecting me—parents, coaches, older teammates. Now that I'm sixteen and prepping for Trials, I have more freedom. It's dizzying sometimes, how fast things are changing, how much more real it all feels this time around. The pressure increases every single day.

But there are perks, like getting to go to the beach with your boyfriend without a chaperone. Harry takes my hand as I knock on Beth's door. I smile at him and think, *I'm so freaking lucky.*

"Curfew is nine-thirty," Beth reminds us, handing me the sign-out clipboard. "Lights out at ten."

"We know," I say. "We'll be on time."

"Don't go too far. Be safe. Keep your phone on," Beth says. "And have fun."

"That's the plan," Harry tells her, grinning. "We're going to the beach."

Beth looks doubtful. "I know it's warmer than home, but the water will be too cold to swim in."

Harry glances at me. "I think we've probably had enough swimming for one day?"

"Actually, I was thinking we could get in a few more hours," I say. "Open water will be a nice change of pace."

"Okay, get out of here," Beth says. "Enjoy your night."

"Can I tell you a secret?" I ask as we walk down the street to the beach hand in hand. We turn a corner and the water comes into view.

"Is it scandalous?" he asks, eyes widening playfully.

"I guess that depends on how easy you are to scandalize."

"Try me."

It's a relief to see him so buoyant and cheerful. Just a few days ago, he was racked with anxiety over getting on a plane. He clutched the armrest in a death grip, wincing with his entire body every time the plane shook. I kept thinking about something Dad said to me on my first plane ride: *The scary thing about turbulence is that it reminds you how fast you're going.* I told Harry this, but he did not find it comforting, so I gave him my hand to hold.

We remove our flip-flops and step onto the beach. The air is spiced with the salty tang of the ocean. I take a deep breath, pulling as much of it as possible into my lungs. The waves hit the sand in a succession of muted crashes, casting white foam out like fingers. The beach is nearly empty; other than us, there are just a few people walking their dogs.

The sand is cool against the soles of my feet, and slightly damp, even this far away from the water. I like the feel of it between my toes. It has the consistency of brown sugar, fine-grained and crumbly.

"I've never gone swimming in the ocean before," I confess.

Harry lets out a theatrical gasp and clutches his chest, kicking up sand as he staggers backward like he's been shot. I punch him in the arm, which probably hurts my knuckles more than his bicep.

"We could remedy that," he says, tugging the belt loops of my jeans. "What are you wearing under these pants?"

"Wouldn't you like to know."

"I would. I absolutely would." He slips an arm around my waist and kisses my neck. "You're going to show me someday, right?"

My laugh is breathy and nervous. "You see me in almost nothing every day of the week!"

Harry makes a fart noise with his mouth and gives me two thumbs-down. "Swimsuits are equipment. Underwear is…"

He smiles instead of finishing his sentence. The look on his face is almost dreamy.

"Underwear is what?"

He gives it some thought before saying, "Sexy."

"Not the kind I wear."

Harry frowns. "Why do you make mean comments about how you look and dress? I don't get it. It's like you're trying to convince me not to want you."

"No, that's not it," I insist. "I don't know why I do it. I guess I…"

"You guess you what?" he presses. "Susie, come on. Whatever you're thinking, you don't have to be embarrassed to say it to me. I told you something I tell almost nobody. I trusted you with the most private part of my life. Don't *you* trust *me*?"

"That's so manipulative," I tell him.

"Is it working, though?"

I sigh. "I'm really worried about having sex and I know you want to and I think I want to, too, but I'm not sure I'm ready and I'm also terrified of getting pregnant and—are you a virgin?"

Harry shakes his head slowly. My heart cramps. I didn't think he was, but getting confirmation of it is a different thing. Was it Fee? Was she his first?

I almost ask, then decide I don't want to know.

"I want you to want me," I say. Harry hums the opening bars of the Cheap Trick song. "But when you talk about sex, even if you're joking, I get all worried about doing it and being ready for it and being bad at it and…sex is a big deal to me."

"It's a big deal to me, too," he says, staring at the ground. My stomach sinks. I feel terrible, like I've ruined everything and hurt him.

"You asked," I say. "I'm just being honest."

"No, it's good," he says. His shoulders relax and he smiles at me. "I'm glad you told me."

"You're not mad?"

"Why would I be mad?"

"I don't know."

"You're not ready to have sex. That's okay, I can wait. And I'll stop bringing it up even as a joke if you don't like it. I'm not trying to make you uncomfortable."

"You're ready now?"

"I feel ready. I mean, I love you, Susie. I have for months. And I'm not in your same situation, where it's my first time. I've done it before, so I'm less scared." He pauses. "But so we're clear, I'm not *not* scared. If we have sex, when we have sex, it's not going to be just any girl. It's going to be you. I don't want to screw it up."

"You love me?"

"Did you even hear anything else I said?"

"Nope, I pretty much stopped listening after that." I'm so happy to hear those words, if I were a cartoon I'd have hearts for eyes. "Did you mean it?"

"Of course I mean it!"

He reaches for me and presses his mouth to mine, gently teasing my lips apart. When our tongues touch, it's like a shock, like being hit by lightning. I'm tingling from my head to my toes. If sex is even half as nice as kissing, maybe we should do it right now.

We're both breathing hard, staring at each other. A smile breaks over his face.

"I love you, Susie," he whispers. He closes his eyes, as if it's too hard to look at me right now.

I kiss his eyelids. "After Trials. If we can table it until then, I think I might..."

He groans. "You don't need to give yourself a deadline for sex."

"I like deadlines," I tell him. "They work for me."

"I know, but it's not something you have to schedule. We can take it as it comes." He squints at me in the fading light. "Right now, we have a bigger problem."

My stomach turns over. "What problem?"

"I told you I loved you," he says. "Twice. Usually, there's some kind of, um, response?"

I squeeze my eyes shut, embarrassed. "Harry, I love you. Obviously. What is wrong with me?"

He kisses me, laughing. "Nothing. You're amazing. I have never felt this way, about anyone."

"Thank you for loving me," I whisper. I didn't realize it until now, but I honestly thought no one ever would. That Harry found something inside me to love feels like a miracle.

Harry looks off to his right, down a long, empty expanse of beach, then turns back to me, grinning. "Race you!" he shouts, scattering sand as he takes off running.

"Seriously?" I chase after him, heart pounding in my chest.

We don't get far before Harry slows down, tiring of the effort or growing bored with the game. He gives himself a triumphant, dorky self–high five as I catch up with him.

"Sorry, Susie. Better luck next time," he says, throwing an arm around my shoulders.

"No fair," I pant. "You had a head start."

"Life's not fair," he says with a laugh.

"It's okay," I say, leaning against him. He presses a kiss to my forehead. "When you win, I win."

His eyes widen with delight. "When you win, I win. It's why we make such a great team."

"Must be." I give him a winner's kiss on the cheek.

Harry sits on a patch of dry sand and tugs me down beside him. We kiss for a long time, sinking slowly down into the sand until we're lying together, me on top of him, then him on top of me. He removes his fleece and spreads it like a blanket, then pushes me down on top of it. My sweatshirt comes off next; he balls it up and places it under my head like a pillow. The light is draining fast from the sky, but we don't need it to see each other. We use our hands instead, our lips, our hips, pressed together so close it's like we're one person, moving in a coordinated, slightly delirious dance.

His fingers creep under the hem of my T-shirt.

"Is this okay?" he asks. He's touched me like this before, but not immediately after a conversation about sex. I guide his hand farther. I don't want a second to pass without his hands on me, without the feeling of his skin sliding against mine. I make my own explorations—slowly, deliberately, enjoying every noise he makes. He tastes like salt and sunscreen and Red Vines, perfectly Harry.

We eventually tire ourselves out, the exhaustion from to-day's hard practice descending like a heavy curtain. He settles down next to me and I curl into him, resting my head on his chest. His fingers trail up and down my arm. I shiver, though I'm not cold. He kisses the top of my head.

"Thank you for loving me back," he murmurs.

We're both tumbling into sleep, and I know we shouldn't, even as it's happening. We have a curfew, and a public beach is not the best place for a catnap. But he's so warm, and I'm so tired. Our breathing slows, and the rest of the world slows with it.

"Susannah," a voice says. Someone is shaking me by my bad shoulder. It's the pain that wakes me. "Susannah, come on, you need to get up now."

I wrench my eyes open. They feel scratchy and dry from the sand and the salt air. Beneath me, Harry stirs. His arm tightens around me as he sits up in alarm.

Beth is kneeling in the sand. In the dark, it's hard to see the expression on her face, but if I had to guess, she's pissed. I fumble in my pockets for my phone.

"It's almost eleven," Beth tells me. "You missed curfew. We didn't know where you were."

"Shit," I say. My hands start to shake. I'm in so much trouble.

"We didn't mean to," Harry says, rubbing his eyes. "We sat down and we were so tired we fell asleep. If you think about it, this is your and Dave's fault for working us so hard today."

"Now is not the time for jokes, Harry," Beth says.

I jab him in the ribs with my elbow. He squeezes my arm in solidarity. He knows how upset I am to have broken the rules.

"What the hell is going on here!" Dave bellows, stalking toward us. It takes him a while because his shoes keep sinking into the sand, so it's more like he's running in slow motion. I would find it funny if I weren't so terrified. My heart is like a hummingbird's, pounding at a thousand beats per minute.

When he reaches us, Dave points at Harry and shouts, "You get away from her *right now*! Get up! I'm not going to tell you twice, Matthews."

Harry glances at me, eyes wide. He doesn't want to leave me, but we both know Dave won't stop until he gets what he wants. Harry scrambles to his feet. I feel like he's been torn away from me, like something is irreparably broken.

Dave keeps going after Harry. "Susannah is a good kid!" he yells, jabbing his finger at Harry. "She always followed the rules, and then you come along, and suddenly she's rolling her eyes and talking back and breaking curfew—"

"It was an accident," I insist. "It's not Harry's fault."

"You mean standing up for herself and living her life and doing what *she* wants rather than what *you* want for a change?" Harry yells back. "Yeah, I'm terrible influence, Dave. She's not a rag doll you can throw around."

"Stop!" I cry. I grab Harry and drag him backward.

He shrugs me off. "He can't talk about you like this."

"Everybody calm down," Beth says. "Let's go back to the hotel and talk about this like adults."

"They're not adults!" Dave says, throwing his hands up. "They're *kids*. Stupid, immature kids."

He rounds on Harry and me. "You two want to grope on a beach in the dark, do it on your own time. Not on a training trip that I brought you on so you could maybe have the smallest shot at being competitive in the most important meet of the year. This is *my* time. My team. And if you want to swim on it going forward, this—" He gestures between Harry and me. "This ends. Right now."

Harry shakes his head. "Not happening."

"Then Susannah can forget about the Olympics," Dave says. He looks at me. "This is over, or you're off the team. I know he doesn't give a shit about swimming, but you do. That's my condition."

I shoot a pleading glance at Beth, who looks stunned.

"And *don't* look at Beth to save you—she works for *me*," Dave snaps. "You're not the only swimmer who's counting on her. Don't ask her to pick you over the rest of them, because she won't."

Dave has been my coach for nearly ten years. He knows exactly what knives cut the deepest, and he keeps them nice and sharp at all times.

I can't look at Harry. He doesn't say anything to me. I don't think he's looking at me, either. The moment stretches endlessly, and everyone keeps waiting for someone to break it, but nobody does.

Finally, Beth puts a hand on my back and says, "We need to take this conversation off the beach. You broke curfew and our trust. We're going to have to talk about that, and about consequences."

Harry glares at Beth. "Making her choose between me and swimming isn't enough of a consequence? We were two blocks away from the hotel and we *accidentally* fell asleep because we swam for eight hours today. Sorry if I'm not interested in being punished for an innocent mistake."

He starts to walk away, up the beach toward the road.

"Harry, where are you going?" I call out. I hate watching him leave. This can't be how it ends. It's barely even begun.

He turns. "I'm not giving him the satisfaction of seeing me watch you pick swimming over us."

Dave scoffs. "Go to bed, Matthews. I better see you in the pool at seven a.m." Then he takes off in the opposite direction, farther down the beach. Harry heads back to the hotel.

I try to follow Harry, but Beth holds me back. "Give him time to cool off," she says.

"Which one?" I ask.

"Both." After a few seconds of silence, Beth adds, "You know, he's not wrong about all this. Dave. You're at a linchpin moment in your career. A boyfriend can only be a distraction."

"Have you been thinking this the whole time?" I ask.

"I know it feels unfair, having to sacrifice normal things for what will be, at the end of the day, a two-minute race," Beth says. "But you can't slack in school. And you can't neglect your family. Those are nonnegotiables. Everything else has to go into the pool. You have to be able to know, no matter what happens in Omaha, that you gave it all you had."

"And you don't think I can do that if I'm with Harry."

"It would be difficult. Speaking from experience," she says. "Grady wouldn't let me date when I was in high school, so the second I was in college and out from under his thumb, I got together with a guy in my dorm. Nothing dramatic happened, but I did not perform well in the pool that year. I deprioritized my swimming and focused all my time and energy on my boyfriend. It put my scholarship and my elite status at risk, two years before the Olympics. If I could go back and do it again, I'd make different choices."

"Harry cares about my swimming," I insist. "He doesn't want me to lose focus. He *helps* me."

"He can do all of those things as your friend," Beth says. "For now."

"Where does it end? You didn't date in high school, then dating in college almost ruined your career. A career *you walked away from*, by the way."

"I remember," she says quietly.

"What am I supposed to do? Be a spinster till I retire? What if I compete into my thirties? Am I never allowed to be in love or have a boyfriend or get married or *anything*?"

I never raise my voice to Beth, but I'm shouting now.

"Of course not. In a few years, you'll be mature enough to handle a relationship and your career. Once school isn't part of the equation, it'll be easier."

"A few *years*?"

"You can't let this incident throw you off your game, Susannah," Beth says. I wish she would stop ignoring my questions. "You've been making great progress. I think you're going to kill it in Des Moines, but you have to stay focused.

It's just this, then Richmond, then Bloomington, then Trials. Each meet has to count."

I know she's right. I'm the closest I've been in years to being ready for the Olympic Trials. I can't lose my focus, and I definitely can't lose my coach.

But I don't want to lose Harry, either.

When Beth and I get back to the hotel, Dave is already there, and he seems to have calmed down a bit. Not enough to go back on his decree that I have to break up with Harry or I'm out of GAC—he stands firm on that—but at least he's not yelling anymore.

He and Beth sit me down in Beth's room and lecture me for a while, but I tune them out after Dave reaffirms his ultimatum. I've heard enough. All I can think about is Harry walking away from me on the beach, how sad he looked with his shoulders slumped in defeat, how devastated he sounded. I keep replaying it in my head, and on every repeat viewing, my heart breaks like it's the first time.

Finally, Dave tells me I can go. Beth tries to comfort me, but I hurry out the door. I'm livid, but I know making a scene won't solve the problem.

Back in our room, Amber and Jessa are waiting for me. "Did Dave and Beth really catch you having sex with Harry on the beach?" Jessa asks as soon as I walk through the door.

"Are you kidding?"

"That's the rumor going around," Amber says. She shows me a series of texts on her phone from GAC people saying they heard from someone who heard from someone who was eavesdropping on Dave and Beth and so on and so forth.

I make a disgusted noise and start changing into my pajamas. "We weren't having sex. We were talking and fell asleep
on the beach."

"Are they sending you home?" Jessa asks. If I didn't know
better, I'd say she sounds almost hopeful. "Are they going to
call your parents?"

I take a deep breath. "Dave says Harry and I have to break
up or I can't be in GAC anymore."

"What?" Amber gasps.

Even Jessa looks mildly horrified. "That seems like an over-
reaction," she says. "What are you going to do?"

"What can I do?" I shrug like it doesn't bother me. Like
the coldhearted automaton Dave wants me to be. "It's the
Olympics."

"Are you okay?" Amber asks. She looks me up and down
as if searching for an open wound. "You care about Harry."

I love him, I want to say, but don't. Instead, I tell her, "It's
only five months. After Trials, and the Olympics, maybe we
can get back together. If he still wants to."

The mere thought of Harry using those five months to get
over me is excruciating.

"Are you sure you're okay, though? You seem strangely
calm about all this," Amber says.

"It's late," I say. "I need to get some rest. Good night."

Jessa is sprawled out on one of the room's two queen-size
beds. It's her turn to sleep on the rollaway, but I don't have
the energy to argue with her about it, so I climb in and turn
onto my side, facing away from them.

Jessa turns off the lights. I'm exhausted, but I can't sleep.
When I hear their breathing slow to the point where I figure
they must be out, I climb out of bed and take my phone into

the bathroom. Sitting on the floor in the dark, I text Harry: We're not over, are we? I can't sleep until I know.

It takes him less than a second to write back. He's obviously just as awake as I am.

NO WAY are we over. I love you, Susie.

I love you, too. What are we going to do?

Hide our relationship from Beth and Dave.

The rest of GAC, too? Amber and Jessa and Avik…if they know, the coaches will, too.

Yeah, it has to be a secret from everyone. Our parents and Nina, too.

I wince. Beth and Dave are one thing, but how can I hide this from my family and friends?

That's going to be really hard, I tell him.

I know. But you can't leave GAC, there's too much at stake. And we don't want to break up. This is the only thing I can think of. Can you talk right now?

I call him and he answers right away.

"I'm in, like, a broom closet in the hallway," he whispers. "Where are you?"

"Bathroom. Jessa and Amber are heavy sleepers." I sigh. "I wish you were here right now."

"It'll be okay," he assures me. "It's five months, six with the Olympics. Once that's over, Dave will drop it. It'll go by quick. We've already been together six months."

"Two and a half months," I say.

"I retroactively count the time since we first met," Harry says. "We were pretty much dating. We were just...negotiating the terms."

I laugh softly. "If you say so."

"You know, it might be kind of fun," he teases. "Forbidden romance can be hot. Meeting in secret, hidden messages. Like Romeo and Juliet!"

"Yeah, because it turned out so great for them."

He laughs. "My priest won't poison you, I promise."

"The priest doesn't poison—wait, *your* priest? You have a priest?"

Harry says, "Yeah, Father Bob. I volunteer sometimes at a soup kitchen he runs in the city. He's been a sort of sobriety coach for me. Nice guy. You'd like him."

"You've never mentioned him before."

"Yeah, well, I try to respect his privacy. I hope you can meet him one day. Because you and I are not breaking up. We're not Romeo and Juliet, either, because we're going to live through this. Okay?"

"Okay," I say, feeling sort of teary. It's almost one a.m. I'm so freaking tired.

"Love you, Susie. See you in the pool tomorrow. Try not to check out my hot bod too much in front of Dave and Beth or they'll know you're not over me."

I laugh. "I think I'll be able to control myself."

"Sleep tight," he says, all soft and sweet.

"You, too. I love you."

I hang up quickly so I'm not tempted to offer to sneak out and meet him somewhere. If we got caught, Dave would *definitely* tell my parents. I sag against the bathroom cabinet. A secret relationship? Can we really pull this off?

Dave must know he can't enforce this ultimatum, but I realized pretty quickly that he thinks he doesn't have to. He thinks he knows me, that the threat of throwing me out of GAC and ruining my chances at the Olympics will scare me so much I won't bother to defy him.

Six months ago, he would've been right. But he doesn't know me, not anymore. I'm angry, and I'm in love, and screw him if he thinks I'll let him take away the one thing that makes me happy. I've lost enough for this sport already.

When I wake up the next morning, I feel reenergized and full of can-do spirit. I can-do this! I can be happy with Harry, even if it has to be in secret for now, and I can kick ass in the pool, too.

As I glide through the water during warm-up, I think about how much progress I've made. I'm swimming better now than I was before my slowdown. I really could go to the Olympics.

I'm going to make it, I tell myself. *I'm going to be an Olympian.*

CHAPTER EIGHTEEN

105 days until US Olympic Team Trials

WE GO STRAIGHT FROM TRAINING CAMP TO THE PRO SWIM Series meet in Des Moines, Iowa. There are only three of these big competitions before Olympic Trials, so each swim is important. Each swim is *everything*.

To ensure they can get the time off to see me swim in Omaha, Mom and Dad are skipping this meet, and the ones in Richmond, Virginia, and Bloomington, Indiana, too. I wish they were here. I'm tired of traveling. I want to be at home with my family and my animals. Nina texts me pictures and videos of them, but it's not the same.

I'm sitting in the ready room, trying to relax before the 200 IM finals, when I hear someone calling my name. I open my eyes and yank out my earbuds to see Beth standing over me. Behind her, there's a giant TV where swimmers prepping for their next race can see what's going on in the pool. I'm too nervous to watch, so I've been ignoring it.

"What's up?" I ask Beth. Her mouth tightens at my tone, which is clipped and impersonal.

Things have been tense between us since that night on the beach. I'm upset with her for siding with Dave and trying to meddle in my personal life, but I'm also worried about what it means that she did. Since I started swimming with her, I've trusted Beth to look out for my best interests. It's hard to convince myself she's not doing the same thing now. And she's almost always right.

I resist it, but the thought keeps nagging at me: *What if she's right about this, too?*

Beth clears her throat. "Harry's 200 back is up in a minute. I thought you might want to watch."

I'm surprised, given all the drama in Texas, that she's telling me this. It's a peace offering, I guess. Maybe an acknowledgment that she doesn't expect me to stop caring about him just because Dave threatened us into breaking up. I'm still mad at her, but I appreciate the gesture.

"Thanks," I say, pulling my chair closer to the TV. She takes a seat beside me.

Harry is standing behind the starting block, dressed in his GAC warm-ups, cap and goggles, a towel hanging around his neck. He strips quickly, tossing his clothes on an empty chair near the judges. In his suit, with his broad shoulders, arms and abs on display, he looks like a god of swimming, a boy made for the water.

As he steps up to the block, swinging his long, muscular arms in wide circles, Beth says—like Harry isn't a touchy subject right now, which is ballsy of her—"He's doing so well this meet."

What an understatement. Harry has three solo events here—the 100 back, 100 butterfly and the 200 back—plus the backstroke leg of the men's 400 IM relay, and he blitzed through the prelims in each one. He missed the finals of the 100 fly by a few hundredths of a second, but he's coming into the finals of the 200 back seeded fourth. If he keeps swimming like he has been, he could win it.

I knew Harry had this kind of talent in him. You can see it in his swims, that he's been holding back, but he isn't anymore. We haven't spoken in person since the night we "broke up," but we've been texting as much as we dare. Last night before lights out, I asked him about the sudden change. Harry admitted he was doing it to spite Dave.

He said I'm not good for you because I don't take swimming seriously, Harry said. Challenge accepted, douchebag.

I'm proud of what he's accomplished here, but I remember what he told me about why he doesn't try harder in the pool. I can't help but worry, but he asked me not to change the way I treat him now that I know he's bipolar. It would never occur to me to raise a concern about it before, so I support his decision and trust that he knows what's best for himself.

The swimmers jump into the pool—the backstroke always starts in the water. As the announcer tells them to take their mark, my fingers itch for Harry's swim log, which is sitting in the bottom of my bag. When the event schedules allow for me to watch him race, I record his splits and final times in the notebook I gave him for Christmas, and he does the same for me. Beth would notice if I did it now. I'll have to look up the official record online and fill it in later.

I don't need the book to know what Harry's capable of,

though. I've already done the math on his times. This is a long-course meet, which means every lap is fifty meters instead of the American standard twenty-five meters or yards. Everyone swims slower in long-course races because there are fewer turns, but this natatorium is one of the fastest pools in the world, built deep with special gutters to minimize turbulence, the sworn enemy of every swimmer.

Which means my calculations are approximate at best. Anything could happen.

"He could win this one," Beth says. I see her glance at me out of the corner of my eye. Is this some kind of stupid test? If it were Dave, I'd say probably. But Beth's not manipulative like that.

"I don't know," I reply. "Jacob Cawley's seeded first, and he's got one of the fastest personal-best times in the country right now in this event. He could blow Harry out of the water if he brings it."

"I don't think he will, though."

"Why not?"

The start tone goes off, and the swimmers fling themselves backward into the water, dolphin-kicking out to the fifteen-meter mark. Beth and I watch the TV intently. My heart clenches, and my stomach does a slow roll.

"There's something up with his back. In the prelims and the semis, it started to cave later in the race, which I think means he's compensating for some pain."

Her eyes flick to me again. I wonder if she's thinking about my shoulder, and how each of my competitors could be having this same conversation about me with their coach right now.

"If he gives in, it'll screw with his streamline and slow him down," Beth continues. "Could open up a gap for Harry to slip through, if he's not too tired by then to take advantage of it."

I lean forward in my seat, as if by getting a few inches closer to the TV I can spot evidence of Jacob Cawley's injury. If it's there, the cameras are too far away to catch it.

What *is* noticeable is Harry's slow start off the block. At the first turn, he's in fifth.

"Come on, stop dicking around," I whisper, forgetting for a second about Beth sitting right next to me. All my focus goes toward willing Harry to speed up.

I know his body. I know the way it moves through the water, its speed, its rhythm. He's pacing himself, saving his energy, but this is not a long race, just four lengths of the pool and back. By the time he decides to kick it into high gear, he might not have enough room to take the lead. Meanwhile, Jacob Cawley is cruising along at half a body length in front of the field.

Then Harry starts to motor. Off the second turn, he overtakes the two swimmers in front of him; they fall back, unable to catch up to him, and I can tell they're done for this race. Now it's just Jacob, Harry and one other guy.

By the time he's halfway down the pool, Harry's second after Cawley, but the third swimmer's still in it, straining to pass them. My gaze flicks to Cawley, but he's in total control of his stroke. Maybe Beth was wrong.

Going into the final turn, it looks like Harry's going to lose, and not just to Cawley—the third swimmer isn't flagging. He could sneak past Harry if he's got anything left in the tank in the last fifteen meters.

But Harry bursts off the wall like he's been shot from a cannon, switching on his mighty dolphin kick and torpedoing out past the flags. In the space of a few heartbeats, he catches up with Jacob Cawley, closing his lead in less time than it takes me to release the breath I'm holding. They're neck and neck coming down the final stretch.

This swim must be breaking Harry. I noticed him do a spot check at the turn; he knows Cawley is winning, so he's throwing everything he's got into the last twenty meters in the hope of muscling past him. And it's *working*. I twist the plastic straps of my goggles around my fingers so hard it cuts off my circulation. He could win. Harry could *win*.

There's a collective intake of breath so loud I can hear it when both boys slam into the wall. Did Harry touch first, or did Cawley? It takes only a few tenths of a second to register the times, but it feels like a freaking eternity. The scoreboard flashes up on the screen.

Beth pats me on the back and flashes me a brief smile.

"That was a good swim," she says. "He should be proud."

I drop my head and cover my face. Happiness sloshes through my body as I grin into my hands. I always knew Harry had it in him to be one of the best swimmers of his age group, but the confirmation is twice as sweet. I want to run out on the deck and grab him, pull him to me, give him the victor's kiss he so clearly deserves. Instead, I'm stuck back here.

I watch as Harry luxuriates over his victory in the pool. He pulls himself up on the lane line and pumps his fist in the air, shouting and crowing. Then he loses his balance and tumbles into Jacob Cawley's lane. Jacob drifts over to shake Harry's hand, even though this loss must be killing him. A single one-hundredth of a second is an absurd, unbearable amount of time to lose by, but in swimming, that's often all it takes.

Dave nabs Harry as soon as his feet hit the deck. He cuffs his hand around the back of Harry's neck and speaks into his ear. Harry nods. Dave gives him a *job well done* pat on the back and Harry lights up like a kid on Christmas morning, which surprises me. I thought Harry decided to swim well to troll Dave. It never occurred to me that Harry might want Dave's approval.

Well, now he has it. Dave can't dismiss him as a slacker anymore. My guts tighten with unfamiliar jealousy. I shake it off and paste a smile on my face, grinning so hard it hurts.

I'm thrilled for Harry. Why wouldn't I be?

Harry's win has stoked my competitive fires. I stride onto the deck in a storm of confidence, wearing my GAC parka like a superhero's cape, or the robes of an arrogant queen. By the time I step up on the block, I know this race is mine.

It happens early, during the second half of the butterfly leg of my 200 IM. There's no warning shot across the bow, no rumbling ache to herald disaster. One second, everything is fine—I'm soaring over the water, skimming along the surface like a stone skipping across a lake—and the next, a lightning bolt of pain lances down my arm, tearing through me like fire racing along a trail of gasoline. A dense cloud of agony mushrooms through my body as I hobble through the rest of the race.

Everything after appears only in flashes as my eyes flutter in time with the pulses of pain that roll over me in unceasing waves. A blur of color as people run along the deck. The rustle of voices like birds' wings against a gray sky. Familiar faces seen only in glimpses as people hover over me at the end of the lane: Amber, Jessa, Beth, Dave.

And Harry, who says, "Hold on, Susie. I'm coming to get you."

The next thing I know, he's behind me in the water. I flinch, thinking he's going to touch my shoulder, but he rests his hand on my waist and puts his lips right up to my ear.

"Relax," he says. "I'm going to count to three, and then I'm going to lift you so Dave can pull you out, okay?"

"My shoulder..." I begin to shiver. The smell of chlorine is so thick I feel like I'm choking on it. I try to pull away from Harry and realize: I can't move my arm.

"I'll be gentle," he says. "I won't hurt you, I promise."

He bends for leverage, resting his forehead against the nape of my neck. He takes a deep breath. "One...two...*three*."

The next time I open my eyes, I'm in the backseat of Dave's rental car as he speeds toward an unknown hospital in an unfamiliar city where I'm suddenly, bewilderingly, alone among strangers, with only the pain to keep me company and remind me that I'm human.

CHAPTER NINETEEN

105 days until US Olympic Team Trials

"LEFT GLENOID LABRUM," DR. PFASTER SAYS, TUCKING A CLIP-board under his arm. "It's a rim of cartilage that surrounds a socket in your shoulder. It helps stabilize the joint where your upper arm bone meets your shoulder blade. You've torn it."

He pauses as his words fall limply into the silence of the room. I'm at the hospital with Beth and Dave, and Mom, whose flight to Des Moines landed an hour ago. She rubs my lower back, partly because it usually comforts me, and partly because she doesn't know what else to do.

She blazed into the room not long before Dr. Pfaster arrived, looking to fix whatever trauma had befallen me. But she couldn't hug me, I wasn't in much of a mood to talk and Beth had filled out most of the insurance paperwork already; they keep that sort of information on file for just such an occasion. Mom ended up with not much to do other than watch me suffer.

I can't stand to be touched right now, but I don't tell Mom, because I'm so grateful she's here I would put up with almost anything to keep her close. I feel guilty for scaring her, for dragging her away from home. I'm almost positive she's missing an exam for this, but she doesn't mention it. She takes my right hand and squeezes my fingers. I fight the urge to put my head on her shoulder and cry.

"I'm sorry," Dr. Pfaster says when nobody responds to his diagnosis. "I was told you're an athlete. A swimmer—do I have that right?"

I nod. Beth is pale, her brow and mouth compressed with worry. Dave looks positively green. I think I might've been crying in the car on the way to the hospital. Most of it is lost in a thick fog of pain, but I have a few shards of memory from the ride here: pressing my wrist to my mouth to muffle the sounds, the city streets as they streamed past my window, a glimpse of Harry sitting in the backseat with me, afraid to come close, head between his hands, helpless as I sobbed in agony next to him.

When I came back to myself in the bright glare of the exam room, Harry was gone, and Dave and Beth seemed completely freaked out.

"What happens now?" Mom asks. She glances at my coaches. Dave folds his arms and stares at the doctor. Beth braces herself, like she knows what's coming.

Having Mom here has been enough for me until this moment, but now I want Harry, with a sudden, fierce ache. Dave sent him back to the hotel in a cab a few hours ago, while I was getting an X-ray. I was devastated when I realized he was gone, but I'm out of tears.

"You'll want to discuss this with a specialist when you get home, but the two options they'll likely give you are surgery or physical therapy," Dr. Pfaster says.

I shake my head. "No surgery."

"Susannah," Mom says. I can tell she's trying hard not to get impatient with me. "We're not making any decisions before we have all the information."

"I've seen what happens to swimmers who have shoulder surgery. They've seen it, too," I say, jerking my chin at Beth and Dave. They exchange a glance. "It could end my career."

Not to mention cost a fortune my parents don't have. Insurance doesn't cover everything.

"Not necessarily," Dr. Pfaster says with a shrug. "But it could limit your range of motion in that shoulder. Do you need a full three-sixty rotation to swim?"

"Is that a joke?" Dave snaps.

"Yes," Dr. Pfaster says, blinking at Dave like he's surprised by his bark but not afraid of it. He has an arrogance about him that I've often noticed in doctors, more cynical than someone like Harry's—haughtier and, if anything, less self-assured.

I decide I don't like Dr. Pfaster, but I do enjoy the way he mostly ignores Dave. Guess there's only space for one blowhard in this room.

"Then again, it could not," he says, like his exchange with Dave never happened and he's been talking uninterrupted the whole time. "There's no telling beforehand how you would recover. There are fewer risks with arthroscopic surgery, and you're young, so it's possible you could regain full use of your shoulder. But I wouldn't promise it."

"You said there are other options," Mom says. "Physical therapy. What would that entail?"

"And what's the recovery time?" I ask.

"You'll have to work out a regimen with your physicians back home," Dr. Pfaster says. Even though he's got a cold, bored way of talking to me, I like that he talks *to me* and not Mom or my coaches. "And there's PT in your future, surgery or no. But if you stick to your program and don't try to do too much too fast, I don't think there's any reason you can't be at close to one hundred percent in about six to eight months."

I take a deep breath in through my nose and let it out through my mouth, fighting off panic. Olympic Trials are in less than four months.

"If anyone can do it, you can," Dave says. We all turn to look at him in surprise. He clears his throat and smooths down the collar of his polo shirt the way he always does when he's uncomfortable. "You're the most stubborn person I know, Susannah."

Dave's not my favorite person in the world, but sometimes he knows exactly what I need to hear.

The hotel the team is staying at is booked up, so Mom gets a room at the first decent place with a vacancy she can find. I wait in the car while she fetches my bags from the room I was sharing with Amber and Jessa.

The parking lot is quiet, and the lights are out in most of the hotel's windows. Everyone seems to have gone to bed. I feel exhausted, wrung out like a damp towel, plus a little floaty thanks to the painkillers they gave me at the hospital. My arm is in a sling and the pain feels distant but unmistakable, a sharp shout into a deep canyon. I rest my head against the window and close my eyes.

I doze off for what feels like hours, but it must be only a few minutes, because when the sound of fingers tapping wakes me, Mom's still gone, and Harry's crouched outside the rental car with his face pressed against the glass. He waves and mimes rolling down the window.

"What's with the charades?" I ask. "The glass isn't sound-proof."

"I'm trying to be stealthy," he whispers, folding his arms on the door and resting his chin on his hands. "I'm supposed to be in my room, but Amber texted me that your mom was upstairs getting your stuff, so I figured you were waiting out here. I had to see you. How are you feeling?"

"Shitty. I tore my labrum," I tell him. Harry winces. He knows what that means; shoulder injuries are common in swimming. "They're talking about surgery."

"Are you going to do it?"

I hesitate. "Do you think I should?"

"I'm not a doctor," he says. "I don't know what's best."

"Me neither," I admit, deflating. "But I've seen people go through this. Surgery could ruin everything. Physical therapy is the safer option. I just don't know how long it will take."

My eyes start to sting. "Is there even a chance I could recover by Trials?"

"If anyone can, you can." The complete conviction in Harry's voice makes me love him even more than I already do.

"That's what Dave said. Apparently, I'm the most stubborn person he knows."

"Not giving up is kind of your brand." Harry frowns. "How much pain are you in?"

"Less than before." I muster a smile. "They gave me some good drugs."

He laughs and leans in closer. We always gravitate toward each other, drawn together in a process as natural as breathing. I can smell his familiar scent of Irish Spring soap and clean cotton, with a lingering hint of chlorine. I take the deepest breath I can without being completely obvious about it, but the pills must be throwing me off more than I realize, because Harry grins and asks, "Are you sniffing me, Susie?"

"I'm smelling the *night air*," I snap.

"Okay, grouchy," he says with affection. "Vicodin does not agree with you."

"I'm allowed to be grouchy. I'm in a lot of pain and I'm very—" I yawn "—tired."

He strokes my hair and I close my eyes. "Yeah, you are allowed," he says softly.

I rest my cheek on his arm and nuzzle against him. This close, his skin smells like bread warm from the oven.

"I'm sorry I didn't stay with you at the hospital. Dave wouldn't let me and I knew making a thing of it wouldn't help you. But I've been thinking about you all night."

"It's okay," I murmur. Then a thought hits me and my eyes fly open. "Harry!"

He jerks back. "What's wrong?"

"You swam *so good* today," I say. He presses his hand to his chest, choking on a laugh.

"God, Susie, I think my heart just stopped." His eyes glitter with pride in the lights of the parking lot. "You were watching today?"

"Of course," I say. "I'm so proud of you."

"Thanks. That means a lot."

I grab him by the collar of his T-shirt with my good hand. His eyes widen as he braces himself against the car door.

"Whoa," he says. "Even injured, you're strong. Almost knocked me over."

"I am *so proud* of you, Harry," I tell him. I have to make him understand this. For some reason, at this moment, it feels vitally important, and I don't think he's listening to me. "I'm proud to be your friend, and I'm proud to be your girl. I've never known a sweeter, better, smarter, more wonderful, more talented person than you. And I love the way you swim. It's like music. Like art."

He looks away as if embarrassed by the compliments, but I know him well enough to see the satisfaction beneath the humility.

"You're only saying that because you're high," he jokes.

"You don't believe me?"

"I believe you believe it," he says, tensing. "Sometimes I worry you see what you want to see."

It's the sort of thing where, if he'd said it on another day, I might've been hurt. But instead of reacting, I stare back at him and say: "I see what you show me."

"Whoa," he says, swallowing hard. "Killer aim with that truth bomb."

"I *am* proud. You showed Dave."

"That's why I did it," he says. "But it felt great. To try for once. To win. I might do it again."

My eyelids are so heavy, like something is pressing down on them. I can feel myself beginning to drift off when I hear the sound of someone clearing their throat. I look up to see Mom standing over Harry, who stands up in a hurry.

"Hi, Harry," she says with a fond smile. "How are you?"

"Hi, Mrs. Ramos," he says. "I'm good. I was keeping Susie company while she waited."

"They're doing bed checks. Might want to get up there before Dave notices you're gone."

He nods. "Yeah, thanks. Good night, Susie. I'll see you at home."

"Okay," I say in a singsong. Man, these pills. I'm never taking them again after today.

As we pull out of the parking lot, I watch Harry disappear into the distance. A sudden, terrible fear of never seeing him again rises inside me, tugging at my heart with invisible fingers, but it fades almost as quickly as it comes. I chalk it up to the painkillers.

"I'll call Dr. Brandywine in the morning and ask for an ortho referral," Mom says. "We'll get you in to see someone as soon as possible and figure out what we're going to do."

I let my head fall back against the seat. "No surgery," I remind her.

"We'll see what the doctor has to say."

"No. Surgery."

Mom stares at me with an inscrutable expression.

"It may not be up to you, Susannah," she says. Before I can reply, I stagger off the cliff of exhaustion I've been teetering on the edge of all night and tumble into a dark and dreamless sleep.

CHAPTER TWENTY

72 days until US Olympic Team Trials

"ALL RIGHT, I THINK THAT'S ENOUGH FOR TODAY," JOAN SAYS, extending her hands. "Give them here."

I surrender the elastic therapy bands I'm holding and wipe the sweat from my forehead. I'm sitting in the center of a mat on the floor of Joan's studio. Exhausted, I lower myself into corpse pose and release a deep breath.

"We still have ten minutes," I remind her, staring at the ceiling. I'm drenched, but there's a fan blowing on me and it feels nice. I probably stink, but I can't smell myself over the vanilla incense wafting out of a diffuser in the corner. I'd forgotten how many unfortunate side effects of working out are masked when you do it in water.

Weird that it's me pointing out the time. Joan is one of the best physical therapists in Chicago; she's treated US senators and professional sports players, even an Olympian or two. Her time is precious, and expensive. She never lets me forget that, and she never lets me waste a second of it, either.

Not that I try. In consultation with my orthopedic surgeon, coaches and parents, Joan brought the hammer down: if I wasn't going to have surgery, and I wanted her to treat me, I was going to have to do things her way. Once I agreed to that, she told me I wasn't allowed to swim for a month. An *entire* month, with the Olympics four months away. I could attend morning practice and kick in the diving well, but my afternoons were to be spent with Joan at her downtown clinic.

"If you want to get better, you have to trust me," Joan said at our first meeting.

"Can you make me better by Olympic Trials?" I asked her.

"I don't know," Joan said. "But I'm sure as shit going to try."

And I'm sure as shit not going to drag my feet. If I'm not back in the pool by mid-April, there's no way I'm coming out the other side of Trials a member of Team USA.

Joan has the foulest mouth I've ever heard on a doctor. When I told her so, all she said was, "I'm not a fucking doctor." At first, I thought the swearing meant that she was pissed at me for something, or that she didn't like me, because on top of all the cursing she has this low, raspy voice that makes her sound like she's annoyed by your very presence. Plus, she's built like a wrestler. It's intimidating.

But Joan is a friendly, easygoing person, with one exception: she hates Dave. She doesn't take any crap from him, so obviously I love her. He and Beth came to the consultation where I first met Joan, and when Dave said—for like the hundredth time—that I should swim through the pain, Joan told him that she was the expert, and if he didn't like her advice he could go right on ahead and fuck himself. Beth comes to PT with me about once a week, but Dave hasn't been here since.

Joan stretches out beside me on the mat. "You're pushing yourself too hard," she says, drumming her fingertips on her stomach. "What did I tell you when we started this?"

I don't say anything, so she presses me. "What did I tell you, Susannah?"

"No shortcuts," I mutter.

"Damn right. You think I don't notice you doing extra reps when you think my back is turned? I'm sick of having to tell you to take it easy and not overdo every fucking exercise. If I wanted you to work harder I would fucking *tell you*."

She sits up and stares at me. "As far as I'm concerned, the human body's ability to heal itself is a miracle, and you can't rush a fucking miracle."

I keep my gaze trained on the ceiling. A couple of tears drip down the sides of my face and into my hair. Joan pats my good shoulder and sings, "Oh, Susannah, now don't you fucking cry," to the tune of "Oh! Susanna" like she thinks she's funny or something. Never heard that one before.

"I'm not crying," I tell her, wiping my face. "My eyes water when I'm tired."

"Sure, let's go with that," Joan says. "You miss the pool?"

I nod. "When can I go back for a full practice?"

"End of next week, I'm thinking."

A flare of happiness goes off inside me. This is great news.

"You're doing well. But I need to make sure you're not straining that shoulder when I'm not there to help you. And I want you to take it easy."

Joan jumps up and hauls me to my feet by my good arm. The sleeve of her T-shirt rides up a few inches and I catch a glimpse of the tattoo that circles the upper part of her bicep. It's in almost the same exact location as Dave's, but instead of the Olympic rings, it's a quote, I think. It's in Latin.

"What does your tattoo say?" I ask. She tosses me a towel.

"Quod me nutrit me destruit," Joan says. "Do you know what it means?"

"No. Do *you* know what it means?" I joke.

"Yes," she says, swatting me with a towel. "I took four years of Latin in high school, thank you very much. It means 'what nourishes me destroys me.'"

"Cheerful."

Joan shrugs. "It's a reminder, for me personally, that I have to pursue all things in moderation. If I love something too much, or give too much of myself going after it, that same thing can hurt me."

"Like what?" I ask.

"Oh, any damn thing. An addiction. A relationship. A job." She pauses. "You could say it about swimming, right? The Olympics? You want it so fucking badly that you injured yourself chasing it."

"I wouldn't put it like that," I say. "Sports injuries are super common."

Joan smiles. "Of course, you're right. Maybe instead you should see it as a suggestion: your PT exercises are making you stronger, but don't fucking overdo it or you could reinjure yourself."

"Noted. Your tattoo is very wise."

"It's Friday night," Joan points out. "Got plans?"

"Probably go home, eat dinner, do my homework."

Joan throws up her hands. "Those aren't plans, that's a fucking routine. What about your boy? You don't have a date tonight?"

I don't mind when Joan teases me, because I know it comes from a place of affection, but I'm feeling sensitive about Harry. Technically, Joan's not supposed to know about him—we're still pretending to be broken up—but he picked me up from physical therapy once in a pinch and she wouldn't stop asking until I told her who he was. I had to swear her to secrecy. Luckily, she's about the last person in the world who would sell me out to Dave.

"We don't usually call them 'dates,' Joan. We hang out."

"So, are you hanging out with him tonight or what?"

"I texted after school to ask if he wanted to meet up, but he never responded."

"Maybe he did while you were here," Joan suggests. When I first met her, I never would've pegged her for a hopeless romantic, but that goes to show you how wrong first impressions can be.

"Maybe." I pull my phone out of my bag and check my texts while Joan watches expectantly. I shake my head. There's nothing new from him. She looks as disappointed as I feel.

Things haven't been easy between Harry and me. When I am in the pool, I'm separated from the rest of the team. When I'm not in the pool, I'm with Joan, or in school, or at home with my family. Harry and I can't spend much time together in public because of Dave's ultimatum, and we can't hang out at either of our houses too often because we're pretending to have broken up.

We decided it would be easier to lie to everyone than to try to keep multiple stories straight or hope that people who know the truth never cross paths with people who don't. It makes seeing each other difficult, though. There are so few places we can be sure nobody we know will spot us. We can't even keep our Sunday diner ritual because my family would definitely notice. I almost believed Harry at the beginning, that sneaking around would be fun and sexy, but mostly I feel lonely.

"I'm sure he'll call tonight," Joan assures me. "Now get the fuck out of here and enjoy your fucking weekend."

The only upside to this whole mess with my shoulder is that I have a car now. Okay, so it's not *my* car, it's Bela's, but she doesn't like to drive and wasn't using it. She offered to let me borrow it for the duration of my recovery, so I can drive myself to physical therapy and doctors' appointments.

The car is older than I am, too big and painted a hideous shade of mint green, but it has fewer than twenty thousand miles on it and runs like a dream. More important, it makes me feel grown up and in control, if not of my whole life, then at least of where I am or could be at any given moment. Theoretically. Practically, I use it only when I absolutely need to, because gas is expensive and, like everything else, my parents pay for that.

With traffic, it takes about an hour and a half to get home from Joan's office in the city. Most nights, I get home just in time to have dinner with my family, but sometimes I'm late and I eat alone at the kitchen table while Mom studies in the living room and Dad putters around in the garage and Nina does whatever she does in her room.

Tonight, nobody will be there. Mom's got class, Dad's working a shift at the restaurant and Nina's seeing a movie with friends. It's the perfect opportunity to have Harry over. But he's not answering any of my texts.

I turn the music up to drown the thoughts that keep swirling through my head: *Is Harry mad at me? Is he sick of sneaking around? Or is he feeling depressed and doesn't want to be around anyone right now?* But the thoughts bleed through the songs.

By the time I pull into the diner parking lot, the high of finding out I'll be back in the pool next week has dissipated. Twenty minutes ago, while I was waiting a stoplight, I made a mobile order for pickup. I'm going to get it, go home, eat dinner in front of the TV and watch a movie.

Even though it's early April, spring is late in the Midwest this year; we got snow last week, and now it's sleeting. I bundle up in my heavy winter coat and race from the car to the door of the diner.

"It's going to be a few more minutes," the server at the pickup counter tells me.

I take a seat in the waiting area near the host podium. I'm trying to decide if it's worth sending Harry another text even though he hasn't answered the last three, when I hear a laugh I recognize.

I turn around on the bench I'm sitting on and peer through the leaves of a plant at a group of people my age sitting a few booths away. I can name every person in that booth, because they're my teammates. But that's not what makes me feel like I've swallowed a hot stone.

Harry is with them, and he looks like he's having a *fucking* amazing time.

I'm not sure what to do. I want to know why Harry's here when he wouldn't answer any of my texts. But I can't confront him with a bunch of people we know within earshot, and anyway, it won't make me feel better. I decide to get my food and go home. There has to be a good explanation, or at least an acceptable one. Harry would never do anything to purposefully hurt me.

It's a fine plan. But when my order is ready, the server at the pickup counter bellows my name, not once but twice. I hurry to the counter and grab the bag from his hand.

"Susie?" I whirl around to see Harry standing behind me. All the blood in my body rushes into my face. I turn back to the server.

"I was sitting *right there*," I tell him. "And I was the only one waiting on an order! Did you have to scream my name like that? I didn't want anyone to know I was here."

"Uh, sorry," the server says. His gaze darts between Harry and me, then he scurries away.

Harry clears his throat and chokes out a nervous laugh. "You didn't want anyone to know you were here? How come? There's plenty of room at the table. Are you avoiding me?"

"I thought you might be avoiding me."

"I wasn't. Should we, um…" He looks around, checking to see if anyone is watching. Thankfully, nobody is. "Let's go outside and talk about this."

"It's raining outside," I argue. "And it's cold."

He flips the hood of my coat over my head. "There, all set. Let's go."

I follow him outside and around the corner of the diner, near the dumpster.

"Susie, what's going on? You seem upset," Harry says.

I sigh. "Nobody's at my house tonight and I texted to see if you wanted to come over and you ignored me." My backpack slides off my arm and I accidentally overrotate my shoulder trying to catch it. "Ow."

"You okay?" he asks.

"I'm fine," I tell him. "I wanted to see you. I never see you anymore."

"Whose fault is that?" His eyes widen as he realizes what he's said. "Shit, I'm sorry. I didn't mean that. It's not your fault. And I didn't see your texts. I forgot my phone at home this morning."

"Okay, but it's Friday night and we haven't—" *kissed each other held each other touched each other really even* talked *to each other* "—been alone in, like, a week."

He rubs his face. "I know. I was going to text, but I thought you wouldn't be home until later and that Nina would be there. So when Sarah invited me and Avik to go out with her and Nash and all them, I... I don't know. I liked the idea of hanging out with everybody. I'm sorry."

I feel foolish. He didn't mean to hurt my feelings. And I can't hold it against him that he's making friends. I've been isolated from everyone for weeks and I hate it. When Harry didn't answer my texts, I should've reached out to Jessa and Amber, but I didn't. He's the only person I want to see, and the only person I can't. But it's not fair to expect him to re-arrange his whole life around my schedule.

"I get it," I tell him. "I just miss you."

Harry hugs me close. He noses my hood off and kisses the top of my head. "Miss you, too."

"Do you think anyone saw us in there?" I ask.

"Nah," he says. "Want me to ditch these guys and come over?"

"That's okay. It's nice that they included you. You should stay and enjoy yourself."

"Want to come in and hang out with us?" he asks. The note of hope in his voice is a balm to my bruised ego, but I shake my head.

"I'm tired and sore. I want to go home and get into my pajamas." He doesn't say anything. "Harry?"

"What? Oh, sorry. Just picturing you in your pajamas. Are we talking nightgown or short shorts or like a two-piece flannel ensemble?"

I laugh. He cuddles me closer. It feels so good to be held by him, to touch him, even though his nose is cold against my skin and a tiny trickle of freezing rain has found its way down the back of my coat.

The thought of Harry seeing me in my pajamas sends an arrow of warmth through my chest. Of course, he's seen me in my pajamas, in hotel rooms during competition travel. And he sees me in much less every day at the pool. But we're rarely alone in those moments. That night on the beach was the closest we've ever gotten to being in bed together.

When I'm trying to fall asleep at night, I fantasize about it. Not sex, although sometimes that's part of the fantasy. But sleeping together. For a whole night. Like a grown-up couple. We probably won't get the chance until we're in college, and that's usually the thought that kills the fantasy, because we don't talk about that stuff. The future is so uncertain. Will we go to the same school? And if so, what school will that be? Those questions inevitably lead to a spiral about where I might be offered a swimming scholarship, if I even will, if he will, too, if he even wants one, and if that might mean we'd be separated.

I try not to think about that, and I definitely don't want to think about it right *now*, not when the near-future is just as unpredictable.

"Sweatpants and a T-shirt," I tell him. "Sorry to disappoint."

"The only disappointment is that I'm never there to see it. Someday, though."

"Yeah," I whisper. "Someday."

CHAPTER TWENTY-ONE

67 days until US Olympic Team Trials

"THIS IS SUCH A BAD IDEA," BETH SNAPS. SHE'S USUALLY CA-pable of keeping it together in front of the team, no matter how much Dave frustrates her, but right now she's clearly ex-asperated beyond the point of self-control.

I don't blame her. Because Dave has announced, with fan-fare and suffocating smugness, that in two weeks we are going to have our first annual GAC Battle of the Sexes meet.

The mezzanine is so silent you can hear the water slosh-ing around in the pool gutters below. The team is stunned. Boys and girls train together at GAC, but we don't compete against each other, and it hasn't occurred to any of us that we might ever have to.

Harry and I glance at each other. His eyes widen. There's no reason for Dave to pit girls against guys unless he's try-ing to create tension. I can't tell, in this moment, who he's gunning for most: the girls on the team, or Beth. Very possibly, it's both.

"You're welcome to your opinion, but this is *my* team. So if you want to coach here, you can keep it to yourself," Dave bites back.

Beth's jaw tightens. It's not the first time he's spoken to her like this in front of us, but it's become more frequent lately. Dave and Beth don't see eye to eye on much—that was never a secret—but they used to keep their bickering private.

I'm not the only person on the team who finds this whole situation unsettling.

"We're not going to win this," Amber says in a low voice as we change out of our suits in the locker room that night after practice.

"Speak for yourself," Jessa says, wriggling into a pair of leggings. "I could take at least half of those boys in a race. But yeah, you guys are in for it."

"Excuse me!" I protest. "I can take them, too. And so can Amber."

Jessa gives me a skeptical look. "No offense, Soos, but you're not taking anybody right now, not with that broken wing."

I bristle. It wasn't until my first practice back that I realized how bad my injury is. Beth altered my workout so that it's mostly legs-only sets, but I'm still swimming through quite a bit of pain. The last thing I need is someone who's supposed to be my friend and teammate smirking at me about it, making me feel even worse than I already do.

Which is why I say—stupidly—"Want to bet?"

We agree to put fifty dollars on whether or not I can beat one of the guy swimmers in one event during Battle of the Sexes.

"You don't even have to win the whole race," Jessa says in

a tone that I guess is supposed to underscore how magnanimous she's being by offering this concession. "Beat one boy. Doesn't matter which one."

"You're on," I tell her. We shake on it while Amber watches, incredulous.

"This will not turn out well," she mutters, shaking her head.

I zip my swim bag closed, then the three of us walk out together. We run into Avik, Harry and Nash leaving their locker room. My heart starts beating rapidly the second I set eyes on Harry. This ruse of not being together, and the distance it has forced between us, has ratcheted up the longing I feel for him to the point where I feel like I can hardly bear it. I wonder if it's the same for him. From the scorching look he gives me over Nash's shoulder, I'm going to go with *yes*.

It's clear from the snippets of conversation I overhear as we catch up with them that the boys are talking about Battle of the Sexes, too.

"It's so *unfair* to you girls," Nash says to us as we make our way to the parking lot.

I'm not in the mood for his shit tonight. Watching Dave and Beth argue so publicly earlier has left me feeling shaken. Amid all the turmoil of my injury, I feel like the only ground I thought was still solid is crumbling beneath my feet.

"Fuck you, Nash," Jessa says lazily.

I flash Nash a smile and my middle finger. He rolls his eyes at both of us, then spreads his arms to slap Harry and Avik on the back.

"It's gonna be a shutout, boys," he says with a laugh.

Harry and I are walking beside each other, doing our best to affect disinterest. Stealthily, he brushes the back of his hand against mine. I can't tell if he's trying to reassure me, or just desperate to touch me after all the time we've been spending apart, but my body springs to attention. I'm surprised nobody can hear the muffled *whoomp* of it going up in flames. It's still cold out, and I can feel my cheeks burning against the chill in the air.

There's nothing I want more than to follow Harry into his car, lean the seats back and put my mouth on his until all this wanting I feel recedes to normal, manageable levels. The frustration rises through my chest to the point where I think it might burst. I hold it together as we scatter to our cars, calling goodbyes almost as an afterthought. I've got Bela's sedan, so I'm driving Amber home tonight.

"Are you sure you should be swimming in this Battle of the Sexes thing?" Amber asks, cranking up the heat. She can't keep the disgust at the mere prospect of the meet out of her voice.

I know she's coming from a good place, but I'm done with having my every move questioned.

"Well, if I shouldn't, I bet a million people are going to tell me so," I say. "I feel like I can't even sneeze right now without everybody having an opinion. Beth, Dave, Joan, my parents…"

"Sorry," Amber says. She doesn't sound that sorry. She sounds irritated. "My mistake. It's not like you were *gravely injured* or anything."

"Yeah," I say, pulling out of the parking lot. "Thanks for pointing that out, I'd forgotten."

Amber and I never fight. I'm not even sure if we're fighting right now, or just sniping at each other because we're exhausted and spent the evening swimming through waters made toxic by Dave and Beth's constant and ever nastier disagreements. Whatever the reason, I don't like it. I take a deep breath.

"I think 'gravely injured' is a bit dramatic, don't you?" I ask, keeping my voice light. "It's not like I'm bleeding from a wound to the gut or anything."

She laughs. "I guess not." Then she sobers, like her mind has snagged on something. "I don't know, though—you didn't see your face in that pool in Iowa. Your expression, it was like…the visual equivalent of a howl. Lost and anguished and hopeless. I'll never forget it."

I shudder, more affected by the hollowness of her voice than I am by anything I recall about that day. "I don't remember much."

"That's probably for the best."

We don't talk as I drive to Amber's house. That's one of the nice things about being alone with Amber—she's an extrovert and I'm an introvert, but we're both happy to sit quietly and listen to music, sunk in our own thoughts like footprints in a snowbank. We've always had more in common than either of us had with Jessa, who never met a silence she didn't feel compelled to break with restless chatter. Pale, blond, pretty Jessa, with her demanding, overbearing parents and high-limit credit card and endless confidence, never an outsider anywhere.

But Amber knows what it's like to feel like you don't belong, like capers on a birthday cake. To feel like you have to fight hard for every scrap of recognition the ravenous machine of swimming, and society at large, resentfully spits out.

"Did you consider quitting?" Amber asks. Her voice is soft, her tongue a bit clumsy, as if she's woken up from a nap. "After you tore your shoulder?"

"No."

The answer comes quickly, because I haven't allowed myself to think about quitting since Des Moines. Before the injury, I used to toy with the idea sometimes, idly, the way you might play with a piece of your hair while watching TV. When the fantasy started to feel too real, I shied away from it, like it might burn me, or like merely thinking it could make it come true.

After Des Moines, I knew that if I let the possibility cross my mind for even half a second, it would take root and flower faster than I could kill it, and then everything would be over. Everything I'd worked so hard for. Everything I believed myself to be. Gone. And I couldn't let that happen.

"I think about it, sometimes," Amber says, examining her cuticle beds as if the answer to whether or not she should quit GAC might be written there. "A lot more, lately. Since you got hurt."

I don't know what surprises me more—that Amber has thought about quitting, or that it has anything to do with me.

"Is everything okay?" I ask. "Is something bothering you?" Because that must be it—she's got some pain, in her knee or her back or maybe her shoulder, too. All common injuries in swimming.

She sighs, then smiles. "Oh, lots of things." I frown at her, not understanding at all. She gives my knee a comforting pat and turns toward the window. "Don't worry, Soos. I'm good."

"How do you feel about this Battle of the Sexes meet?" I whisper into the phone that night. My eyes are closed, the better to imagine Harry's lying right here next to me instead of in his own bed across town, but I'm not the least bit sleepy.

Harry hesitates before answering. "I don't know," he says. "Not good?"

"That didn't sound convincing," I say a bit too loudly.

"Shh," he says. "You want to wake up your parents?"

"You think this is okay? Pitting boys against girls like it's some kind of fair fight?"

"I think Dave's trying to shake us all up," Harry says, calmly, like he's trying to keep me from getting upset. I hate when guys talk to girls like that. "You and I used to practice together all the time. Are you saying that didn't make us both better?"

"That's practice, this is competition," I remind him. "There's a reason men and women don't race together. The only point of making us swim against each other when the clock is running is to show Beth that her girls can't possibly stand up to Dave's boys. Or to make us girls feel bad. Or, hey, two birds, one stone."

"I don't think that's what this is supposed to be," Harry says. "You could outswim half the boys on that team."

"It's the other half I'm worried about! You included."

"We're a team, Susie."

"*Sometimes* GAC is a team. But most of the time, we're all looking out for number one."

"I'm not talking about GAC," Harry says. "I'm talking about you and me. When you win, I win, and—*hopefully*—vice versa."

"Of course. When you win, I win." But I can't shake the feeling that this is more than just an exercise, and I don't know why Harry can't see that.

"So, you know, whatever happens in this dumb meet, it doesn't matter."

"It matters to me," I insist. "I don't understand why you're giving Dave the benefit of the doubt. He's the one who made us break up, remember?"

"You think Dave is doing this to spite you?"

"No, but I do think he's doing it to spite Beth. He doesn't like her because she's different from him and she has her own opinions and he's afraid she's a better coach."

He scoffs. "She's not a *better* coach."

"How would you know? She's never coached you. They've both coached me and I'd choose Beth over Dave any day of the week."

"I'm sure you would."

"What's *that* supposed to mean?"

"Stop yelling. You're going to wake your whole house and then they'll know we're still together." After a beat of silence, he asks nervously: "We are still together, right?"

The giant bubble of anger that's been expanding in my chest suddenly deflates. I laugh softly.

"Yeah," I say, dropping my voice to just above a whisper. "But I wish you wouldn't defend Dave. I know you think he's on your side, but there's only one side with him. *His*. I don't want you to be his catch of the day."

"Uh…what?"

"It's what Jessa calls it when Dave latches on to a specific swimmer for a while, giving them all this attention and making them think he sees something special in them," I explain. "In the end, he always throws them back."

"Yeah. God forbid anyone ever sees anything special in me."

"You know that's not what I mean."

"He's not doing that," Harry says defensively. I don't want

him to question his talent, or that he's deserving of a coach that believes in him. I just don't trust Dave to be that for him. But I know that I've got my own issues, and maybe I am projecting them on Harry.

"Okay," I say. "Let's forget it. I need to sleep or I'll be lead in the water tomorrow."

"Today," he says. "It's after midnight."

"Today, then." I yawn. "Good night, Harry. I love you."

"Love you, Susie."

I'm so beat I expect to fall asleep instantly, but while my body is exhausted, my brain is wide-awake, spinning my conversation with Harry into troublesome knots. Why doesn't he see what's going on here? I don't get how he could not be bothered by the way Dave is gunning for Beth. I can't stand it that he's getting drawn into Dave's web.

It's not that I'm jealous that Dave's paying attention to Harry and can't be bothered with me. I'm *not*. But I am protective of Harry. I'm afraid that Dave's using him. I really hope that's not true.

CHAPTER TWENTY-TWO

53 days until US Olympic Team Trials

"I DON'T WANT YOU SWIMMING IN THIS BATTLE OF THE SEXES meet," Beth tells me as soon as I sit down in her office for our weekly meeting. She's careful not to talk negatively about Dave to me, but I can hear the unspoken disgust in her tone: *This dumbass Battle of the goddamn Sexes meet.*

"Well, don't beat around the bush about it," I say. "Tell me what you really think."

"I'm serious. The PT is starting to pay off. You're improving more rapidly than I expected, and the last thing we need is for you to reinjure your shoulder and set yourself back," Beth says.

"But don't you think this is a good opportunity to test myself in competition? It's less than two months till Trials. I need to keep my body race-ready."

Beth shakes her head. "It's too soon," she insists.

"It feels like Dave is having this stupid meet to humiliate the girls," I grumble. "It's unfair. We're working our asses off. It's like he's trying to break our spirits, setting us up for failure like this."

"I'm sure that's not his intention," Beth says tightly. I can tell she doesn't believe that. "Let's go over this week's—"

"How many of us do you think could beat the fastest boys in a head-to-head race?" I ask her. "Five or six? Sarah and Trinity and Gwen and Lilly, maybe Jessa? I think I could, but if I'm not swimming...that's not enough to give the girls a fighting chance. I feel guilty, not helping the team." I give Beth a look. "Don't you think that could be bad for morale?"

Beth sighs. "You're not going to let up until I agree to let you race, are you?"

"Nope."

"One event. Only the 200 IM. Will that be enough to make you feel like you're contributing meaningfully to the team effort?" Beth asks, staring at me over the tops of her glasses.

"Yes!" I grin. She shakes her head, like I exasperate her, but I think she appreciates my stubbornness. Beth likes that I'm not a quitter. Sometimes I wonder if that's because of the way her own swimming career ended—abruptly, out of anger and resentment, and without closure.

"You have to promise me you won't push yourself if you start to feel pain," Beth insists. "This is not the time to be playing fast and loose with your health. If your labrum were to tear again, or God forbid some other muscle or ligament in your shoulder, you'll have to sit out Trials."

I know this, but hearing her say it so bluntly sobers me right up.

"I'll be careful," I promise.

Dave's Battle of the Sexes scrimmage is scheduled for the first Saturday in May, which also happens to be my seventeenth birthday. Harry and I have plans to celebrate after the meet with dinner at a fancy restaurant all the way downtown. He's been saving up for it, doing odd jobs for family members and neighbors. I wish I could say it matters to me where we eat my birthday dinner, because it matters so much to him, but as long as I'm with Harry, I could be eating sawdust for all I care.

Our relationship is still a secret, so I had to lie to my parents about spending Saturday night at Amber's house, because I know they won't check up on that. Friday evening is reserved for a family celebration with my parents and sister, plus Bela.

On Friday afternoon, Mom picks me up from school to drive me to my physical therapy appointment—Dad's car is in the shop again, and he's borrowing Bela's for the day.

At least, I think we're going to physical therapy, but Mom turns out of the school parking lot going the opposite direction.

"Hey, uh, Mom?" I say, tapping her arm. "It's the other way."

"We're not going to Joan's today," she tells me. "I canceled that appointment and scheduled a different one. With Dr. Galletti."

"You're taking me with you to the gynecologist?" I ask.

She glances at me out of the corner of her eye and I realize what's happening. "Oh."

"Yeah. I don't know who you think you're fooling, but it's clear that something's still going on between you and Harry. I'll remind you, my darling dummy, that your phone bill comes to me."

"We never broke up," I admit. I decide not to tell her about Dave's ultimatum, because it's the sort of controlling behavior she'd get all fired up about and want to fight. Everything is too precarious right now for that, and I don't want Dave suspecting Harry and I never did what he instructed.

Instead, I err on the side of vagueness. "Dave doesn't like swimmers dating each other. We decided to keep it quiet so he wouldn't get on our case."

"I don't see why 'keeping it quiet' necessitated lying to your parents."

"I'm sorry. I didn't want to. But we thought it would be simpler if we stuck to one story."

"This devious streak is a side of you I've never seen before, Susannah, and I'm not happy about it." She narrows her eyes at me. "Where are you really spending tomorrow night after the meet?"

"Harry's taking me out to dinner downtown," I tell her grudgingly.

"It's serious between you two, isn't it?" Mom asks. I nod. "I didn't think you'd lie to us like this for anything less than complete and total infatuation."

"It's not infatuation," I reply. "I'm in love with him."

"I see," she says. I can't tell if she's mad about this or not. She seems calm, but Mom does not tolerate lying or rule-breaking from Nina and me. I bet she's boiling inside, and also shocked to be dealing with this from me.

"Well," she adds, "that's why we're going to see Dr. Galletti. I should've done this back when you first started going out with Harry. As much as I'd love for you to stay my little girl forever, your body is not just a machine that swims. You need to know how to care for it."

"Please tell me you didn't talk to Dad about this." It's one thing to have my mother speculating about the status of my sex life, but the idea of her having conversations about it with another person embarrasses me.

"Of course I did! You're forgetting, Dad and I were high school sweethearts, too. We know what we got up to when we were young and falling in love. We want to make sure you're being safe and—no offense to Harry, but—we can't assume he'll be responsible enough."

"I hate this conversation," I mutter.

"Too bad. Honestly, if I had my way, you two would wait—although I guess I shouldn't assume..." She glances at me. "Have you already had sex, Susannah?"

"No! Mom, can we please stop talking about it?"

"You don't have to go into detail with me or anything, but no, we can't stop talking about it. Becoming sexually active for the first time is an important threshold in a person's life. I want you to feel informed and prepared and in control when you decide to take that next step—whenever and with whomever it happens someday."

I put my palms to my cheeks—they're fever hot. The thing is, Harry and I haven't talked about having sex on my birthday, or made plans for that to happen. I can't say I haven't thought about it, though, or figured that maybe tomorrow night could be The Night. And I guess, in those imagined scenarios, I assumed he'd bring condoms. I haven't bought my own or anything. So maybe what I'm really embarrassed about is that I didn't think more ahead about this.

It's unlike me. I worry and strategize about everything. I crave constancy and hate surprises. But deep down, I'm avoiding thinking about our first time because I'm afraid of disappointing Harry with my inexperience. If I give the possibilities too much consideration beforehand, there's a real chance I'll freeze up and chicken out in the moment, and that's the absolute last thing I want.

Can't say I'm not grateful to Mom for forcing the issue, though. She's saved me a lot of sweat about how I'm going to deal with birth control. After a routine exam, Dr. Galletti talks with me privately about my options, then gives me a prescription for the pill. Mom and I go right to the pharmacy to have the prescription filled, and while we wait, Mom makes me buy a pack of condoms—by myself, with my own money—to get me in the practice of doing it myself.

"Never count on anybody else to ensure the quality of your reproductive health," Mom tells me on the drive home from Walgreens. We're stopped at a red light and I'm seized by the urge to hug her, so I do, quickly before the light turns green. She squeezes me tight, then lets me go.

"Thanks, Mom," I say, feeling teary. I have such a great family.

Mom smiles. "You're welcome, mija. I'm not thrilled by the prospect of you having sex, but it's *my* responsibility to take care of you, and to teach you how to take care of yourself. I take it seriously."

"You're doing a good job," I tell her.

"Thanks," she says. "Lucky for you, I got to practice with Nina. That was a disaster, but it seems I've worked the kinks out."

That night, I lie in bed with my eyes closed, thinking about the packet of pills in my nightstand drawer and the box of condoms beside it. Frick and Frack are curled up near my head; I can hear the soft sounds of their breathing, feel the tickle of tails against my neck. It's like there's a heavy weight on my chest, a pile of bricks stacked haphazardly in the corner of a half-built house. When my phone lights up, I answer right away. I'm desperate to talk to Harry about this.

A year ago, I had no idea he existed. Now, nothing seems to have really happened until I've told him about it.

"My mom thinks we're going to have sex tomorrow night," I whisper into the phone.

"Hi, Susie," he says with a teasing smirk in his voice. "Sounds like you had an exciting day."

"Hi," I say. I picture him lying in bed, shirtless in boxers, basically the same amount of clothing he's wearing in seventy-five percent of our interactions. But the image sends a shiver of carbonated lust up my spine, and I remember what Harry said to me on the beach in Texas: *Swimsuits are equipment, underwear is sexy.* I bought a new dress for my birthday dinner but have given zero thought, until this moment, to what I should wear underneath it. That will have to be revisited.

"What's this about us having sex?"

"My mom kidnapped me this afternoon and took me to the gyno instead of PT," I tell him. "I'm on the pill now. Oh, and she made me buy a pack of condoms."

"You told her about us? It was supposed to be a secret." Harry sounds panicked. A month ago, I would've thought he was worried about putting my career in peril if Dave finds out we're still together. Now I wonder if he's not just as concerned for his own.

"She figured it out. I guess I haven't been as subtle as I thought. I'd make a terrible criminal."

"Well, that's a relief," he says. "Cool of your mom to take you to the doctor instead of, like, locking you in a tower and throwing the key in the moat."

"I don't think she's so much cool as she's a woman married to the guy that she fell in love with when she was fourteen. Plus, they filled in the moat last summer. They're more trouble than they're worth, a breeding ground for mosquitos, basically."

He laughs. "I have a box of condoms, too. Just so you know."

I clear my throat. "Uh, good."

"My mom's a nurse, so I had a similar experience a few years ago."

"How old were you?"

"Twelve." He hesitates, then adds: "Hypersexuality is a common enough trait among people who are bipolar that she felt it was important to teach me about safe sex as soon as possible." He coughs. "I think I'm as sexual as the next guy my age, though. Pretty average on that front."

"Oh, well…that's…good," I say.

"I wasn't planning to seduce you tomorrow night or any-thing," Harry says. "I was mainly focused on dinner. I'm ex-cited to eat at this restaurant. But I'm ready if you're ready."

I exhale slowly. My skin is sensitive to the touch; Frack's tail brushes my shoulder and my body lights up like a struck match. Even though he's not here in my room, I can sense Harry all around me. I can almost smell his soap. In my imag-ination, he's lying on his bed with the covers thrown off and the window slightly cracked because he likes the fresh air, his hand splayed across his bare stomach just above his navel where the trail of soft blond hair begins, fingertips drum-ming against his abs to the beat of a song only he can hear.

Something has changed since the beach in Texas. I wasn't ready then, but I am now. At least, I think I am. How am I supposed to know when I'm ready? But I think about it all the time.

"Susie," he says, "promise me that no matter what happens at the meet tomorrow, it's not going to change us." He lowers his voice and says, "We exist outside of that pool."

I pause to think about that. Sometimes I feel like *I* don't exist outside of the pool, like when I'm not there I'm some-thing less than myself. Like I might disappear. But I want to believe Harry. I give myself over to the fantasy that I can be who I'm meant to be on dry land, too.

"Yes," I say. "I promise."

CHAPTER TWENTY-THREE

50 days until US Olympic Team Trials

THE NEXT MORNING, AFTER OUR PREMEET WARM-UP, ALL THE GAC girls are crammed in the women's locker room for Beth's final pep talk. We're sprawled on the floor, squeezed together on benches, leaning against the lockers, waiting for her to say something inspirational, something that will help us believe that we could beat the boys despite the odds stacked against us.

She sweeps her gaze across the huddled mass of us, making eye contact with each of us in turn, clutching her clipboard to her chest. It's humid in the locker room, and her glasses are foggy, but she doesn't seem to notice. Her hair is in its typical tight ponytail, and it swings across her shoulders like a metronome as she paces back and forth.

"Girls," she begins. Her voice echoes through the room. "Lately I've been thinking about valor. I was a history major in college, and I wrote my senior thesis on the role of the gladiator in Ancient Rome. Many gladiators were slaves, men and women whose lands and cultures were crushed and consumed by the might of the Roman military. Some were criminals, or Christians, which amounted to pretty much the same thing. Some were volunteers who risked their lives for the chance at glory the arena provided.

"The significance of gladiators in Roman culture, and the fascination the Romans had for them, is a contested topic among historians. Some say the gladiatorial spectacles are evidence of the endemic sadism of human nature, our innate bloodlust and gruesome bent toward violence. Others believe the games reflected the harshness and brutality of Roman life and were a reminder of the government's power, to ensure no one ever doubted their right to punish those who dared defy the patriarchy.

"There are other theories, but this one is my favorite. Some scholars believe that the gladiators embodied one of the highest ideals to which a person could aspire: the ability to face defeat with grace and bravery. Their circumstances were very nearly hopeless, and yet they stepped out onto the sand and held their heads up and walked calmly toward their fate. They were heroes.

"For gladiators, the future did not exist, only the present, and by setting aside any hope of survival, they also shed any fear they had of dying. Though they were considered despicable by society, in the arena they regained their power, because knowing how to lose with dignity and without regret is the best weapon against despair. And fighting, not for the promise of a reward but simply for one's own satisfaction is the greatest glory a person can attain.

"I believe we have it in us to prevail," Beth says, "just as countless gladiators did, but I won't condescend to you by saying that with a little pluck and good teamwork, victory is certain. What I will tell you is that *the future doesn't matter*. Not today. Today, we do as the gladiator does—enter the arena, heads held high, and take back our power. Today, we swim with joy."

Beth tucks her clipboard under her arm, gives us a tight, determined smile and walks out of the locker room. Without a word, we follow her.

The 200 IM is scheduled for the second half of the meet. By the first diving break, the boys are beating us, but not by much. Most of us spent the week griping about having to swim against them, but a change has come over us since Beth's speech. I can see determination in the set of everyone's shoulders and purpose in the expressions on their faces.

The energy on the pool deck is strange, different than usual. At other meets, even the most serious swimmers find time to chat and joke with teammates between races, but nobody's doing much of that today. The boys look uncomfortable—even Nash, who crowed about how they were going to crush us to everyone who would listen, seems subdued.

I keep trying to catch Harry's eye across the pool deck, but he's deliberately avoiding my gaze. There's a jittery feeling in my limbs, like something is vibrating under the surface of my skin. I don't know what I'm nervous about. It's not like this is a real meet. But I can't stop thinking about what Harry said last night, the way he begged me not to let this meet change us. I hate this feeling.

Why does it matter so much to me? We agreed that this

whole Battle of the Sexes thing was stupid and insulting. If the boys beat us, who cares? If we beat them, what does it change? It has nothing to do with Harry and me. But reminding myself of this doesn't make me feel better. I wish he would *look* at me.

Because Harry *won't* look at me, though, I watch him instead. He can't stay still. He keeps sitting down on benches, then getting up and finding a different seat, only to move again a minute later. The other guys aren't paying attention; nobody seems to think it's weird, or even notice him doing it. He's clearly agitated. Even when he's sitting, he drums his fingers restlessly against his knees and picks at the edge of his jammers and rhythmically scrubs his fingers through his hair.

I wonder if something else is going on here, if this isn't simply his nervous reaction to the tension of the meet. Harry tries to keep all outward signs of his depression away from me, but I can tell when he's sad, and I can guess what's happening when he retreats. I've never seen him in a hypomanic state—I don't know what it looks like.

You're going to worry about me all the time, he said when he told me he was bipolar, and I do worry sometimes. But I can't tell if it's because of what I know, or because I'm always waiting for the other shoe to drop in every corner of my life. Am I making something out of nothing, projecting my anxieties onto him? Or is something really wrong?

I feel increasingly uneasy as my event approaches, but I force myself to believe that everything is fine. I cheer my teammates on from the sidelines, and I cheer Harry on in my head. He wins two out of his three races with one to go, and

I can't help but feel a flush of pride when he edges out both Nash and Jessa to take first in the 100 back.

Jessa is, predictably, steamed about it—she hates to lose, and she's always quick to assign blame everywhere but herself. As soon as she's out of the pool, she marches up to me wearing a face like a storm cloud.

"Your...boyfriend—" she pants, pointing an accusatory finger at me "—*sucks!*"

My heart stutters—if my parents figured out Harry and I were only pretending to be broken up, it's possible Jessa has, too.

Amber steps between us and says, "It's not Susannah's fault he beat you. They're not even together anymore."

"Oh, come on. Do you think I'm stupid? Everyone knows something's still going on between you two," Jessa hisses. "We have *eyes*."

"Keep your voice down," I whisper. Amber glances at me in shock.

"We'll see how you like it when *you* have to swim against him," Jessa says. "Don't forget our bet."

"I'm not competing against Harry. He's not swimming in the 200 IM."

A smug grin slowly spreads across Jessa's face. "Are you sure about that?"

Amber and I exchange a wide-eyed look, then hurry to the bulletin board where the heat list is posted. I hadn't thought to look at it today, because I knew when my event was scheduled and who I would be swimming against. But Jessa's right. Nash's name has been removed and Harry's has been added in its place. I've been assigned lane four, and he's in lane five.

Not only will we be racing against each other, we'll be swimming head to head.

When I think back to our conversation last night, I realize that Harry already knew about this. That's why he's been avoiding my eyes all morning. He knew what I would think if I found out. It's not like Harry never swims the 200 IM, but it's not his best event, so there's no good reason Dave would put him in it. Unless he wanted us to compete against each other.

I can't believe Harry mocked me for thinking this meet had anything to do with me, because it *did*, if only in this small way.

"Harry didn't tell you?" Amber asks.

I shake my head.

"Is Jessa right?" she asks. "Have you been together this whole time?"

I look down at the tiles of the pool deck as my vision blurs. "It's not really anybody's business."

"No, it's not," Amber says. "It's your relationship. I'm just surprised."

"Dave was going to kick me off the team," I remind her.

I search for Harry across the pool deck, and this time he's looking right at me. I can tell from the expression on his face that he knows I've figured it out.

If I had to explain to a stranger right now why this means so much to me, I don't think I would be very convincing. *It's just a stupid fake meet*, the imaginary stranger would say. *It doesn't matter.* I feel like a toy Dave has grown tired of yet doesn't want anyone else to play with, and if that were the only thing going on, this wouldn't hurt so bad. The fact that he's using Harry as a tool to humiliate me, and that Harry is going along with it, is the part that feels like a blow to the stomach.

I shake my head in disbelief. He starts to mouth something, but I turn away. We can deal with this later. Fifteen minutes before our race is no time to lose focus.

"I think Harry's trying to get your attention," Amber tells me as I strip out of my warm-ups and put on my goggles.

"The next time Harry Matthews speaks to me, he better be congratulating me for beating him," I say. "And I hope Jessa brought cash, because I'm going to win that bet."

Amber smiles. "That's the spirit! Today, we swim with joy."

"Yeah," I reply. "Joy." And maybe a splash of vengeance.

I take comfort in the knowledge that the 200 IM is not a race that plays to Harry's strengths. His breaststroke is weak. As long as my shoulder behaves, I might be able to pull out a victory. It would close the point gap in the last third of the meet. We could win, and even if we don't, a first-place finish in the 200 IM would help us save face.

In the diving well, I swim a set of slow, careful laps to test my shoulder. I'm feeling some pain, but it's nothing I can't push through. I'm tired of holding back in the water, of being gentle and taking care. I know why it's necessary, but it makes me feel like a falcon on a tether, safe and secure and confined when all I want to do is soar.

Dave intercepts me on the way to the diving blocks.

"Just wanted to wish you luck," he says. Then he lowers his voice. "You wanted to work with Beth? You thought I had nothing more to teach you? This is your chance to prove it was worth it."

He leaves me standing there, stunned. He didn't think I had what it took to go to the Olympics. He should be happy I'm someone else's problem now. But I know Dave well enough to suspect that isn't the point. In his world, he decides who matters and who doesn't. He would rather my career gutter out and die on his watch than see me try to resurrect it with another coach. My decision to swim with Beth was a repudiation of his godlike status. And the fact that I got faster when I was out from under his thumb? Well, that was just salt in the wound.

When my event is called, I step up to the block, staring straight ahead as if I'm wearing blinders, not bothering to look at the competition. I watch the water ripple with the memory of the previous race, but out of the corner of my eye I notice Harry bend down and scrape his palms against the rough plastic of the gutters. Some people think the new skin exposed by abrading the hands before a race helps catch the water better, but I remain skeptical.

As we mount the blocks, Harry whispers, "Susie, I—"

"Not now," I say.

"Take your mark—"

My body slices through the water like a knife. Right away, I feel a twinge of pain in my shoulder, but I cruise through the butterfly, concentrating hard on my underwater pulls, determined not to create any extraneous drag. My backstroke is smooth, and my supercharged kick does its job off the turns— all those legs-only sets are starting to pay off. I careen up and down the pool, certain I'm in first place, but in the back of my head a voice whispers, *Pace yourself.*

By the second lap of the breaststroke, my shoulder is complaining. Loudly. *You're fine, you're fine, you're fine*, I think as I push off the wall and switch to freestyle. Then fatigue settles over me like a lead blanket, and it's as if I've forgotten how to use my legs. They drift sullenly behind me, heavy as concrete, dragging me down as my arms do all the work. Stupidly, I blew all my energy on the first half of the race and now I'm running on fumes for the finish.

Stay calm, I command myself, but my shoulder is screaming. I bite down hard on my lower lip and taste blood. I'm slowing down. I'm flailing. But I set an excellent pace during the fly and back fifties, and Harry has surely been slowed by the breaststroke. All I have to do is finish strong on the last lap and I'll win. I'm sure I'll win.

Why won't my legs move? My shoulder will tear again if I keep this up. I imagine the flimsy ligaments ripping like a piece of loose-leaf paper and feel the tight grip of panic in my chest. I can't reinjure my shoulder. If I do, it's all over. No Trials. No Olympics. The yellow touchpad at the end of the lane beckons. I force myself to concentrate on the finish.

Fifteen…ten…five… I count the yards like I'm making promises. As I approach the wall I burst forward with one last Hail Mary kick and slam my right hand as hard as I can against the touchpad before drifting to a stop and looking to the scoreboard.

I'm so sure I've won that, for a second, that's exactly what I see: *1. Ramos.* But it's a trick of the light, or my brain. I blink and the 1 has been replaced by a 5. *Fifth.* But what's infinitely worse than losing so badly in my best event after all the work I've done and all the pain I've suffered is what I see when I look for Harry's name.

1. Matthews.

Harry beat me by five full seconds, even with his subpar breaststroke and my improved kick. I'm in so much pain I think I might pass out.

A wave of nausea rolls over me as Harry slips beneath the lane line that separates us and drifts over to me. "Susie," he says, but I turn away from him. If I don't get out of here right now, I'm going to throw up in the gutter.

I look up to see Jessa and Amber standing over me on the deck wearing identical expressions of concern. It must've been obvious to everyone what was happening to me. I feel so ashamed.

"Will you please help me?" I gasp.

Amber and Jessa grab hold of me awkwardly to avoid touching my shoulder. They haul me onto the deck like a fisherman's catch. Harry lifts himself out of the water and reaches for me, but I struggle to my feet on my own, using the block for ballast.

"Don't touch me," I snap.

I escape to the locker room where I throw myself down on a bench, bury my face in a towel and let loose a frustrated, anguished scream. I gulp down air, choke on it, cough it out, feeling my lungs flatten like paper bags in my chest.

Get ahold of yourself, I command myself savagely. I test my shoulder, rotating and stretching it to assess the extent of the damage. At least I can move it.

My muscles relax in relief. It hurts, but I don't think I've torn my labrum again. This might be a setback, but it's not a permanent one. Not a career-ending one. I almost cry all over again when it crashes down on me, the realization of how lucky I am to have skirted disaster.

"Susie?" Harry is standing next to me, twisting his goggles in his hands. I didn't even hear him come in. The sound of my sobs must've drowned out any noise he made.

"Leave me alone," I mutter wetly into the towel.

"I want to make sure you're okay."

"You need to leave. This is the girls' locker room. You can't be in here."

He sits down next to me on the bench and rubs his knees. "I'm sorry."

"For beating me?" I scoff. "Screw you, Harry. I don't care."

What a liar I am. I care so much, and I don't even know why. Why can't I just *not care*?

"What happened to 'It's just a race'?" Harry asks.

"There's no such thing as 'just a race.'"

"Then what happened to 'When you win, I win'?" he asks. "Did you even mean that, or does it only apply when it's convenient for you?"

"Shut *up*, Harry! I don't want to talk to you right now, and I sure as hell don't want to talk to you about us." I take a deep, jagged breath. Tears leak from my eyes. "Can't you see I'm in pain?"

"*Yeah*, I *can* see that! I want to help you, but you won't let me."

"I don't want your help. You're only going to make it worse." What I mean is that if he touches me it'll only hurt more, but that's not how he takes it. I'm feeling mean and angry and hurt. Like a cornered animal, all I can think to do is lash out.

He stands. "I swam my best," he shouts. "That's what I'm supposed to do. Should I have let you win? Because you're my girlfriend? Would you have liked that?"

"Of course not!" I almost tell him to keep his voice down, Dave might hear, but I realize that doesn't matter now. After this drama, nobody's going to be fooled into thinking we're just friends.

"I couldn't stop it. It's not my fault."

"I know," I say. "Please just go. *Please.*"

"Your shoulder—"

"MY SHOULDER IS FINE."

"No, it's *not*, so stop fucking saying that. Look at yourself!"

I'm cradling my arm and my breath is labored. I used up everything I had in that race, and this fight is taking my final wind. I want to stand, to look him in the eye, but I know that if I get up I'll fall.

"You have to stop lying to everyone, and you have to stop lying to yourself," Harry says. He grows scarily quiet. "You are injured. You cannot do the things you used to do, not right now. And yelling at me, or resenting Dave, or ignoring Beth's advice, is not going to change that. You have to accept it. You have to face it. And you have to stop blaming everyone, including yourself."

I hang my head. "Go away, please, Harry. I'm begging you. I can't do this right now."

"Why are you so mad at me?"

That is the worst thing he could possibly have said. A tsunami of anger surges up inside of me.

"Why am I so mad? For *years*, no matter how I felt, no matter how hard it was, I put in the work, I did the laps, I swam the races," I tell him. "I put up with Dave and I did Beth's stupid affirmations and I volunteered as a lab rat for her training experiments. I feel like a fool and failure *all the time*. I worked so hard I literally broke myself. Then you come out of nowhere and with the tiniest bit of effort you manage to do everything I wish I could do. And *you don't even care.* You don't even want it."

"That's not true," he says coldly. "You know why I don't push myself. I told you why."

"So why are you doing it now? Why did you have to do it out there?"

"To show Dave I'm not bad for you! To prove to him that I can be serious about swimming and play by his rules, and that I'm not going to drag you down."

I release a ragged breath. "That's never going to work. He doesn't care about my career—he cares about control! Dave used you to humiliate me. *And you let him.*"

I fling the words like rocks. Right now, I hate Harry. I hate him the way you can only hate someone you love when you think they've betrayed you.

"What?" Harry barks, sounding genuinely surprised. Whatever he thought I was upset about, I can tell he had no idea that was it. "Why do you keep insisting that this stupid meet is about you?"

"He told me, right before the race. I wouldn't listen to him and I left him to swim with Beth *and then I got better.* He'll never forgive me for that. His pride won't let him. So he did what he thought would hurt me most. He made my *man* put me in my place. Do you know how that makes me feel?"

"That's ridiculous. He doesn't even know we're still together!"

"*Everyone* knows. We were fools to think we could hide it from people we see every single day."

"You think I would do something to deliberately hurt you?

That I would side with Dave against you? We agreed that this meet was stupid and meaningless. Yet you're brutally injured and you destroyed yourself out there so you could have the pleasure of beating me. What the hell is that? You think I'm worthless? You think you're the only person who's ever worked hard at anything?"

"No, that's not what this is about." This conversation is getting out of control. I have to stop it, but it feels like an avalanche that's about to bury us both. "And if it means nothing, why didn't you tell me he'd put you in my event?"

"It's not *your* event! You don't own it. And I didn't tell you because I knew you would get all in your head about it. Why does everything always have to be about you? Your swimming, your dreams. I worked my ass off to be able to do what I did out there tonight. You saw that time. I earned it."

He's right. And even now, I'm so proud of him. But I've spent the last few years telling myself the pain and exhaustion and fear were going to be worth it someday. What if they won't? What if I was right that the only way I was going to get to the Olympics was to put aside everything else? When I decided to be with Harry, swimming stopped being the only thing that mattered. He told me that my swimming was more important to him than his own. Maybe we were fools to believe that.

Devastated, I say, "I knew this would happen."

"What are you talking about?"

"This is why I had rules, Harry. This is why I told you we couldn't be together, why I couldn't think or care about anyone or anything except swimming. Everything I worked for, everything I was trying so hard to do, it's all ruined."

Harry's face is a portrait of agony, like I've reached into his chest and torn his heart out. Like I'm holding that still-beating, bloody chunk of muscle in my hands. My own heart folds in on itself, crumpling like a sheet of wet paper. I want to take it all back, everything I said, but the words fell out of my mouth so thoughtlessly and there's no cramming them back in now.

"That has nothing to do with me and you know it," he says.

I suck air into my lungs, trying to calm down. My heart is racing and my body is shaking and my shoulder is throbbing. I feel like I'm about to fall completely to pieces.

"I know," I say. The anger has ebbed. All that's left is the gritty silt of regret. "I'm just so sick of being a loser."

"You're not a loser," Harry says. His shoulders slump under the weight of everything we've dumped on each other tonight. He looks miserable. "You just lost. But you are being a real asshole. I love you, Susie, but I'm so fucking mad at you right now."

He walks away, disappearing behind a row of lockers.

"Harry, wait," I call after him, but he doesn't come back, and when I get up to follow him my legs won't hold me.

I slide into a heap on the floor and press my face into my hands. I feel like a ship caught on a rocky shoal, half-drowned and wrecked and abandoned. I don't know if my body can come back from this, but I'm certain that, after tonight, there's no hope that Harry will ever forgive me.

CHAPTER TWENTY-FOUR

49 days until US Olympic Team Trials

HARRY WON'T ANSWER MY CALLS. HE WON'T RESPOND TO my texts. I stay up all night, trying to get ahold of him and tumbling down a shame spiral. I can't believe I said those awful things to him, that I blamed him for my problems, told him he was responsible for *my* struggles. In the morning, I drive over to his house and ring the bell—desperate to talk to him, to apologize, to beg for forgiveness.

But there are no cars in the driveway, and nobody answers the door. I sit at the curb in my car for over an hour, hoping to catch one of the Matthewses coming home, or Harry leaving the house, but the windows are dark. At one point, I think I see a curtain ripple in Harry's upstairs bedroom, but then I figure I must've imagined it.

I fold my arms over the top of the steering wheel and rest my forehead in the crook of my elbow, fighting back panic.

I can't even cry. Terrified thoughts cycle through my mind on an endless loop: *What if our fight did more than hurt his feelings? What if he's not okay?*

The house is quiet when I get home. Dad is at the restaurant, helping Miguel prep for the dinner rush, and Mom is in class. Nina, I assume, is still asleep, but as I trudge up the stairs I hear voices coming from her bedroom. I assume she has a friend over, or even a new boyfriend, but then I recognize one of the voices: Amber.

Maybe she's here to check on me after all the drama of last night. Harry and I were alone in that locker room, and I refused to talk to anyone about it after, but I'm sure people standing near the door could hear us. It's no secret to anyone on the team that we had a massive fight.

But there's only one person I want to see right now, one person I want to talk to about what happened between Harry and me, and I can't get through to him.

Nina's door is partially closed. I knock, then nudge it open. I'm not at all prepared for what I see.

Amber. And Nina. One of my best friends, and my sister, *making out* on Nina's bed.

I take a step back and turn my head, shouting, "Sorry!" Then I hurry across the hallway to my room and slam the door. I was so startled by the sight of Amber and Nina kissing that I'm breathless. Talk about a surprise.

I've known Amber for as long as I've been at GAC, and she told me she was gay as soon as she'd figured it out herself. That was when I realized that we were truly friends—not just teammates, or acquaintances, but real friends, the kind who trust and confide in each other. Now, of course, everyone knows. She's been out since we started high school.

But Nina! As long as she's been old enough to have crushes or be attracted to people, it's always been boys, or at least I think it has. Now I feel stupid for assuming. She's only ever brought boyfriends home, but that doesn't mean she hasn't had girlfriends, too. Maybe she never invited them over or told us about them because she didn't know how we'd react, what Mom and Dad and Bela and the rest of the family would think or do if they found out she wasn't straight.

Something else occurs to me: this is not the first time they've done this. What I saw of that kiss tells me they've had some practice. Which means they've been together for at least a few weeks, if not longer, and I didn't even notice. I've been so focused on swimming and Harry that I missed something that was probably right in front of me.

For some reason, it's this, not the situation with Harry, that moves me to tears. It's a comfort to cry. It reminds me I'm not completely broken inside.

There's a knock at the door. "Susannah?" Amber calls. "Can we come in?"

"Yeah," I say wetly, wiping my face. The door creaks open, but Nina and Amber stay in the hallway, looking at me warily. "I thought you were coming in?"

Amber exhales and forces a smile. "We weren't sure if... how you were feeling, you know. About what you saw?"

A fresh wave of tears bursts out of me. Nina rushes over and puts her arms around me, hugging me in a way she hasn't in years. "What's wrong?" she asks, brushing the hair out of my face.

"I don't know," I sob, pressing my face into her shoulder. She rubs my back and shushes me softly. I don't think Nina has ever been this gentle with me. It only makes me want to hold on tighter.

The room is silent except for my sniffling. Then Amber starts laughing. I lift my head, blinking at her for a few seconds, trying to see the humor. Then it hits me how melodramatic and silly this is, and I start to laugh, too. Nina joins in, and then we're all laughing. Before I know it, my tears have dried up.

Nina hands me a tissue. "Wipe your nose, Booger," she says. She glances at Amber. "Susannah always had the runniest nose as a kid."

I blow my nose a few times. "So, what is *happening*?" I ask Amber. "Don't tell me I walked in on you helping her run lines for the play."

Amber shakes her head. "We're…" She shoots Nina a look. "Hey, we haven't really discussed what we are, have we?"

"Not as of this exact moment, no," Nina replies. "But I guess, if I had to define it without any prior conversations with Amber…"

"Yes?" Amber and I ask.

Nina shrugs. "I guess I'd say we're together. Like, girl-friend and girlfriend. Is that what you were thinking?" she asks Amber, whose face-splitting grin is confirmation enough.

"Since when?" I ask.

"Around Christmas," Nina confesses. My eyes practically bug out of my head. That's almost five months! Harry and I haven't been together much longer than that. "It was, um, you know, casual at first but I think we like each other."

Amber's eyebrows shoot up. "You *think*?"

"She broke up with her boyfriend," Nina says. "I'm trying not to rub it in."

I jerk away from Nina. "I can hear you, you know. And we didn't break up. We had a fight. Harry and I—we're not something that just *ends*."

Nina and Amber exchange a look I can't interpret. It's like they have some information I don't.

I gesture between them. "What's this? What's happening?"

"Amber, didn't you have something you wanted to talk to Susannah about?" Nina asks, bouncing off my bed and over to the door before I can blink.

"Now is not the time," Amber tells her through gritted teeth.

"Tell me what?"

"Oh, don't worry about it," Amber says with a breezy, dismissive wave of her hand. "It's nothing. It can wait."

"It's actually *not* nothing, and it *can't* wait," Nina says. "Tell her. She'll find out on Monday, anyway." She gives Amber an encouraging kiss on the cheek. "I'll talk to you guys later."

"What—" I start to say.

"And, Susannah?" Nina cuts me off, pointing her finger at me. "No telling Mom and Dad about me and Amber. I'll be the one to tell them, got it?"

"When exactly will that be?" I ask.

"Yeah, when exactly will that be?" Amber asks.

"Tonight," Nina says with a smile. She taps her temple. "I've got it all worked out."

She leaves, closing the door behind her. Amber and I are alone. My eyes are puffy and red, I'm sure; they ache and burn from all the crying. Amber takes my hand and squeezes.

"I'm sorry for lying to you about Nina," she says.

I shake my head. "You didn't lie. I never asked. And you don't owe me an explanation. Of all people, I get that there might be reasons to be private about a relationship. I was shocked, is all."

"You burst out crying!"

"It wasn't about that." I close my eyes, pinching them shut, trying to push aside the memory of Harry's face as I hurled accusations at him. "I miss Harry."

"Have you talked to him since last night?"

"No, he won't pick up when I call or text me back. I tried going over to his house but he's either not there or not answering the door. We've never had a fight like this before," I tell her. "I don't know what to do. I don't know how to make this better."

"He adores you," Amber assures me. "But you hurt him. Give him time to cool off."

"I hope that's all it is," I say, but I can't tell her about my worst fears, that Harry's bipolar disorder might affect how he reacts to all this. It's not my right to share.

"If Harry's half as devastated as you are about this fight, I predict he'll be blowing your phone up in no time, begging to see you," Amber says. I give her a small, watery smile.

It's a relief to be with someone who knows and cares about me, who doesn't give a shit what I look like or what I swim like or what I said last night to my boyfriend. In the many years since we met, Amber and Jessa and I have been a trio, so I've always thought of everything as equal, no relationship stronger or closer than the others. But the truth is that Amber has always been the best of us, and the person I trusted most before Harry came along. I'm lucky to have her in my life.

I press my face into her shoulder. "I hate feelings."

"I know," she says, patting my head. "You just want to be one of Dave's heartless robots."

"I don't," I insist. "I'd rather have my heart broken than pretend I don't have one at all."

She pulls back, eyebrows raised. "Wow," she says, "look who's growing."

"Okay, enough. I'm sick of talking and thinking about myself. What did you want to tell me?"

Amber's expression changes. One minute, her face is open and sympathetic, and the next she looks closed off and nervous, even a bit scared. We're sitting cross-legged on the bed, facing each other. I nudge her, trying to get her to look at me, but she's staring over my shoulder with obvious discomfort.

"Is something wrong?" I ask her. "Did something bad happen?"

"No, something good," Amber says, swallowing hard. "I'm quitting GAC. Actually, I'm quitting swimming. Entirely. As of today."

It's like I've taken a cannonball to the stomach. This is the last thing I expected her to say. Amber has been swimming competitively longer than I have. She's one of the best swimmers at GAC, not to mention one of the only girls of color on the team besides me. She can't *quit*.

"Is this because of Nina?" I ask, feeling all the old resentment left over from when my sister quit GAC bubbling to the surface. This is my experience: I'm close to people, then they stop swimming, and we aren't close anymore. I don't want that to happen with Amber. She's too important to me.

"Nina has nothing to do with this," Amber says. "In fact, your sister's the reason I haven't quit already. She told me to give the sport a chance to convince me to stay before making any final decisions. I think she misses it."

"So why are you quitting?"

"Is this really such a surprise to you?" Amber asks. "I thought it was obvious. It's all I've been able to think about this year, how much I want to be done with GAC."

"I had no idea," I tell her. But snippets of conversations we've had start floating back to me: *If a girl I was into liked me back, I'd quit GAC tomorrow… Don't you care about qualifying for Trials? Not really… Did you consider quitting? After you tore your shoulder? I think about it, sometimes…*

She's been trying to tell me for months—the entire season—but I wasn't paying attention.

Amber chews her thumbnail. "Swimming doesn't make me happy anymore. It hasn't for a long time. But I wasn't sure I was ready until yesterday, when I realized it might be bad for me."

Her eyes meet mine. "The way Dave treated you and Harry was atrocious. Manipulating you like that, lording his authority over you, playing God with your lives and careers. You could see on his face how much he enjoyed making you both squirm. He hurt you to watch you hurt, even though there was a very real chance you could aggravate your actual physical injury. I don't want anyone to have that kind of power over me."

"Plus," she concludes with a shrug, "there are other things I want to do with my time."

"Like hang out with Nina?" I envy her. I wouldn't be in this situation with Harry right now if I'd put our relationship before my own pride. I don't think I could ever give up swimming for him, but I wish I could go back and make some different choices.

"Partly," she says. "I've always wanted to be in the color guard, ever since my cousin Steph joined when she was in high school. And I'm thinking about trying out for the fall play."

"That sounds great," I tell her.

She laughs like she doesn't buy it. I know how full of false cheer I sound, but I'm reeling from the shock of all this. With Harry not speaking to me, Jessa drifting away and Amber leaving GAC, my list of allies in the pool has narrowed to one: Beth. What will I do if she disappears, too?

But there's also a weird feeling in my stomach, a tiny black hole that opens up and whispers: *I wish I could quit, too.* I stifle it immediately. There's a possibility that I have already lost Harry. If I lose my Olympic dream, I won't have anything left.

"You're taking this better than I expected," Amber says.

"You've clearly given this a lot of thought. If you're happy, that should be enough for me. Would you like me to tear my clothes and wail inconsolably?" I joke.

Amber smiles. "It's not that big of a deal."

Swimming is our lives, which means that life as she knows it is over for Amber—that seems like a big deal to me, even if she is happy about it. But that is one hundred percent not my business.

"Harry will come around," Amber assures me.

"I hope you're right," I say.

CHAPTER TWENTY-FIVE

42 days until US Olympic Team Trials

IT'S A WEEK BEFORE I HEAR FROM HARRY. HE SKIPS PRACTICE, which pisses Dave off. He hauls me into his office on Thursday after practice to grill me about where Harry's at and just what the hell he's up to.

"I don't know," I say, fists clenched at my sides. I don't want to be in the same room as Dave. "He won't talk to me. I asked his best friend what's going on, but he hasn't heard from Harry, either."

I'm not sure I believe Tucker. He has no reason to be loyal to me. I don't even know whether Tucker would tell me if something was wrong with Harry beyond what happened between us, which is what I'm really worried about. When he didn't show up for practice, or school, I became increasingly frantic. What if it's worse than our fight?

"When you hear from him, you tell that kid if he doesn't get his ass back into this pool ASAP he's off the team," Dave says. "I'm not going to tolerate any crybabies. I mean, look at you."

"What *about* me?"

If he's calling me a crybaby, I'm going to straight up punch him. Practice without Harry and Amber has made me feel especially on edge. Jessa only makes things worse. There are so few weeks left before Trials, and there's so very much at stake—she's constantly reminding me of that. It's gotten to the point where we're pretty much not speaking.

The pressure is crushing. I used to think I carried my burdens alone, but now I realize my friends were holding some of the weight. I've never felt so grateful, or missed them so much.

I miss Harry so, so much.

"Even after everything, you're still here," Dave says with a shrug. Then he walks off, and I can almost see the last remaining shreds of my dignity clinging to his shoes like toilet paper.

Even after everything, I'm still here, taking what he dishes out, swimming through the pain. What is it about this dream that makes me willing to endure it all? I can't rationalize it anymore, even to myself. It's gone beyond reason, a logic only the heart knows.

Not, actually, unlike my love for Harry. I can't explain it. It just *is*.

What I still can't figure out is how many loves you're allowed to have before you run the risk of losing them all.

Finally, on Sunday, over a week after the Battle of the Sexes meet, my phone rings and Harry's name pops up on the screen. I stare at it, stunned both by the fact that he's calling me and the realization that I'd resigned myself to the possibility he never would. I feel relieved and anxious all at the same time. I answer the call before it clicks over to voice mail.

"Hello?"

I wait for Harry to speak. There's a long pause, then his voice crackles through the phone. It sounds strained. A rope tightens around my heart. Something is wrong.

"Susie?"

"Harry." I exhale his name. "I'm so sorry. Please don't hate me. I've been calling and texting—I even came by your house. I left messages. I've been so…" A thousand different words get stuck in my throat. Distraught. Worried. Anguished. *Sorry, so sorry…* I don't think I'll ever be able to say it enough.

"Uh—" He hitches in a deep, ragged breath. I brace myself, certain I know what's coming. He's calling to break up with me. It's over.

But after all the agonizing I've done in the last nine months over whether or not I should be with Harry, I don't feel anything close to relief. I feel terrified. I don't want to lose him.

"Susie," he says. His voice is horribly flat. "I did a bad thing."

"With who?" I ask, picturing Fee.

"No—I—" Another deep breath. "I didn't mean to do it."

"Harry, what happened?"

"I didn't mean to. I was just trying—" he sounds like he's fighting for every word "—to make it better. But I cut too deep," he says, and it's like I've suddenly walked off a cliff, or been yanked from the safety of a beach by a strong and vicious current. Falling, sinking.

"Too deep?" I repeat. My whole body goes numb.

"There's blood," he says. His voice is getting softer, like a fading radio signal. "I need…help."

I snap into crisis mode. "I'm going to call 911 and then I'm coming over. Okay?"

"Yes," he whispers.

"I'm going to stay on the phone the whole time—don't hang up."

We have a house line—it came with our cable package—but we never use it. Right now, it's as if this is the reason we have it, because the universe knew one day I would need it. I dial 911. It feels like my hands should be shaking, but they're steady as I punch in the numbers. A strange sense of calm floats down over me. My mind is sharp and clear, focused on this critical task.

"Nine-one-one, what's your emergency?"

"I think my boyfriend might have hurt himself," I tell the operator.

"What is your current location?"

"I'm not with him. I'm at my house, but I'm heading over there now." I rattle off Harry's home address. "He cut himself, and he said he did it too deep. He called me and he sounded weak on the phone. He's afraid."

My voice breaks on the last two words, shattering the calm feeling. She tells me to stay on the line as I run to the car, but I tell her I can't—it's a landline, and I'm leaving—then hang up. My parents are out, and Nina's with Amber somewhere. Part of me is grateful there's nobody to ask questions and slow me down. Another part wishes there were someone, anyone, here—someone more capable than me.

There's nobody to talk to now but Harry, who only says, "Yes," when I ask if he's still there.

I reach Harry's house before the ambulance arrives. Paula

must be on shift—her car is gone—and Bruce isn't home, either. The front door is locked, but Harry told me once where their spare key was hidden. I reach into the mouth of a large ceramic frog near the door and feel around with my fingers until I find it.

"Harry?" I call as I enter the house. There's no answer.

I climb the stairs and peer into his bedroom. He isn't there, but it's been ransacked: lamps overturned, sheets torn off the bed, books everywhere. His laptop is sitting half-open on its side in a corner of the room. It's like he tore the place apart. There are travel-size bottles of alcohol scattered underneath Harry's desk. Understanding creeps over me like a cold shadow.

The bathroom door is open, and I can see Harry inside, slumped against the toilet. His skin is pale and translucent as velum, and his eyes are closed.

"Harry?" I swallow hard against rising bile. It burns my throat. My vision begins to waver as panic puts me in a choke hold, but I dig my nails into my palm and the dizziness recedes.

"Susie?" His eyes flutter open. They're bloodshot and red, unfocused.

Adrenaline focuses my mind the way the strong smell of peppermint can clear the sinuses. Like most swimmers, I've taken lifeguarding courses, so I'm CPR and first-aid certified. I tend to him the way I've been taught, forcing myself to stay calm.

"I'm here," I tell him, because when I was afraid and hurt the thing that made it all so much worse was how alone I felt, how isolated by the pain. I brush the hair off his sweat-drenched forehead and caress his hot skin with my thumb. "I'm here, Harry. You're going to be okay."

An ambulance wails in the distance. *Please be for us*, I think as the sirens grow louder, entering Harry's neighborhood, turning down the street.

Anticipating the paramedics, I left the front door wide open when I came in. I call out our location as they rush into the house and up the stairs. I stand aside while they carry him on a gurney down the stairs. It takes me a second to realize I should go after them, that I can even move. Nobody gives me permission to go with him in the ambulance, but nobody tries to stop me as I climb in. I spend the ride frozen in my seat, watching through a tiny window as they work on him. There's a burning in my fingers and toes, like I've been electrocuted.

When we get to the hospital they wheel him through a set of swinging doors. I try to follow, but someone stops me with a gentle hand on my chest—a woman dressed in scrubs, who has obviously vacated the spot behind the empty intake desk. Harry sits up on the gurney like a jack-in-the-box, and our eyes lock from all the way down the long hallway before the doors completely shut.

Desperate to get to him, I feint left in an attempt to get past the woman who kept me from following him, but she grabs me and pulls me back firmly.

"You have to stay out here," she tells me.

She guides me to a waiting room, where I fall into one of the hard plastic chairs. The woman returns to her desk to fetch a clipboard stuffed with forms, which she brings over to me. She sits beside me and asks me questions, only some of which I can answer. *Harry—no, Harrison Matthews, his mom is a nurse here, you have to call her.* I tell her his address, his birth date, but there are things I don't know: his social security number, his insurance provider, the medications he's taking, his middle name. Why don't I know his middle name?

She writes down what I give her, then gets up to notify Paula.

"Can I call someone for you?" she asks.

Sometime later—I'm not sure how much, it passes both quickly and slowly, and I lost my phone somewhere along the way so I can't even check it—Mom appears. She wraps her arms around me and rocks me as I sob into her shoulder, muttering over and over, "It's all my fault, it's all my fault."

"Oh, sweetheart," Mom whispers, rubbing my back in wide, slow circles. "It's not."

I wipe snot and tears off my face with the sleeve of my sweatshirt. "I hurt him."

"People fight," she says. She pulls back to look in my eyes, taking my chin in her palm. "Couples fight all the time. We say awful things to each other out of frustration and fear and even love. You didn't know that this was what would happen."

I didn't know for sure, but I should've anticipated it. I knew he'd done it before, when he was under stress. He'd told me his doctor had been adjusting his medication. That was why he was sick back in October, why he didn't come to California with the rest of us. He could have been struggling all this time without me knowing, for the same reason I didn't realize swimming made Amber so unhappy or that she was falling in love with my sister: *I wasn't paying attention.*

I've been so consumed with my own problems that I failed to see or wonder what was going on in the lives of the people I love. Shame and fear pour over me. I gulp air like I've just resurfaced from the deep, dark bottom of a lake, but there's

no relief in filling my lungs. Breathing feels like drowning.
I have no control over anything.

I stare at my hands like I don't remember how to use them.
They feel heavy in my lap.

"It's going to be all right."

I raise my eyes to meet Paula's. "Is it?" I ask, blinking away
tears.

My eyes feel like they've been scrubbed with sandpaper.
I'm exhausted. It's been hours since I discovered Harry in
that upstairs bathroom, since the ambulance delivered us to
the emergency room doors. Mom hasn't left my side. Harry's
parents got here as soon as they could.

"Yes," Paula assures me with the confidence of someone
who's been through this before. But beneath the bravado, I
can glimpse the fear of a mother whose training and rational-
izations fail her when the patient is her son. "He's stable now.
They've stitched him up. There was a lot of blood, but the
cuts were mostly superficial. They have him on some mild
tranquilizers. He's sleeping."

I take a deep breath and let it out slowly. These are the
exact sorts of situations in which I do not shine. Give me a
crisis, an urgent need for my assistance, and I'll immediately
spring into action, do what needs to be done to the best of
my ability. But when the dust has settled and it's time to sort
through the rubble, all that resolve and focus crumbles, and
I dissolve into a pathetic, worthless mess.

I force my attention back to Paula. "Do you think he did
this because of our fight?" Mom's arms tighten around me.

"I don't know everything that went on between the two
of you," she says. "But I could see that whatever happened at

that meet put him under a tremendous amount of stress. He may have walked away from your argument thinking that you blamed him for things he has no control over, even if that wasn't your intention. Your good opinion is so important to him. If he thought he'd lost that, he may have felt the need to rely on coping methods that made sense to him once before."

Bruce walks into the waiting room looking like someone's hit him over the head, which is how I know he's come from Harry's room. He was on a business trip in New York, but he took the next flight out as soon as Paula called him. He's still wearing a suit, but it's rumpled and creased.

"What happens now?" I ask.

"We're moving Harry tomorrow," Bruce explains, taking Paula's hand. "They found a bed for him at a hospital that specializes in more long-term care. It's a place he's been before. They'll get him back on his feet."

This isn't what I expected. I thought that once he was okay, he would get to go home. "How long will he be there?"

"As long as he needs," Paula says. She looks as though she hasn't slept in days. "One of the drugs Harry was taking had some very unpleasant side effects, and he wanted to go off it. We were working with his doctor to find a more palatable solution, but it's been a challenge. For the last few months, Harry's medication has been less effective at controlling his moods."

"We're going to set him up at Regency," Bruce tells me. "It's a psychiatric hospital for minors. There will be other kids for him to talk to, and doctors who understand the way bipolar disorder manifests in teenagers. They'll help him there."

I'm out of my depth here. All I can do is nod and trust that they're doing what's best for Harry.

CHAPTER TWENTY-SIX

30 days until US Olympic Team Trials

FOR THE FIRST WEEK AND A HALF OF HIS INPATIENT TREAT-ment, there's no opportunity for me to visit Harry. His days are scheduled from morning until night with recreational and group therapies, medication management sessions, consultations with his psychiatrist and meetings with his social worker—all tailored to his specific needs. I talk to Paula every day after I get home from practice, eager to know how he's doing. Given everything that happened, I'm grateful he's given her permission to discuss his progress with me.

"When you enter inpatient hospitalization, a case manager evaluates the severity of your situation," Paula explains. "Harry's case manager doesn't believe he poses further danger to himself, and he's been taking his medication and following the program. We're hoping that at our next family therapy session, the doctors will tell us he's recovered enough to start outpatient treatment."

This means that Harry will be able to go home at night, but he'll still spend his day at Regency, learning how to cope with his symptoms and manage his illness. He'll also receive daily psychiatric evaluation, to track how the new medications are working.

"Harry spent most of that weekend you found him in a mixed state," Paula tells me. "In the daytime, when I was home, he was significantly depressed. He'd sleep a lot, wasn't eating much, and now I know he was drinking. At night, after I left for my shifts, he became hypomanic. Bruce was traveling for work, so there was nobody home with him. He was journaling frantically. He wrote all over that swimming notebook you got him for Christmas."

I ask what he wrote, but Paula tells me most of it is illegible. I wonder if she knows that the notebook isn't his, it's mine, and if that means anything, but I don't want to interrupt her. She says Harry also engaged in other hypomanic behaviors. He spent hundreds of dollars online and took long runs around town in the dark to quiet his racing thoughts.

"You have to understand, Susannah," she says. "In the time you've known him, Harry's been more stable than I've ever seen him. He has learned to manage his illness quite capably, and what to do if things get bad, if he thinks he might hurt himself or need medical intervention. He seemed in control of his situation, even though he was feeling depressed. But that all changes if he's not sober."

I remember what Harry told me, how alcohol impairs the effectiveness of his medication.

"If I'd known he was drinking," Paula continues, "I never would have left him alone."

Her voice breaks, and my heart goes out to her. It can't be easy to protect your kid at the same time you're trying to let them grow up.

Paula warns me that Harry's mixed state is over, the euphoric high of hypomania gone. He's suffering from a depression that will not abate.

"His doctors are still adjusting his medication, trying to find something that works the way the old combination did," she says. "He's starting to feel better, but he's still low energy, exhausted and deeply sad. I'm telling you all of this so you aren't surprised when you see him. More than anything, the best thing we can do as the people who love him is show him support and understanding."

Regency has rules about who can visit someone who's going through adolescent inpatient treatment—family only. But Harry's been asking for me, and Paula requested that an exception be made given how well he's progressing. She thinks it will be good for him to see me, and his doctor and social worker both agreed. I want to see him, but I'm worried that it will trigger upsetting memories of our fight. More than anything, I don't want to cause him any more pain.

"You won't be left alone with him," Paula assures me. "The hospital requires visitors under eighteen to be accompanied by a parent or guardian. They'll be in the room with you the whole time, and the door will be propped. The meeting room is close to the nurses' station and they'll be keeping a close watch. If he's not feeling up to it the day you visit, or his caretakers believe it would harm him to see you, they won't let you in. But every time we see him, he asks about you, more than anyone else."

"Will you tell him I'm excited to see him?" I ask. Paula promises she will.

My visit is scheduled for Friday after practice, which I spend in a fog so dense I don't even notice that Dave and Beth aren't speaking until Jessa points it out.

"They're either secretly dating, or plotting each other's murders," she says under her breath during a break between sets.

"Pretty sure it's not the first one," I mutter.

Their dislike of each other has only escalated since the Battle of the Sexes meet. It's putting us all on edge. I hope like hell they can keep it together until Trials.

At least I have swimming to pour all my frustration and worry into. In the water there's only one way forward. The simplicity of swimming has always been one of my favorite things about it.

Mom agreed to come with me to Regency. As we drive to the hospital, I think about something Paula said to me last night on the phone.

"Several factors contributed to this," she told me in a calm, steady voice that must serve her well as a nurse. "Harry's meds were off. He was upset. He started drinking. Depression tells you that you're worthless, that people hate you, that you can't do anything right. It convinces you that you deserve the pain you're experiencing. Harry knows that you care for him, in spite of the argument you had, but his depression did everything it could to make him believe otherwise. I know you feel guilty—we all do. You did not do this to him, but it's important to treat people with compassion, whether they have a mental illness or not. We can never truly know what someone else is going through."

I hate thinking about that night at the meet, the horrible words I flung at Harry—blaming him for things that weren't his fault, lashing out at him because I was angry and afraid. I know better than to act that way toward someone I love, but I did it anyway, because I was overwhelmed by my own suffering.

It wasn't him I was mad at—it was me. When I decided to be with Harry, I thought I knew what it meant to let a new person in my life, someone with their own needs and wants and struggles. I believed I could handle it, because I believed I could handle anything life threw my way. Hadn't the last few years been proof of that?

The truth is, I was still the center of my own universe, locked in a prison of my own making. I couldn't find a way to break free of it. Throwing myself against the bars of my cage won't accomplish anything, and neither will pushing away everyone I love. There has to be a better path. I hope that I can find it, and that—if I do—I'll have the courage to take it.

But blaming myself won't help Harry, or change what happened. I need to listen to him, and let him tell me what he needs. Maybe, through focusing on someone else for a change, I'll figure out what I need, too.

I bring Red Vines to Regency. Food is allowed, but only if Harry consumes it during our visit. He's not allowed to take it back to his room. I wish I could think of something to give him that he can keep, to remind him that I'm thinking about him, but between the regulations and the limits of my own imagination, I'm drawing a blank. If I could fill his entire hospital room with rubber ducks, I would.

Once we're checked in, Mom and I take a seat in the waiting area. There are signs posted that list the objects visitors cannot bring in to see a patient: weapons or sharp objects, drugs, alcohol, cigarettes or anything with strings. I'm wearing gym shoes, so I remove the laces and hand them to the nurse, who locks them away in a drawer.

Harry is already with a visitor, so I have to wait for that person to leave before I can see him. Paula and Bruce were here earlier today, so it must be Tucker. He must've found out from Harry, or maybe Jessa, what happened at the Battle of the Sexes meet, and the few times I've seen him in the halls since then he's pointedly ignored my attempts to talk to him. I'm nervous about running into him here.

Mom goes to the bathroom. I try to read a book for school, but my mind keeps wandering. I stare at the pages until the words blur together in a series of gray lines.

A tall white man enters the waiting area and speaks briefly with the nurse. He's wearing black pants and a black long-sleeved button-down shirt, and he has a light jacket draped over his arm. His back is to me, but when he turns I notice he's wearing a Roman collar. He thanks the nurse and starts toward the door, but stops when she calls my name and tells me Harry can see me now.

"Susannah?" he says, like he knows me. It takes me by surprise. My parents were raised Catholic but they're not much for church. We don't even belong to a parish. I don't know any priests personally.

"Yes?"

"You're here to see Harry Matthews."

I nod. Harry mentioned a priest to me once, his sobriety coach. This must be him.

"Hi," he says, extending a hand for me to shake. In the other hand, he's holding a book, but I can't see the cover. "I'm Bob."

"*Father* Bob?"

He tilts his head and smiles warmly. "Sure. Or just Bob. Whichever you prefer."

"I don't think I have a preference," I tell him. His smile widens.

"Let's stick with Bob," he says. "Unless you have something you'd like to confess."

I feel all the blood drain from my face. Does he know what happened with me and Harry?

"I was only kidding," he says. "I'm sorry, I didn't mean to upset you."

"You didn't," I lie. "How is Harry?"

"He's been through a lot, so if you take that into consideration, he seems well," Bob says. "They're helping him here. He's determined to recover, and I have no doubt he will in time."

There's something about the way Bob says it that makes me believe it. Maybe it's the confidence that comes with being a man of God, though I'm not sure I believe in God, or the wisdom of priests for that matter. The closest I've ever come to a religious experience is a really great race.

Maybe that's where my god lives: in the water, watching over me from inside the grates and gutters of an Olympic-size pool.

I nod at the book in his hand. "Were you reading to him

from the Bible?" I've never known Harry to be religious. I doubt he would enjoy being preached to, even by someone he likes.

"Oh, no, this isn't the Bible," he says, turning the book so I can read the title. *Pale Blue Dot* by Carl Sagan. It's got a big picture of the planet Jupiter on the cover.

"This book made a big impression on me as a young man," he explains. "I thought Harry might get something out of it."

"Did he read it?" It doesn't look like the sort of thing Harry would pick up. He's more of an airport-thriller sort of guy.

Bob laughs. "No. Brilliant book, but dense. It's not for everyone, I guess. We talked about it for a while today instead."

He turns to a page in the book and hands it to me. It's a photograph taken—the caption tells me—by the *Voyager 1* space probe from almost four billion miles away from Earth. The blackness of space is striped by streaks of colored light. In the middle of a brown band to the far right of the picture, there's a tiny mark that looks white, not blue, to me. Apparently, that mark is Earth. Looking at it makes me feel incredibly small.

"'A point of pale light,' that's how Sagan described the way Earth looks in this picture," Bob says. "I was trying to explain to Harry about perspective, but I don't think he grasped my meaning."

I close the book and hand it back to him. "Perspective?"

"There are two ways to look at that picture," Bob says. "I think Harry chooses...not the wrong way, necessarily, but not the way I meant when I showed it to him."

"How so?"

"He thought I was saying our lives are insignificant because they're small and short. I confess that seeing a vast and varied world like Earth as a tiny speck of dust in the midst of such great darkness might lead you to that conclusion. But what I was trying to tell him is that the speck is *important*, precisely because it is *there*. That was what Sagan was saying, too."

"I'm not sure I understand," I admit. These aren't the sort of things I spend much time thinking about. To an athlete, the arena is the universe. Everything else often feels like a movie set.

"Humans are alone in the universe, or if we're not, it's unlikely we'll ever know otherwise. The pale blue dot is the only one of its kind, the only home we'll ever have. Harry is the only one of his kind there has ever been, and that there will ever be. So are you. So am I.

"No matter how deeply he might sometimes loathe or fear or doubt himself, I was trying to make him understand that he must love himself, too, be kind to himself and do right by himself as much as he possibly can. We're all points of pale light swimming in our own seas of darkness, so it's our responsibility to take care of ourselves, and each other. That's what I wanted him to see, and I think someday he will."

I consider what he said, then tell him, "I like that."

"I'm glad you find it comforting."

"I don't know if *comforting* is the right word."

Bob laughs. "You reminded me of someone just then. I met her when she was around your age." He tucks the book under his arm. "What don't you find comforting about the profound and heartfelt speech I just gave?"

"It doesn't change anything. People still get hurt. They lose things—and people—that mean everything to them. We don't always take care of each other the way that we should."

I fight back against the tears that spring to my eyes. "So how is being a point of pale light floating in a sea of infinite blackness supposed to give us comfort?"

"It's not."

"Then why—"

"If it did, I would of course be pleased—as a priest I'm nothing if not a peddler of hope, and like all good peddlers I feel proud when somebody buys what I'm selling. But, Susannah, it's terrible, the things that people suffer. It takes more than cosmological philosophy to change that reality."

"What about God's plan? Don't you believe in that?"

"The world isn't governed by God's plan," Bob says. "That's precisely what's wrong with it. The downside to free *human* will is that people can and do make choices that hurt themselves and others."

It's hard not to think of the hurtful choices I've made. He's right about that part at least. But: "Harry's illness isn't a choice."

"No," Bob agrees. "And it isn't his fault. I can't tell you why he has it. I can't even say if there *is* a reason. But I do know that Harry fights against the pain and hardship it causes him, that he's determined to live with it and makes choices that increase his happiness even as sorrow tugs at him. In the process, he makes others happy, too. If that's not an act of being light, I don't know what is."

"What's a priest doing reading cosmology for fun?" I ask.

"I used to be a physicist," Bob tells me. "You're aware of how Harry and I know each other?"

I nod.

"Scientific study is competitive," Bob explains. "The pressure to produce brilliant, groundbreaking work is overwhelming. I wanted to be the best, and when I started to suspect I couldn't be, I tried to drown those feelings, to blunt them with whatever I could find. But they never went away.

"When I got sober, my sponsor told me something that changed my life. She said that failure is an intersection. You have the option to move forward, to try again, but you can also turn and follow a new path. Religion gave me solace during that hard time, so I became a priest. At least then, I figured, my life wouldn't be—couldn't be—all about me. What I could achieve became directly related to how many people I could help, not what I could do for myself. Maybe it was another way of distracting myself from failure. But it's a lot better than what I was doing."

I feel light-headed all of a sudden, and like the ground has disappeared from under my feet.

"Failure is an intersection," I repeat softly. I've never thought of it like that. To me, failure has always been a wall I slam myself against over and over again, desperate to force myself through it. Changing course never felt like a real option. But if my single-minded focus has made me selfish, and turned me into a person I don't want to be, what value will success even have?

"Susannah?"

Mom is back from the bathroom. She gives Father Bob a questioning look. I wonder how much she overheard. I realize that I've said more to Father Bob about what I'm feeling than I've shared with my own parents.

"I'm going to see Harry now," I tell Father Bob.

He smiles at me and departs through the main doors without introducing himself to my mom or saying goodbye. It's surprising how quickly he disappears, one minute there, the next gone. I wonder if, later, I'll entertain the possibility I might've imagined him.

A nurse escorts us to the meeting room where Harry is waiting. It's small, but there's no one else in here right now, so we have some semblance of privacy, even with my mom hovering and the door open all the way. The room is mostly empty, just a table and a few chairs in one corner and two brown leather sofas in the other.

Harry's sitting at the table. He looks tired and pale, and his hair has grown out enough that a lock of it falls across his forehead.

I can feel my heartbeat in my throat, and my hands are shaking so badly that the Red Vines package crinkles, but my stomach wheels like a flock of birds in the sky. It's so good to see him.

"Hi," Harry says. I give him my warmest smile.

"You can sit," he says, nodding at the chair across the table. I take it, feeling shaky. When I get anxious before races, I bounce on my toes, swing my arms, adjust my cap and goggles a few times to release my nervous energy. I have no rituals to fall back on here.

Mom settles at the far end of one of the couches. "Pretend I'm not here," she says. "It's wonderful to see you, Harry."

"Thanks, Mrs. Ramos," he says, ducking his head nervously.

We sit for a few seconds in silence. Harry avoids my eyes as I continue to smile at him. I breathe slowly, carefully, desperate to calm the frantic pounding of blood through my veins. Now is not the time to give in to awkwardness or uncertainty or—worse—panic at feeling so helpless in the face of Harry's pain. I have a plan. Focus on Harry. Let him tell me, with his body language and his words, what he needs. Do whatever I can to help.

I always do better with a plan.

"Tell me something, Susie," he says.

"What do you want to know?" I ask gently.

"Anything. What's going on out there?" he asks, glancing at the window that looks out over the park. "In the world."

A stream of bad news about wildfires in California and hurricanes in Florida and corrupt politicians getting away with their crimes shoves its way into my brain, but I stop it before it reaches my mouth. I don't think that's what he's asking. He doesn't want to know about *the* world. He wants to know about *our* world.

"Amber quit swimming," I tell him. He nods solemnly, but he doesn't seem surprised. I wonder if I was the only one who couldn't tell how miserable it made her. "She doesn't seem to regret it at all."

Harry picks at a scratch on the surface of the table with his fingernails. "You must miss her."

Not as much as I miss you, I think. But I can't dwell on that, not here. I'm with him now, and I have to focus on being in the moment. It's never been an easy thing for me to do, but I'm trying.

"Oh, and Amber was secretly dating my sister for, like, five months," I tell him. "They're public now, though. It's excruciatingly sweet."

As she promised, Nina came out to my parents as pansexual, and told them about Amber. They're open at school, too, holding hands as they walk down the hallways and kissing between classes. Amber and I haven't been hanging out as much, not with Trials a month away, but every time I see her it's like someone turned on a light bulb inside of her—she radiates joy.

I'm glad for her, and for Nina, but seeing how content Amber is now that she's done with the sport has been bringing up some complicated feelings. Sometimes I wonder whether, if I'd done the same thing, I'd be happier, too.

Harry's eyes widen in surprise. "Really? Then they were way better at hiding it than we were."

"Thank you!" I relax a bit in the chair. "Jessa claims she suspected, but I knew I couldn't be the only one who didn't see it coming. Seems obvious in retrospect, though."

"Jessa didn't know," he says, flicking a piece of fluff off his sweatpants. "She said that because she always has to make you feel like you're not as smart as her, or as good of a swimmer. It's how she tries to control her fear that you're better than she is."

I raise my eyebrows at him. I knew he didn't like Jessa, but he rarely criticized her in front of me. "How long have you been holding that one in?"

He mimics my expression. "How long have you been letting her get away with it because you're secretly afraid she's right?" he asks sharply.

I exhale slowly. "You have every right to be pissed at me."

"No," he says, sounding defeated. "You're pissed at me."

"*No,*" I insist. "I'm not. Not at *all.*"

"You told me I ruined your life," he says, turning back to the window, like it's too painful to watch the expression on my face as the accusation lands. It's so hard to hear, and even harder to remember, because I *did* say it. Even if I didn't mean it.

I think of Mom over in the corner, pretending not to listen. She only knows that we fought. She doesn't know what I said. Looking back on that ugliness isn't easy, but it's the truth. I've been lying to myself, and everyone else, for so long, about what I can handle without wanting to break. It's almost a relief to look a moment I'm not proud of in the face and realize it *won't* break me. I have to hope that it will only make me better.

"I didn't mean it," I say softly. "If I could take it back, I would."

"I know," he says, bracing himself. "But you were right."

"I was not right," I tell him. "You didn't ruin my life. You woke me up. I was in pain when I said those things, and the pain made me angry and mean. But that's not an excuse. The pain wasn't your fault, and I never should've taken it out on you. It wasn't fair."

He lifts his eyes to meet mine. "I knew Dave wanted me to race against you, and I didn't say anything. You were right to hate me."

"I don't hate you," I say. "Not for that, not for anything. You should swim in any race you want. I never wanted to be the sort of person you can't tell things to because you're afraid of how I would react, but I became that person anyway, because I was so caught up in myself I couldn't see straight. Dave knew that about me. I'm pissed at myself for proving it, but that isn't your fault, either. I should've known better. I did know better. I just let myself forget because forgetting was easier than figuring out how to change."

I keep thinking about that meet, how everything would've been different if I'd done what I'd promised and treated it like it didn't matter. If I'd laughed when I found out Harry

and I were going to compete against each other, if I'd taken seriously the anthem that has carried us through so much: *When you win, I win.* If I'd listened to Beth and decided not to swim at all. If I'd decided to show Dave he couldn't push me around, or—better still—not given him a single thought.

But there are no do-overs. If nothing else, swimming taught me that. All you can do is get back up on the block and try again.

Harry closes his eyes. "I wasn't trying to kill myself," he says in a voice so low it's almost a whisper. "I promise, Susie. That wasn't what I wanted."

"Can you tell me what you were feeling?" I ask, choosing my words with care. It's like I'm picking my way across a rope bridge hanging over a canyon, trying to stay upright as it sways and sways. I'm terrified of stepping through a rotted board and plunging into the yawning gap below.

"I wanted a release. Something to distract from the pain in here." He presses his hand to his chest. "Handle it in the only way that made sense to me at the time."

He speaks slowly, as if every word hurts on its way out. "I wasn't sober, and I was having trouble with my medication, and I cut too deep."

My mouth goes dry. I'm scared for him, scared of how unprepared for all this I am. Outside smoke isn't always a good thing. Bad things come out of nowhere, too.

I want so badly to be here for him in the right way, to say all the right things. I've been reading about how to support a loved one who is bipolar, something I should've done a long time ago. All the resources I've found say that it's important to let the person know that an episode doesn't affect how you see them. That you still love them as much as you ever did.

"I'm so sorry you went through that," I say. "It doesn't change what I think of you, or how I feel about you, in any way."

"Really?" he asks, rubbing his face. He hangs his head and massages his temples with the heels of his palms.

"Really," I say. "How are you feeling now?"

Harry shrugs. "Tired. Weak. Slow. Like I'm walking through mud." His attention shifts slowly to the package of Red Vines in my hand. I'd forgotten them entirely. "Are those for me?"

I place them in front of him. "It's silly. But you love them so much. You're the only person I know who does. They remind me of you."

He fiddles with the package for a moment, playing with the sealed plastic edge. Then he opens them and pulls one out, but he doesn't eat it. He coils the strip of red licorice around his finger and presses his thumbnail into the soft candy.

"You didn't have to come," he says. "Did my mom tell you that? I told her to tell you."

I put my hand on his, completely forgetting about the no-touching rule. The sudden contact shocks him into looking at me, his blue gaze pinning me down. I squeeze his fingers, trying to telegraph that I'm here with him.

"She said you were asking for me," I reply.

"I had to see you, but I didn't want *you* to see *me*, not like this," Harry says. "I never wanted you to see me like this."

"I wanted to come," I tell him. "I always want to see you. You're my favorite—" Emotion makes my voice wobble. "My *favorite* person, in the entire world."

Harry's eyes flicker across my face, then he stares at the floor again. There are tears in his eyes. He's overwhelmed. His broad shoulders bow inward and he bends slightly forward, as if he's being crushed beneath a massive weight. The bigness and strength that propel him through the water seem diminished by his circumstances. He's exhausted. I ache for him.

"This is so fucking awful." He nearly chokes on the words. "I hate it here. I hate myself. I hate what I did. I hate that you saw." His voice breaks. "I want to go back."

"I know," I whisper, wiping my eyes. I have no wisdom to share, only the one thing I know to be true. "We can't go back. But we can start over. You'll feel better someday. And I will be by your side, with you, as much and as long as you want me there."

"I already fucked up once before," he says. "Swimming, changing schools, being with you—this was supposed to be my second chance, and I ruined it."

"You didn't ruin it," I assure him. "And you don't get just one second chance."

"Yeah, you do," he says with a sigh. "It's in the name."

"So we get third chances, and fourth chances, and fifth chances," I tell him. "And on and on, as long as we don't give up."

"Since when are you the optimist in this relationship?" he asks. Then his face crumples. I wish I could see into his mind. I want to help him, to bear his pain with him, but I'm here on the outside, and I don't know if, by relentlessly peddling hope, I'm only making things worse.

"I was so angry," he says. "After the meet. At you, at me, at Dave, at the whole fucking situation. I was driving and thinking about us and how much you must hate me, and I was spiraling down into this well of despair, hearing you say over and over again, *my man*, like I was something to be ashamed of, and I felt so shitty. I was driving like a hundred miles an hour down that dark road near school, thinking: *She doesn't love you, why would she love you, you're a loser, you're crazy.*"

"I thought the same things on the way home from that meet," I confess. "*He doesn't love you, why would he love you, you're a loser, you're a failure, you're broken.* But I'm not broken, and you're not crazy. We aren't perfect, but we are doing our best."

He sighs. He looks even more tired and drawn than he did when I arrived. The effort it's taking to talk to me about all this is draining him. I should probably leave soon, but I don't want to go.

"Maybe some of it is true," he says. "Maybe I am crazy, after all. Just like my dad."

"You're *not*," I insist.

"Maybe," he replies. "Or maybe this is the start of a lifetime in and out of places like this one. That's how Jeremy is. He can't hold down a job, he's destroyed all of his relationships… This place is just like the place they put him in, and I'm no different than him."

"That's not true."

"You don't know. You've never met him. Trust me, he and I, we're the same."

"You're not the *same* as anybody."

He growls in frustration, but I keep holding his hand. He's using the other one to rip the Red Vines I brought into little pieces. They're scattered like confetti all over the scuffed wooden table.

"I'm here," I tell him. "I'm right here with you. What can I do to help?"

"I don't know how long it will take for me to recover,"

Harry says. "I have good days, and bad days. My doctors are still experimenting with my medication. Sometimes I can barely get up the energy to walk down the hall to group therapy, or pick up a crayon during the art sessions. I meant it when I said I wasn't trying to kill myself, but sometimes I don't want to be alive."

It takes all my bodily control not to flinch at that. Memories of the day I found him shove their way into my head, but I push them away and concentrate on what Harry is saying.

"I know that's the chemicals in my brain talking, Susie, but knowing that doesn't make it feel any different," he says. "And it's the fucking worst. I don't want you to have to deal with it. I can't put you through that. It's bad enough my mom and Bruce have to see it. We have to break up. It's not good for either of us to be together. You're better off without me."

"I'm not better off without you," I say. My throat feels like it's about to close up. "I was miserable when I met you. Having you in my life has made me the happiest I've been in years."

"This can't possibly make you happy. Can't you see how hard it is, Susie?" he asks. His face is tear-streaked and pale. "How hard all of this is?"

"I can see it," I tell him. "I'm still here."

"You told me I was a distraction."

"I was wrong to say that. I'm sorry. I was jealous, and stressed, and I missed you."

He shakes his head. "We have to break up."

I look him in the eyes. "That's what you want?"

"No," he says wearily. "It's just what I need. And it's what you need, too."

"Don't worry about what I need," I whisper, thinking, *What I need is not to lose you.*

"You want to help?" he asks. I nod. "Then don't do what you do—don't fight. I want to recover, and I know it sounds selfish, but it will be so much harder if I have to worry about someone else."

I let go of his hand and sit back, hugging myself as if to protect against a sudden chill. Every scrap of feeling inside me recoils against this, but I'm not the only person in this relationship. The thought of the tie that binds us breaking and falling away is so awful I can barely stand it.

It's a struggle to figure out how to respond. I can't say what I want to say, which is that I don't want to let him go. But as I play through every other thought that whirls through my head, imagining them coming out of my mouth, they sound so inadequate. I dig my nails into my palms to keep from tearing up and say: "Okay."

"Okay?" His shoulders slump, like he's disappointed, and I wonder if there was a small part of him that wanted me to fight. But maybe I'm seeing what I want to see.

"It's not selfish, wanting to focus on your recovery," I assure him, relieved to have gained control of my tongue. The more I say, the stronger I feel, because I just realized something completely obvious—I don't have to be his girlfriend to love him. "I want that for you, too. I want everything for you, Harry. Whatever will make you healthy and happy, you deserve to have it."

"Thanks, Susie," he says, staring at his hands on the table.

I force some lightness into my voice. "But I'm still your best friend. And best friends visit each other in the hospital. So I'll be here on Tuesday and you better brush your hair and wear your best shirt because you're not fit for company looking like this, and now that I'm not your girlfriend, I don't have to put up with that crap anymore."

Harry laughs. It's a soft, breathy chuckle, nothing like his normal happy laugh, but hearing it is worth the pain of knowing that we're breaking up.

"You're tough," he says. I kiss him on the forehead, which he doesn't so much allow as endure. "If you change your mind, that's okay."

"See you Tuesday," I say.

I don't remember deciding to stand, but suddenly I'm on my feet. Mom takes this as her cue, and in a second she's by my side. Our goodbyes feel absurdly formal and hurried. Mom cleans up the torn Red Vines and pockets the pieces, along with the abandoned package. When we're halfway out the door, I look back at Harry. He's staring out the window again.

Mom waits until we return to the nurses' station to take my hand and pull me in for a hug.

"I'm so proud of you, mija," she whispers, wrapping her arms around my shoulders. I close my eyes and breathe in her familiar smell of bergamot and vanilla. "I know how hard it is to see someone you love in pain."

"Do you think he's going to be okay?" I ask her, pressing my face into her shoulder.

She hesitates. "He seems determined to get well," she says. "All you can do is be there for him, in the way that he needs you." She pulls back and looks at me, smoothing my curls away from my forehead. "But you have to take care of your-self, too. You can't be strong for anyone else if you neglect your own health."

I nod, thinking of my shoulder. Pushing it before I'd healed was so stupid. "I'll be better," I promise her. "I'll do whatever Joan and Beth tell me to do. I'm done taking chances."

"I'm glad to hear it, but that's not what I mean," Mom says.

"If this is about surgery, it's too close to Trials—"

Mom shakes her head. "What Harry has been going through made me realize that it's long past time you had someone to talk to," she says. "Someone you can confide in without worrying about being judged or seeming weak. Dad and I have been doing some research. We're going to find you the right person, whatever it takes."

I expect to feel defensive, for the words *I'm fine* to leap off my tongue. But I'm relieved. The weight I've been carrying around on my back temporarily lifts, and for the first time in a very long time, I feel like I can breathe.

"Thanks, Mom," I say, hugging her tighter. "I love you."

"I love you, too," she whispers.

CHAPTER TWENTY-SEVEN

19 days until US Olympic Team Trials

A LOCKER ROOM BEFORE A MEET FEELS LIKE ONE OF THE LOUD-est places on the planet. Everyone's revved up and excited to race, chatting and yelling and laughing like nothing could possibly be wrong in the world. But I don't have the energy for any of it today. It's my first competition since Battle of the Sexes, my shoulder hurts and Harry isn't here.

I dress silently in an empty corner—struggling into my tight suit, tucking my hair under my cap, adjusting my goggles. Nobody tries to talk to me. Rumors about Harry's prolonged absence are flying through GAC, but I've made it clear that I'm not taking questions. Jessa's pissed I won't tell her anything, but I refuse to slake her thirst for gossip. The thought crosses my mind that she must miss having Amber here as much as I do, but I can't fix that.

After what happened at Battle of the Sexes, I should be

nervous about today's races. It's a small meet with some local clubs, nothing major, but there's no telling what's going to happen in that pool. Will my shoulder hold up, or will it give out? This is my last chance to test it in competition before Trials. If the pain is too great, that's it—I won't be able to recover before Omaha.

But I can't get my head in the game. Swimming seems so pointless. What am I even doing here?

All through warm-up, my body is on autopilot. I let it lead me through the sets, then climb out of the pool and curl up on a bench in my parka with the hood pulled down over my head. I don't want to see or speak to anybody. I just want to swim and go home. My mind is miles away.

When it's time to step up onto the block, I feel myself shaking out my shoulders, swinging my arms to test the pain level of rotation, cracking my neck from side to side—all my normal prerace rituals. But it's as if somebody's operating me from afar. I don't consciously decide to do anything. I'm preprogrammed, following a protocol that was coded into my limbs and muscles a long time ago.

After I touch the wall, I don't look up at the scoreboard to check my time. I know I came in first. I can tell from Beth's relieved smile that I had a good race. I warm down as instructed, then crawl back into the comforting warmth of my parka and wait in silence for the meet to end.

The end of the semester is looming, which means Harry's not going to finish it out with the rest of us, and I can tell that bothers him. He has continued to progress in his recovery, so he's transitioned into Regency's outpatient program.

This means less time at the hospital and more time at home, more time to think about where he would be if things were like they were before. I rearrange my physical therapy schedule so that I can visit with Harry in the afternoon, when he comes back from treatment.

I know it's the worst time to be skipping workouts, even if only occasionally, but the tension between Dave and Beth is suffocating, and I want to prove to Harry that swimming isn't the only thing that's important to me. That he's important, too.

"I had a physics test today," I tell him, settling on the couch with a bowl of popcorn Paula made for us. Harry's sitting opposite me, in mismatched sweats with a blanket pulled over his lap. I offer him the popcorn, but he shakes his head. "It was rough."

"How do you think you did?" he asks. He seems to be having a good day, as evidenced by the fact that I'm here. Sometimes on mud days he won't leave his bed, and he doesn't want to see anyone.

He's still not totally comfortable with telling me how he's feeling. He's convinced it's a burden to me to hear when he's having a hard time. A special language has developed between us, one that lets him communicate without making him feel too exposed. When he's struggling, it's a mud day, a day when he's slogging through the quagmire of his own emotions. When he's feeling better and has more energy, it's a good day. He rarely wants to see me on mud days.

But even on good days, he doesn't talk much. Neither of us wants to discuss swimming, so we never do.

"Fine, probably," I say. I point to myself and say, "Dumb jock, remember?"

Harry sighs. "Another semester of school missed. Can't wait to be a twenty-one-year-old senior."

"You'll make it up," I assure him.

It's clear that beneath the weary jokes at his own expense, Harry is unsure about leaving Regency. He hates it there, because he says it makes him feel crazy—his word. But it makes him feel safe, too. Paula has taken a leave of absence from work to tend to Harry, his adjusted medication seems to be helping and he's worked out a therapy schedule with his doctors, but there are still so many variables. Anything could happen. And that scares him.

He's not alone. Unused to all this as I am, I hoped that once he left Regency he'd recover fast and things could go back to the way they were before. The relentless emptiness of the place seemed to be part of what was getting him down. But Harry's depression is chemical and fierce; it's not letting go of him without a fight.

The longer Harry is home, the less I see or hear from him. It's not unusual for a week to go by with no communication at all. I check in with Paula every day, and I visit him as much as he'll let me, but more often than not he isn't feeling up to seeing people. Mud days multiply, and good days are few and far between.

When I do see Harry, it's always at his house. He never leaves it except to go to treatment. We curl up on the couch and watch a movie or reality television with his light box humming nearby. Sometimes I read him poetry, because he's often too tired to read himself.

One time, he falls asleep while I'm reading, and even though he is careful not to touch me when he's awake, his head ends up resting on my good shoulder. I'm exhausted, too, from the long workout I endured before I came over, so I close my eyes and drift off.

Twenty minutes later, I wake to find his nose pressed against my neck and his hand tucked between my thigh and the couch cushion, as if he's trying to keep his fingers warm.

His nearness is at once a comfort and a torment. The fact that his body seeks mine out in sleep is a knife in the heart, evidence of an enduring affection that cannot make any promises. I disentangle myself and leave the room quietly so I don't disturb him. There are no words to express how much I miss being with him, and how painful it is to know how much he's suffering, how far he is out of my reach.

CHAPTER TWENTY-EIGHT

15 days until US Olympic Team Trials

IN THE MIDDLE OF MAY, JOAN CLEARED ME FOR MORE RIGOR-
ous training, however reluctantly, but I still have to go to
physical therapy a couple times a week right up until I leave
for Omaha. As for the other type of therapy, Mom and Dad
have been exploring the options our insurance will cover. I
convinced them to table it until after Trials, and they agreed,
but I still see Dad on the computer late at night, scouring the
internet for the right fit.

"You know I think the safest thing would be to skip Trials altogether and take it easy through the summer," Joan
tells me during a deep tissue massage at the end of a session.

"Not going to happen," I tell her, wincing as she works
out a knot near my neck.

She sighs. "You're so fucking stubborn, Susannah. Sometimes I don't know whether to hate you for it, or admire you."

"Whichever one gets me back to where I was."

"Swimming in that meet before you were ready was the stupidest fucking thing you've ever done," Joan says. It crosses my mind to shoot back that she only says that because she hasn't known me very long, but I keep my mouth shut.

"But I've worked with professional athletes who complain a thousand times more than you do about injuries half as bad," she continues. "And I'm proud of you for sticking up for yourself—even if it *did* set your fucking therapy back."

"Look at it this way," I said. "More money for you. I don't have NBA millions but my insurance always pays on time, right?"

Joan doesn't respond to that, but she does push harder on my muscles, which I suppose is a sign that she doesn't appreciate the joke.

Returning to full workouts is like being let off a leash. I'm practically flying through the water now. But I don't just want to attend Trials. I want to crush them.

I know that my chances of making the team are slim. They take two people per event, and the competition is near-unbeatable. But if I'm going to do this, I can't admit defeat before I even set foot on that deck. *I'm going to the Olympics*, I tell myself. I'll deal with the future when I get there.

Beth believes I can do it. Dave is not so sure. It's one of the many things they continue to fight about. Their constant bickering is wearing on me. Realizing this, Amber stages an intervention.

"You need to have some fun," Amber says at lunch one Saturday after practice. It's just me, her and Jessa, who I haven't hung out with outside of the pool since April. I haven't hung out with her much inside the pool, either.

Amber arranged this lunch, supposedly because she misses

us now that she's not swimming anymore, but she's always at our house. I'd have to be stupid not to figure out what's really going on.

It bothers Amber that Jessa and I are no longer close, probably more than it bothers Jessa or me. The closer we get to Trials, the further apart we drift. I'm not the only one who's noticed Beth and Dave squabbling over me, and Jessa was never the sort of person to cede the spotlight to anyone. She resents the attention I'm getting from the coaches, and the times I'm clocking postinjury. Doubtless she assumed that when I tore my labrum I was no longer a threat to her, and my refusal to float off to whatever desolate island swimmers go to when they break seems, to her, like a sort of betrayal.

She hasn't said any of this to me, but I know her well enough to guess.

"There's a party tonight at Nash's house. We should go," Amber suggests. I look up from my salad in surprise. She quirks an eyebrow at me. "What? I'm still on all the group emails."

"I can't. Harry and I sometimes hang out on Saturdays. He might want me to come over."

"You can't jump whenever he deigns to talk to you," Jessa says in the same sharp tone she uses whenever she speaks to me these days, no matter what she says. "Have a little dignity."

I dismiss that with a shake of my head. "I want to be there for him."

"He broke up with you."

"That's not what it's about," I say defensively. "He needs to know there are people he can depend on. I want to be there *as his friend*."

"I know you do," Amber says. "But you need to take care of yourself, too."

"Don't you think you should find a boyfriend who doesn't make you feel like shit?" Jessa asks.

I bristle. "He doesn't make me feel like shit."

That's a lie. I feel like shit constantly, but not for the reasons they think. Sometimes I feel like I can go on like this for a long time, but I'm running on fumes. Swimming is all-consuming, and I'm still struggling to figure out how I fit into Harry's life.

"We're going to the party," Amber says. "Come with us."

"I don't know."

"If you're waiting on Harry, don't," Jessa says. "You'll probably end up sitting at home."

"Just say you'll think about it," Amber pleads. "It could be good for you."

"How will a party be good for me?"

"You'll dance and hang out and have fun," Jessa says. "How could that *not* be good for you?"

I don't want to go—some things never change—but I know what Jessa said is true: I'll probably end up watching TV on the couch, staring at my phone, willing Harry to call.

So later that evening, I let Amber and Nina dress me and make me up, and when Jessa honks her horn in my driveway I'm ready to go.

Nash's house is not the sort of place I'd expect a six-four, broad-shouldered swim god to live. The house is on the smaller side, with low doorways Nash must have to duck under every day. His mom has a thing for cows and they're all over the place: ceramic cow figurines, cross-stitched cow pillows, cow paintings, stuffed cows…it's like partying in a Cracker Barrel, which isn't altogether unpleasant.

It's a modest home that reminds me more of my house than the McMansions Jessa and Amber live in. I never imagined Nash and I might have more than swimming in common, and it's a bit humbling to realize I'm not the only person on the team who doesn't come from money.

"What's going on in there?" Jessa asks as we walk through the front door. Everybody has congregated in the living room and the music is blasting. It takes a second, but I recognize the song.

Amber glances at me, eyes widening. "I thought you said he doesn't go anywhere."

I push through the crowd, determined to prove to myself that Harry's not here, that the fact the stereo is blasting his Flow song is a coincidence. But there he is, eyes closed, dancing in time with the beat.

All around me, people are singing along, cheering him on as if it were nine months ago. Our teammates, who gossiped about him for a week and then forgot about him. But his spirits seem as high as I've seen them since before Battle of the Sexes, like he's absorbing the energy of the crowd.

"The Flow is back!" Avik cries from behind me. I want to throttle him. Where was he when Harry was in the hospital? I know from Paula that Tuck and I were the only people from school who came to see him.

When the song ends, Harry's shoulders slump. He heaves a big sigh and opens his eyes. I give him a small wave. He pushes through the crush of people to reach me, accepting back slaps and compliments with grace.

"Hi," he says, shoving his hands in his pockets and rocking back on his heels. His hair sticks to his sweaty forehead and he's slightly out of breath.

"Good day?" I ask.

He nods, smiling tentatively. "Yeah. Good day."

An emotion I can't identify sits like a balloon in my throat, cutting off my air supply, and I realize it's been there for weeks, slowly inflating as the pressure increased. What is going on with me? It's great that he feels good enough to go to a party and hang out with his friends. That's what I want for him. I press the heels of my hands against my eyes, digging in until fireworks burst behind my eyelids and tears wet my lashes.

"Susie," he says in surprise. "What's wrong?"

"It's fine, everything's fine," I tell him.

"You don't look fine," he says softly. "You look sad."

I take a deep breath. "I didn't expect to see you here."

"I tried calling you," he says.

I take out my phone. "It's dead," I tell him.

"I wanted to see you, and I thought maybe you'd be here, so I came," Harry tells me.

"I called you earlier today—you didn't answer."

"I was at therapy," he tells me.

I nod. "How did you know about the party?"

"Avik texted me. Why didn't you tell me about it?"

"I didn't think you'd want to come," I say. "*I* didn't want to come. Amber and Jessa made me."

It's such a relief to hear him laugh. "I should've known."

This feels so familiar, a looking-glass version of our conversation at Tuck's party all those months ago. I'd give anything to pass through the mirror and be back there. But there's no use thinking like that. Maybe that's what all these tears are about—yearning for the relative simplicity of the past.

"I'm sorry, Susie," Harry says.

"Don't be sorry," I say. "I'm happy you're here."

"It's so hot in here," he says, rubbing his temples. "Let's go outside."

He closes the front door firmly behind him and gestures to the empty porch swing. "Want to sit?"

For a while, we rock back and forth in silence. Neither of us seems to know how best to begin.

"It must've been a shock to find me here, doing the Flow, like everything is normal," he finally says. "After the way I've been feeling lately, it was a shock to me, too, that I wanted to go out and be around people. I haven't wanted that in a long time, so I embraced it. I was hoping you'd be here."

"Can I be honest?" I ask.

"Of course. Sure."

"I came here to forget for a few hours that we aren't together anymore," I say, shaking my head at the irony. "Instead, you were here, perfectly happy without me. That makes me feel... I don't know. Irrelevant, I guess. Which is stupid and selfish, I know, but I can't help it. I'm not perfect."

He balls his fists up in his pockets, as if he's trying to resist the urge to reach for me.

"I'm not happy without you. I miss you. But I miss me more, who I was when my medications were working well and I didn't feel so lonely and empty and miserable all the time. I'm trying to get back there, and sometimes—like tonight— I do. I seized the moment."

"I want you to enjoy feeling good. I miss you, too, that's all. I want to be there for you, but sometimes it doesn't seem like *you* want that."

"It's not that," he says. "Knowing that people like you care is the only thing I have to remind me what I'm fighting so hard for sometimes. But so much of this I can only do by myself. And I don't want to keep you on the hook for months or years while I sort it all out. I can't have a girlfriend right now. I can't have a *goldfish* right now."

He turns to look at me. "For the record, I don't think you're selfish. I think you're focused and driven and you're doing your best. Nobody expects you to be perfect, least of all me. You're trying to achieve something only a few people in the world ever will, and you need support, too. I wish I could give it to you right now, but I can't."

"I know," I say. "But I appreciate you saying that."

The front door creaks open and Amber peeks out.

"Sorry to interrupt, but I heard a rumor that the neighbors threatened to call the cops," she says. "Susannah, I'm going to Jessa's house. You should come."

I nod. Jessa and Amber file out the door. "Give us a minute."

"We'll wait for you in the car," Amber says. "Hi, Harry. It's good to see you."

Harry smiles at her politely, but his eyes don't leave my face.

"I know we broke up," I tell him. "I know that's what you want, and I respect it. But sometimes it's so hard to believe it's actually over."

"For now, it has to be." He looks out at the street, at Jessa and Amber climbing into Jessa's car. "Swim your race, Susie. Win it for both of us."

"When I win, you win?" I say with a sad smile.

He gathers me into his arms and hugs me tight. "Exactly."

CHAPTER TWENTY-NINE

13 days until US Olympic Team Trials

"WHERE'S BETH?" I ASK DAVE.

It's a quarter to six in the morning. Practice has already started, and Dave's swimmers are in the pool warming up. The rest of Beth's swimmers and I are huddled near the diving boards like a flock of lost ducklings. We should be in the pool, too, but hitting the water is the hardest part of every practice, and we're always on the lookout for an excuse to delay that first dive. A missing coach is as good an excuse as any.

Dave ignores my question. "Get in," he commands us, jabbing a finger at the water.

The other girls and I exchange bewildered glances. A few of them give me looks like, *Say something.* I don't know when I was elected spokesperson for this group, but I don't like the way Dave is evading the question.

"She's never been late to practice before," I remind him. "Did she say when she'll be here?"

Dave shoots me a dark look. "Stop causing trouble and start swimming. You of all people should know how important these last few weeks are. You're going to need every second, so get in. *Now.*"

I square my shoulders. "Not until you tell us what's going on with Beth."

"It's a family thing," Dave says, suddenly focused on the whiteboard where he's been writing today's sets. The way he refuses to look at us doesn't inspire much confidence.

"You're lying," I say. Maybe it's stupid to push him, but I'm fed up with this garbage. I got zero sleep, my shoulder hurts, I have my period and I'm exhausted—body, mind and spirit. I have reached the frayed end of a very long rope.

Dave fixes me with an expression that's not so much angry as astonished. It's unnerving, but then this whole thing is. The second I noticed Beth was missing, I knew that, whatever the reason, it wasn't going to be good.

"That's quite a thing to say to the person who's trying to protect you," Dave says in a low voice.

"Protect me from what?"

"The fact that your coach has abandoned you," Dave says. He drops the marker he's holding into the whiteboard's silver tray. "Beth's not coming, Susannah. She doesn't work here anymore. Now get in the pool—you're five hundred yards behind everybody else."

"That's it? She's *gone*? With no explanation." My panic level is skyrocketing. I can't do this without Beth. "She wouldn't do that!"

"Maybe you didn't know her as well as you thought you did."

I know he's saying that to hurt me, for whatever reason he feels compelled to do so, but it works. My relationship with Beth has always revolved around me. I've learned some things about her past, and once I knew who she really was I found out other things by Googling, but as for who she is now... I've never made much of an effort to find out.

Dave lifts his eyes to take in the group of swimmers behind me, twisting their goggles in their hands and shooting each other looks of discomfort.

"Time for practice," he says, and it's clear to everyone he's talking to them, not to me. They nod and hop in the pool without further protest. I'm the only one still standing on the deck.

It's not like this situation is new to them. We've lost several assistant coaches in the years I've been with GAC because they "weren't working out"—meaning they wouldn't bow to Dave's every whim. It's shocking he kept Beth around this long; I've never seen anyone stand up to him the way she did. But I'm not going to cave like the others. I head for the locker room.

"Hey!" Dave shouts. "Where the hell do you think you're going?"

"To call Beth." She wouldn't voluntarily leave, not now. Not when there's so much at stake. I need to find out what's going on.

"Don't you dare," Dave says. "You step off this deck, you don't come back. You have fifteen seconds to get in the water, or you're off this team for good. Do you understand me?"

I stare at him. "Insofar as I speak English, yes."

"Then why are you still standing here?"

"Maybe I don't want to be on this team," I say. It's not smart to tempt Dave. Right now, GAC is my only path to the Olympics. But still I say, "Maybe you'd be doing me a favor."

"Oh, yeah? Well, forget Trials, then. I'd like to see you swim in Omaha without a coach."

Trials are two weeks away. He's right—I can't go that long without coaching if I want to perform well. I can't go two days without coaching. Even if Beth was willing to work with me privately, we'd be handicapped without GAC's resources and facilities. Where could we even get pool time? That isn't the experience Beth would want for me. I don't want it for myself, either.

"Come on, Soos," Jessa pleads. "Don't be stupid."

She's looking up at me from the water. The nickname startles me. The night of Nash's party notwithstanding, Jessa hasn't been much of a friend to me lately. My already wavering resolve continues to crumble.

"But I need her," I tell Jessa.

"What you need is to get in the water and swim," Dave says. He starts counting off on his fingers. "Five. Four. Three. Two…"

I jump into the pool before he can finish. I'm angry at myself for folding, but that's what Beth would want me to do. I swim to the other end of the pool underwater, pushing off the wall and shooting beneath the lane lines as my teammates finish their warm-up overhead.

My chest feels hollow and achy, like I'm one of those children's puzzles with a giant piece missing. It occurs to me that the saying *When you have nothing, you have nothing to lose* is total horseshit. There's always something left to lose.

After practice, I text Beth and she agrees to meet me at the diner. I can't take Dave's word for it that she quit GAC without warning. I have to hear it from her. To my utter lack of surprise, his story is not the full one.

"He got sick of me challenging him, I guess," Beth says, pouring cream in her coffee. "We were arguing a lot, you know that. We're from different generations, different schools of thought. He's been in the sport for a long time, and he's so traditional..."

Beth shakes her head. "Traditions aren't all bad. Sometimes, accepted wisdom does bear out. I respect that. But that doesn't mean you should shut yourself off from any experimentation or new ways of thinking. Look at what changing your strategy did for you."

"How do we convince him to hire you back?"

Beth frowns. "I don't want to be hired back."

"Why not?"

"Because I'm good at what I do," Beth tells me, "and I don't think I should settle for being someone's assistant when I could have my own program somewhere, do things my own way without being dismissed and berated all the time."

"Do you have a new job?" I ask, feeling hurt. Was she going to leave me, Dave or no Dave?

"No," Beth says with a sigh. "But that's what I'm looking for. A place I can run according to my own philosophies, without interference. I believe in the importance of debate, but I don't want someone treating me as though my experience and opinions have no value."

Even though I'm terrified of losing her, I can't blame her. After all, isn't that what we all want? To do what makes us happy without apology or shame?

Every day, I wish it was just swimming I loved, but I have to admit, to myself if to nobody else, that the race is an important part of that love. If I only wanted to swim, I could do that alone, and no one could make me feel worthless or contemptible over it. But I want to be part of something bigger than myself. I want to compete, to win, to demonstrate the skills that I'm so proud of. To do that, I have to open myself up to the censure of the world, which will judge me according to *its* standards, not mine.

That censure, when it comes, has to go somewhere. So, it goes into me, and because of that I'm never swimming alone. It's always there, with me, living in my heart and mind like an unwanted guest who has long overstayed his welcome.

"I hope you find what you're looking for," I tell Beth. "I'm just not sure it's out there, not quite the way you imagine. This sport hates change."

She smiles—not in a condescending way, like I've said something adorably naive, which is sort of how I feel, but like she's had the same thought many times herself and refuses to accept it. "What institution doesn't?"

I take a deep breath. "I don't know how to do this without you."

Beth fixes her gaze on me. "Susannah, you were always doing it without me. I'm not some crutch that's been propping you up, and you weren't some unformed lump of clay that I molded. You are an *excellent* swimmer—you were when I met you. Yes, I taught you some important things, and I hope you'll keep training as we have been because I think it's what's right for you. But I'm pretty sure the most important thing I did was give you permission to believe in yourself by believing in you first."

"Thank you for that," I say. "For all of it."

"You are going to do amazing things," Beth says, leaning in and putting her hand over mine. "Whatever competition you find in Omaha, remember that you are equal to it. And whatever happens at Trials, believe that you have a promising career ahead of you. That is the best advice that I can give you. No amount of coaching can help you if you don't have faith in yourself. But if you ever falter in that faith, I hope you know that lots of people believe in you. Perhaps more than even you know."

That night, I lie sleepless in my bed, turning my phone over in my hand and listening to Frick and Frack purring three inches from my head. I'm desperate to text Harry, or call him. I miss the sound of his voice. We haven't spoken at all since the party, and the only thing that's done even the slightest good at distracting me is swimming. But I've started my taper, which means less time in the water and more time to think. To worry.

I wonder about Harry all the time. What he's doing. How he's feeling. I keep thinking, *Just one text*, but he told me to focus on winning my race. I owe it to both of us to try.

Still, there's no one I'd rather talk to about Beth leaving than Harry. He's not the only one who'll understand. Amber certainly does. But he's the person I tell things to in order to make them feel real.

A rustling sound surprises me, and I flinch, thinking someone is in the room, but it's Frida moving around in her cage. When I was younger, I was afraid of the dark; Dad enjoys telling scary stories, and I like them well enough in the light, but at night my imagination would spin out ghastly fantasies about vampires entering through open windows and witches flying out of closets.

I'm embarrassed to admit I never got over it, the dread the darkness brings. It's the unknown I can't stand. The inability to see. And the loneliness of lying there, waiting for dawn.

I climb out of my bed and cross the hall to Nina's room. Moonlight filtering through the blinds paints stripes across her sleeping body. The floor creaks underfoot as I make my way to her bed. She wakes, confused but calm, and peers at me through bleary eyes.

"Susannah?" She flips a piece of hair out of her face. "What's wrong?"

"Can I sleep in here tonight?" I whisper.

When we were little, I would come into her room all the time, fleeing the nightmares my own mind kicked up like dust clouds, and we would squeeze together in her twin bed. Only then, with the comfort of another person in the room, could I sleep. After we got bigger and no longer fit, she would surrender the bed to me and take a pillow and blanket to the floor.

Nina has a double bed now; we're both tall, so it'll be tight, but she lifts the corner of her comforter and I slide in beside her.

"What's wrong, baby sister?" Nina asks sleepily.

"I don't know what's going to happen in Omaha," I tell her. "I'm afraid."

She puts her arm around me and hugs me close.

"Don't worry," she says. "Win or lose, you're still our Susannah. We'll love you just the same."

Exhaustion cascades through me, dragging me away from the shores of wakefulness. As I drift off to sleep, I wonder if what my sister said is true. Will I be the same person after Trials? Or will it change me, in some fundamental way that can only be seen by someone else if they look hard for it?

When your biggest fear and your greatest dream are one and the same, once you face it, can you ever go back to the way you were before? And more important, will I even want to?

Countdown to Olympic Trials: Can This Former World Champion Rise from the Ashes and Fly to a First-Place Finish?

By Kris McNamara
Posted June 9

So much has been written (on this site in particular) about those swimmers whose names we know well. Darby Phillips, Zachariah Nelson, Maya Chen, Rodrigo Garza. You've watched them for years now, you know their times by heart. But what about the dark horses poised on the edge of something magnificent—who is writing about them?

We think there's something to be said about those swimmers who make it to Trials by the skin of their teeth, grasping for the golden ring, the ones who nobody's watching. One such swimmer is seventeen-year-old World Champion Susannah Ramos of the Gilcrest Aqualions Club in Gilcrest, Illinois. Many of you in the comments have wondered for years now if her gold in Budapest was a fluke.

There's no denying it—Ramos has a steep hill to climb. For those of us who remember her dramatic in-pool injury at the Pro Swim Series meet in Des Moines, it seems there's no coming back from that. A torn labrum is nothing we haven't seen before, and it has felled better swimmers in much less competitive times.

But the facts are these: Ramos's slowdown didn't sink her. Before her shoulder gave out, she was clocking some of her best times, out-racing some of the most promising names in the sport. She won't be the youngest female swimmer at Trials, but she's younger than most of the people we consider safe bets, and the fact that she's coming to Trials at all means she thinks she has a shot at making the team.

Unpopular opinion, but we think she's got a shot, too. If she's recovered enough, if she can swim her best and if her first time at Trials gives her a little dose of magic we've seen many times in this pool, she just might make it. So watch your shoe-ins, your two-time Olympians, your NCAA favorites. We'll be watching people like Ramos, who defied all odds to be here.

No matter what, it's sure to be an interesting show.

CHAPTER THIRTY

2 days until US Olympic Team Trials

MOM TAPS HER WATER GLASS WITH A BUTTER KNIFE. RAISING her voice, she says, "Quiet, please! I would like to give a toast."

"No, Mom, this really isn't necessary," I groan, covering my face with my hands.

My parents insisted on having a celebration before I leave for Omaha, even though—as I pointed out several times—we don't have anything to celebrate yet. I don't like being the center of attention. I'm not into birthdays, and I despise being fussed over. Plus, it feels like tempting fate. But when Mom puts her mind to something, she can't be deterred, and everyone else thought it was a fantastic idea, so I was outnumbered.

"You made it to the Olympic Trials!" Nina said when I balked. "How many people can say that?"

"Hundreds," I replied. "There will literally be over eighteen hundred swimmers competing for a handful of spots on the team."

"Handful?" Nina scoffed. "There's like fifty people on the roster."

"Not quite fifty. And half of them are guys."

"Boy, Susannah, you really know how to take the fun out of everything," Nina shot back.

That hit close enough to home that I agreed to let Mom throw me this celebratory dinner, but only if we had it at Miguel's restaurant. The food is good, and I know we'll get a family discount, which is important because Mom invited pretty much everyone we know. She even asked me, tentatively, if it was okay to invite Harry, but I didn't want to put him in the position of having to say no. I wish he were here, though.

Mom turns to me now with a big smile on her face. "I was in labor with you for twenty-one hours, Susannah, and by God, you are going to listen to this speech, you're going to be inspired and you're going to applaud at the end. Okay?"

I put up my hands. "Okay, okay. I surrender. The childbirth card trumps all."

"That's right." She stands, and I'm grateful beyond words that Miguel gave us the entire back room tonight. "I always wanted to be a mother, but when I was pregnant for the first time, and I found out we were having a girl—"

Nina wolf whistles from down the table where she's sitting with Amber. Mom tips her glass in my sister's direction.

"When I found out we were having a girl, I was nervous. As anyone who knows me can tell you, I'm not a religious person, but I prayed to a god I'm not even sure I believe in that I would be the sort of mother a little girl could look up to. I wanted to inspire my children, to make them believe, through my example and my love, that they could do anything they set their minds and hearts to."

Tears prick the back of my eyes. I have the best parents in the world, but Mom in particular inspires me every day. She works hard to give us everything we could ever want, and she never loses sight of herself. If I grow up to be half the person she is, I think that'd be an amazing accomplishment.

"It's not easy to be a brown girl in this world," she continues. "Nobody's lining up to give you anything. Nobody's inclined to cut you any slack. You have to earn every single inch on the road to success, and even then, there are people and circumstances waiting around every corner to tear you down and make you feel like you don't deserve what you want most. So that was my wish for myself, and for my girls. *Make me the sort of mother who gives her daughters something to believe in.*"

She pauses to collect herself, then says, "It never crossed my mind that my girls would be the ones to inspire me."

Mom turns to face me. "Dad and I got you something."

"You didn't have to do that," I say, thinking of all the money they've spent to get me here, how much they've sacrificed so I could have a shot.

Mom winks at me and says, "I know."

Dad pulls a box wrapped in silver paper out of his pocket and hands it to me.

"Congratulations, mija," he whispers. "We love you."

Mom gestures for me to open the gift. Inside is a small honeycomb pendant on a delicate gold chain. It's so pretty and perfect my breath catches in my throat.

"Thank you," I croak as Dad fastens it around my neck. "I love it."

"We thought long and hard about what to get you as a memento of this moment," Mom says. "I wanted it to be something you could carry with you, something you could wear, to be your armor or your badge of pride. A reminder of how far you've come, and everything you have to offer the world. But all the swimming stuff we looked at was ugly, so we had to get creative."

I laugh. I own a lot of swim swag and it is, for the most part, hideous.

"Bees are a symbol of industry and commitment, determination and teamwork. I know it hasn't always been easy, but you've given one hundred and fifty percent in the pursuit of excellence, day in and day out, year after year. You have fought and you have fallen and you have conquered and you have kept going, no matter what fate threw your way."

Until now, my tears have been relatively dignified, but I'm about to start sobbing all over the place from gratitude and embarrassment and fear of letting my parents down. I dig my fingernails into my palms in the hopes of stopping the floods. Bela notices and takes my hand, squeezing it tightly. I rest my head on her shoulder.

"Words cannot express the feeling Dad and I get when we watch you swim," Mom says. "It's pride, of course, but something more, too. It's faith. Faith in ourselves, that we were able to raise a girl who doesn't let people tell her she can't. Faith in you, that you will always fight for yourself, no matter how many times people try to make you think you're not worthy of your own dreams. And faith in the world, that there is enough room in it for everyone who wants to achieve something great."

Mom's getting choked up now, too. There are tears gathering in her eyes, which I can see through the tears in mine.

"I don't know what's going to happen in Omaha, Susannah," she says. "I can't predict the future. I can only believe in you, and trust in all the wonderful things you're made of. But I know you're going to walk out of that pool the way you walk in—with your head held high, a heart full of pride, and the faith of your loving family draped across your strong and able shoulders."

She lifts her glass. "To my beautiful daughter—our beautiful dreamer—and her beautiful dream."

CHAPTER THIRTY-ONE

US Olympic Team Trials—Day 1

AFTER YEARS OF WAITING, OLYMPIC TRIALS BARREL DOWN ON me all at once, like a train that for so long appeared far off, then suddenly comes within inches of running you over. I can't wrap my head around the fact that this is happening, that I'm here, but with every hour that passes, it becomes harder and harder to ignore reality.

Chicago is close enough to Omaha that my family can drive, but I fly with Dave and the other GAC swimmers. It's my first time on a plane since the flight back from Des Moines after I tore my shoulder, but it's the one to Texas that I can't stop thinking about, the way Harry gripped my hand, convinced we were going to crash. My mind inevitably wanders to what he might be doing now, if he's paying attention to Trials, if he'll watch me swim on TV. I resist the urge to text him when we land.

I keep trying to tell myself that this is just another meet, but it's impossible to ignore the evidence that it's not. Usually, when I travel with GAC, the group is large and rowdy, but at Trials we're a skeleton crew, each of us so tangled up in our own thoughts and anxieties that we're quiet and subdued. Jessa is here, but we don't say much to each other on the ride to the airport, or on the plane, or even as we're waiting in the hotel lobby while Dave checks us all in.

If this were any other meet, we would share rooms, and Jessa would probably be my roommate, but at Trials we each get our own. Jessa and I ride the elevator to the fourth floor together in silence. It's not until we realize our rooms are right across the hall from each other that the ice thaws between us for an instant, and we both crack a smile.

"It's a good thing we're not swimming in the same events or I'd be afraid you might kill me in my sleep," Jessa jokes. "The proximity alone would make it hard to resist."

"That's really more on brand for you, don't you think?"

She laughs. "I guess so. See you in the pool tomorrow?"

"Probably. I don't have much else going on," I say with a playful shrug.

She smiles at me, and I smile back. Our friendship might be waning, but I know that deep down Jessa wants what's best for me—as long as it doesn't get in the way of what's best for her. In these final days, I hope we can get back some of the camaraderie we lost this year, and end up cheering for each other from the sidelines.

"Good night, Jess," I say, swiping my key card and pushing open the door to my hotel room.

"Good luck, Soos," she replies.

★ ★ ★

US Olympic Swimming Trials are ten days long, and the 200 IM prelims are two days from now. That's a lot of waiting and watching other swimmers win or lose—let's face it, mostly lose. Part of me would rather get it over with, but I need every practice and I'm lucky to have a few of those left.

I recognize a lot of the swimmers here from meets and camps and teams throughout the years, but there's nobody I'm particularly close to, so I spend most of my downtime before race day with my parents and Nina. The night before the prelims, we eat dinner at an Italian restaurant filled with what seems like all the major talents from the US swimming world—former Olympians, college hotshots, even some buzzy young superstars my own age. When I look around and realize who the host seated us next to, I almost fall out of my chair.

"What's wrong?" Dad asks when he sees my face. "You look like you swallowed a bug."

"That's Darby Phillips," I hiss, angling my head behind me in what I hope is a subtle way. Mom, Dad and Nina exchange puzzled looks. "She's a three-time Olympic champion! She has seven golds, three silvers and a bronze. She's probably the greatest female US swimmer in recent history, and she's sitting five feet away from us."

"Really? You should ask for her autograph," Dad suggests.

I snort. "Uh, no."

"Why not? You might never have the opportunity again."

Nina makes a slashing motion across her throat. Mom smacks Dad on the arm and shoots him an *I can't believe you just said that* glare.

"I don't mean that you'll never go to Trials again," Dad

says. "I mean, you know, how often do you sit next to your idol at dinner?"

"She's not my *idol*," I say, flushing with embarrassment. I hope Darby Phillips is too engaged in conversation with the people at her own table to overhear any of this. "I just think she's great."

"How is that different?" Nina teases.

"Well, if you're not going to ask her, I will," Dad says. And then, to my horror, he turns around and taps Darby Phillips on the shoulder.

"Dad, no!" I cry, but it's too late. She swivels to see who's trying to get her attention.

"Hi, Ms. Phillips?" Dad says. "My name is Hector Ramos, and this is my daughter Susannah."

He gestures to me and she smiles. Darby Phillips smiles at *me*. I feel like I'm going to pass out, or maybe throw up. Either way, it'll be undignified.

"Hi!" she says brightly. She doesn't seem unnerved at all, and it occurs to me that this must happen to her a lot. I can't help but wonder if it will ever happen to me.

"Susannah is competing in the 200 IM," Mom says proudly. "This is her first time at Trials."

"Mom!" I squeak. Why would *Darby Phillips* care about some silly kid who's only swimming in one event, and probably won't even make it to the finals?

No, I tell myself, squashing the thought. *You're making it to the finals*.

"Congratulations," Darby says. She sounds genuinely pleased for me. "I'm in the 200 IM, too."

Of course she is! She's won two silvers and a gold in the event at previous Olympics.

"That's awesome," I say. What is wrong with my brain? I can barely form sentences, and everything I can think of to say is totally inane.

I wish Harry were here, I think, feeling a sudden twinge of sadness.

"Can Susannah have your autograph?" Nina asks, getting into the spirit of things—and by that, I mean my utter humiliation. She pulls a small notebook and pen out of her purse and shoves it in Darby's direction. "It would mean a lot to her."

"I'm so sorry about this," I whisper to Darby as she scrawls her name on a blank page of Nina's notebook and hands it back to me. My parents and Nina turn to their menus and pretend they're no longer paying attention.

"Why? Your family is clearly proud of you," Darby says.

I smile. "Yeah. They are."

"Well, it was great meeting you," Darby says, and starts to turn back around.

"Wait—Ms. Phillips? Can I ask you a question?" I feel so stupid, but there's something I want to know, and Dad's right: if I don't ask now, I'll probably never get another opportunity.

"Come on, call me Darby," she says.

"Okay. Darby." I dig my nails into my palm. *No fear*, I tell myself. *She's just one of the best swimmers in the world. It's no big deal.* "How did you, like, do this? For so long? I mean, these are your fourth Olympic Trials—"

"Fifth," she says. "I didn't make the team the first time."

"Your *fifth* Olympic Trials. And you had that back injury a while ago, and that bad case of mono…" I know everything about Darby Phillips's swimming history. I've probably read every blog post and article that has been written about her. "Did you ever think about giving up?"

Darby shrugs. "Of course. We all seriously consider quitting, like, once a week, don't we?"

I love the way she says *we*, like she and I are the same, even though she's so far out of my league she might as well live on the moon.

"If you want to do this for as long as I have, you've got to know the answer to two important questions. One: How hard are you willing to work? And two: Who's got your back? Do you know the answers to those questions, Susannah?" Darby asks. She frowns. "It is Susannah, right?"

"It is," I say. I glance at my family, still hiding behind their menus. "And I think I do."

"Then you already have everything you need to get where you want to be," Darby tells me. "The rest is just luck."

Tuesday is my first competition day, with 200 IM prelims starting at ten a.m. and semifinals starting at six-forty-five p.m. If I don't make it into the finals, which will be held on Wednesday night, Tuesday will also be my *last* competition day.

So it's no wonder I can't sleep on Monday night, even though my body is exhausted. I can't stop thinking about what Darby Phillips said. I know who's got my back, but have I worked as hard as I possibly could? I could've practiced more. I could've taken better care of my shoulder. I could've trusted Beth earlier, started training with her as soon as she started at GAC. I could've followed my first instinct and never fallen in love with Harry.

But I didn't *let* myself fall in love with Harry—that would've happened no matter what. All I did was allow myself to act on my feelings, and I'm not sorry I did. Our relationship was one of the most important things in my life, not in a way that hurt my swimming but in a way that enhanced it. It feels so strange to be at this moment in my career alone, considering how much more difficult it would have been to get here without him.

As we said our final goodbyes the night of Nash's party, he pulled something out of his back pocket and handed it to me—my swimming notebook, the one he gave me for Christmas. There were several pages ripped out, but all the ones he'd faithfully recorded my times on were still there. When I'm feeling lost, I flip through it, watching the numbers diminish as my times got better, remembering where I started and how far I have come. But for Harry and Beth, I don't know that I would be here—not only because they helped me, but because they believed.

On the nightstand, my phone begins to vibrate—not with a text, but with an actual call. I get so few of those, especially at this hour, that it startles me. I grab the phone. As if by thinking about Harry I managed to summon him, it's his name on the caller ID.

I hold the phone for a second, not sure if I should answer it. I want so badly to talk to him about all the things I'm feeling right now, on this night before the biggest day of my career, but I'm also afraid it will throw me off balance. I've just started getting used to his absence. Will his momentary presence shake me in a way I can't come back from by morning?

But what if something bad has happened? What if he needs me?

I answer. "Harry? Is everything okay?"

At first, there's no response, and my imagination immediately leaps to the worst-case scenario, remembering another day, another call, and everything that followed. But then I hear a voice—not Harry's, but familiar nonetheless. Freddie Mercury's voice croons through the speaker.

I shut my eyes and let "We Are the Champions" wash over me. Halfway through the second verse, I hop out of bed, suddenly energized, and mouth the words into the phone like it's a microphone. By the end of the song, my tangled curls are hanging in my face and I'm out of breath. I look at the phone and see that the call has finished.

For a second, I'm disappointed, but Harry called to play me a pump-up jam tonight for a reason—he knows my races start tomorrow. Which means he's paying attention to Trials.

When I lie back down, sleep comes easy, because I know that no matter what happens, Harry will be watching.

CHAPTER THIRTY-TWO

US Olympic Team Trials—Day 3

DESPITE YEARS OF GETTING UP AT FIVE A.M. FOR PRACTICE, I'm not much of a morning person. But on the day of a big competition my eyes always open before the sun is up and I'm unable to sleep after that. Today is no exception. I climb out of bed within seconds of waking and head to the bathroom to begin my race-day ritual with a shower, humming "We Are the Champions" as I go.

I shave every last millimeter of hair off the parts of my body that will be exposed by my racing suit. When I'm finished, I stand in front of the mirror, wrapped in a towel, and braid my thick, curly hair into a tight plait to keep it from springing out all over the place and bunching up under my cap. At least, I *try* to braid my hair, but even though I don't feel anxious or uneasy, my fingers are trembling too hard for me to do it right, so I leave it for now.

I fasten the honeycomb necklace my parents gave me around

my neck. I won't be wearing it in the pool—no jewelry allowed, and anyway, I'd be worried about losing it—but I've gotten in the habit of touching it when I need reassurance, and I want to draw as much strength as possible from the reminder of my family's love before I have to surrender it to swim.

The hotel restaurant opens at six, so I head down for breakfast alone. My family won't be up for hours yet, and I probably won't see them until after finals tonight. As I leave my room, I notice a hotel employee heading toward Jessa's room with a breakfast tray and curse myself for not thinking of that. But I don't want to be cooped up in my room this morning. My muscles feel jittery with the need to move and breathe new air.

I recognize a few swimmers in the restaurant, including—awkwardly—Darby Phillips, but I don't speak to anyone. We smile and nod at each other in understanding and sit at separate tables. I order a large breakfast that's protein-rich enough to get me through the morning, but not so heavy that it will weigh me down in the pool or make me nauseous.

Back up in my room, I remember what's convenient about having a roommate at away meets: there's always someone to help you wriggle into your suit. Women's racing suits are jammers that end a few inches above the knee, and they're tight, to make the body more hydrodynamic. I'm standing in a bathrobe and plotting how best to put it on without suffocating when someone knocks on my door.

"Oh my God!" I cry when I see Beth. "What are you doing here?"

"We had to apply for our coach badges months ago," Beth tells me, stepping into my room and closing the door. "I did a lot of the admin stuff for Dave, so I thought it might not have occurred to him to cancel mine. Sure enough..." She holds up the badge around her neck for me to see.

"Guess it serves him right," I say, hugging her. "It's so good to see you. Can you *please* help me get into this suit?"

Once I'm dressed and have tamed my hands enough to braid my hair, Beth leaves, wishing me good luck and promising I'll see her in the coaching area.

"If Dave doesn't like it, that's his problem," she says. "I'm going to watch my swimmer swim."

"Yeah, you are," I say, feeling buoyant with excitement where before there was only a strange sort of weary dread. I'm ready for this race. Even more than that—I'm looking forward to it.

There are one hundred and thirty women competing in the 200 IM at Trials, split into twelve heats for the prelims. According to the official Trials psych sheet, my qualifying time means I'm seeded fifteenth. This may be my first time at Trials, but I'm not unaware that even this relatively high rank means I'm not guaranteed to make it to the finals. The eighth-place finisher in the women's 200 IM finals four years ago came into Trials seeded eleventh, and she had the lowest seed in that group.

That reality sank in long ago. Today, I'm going to defy it.

I've been assigned to the second to last heat, so I spend most of the morning at the warm-up pool, loosening up my muscles and testing out my shoulder. Thanks to Joan, it's in pretty good working order. I don't know if it'll ever stop hurting entirely, but I feel strong and capable, which is all I can ask for after so grievous an injury so late in the game. Dave is remarkably calm as he puts me through my paces, and when I climb out of the pool, he pats me on the back and smiles.

"You're going to do great," he tells me. For a second, the look on his face makes me think he might say something else, but instead he pulls me in for a one-armed hug. I'm probably imagining it, but he sounds sort of choked up as he says again, "You're going to do great."

I wonder what he would think if he knew Beth was here, but of course I do not tell him.

I head to the ready room in the main pool, where I sit in my GAC parka with a pair of noise-canceling headphones on, blaring my pump-up music and staring at a nearby television without really watching the other heats. Darby Phillips is sitting ten feet away from me doing the same thing, but I avoid looking at her. I don't want to think about my competition.

I close my eyes and visualize the race to come—my pacing, my stroke, my breaths, my turns, over and over again until I feel breathless with imagined exertion.

When they call my heat, I get up and follow the other nine swimmers to the door, where we arrange ourselves in a line based on seed order. My qualifying time puts me in lane two—not exactly the highly coveted center of the pool, but at least I won't be riding the gutter.

As we file out onto the deck, the spectators on either side of the entrance lean over the railings with their hands outstretched. I high-five as many as I can, especially the little girls, feeling the sudden thrill of celebrity like a jolt of electricity. I smile at the cameras and wave to the crowd, then head to my lane and shuck my parka and warm-up clothes. I adjust my goggles, my cap, my shoulders, swing my arms in wide circles and jump to get my blood pumping. All those old rituals, still constant after all this time.

The whistle blows and I climb onto the block. At *"Take your mark,"* I bend to grab the front of the block with my fingers and fill my lungs with as much air as they can hold. For a half second, I close my eyes and envision myself touching the wall. The horn sounds and I dive, hitting the water with the force of a bullet and disappearing beneath the surface.

It's incredible, how fast I feel in this pool. Out of the corner of my eye I notice the underwater cameras darting along their tracks. Every time I lift my head out of the water, I hear the roar of the crowd, and the bright lights flash across my field of vision. It's the closest I've ever gotten to being a rock star on stage at the Staples Center or a starting quarterback at Soldier Field, and the buzz it gives me is almost intoxicating.

But Beth and I talked about this. I know it's an illusion. I can't trust what I'm seeing and hearing, or—even worse—let it influence what I'm feeling. The only thing I can rely on is the body knowledge I've built up over the course of the last year, my sixth sense, my north star, so I let it guide me through all four strokes until the last twenty-five meters, when I abandon all sense and break like mad for the finish. After punching the time pad, I glance frantically at the scoreboard.

I clock in at almost a full second off my qualifying time and third in my heat, with one heat left to go. A good time, but not what I was looking for, and quite possibly too slow to earn me a place in the semis. I won't know until after the last heat if I've made it, but Darby Phillips is in that heat, and so are three of the best swimmers in the country.

Back in the ready room, I grab my phone and join the crowd of swimmers watching the next race. I have a text from Beth: 6th overall coming out of that heat. You're in.

My vision swims and I turn away from the television. I feel like I'm going to collapse. Even if all ten swimmers in the heat happening right now finish with times faster than me, I'm going to the semifinals, but I'll be seeded dead last.

For a fraction of a second, I'm disappointed. Accepting a dignified defeat seems easier right now than having to claw my way past a dozen superstars just to earn a place in the finals, only to have to do it all over again for an Olympic berth. What if I'm not up to it?

"What the hell is wrong with you?" I whisper to myself. I don't want a consolation prize. I want to go to the Olympics. I turn back to the TV to catch the final seconds of heat twelve and gasp audibly in astonished relief when I see the times. I'm not going into the semis seeded sixteenth.

I'm going in seeded ninth.

"What the fuck are you doing here, Beth?"

Dave's enraged outburst carries all the way down the hall. From where I'm standing, I can see him and Beth facing off outside the entrance to the warm-up pool locker room. I want to turn around and find another way onto the deck, but this isn't something I can run from.

"Can you guys not fight right now?" I ask. "This is kind of a big day for me."

They turn to look at me, all kitted up in my cap and goggles, GAC sweats and parka, swim bag slung over my shoulder. I wonder how I must look to them, what they see in me, and it occurs to me that every coach must pour their own dreams into their most promising swimmers, even if only a little.

But I refuse to be a vessel for anyone's dreams but my own.

If they want to continue their petty squabbling, they can do it far, far away from me.

Dave rounds on Beth. "You're not supposed to be here," he says, jaw clenched, arms folded across his broad chest. "I fired you."

"I'm not here for you, or for GAC," Beth replies. "I'm here for Susannah."

"Yeah, well, Susannah doesn't *need* you," Dave says. "I've been her coach since she was a guppy. I made her a world champion. We were doing fine before you came along."

"No, we weren't," I interject. He glares at me. "Come on, Dave, we weren't! Beth helped me get here. I'm not going to let you pretend that's not true. If you want her to leave, then you can, too."

Dave stares at me, trying to figure out how serious I am, but he must realize how much I've changed, how little he really knows me now. I'm not the girl he put on that winner's pedestal at Budapest. I'm something else. Something different. A sword melted down and newly forged.

He throws his hands up in defeat. "Okay. If that's what you want, Susannah. I'm not going to waste time fighting about this when you've only got a couple of hours before the semis. But this doesn't change anything. You're still fired, Beth."

"And I still quit, Dave," Beth says, looking relaxed and pleased.

He points at me. "I'll see you on deck in ten minutes."

"So will I!" Beth calls after him.

"This is promising," I mutter, hitching my bag up on my shoulder. Maybe this was a stupid idea. Having them bicker on deck won't be much of an improvement over having them bicker in the hallway.

Beth shakes her head. "Don't worry about it, Susannah. He won't get into it with me in front of all those other swimmers and coaches. And besides, Dave's no fool—he knows you're here because of what we were able to do together. He's not going to let his pride get in the way of that."

"Yeah, right," I reply, unconvinced.

"Dave's number one goal is sending a GAC swimmer to the Olympics," Beth says. "Nothing matters to him more, and you're not his only iron in the fire. He'll leave us alone."

I should've learned a long time ago not to doubt Beth. She's right about Dave; he stands back and lets Beth take me through my warm-up. It feels so good to swim for her again, like slipping in the final piece of a puzzle. When it's time for me to go to the ready room, they walk me there together, and it makes me feel calmer, watching them pretend to tolerate each other for my sake, like it's a sign that the old me and the new me can coexist.

Or maybe I'm looking for omens in everything to escape the bruising randomness of fate. Whatever it is, it seems to be its own brand of magic. I crush it in the semifinals, squeaking through to the finals seeded eighth with a time that's faster than my prelim time *and* my qualifying time, a long-course personal best for me.

Dave agrees to let Beth stick around through the finals. I'm going to need all the help I can get, swimming in one of the farthest lanes, against seven women who could easily make it to the Olympics, some of whom have already qualified for Team USA.

I wonder how much experience they have with outside smoke.

CHAPTER THIRTY-THREE

US Olympic Team Trials—Day 4

SWIMMING IS A FAIRLY ANONYMOUS SPORT AS FAR AS THE public is concerned, but there's a pageantry to Trials that makes me feel like everyone in the country is paying attention. I make the mistake of watching recap coverage of yesterday's races. The media is trumpeting me as the dark horse of this year's Trials. Hastily assembled profiles of me revolve around my quick rise and quicker fall, then my determined climb back to elite status. It's embarrassing, frankly, and it makes me wish finals were in the morning, so we could get it over with. But no. A race like this needs to be shown in prime time.

At a loss for how to spend the time leading up to the race, I let Jessa talk me into getting a massage in the morning, provided gratis by USA Swimming, and take a walk with my parents along the riverfront. Mom and Dad are so excited for tonight's race they're practically vibrating, but Nina, who can always be trusted to provide a hard dose of reality, is more circumspect about the whole thing.

"Seeded eighth against the country's best swimmers in this event?" she says, snatching the water bottle from my hand and taking a big sip. "Damn, sis. That sounds tough. What's your fallback plan?"

Later, at the warm-up pool, I'm floating at the end of the lane when Dave bends down to talk to me privately. He's been here the whole time, but he let Beth run me through a light workout without interfering. Beth stepped out to go to the bathroom, so I guess he noticed his chance and went for it.

"How's all the attention feel?" he asks. "I assume you watched the coverage last night."

"Yeah," I say, playing with the straps of my goggles. "It's a lot of pressure I wasn't expecting."

"You know," he says, "Beth and I don't agree on much."

"Really?"

"I'm trying to have a heart-to-heart with you, and you're ruining it," he scolds me.

"Sorry. Go ahead."

"Beth and I don't agree on much, but something she said about you once stayed with me. She said that some swimmers are like goldfish: the bigger their bowl is, the larger they grow. She thought you had enough talent to be huge, we just needed to give you room to prove it. Well, this is one big bowl, Susannah." He smiles. "Time to see if she was right."

Tonight, in the ready room, it's like déjà vu. Same suit, same music blaring through my headphones, several of the same people milling around, waiting to be called for their race. But the air in here is thick with a new tension, and a sort of nervous energy that's hard to define. I feel as if I can see everyone's thoughts spiraling through the air like threads cast from a spool, their mantras and doubts, fears and hopes. I wonder if they can see mine.

None of us knows what's going to happen out there. So many races have been won and lost in this pool already. Shoe-ins have triumphed and slunk home in defeat, up-and-comers have toppled icons and faded into obscurity. But there haven't been any real surprises yet. We're all aiming for one of those two Olympic spots, but I don't just want to win. I want to take their breath away.

When I step up to the block, a calmness like none I've ever known before settles over me like a light blanket. There's a peculiar feeling in my shoulders—not pain, but rather a slight, comforting weight, as though fate has settled its hands on me. It feels like a benediction, a sign of what I've suspected since the prelims: that my destiny has finally caught up with me. Now that we're together again, my dream is ripe for the plucking.

I am going to the Olympics.

The air is alive with thousands of voices murmuring specu-latively in the vast cathedral of the natatorium, but in my head, everything is quiet. I look around, mapping these last seconds of possibility with clear eyes: the lights and the cameras, the coaches and the crowd. Judges take their places at either end of each lane, on a sharp lookout for infractions. The water rip-ples in slow motion beneath me, calling to me in a language only we share. *Come and find yourself here*, I imagine it saying.

"Take your mark," the announcer commands over the loud-speaker.

A sudden hush cascades through the arena. I bend and take the block in hand, running the pads of my thumbs over the rough nonslip coating as I remember the way Harry used to scratch his palms up before a big race. It always struck me as a strange ritual, the swimming version of an old wives' tale, for someone who wasn't superstitious and didn't usually swim to win. Maybe he wanted it more than even he thought.

I'm here for both of us. I hope he's watching.

Even as my heart tells me that I'm going to climb out of this pool an Olympian, my head can't help but tally up the strikes against me. I'm coming into this event with the slowest time of the pack by half a second, which in a race this short is a lot. My position out in the hinterlands of lane eight is one of the two worst in the pool. I have a strong IM overall, but I don't have a stroke specialty to give me an edge, not like Caitlin Pierce's sleek breaststroke or Darby Phillips's powerhouse back.

And then, of course, there's my shoulder.

I'm the youngest swimmer in the pool, which seems like an advantage until you factor in the combined experience of my rivals—how many international meets they've competed in, how every one of them has a box full of records and championships under her bed. I'm not swimming against my peers; I'm like a mortal who somehow wandered up a cliff side to Mount Olympus and is looking for a place to sit among the gods.

It was like that at Worlds in Budapest, too, but back then I was too young to grasp it fully. Now that I can see what I'm up against, I'm glad I've always had my head underwater, too self-absorbed and stubborn to take in what was going on around me. If I had known, really known, what it would mean to be here—not just what it would require or cost, but how disorienting and scary it would be to reach the summit only to have nothing steady to hold on to at the top—I'm not sure I would've had the guts to try.

But all of these thoughts dissolve the instant the water touches my skin. So many times, in the past two years, no matter the result at the end, my body has felt heavy and cumbersome in the water, but today I'm a feather coasting on a current of air, a particle of light shooting through the vacuum of space. My arms sail forward like wings, then pull back again, pushing me forward in the strong and steady rhythm of the butterfly. The ease of it is exquisite, the lack of strain or struggle, but I hardly have time to marvel at how good it feels before the first fifty meters are over and I'm into the backstroke.

Everything is going so fast I can't manage complete thoughts, only fragments that zip through my mind before disappearing. I remember Harry standing over me in the JCC pool, telling me to brush my ear with my bicep to keep my bad shoulder from pushing my stroke wide. Sharp shocks of pain telegraph down my arm, but I'm not giving in to them, not here, not now. I'll cut the whole damn thing off after this if it can hold out for two more laps.

The water churns around me with the fury of a sea in a storm, obscuring my vision so thoroughly I miss the flags at the fifteen. Instinct takes over and I flip just in time to get a strong push off the wall.

I immediately feel a shift as I switch into the breaststroke. Never my favorite, the breaststroke is a place where I shine only if you're going by technicalities. My form is good, my execution nearly perfect, but there's something bloodless about the way I swim the breaststroke that I've never been able to change. Even now, in the most important moment of my life, the spark that animated me through the backstroke and the butterfly gutters and dies. The lightness I felt in the first two laps is gone; my limbs feel thick and rubbery. I try not to panic, but I can feel myself thrashing, and in the breaststroke that will sink you—it's suddenly as if I'm not moving at all.

Water doesn't fight, water flows, I tell myself, clinging desperately to the thought like a fallen climber scrambling for purchase on a rocky cliff. I try to relax my limbs. *Be like the water. Arms like water, hips like water, legs like water, breath like water.*

A wail rises up inside of me, pressing against my ribs until I have to let it out. I scream into the water, lunging for every last foot as all the shitty things I've ever thought about myself cycle through my brain. *You can't do this. You never could. You should give up.*

I shove those thoughts away, rejecting their premise: I *can* do this and I am *not* going to give up. I'm too close. It's too possible. I'm going to gut this out to the finish.

A split second later, I hit the wall and escape into the refuge of freestyle.

Pace yourself on this one, I imagine Beth saying as I come out of my streamline. *Don't blow all your reserves.*

I resist the urge to give everything I have right away, pushing back against the illusion that a burst of speed will last me the whole fifty meters. I haven't checked my peripherals once to gauge the position of my competition; I can't spare the energy or the brain space. I can only trust what I feel: that I'm poised for a win, and all that's left for me to do is reach out and grab it.

With twenty meters left, I make my final charge. It took me four long years to get here, thousands of laps up and down the pool, hundreds of early mornings and late nights and long flights. It was hard and it was hopeless for so long, full of agony and despair. There were times when it felt literally impossible to go on, and equally impossible to quit. I pour everything I have into this last twenty meters—not for Dave, or Beth, or my parents, or even for Harry. I do it for me.

These last twenty meters, they belong to *me*.

When I touch the wall, I don't hesitate to look at the scoreboard, sure of what I'll see. It seems impossible that an outside smoke upstart like me won the whole thing, but I'm confident I snuck through in the second-place spot. I hear a shout of jubilation from my right as my eyes find my name.

7 RAMOS SUSANNAH GAC-IL 2:13.30

CHAPTER THIRTY-FOUR

35 days since US Olympic Team Trials

THE DOORBELL STARTLES ME FROM MY NAP. ACROSS THE LIVing room from where I'm sprawled on the couch with the cats draped all over me, the TV is asking if I'm still watching *The West Wing*.

"Don't judge me," I gripe. I'm alone in the house. Mom is with her study group, Dad's at the restaurant and Nina took Lulu on a hike with Amber. I want to doze to the sound of smart people fast-talking about politics—is that so much to ask?

At least I took a shower this morning, so I'm not *un*fit for company. Probably not very fit for it, either, but that's not something I can bring myself to care about right now. The cats bolt out of the room when I sit up. I go to the front door and open it without looking through the peephole, something I regret as soon as I see who's waiting on the porch.

If I had known, I would've changed.

"Hey, Susie," Harry says, easy as a summer day, as if his presence here isn't completely unexpected. He rocks back on his heels, hands shoved in the pockets of his jeans, handsome as the first time I met him. He smiles at me, and it's like the sun gets brighter in the sky.

My heart pounds against my rib cage and my whole body erupts in goose bumps. It's been a long time since I've seen him in person, but absence hasn't dampened his effect on me in the slightest.

Extremely inconvenient given the fact that he's not my boyfriend anymore.

"Hi," I reply, struck stupid with shock. "Is everything okay? How are you feeling?"

"It's a good day," he says.

His smile widens, but even the force of its beam, however diminished, can't distract from the dark circles under his eyes and the pallor of his skin. My guess is he hasn't been sleeping well. His hair is longer and shaggy; he keeps having to brush it out of his eyes, and the humidity is making it curl at the ends. He always kept it short, to mitigate the sting of constant swim cap removal, but there's no need for that anymore.

The evidence of his struggle makes my heart ache, but it's so wonderful to see him I can't quite regret whatever has brought him here.

As if I didn't know.

"I wanted to see how you were," he says, choosing his words with care. I wonder if he rehearsed his side of this conversation.

"I should've come sooner," he says, looking sheepish and,

at the same time, resigned. "I know I should've come sooner. Only I wasn't sure…"

If you wanted to talk about it. If I could be there in the way you needed me. I hear all the possible conclusions to that sentence in the silence that follows. It makes me want to weep. From the first time we met, Harry seemed to know what I needed, and what I needed him to say, even when I didn't. It was me who couldn't see past my own nose, or think about anyone besides myself. Now we're both at a loss for words.

I've spent the last few weeks building up a callus around the wound of Trials, practicing the art of forgetting, of pretending not to be devastated by the loss. I haven't watched any coverage of the Olympics, which aren't even over yet. As we stand there on either side of the door, looking at each other, trying to puzzle each other out, I begin the painful task of dismantling my walls and protections, everything that has served to separate me from the recollection of that failure and—perhaps even more painfully—the death of the certain knowledge that I would succeed.

When I feel ready, when my vulnerabilities are at the surface to be exposed, I say to him in a quiet voice, "I lost, Harry. I thought I would win and I lost."

He makes a small noise in the back of his throat. "I thought you would win, too."

My eyes hurt with the effort of holding back tears. "Were you watching?"

"Of course," he says, sadness curdling his smile. "When you win, I win, remember? I wanted it for you almost as much as you did."

"I was never going to win," I say, fighting to get the words out. It's so hard to admit, but it's the truth. Outside smoke was a fairy tale I told myself to avoid having to face the real height of the odds stacked against me. "What was it all for?"

The work. The pain. The wedge my ambition drove between us. The selfishness it surfaced in me. All the things I'm proud of, and all the things I'm not.

"What do I do?" I ask. "How do I begin again knowing it will probably all come to nothing?"

"I don't know," he says. Then he steps into the house and puts his arms around me.

I sag against his body, relieved by his solidness, his warmth. He smells the same, like Irish Spring and warm cotton, and a bit like chlorine, though he can't have been near a pool in months. It never really leaves us. Even when we abandon it, the water remains.

Harry kicks the door closed, and for a while we hold each other at the foot of the stairs. It's so quiet I imagine I can hear the blood thrumming through Harry's body, propelled through veins and arteries by the ragged beating of his heart. Though it could be my own I hear, or maybe they're synchronized so that I can't tell one from the other.

At first, I think it will be only this—a tender, almost familial embrace that ends with sad smiles and a permanent goodbye. But as the seconds tick on and neither of us pulls away, as we travel far past the marker for how long a normal hug should last, the space between us heats up despite the blasting AC and a familiar emotional energy builds—the kind that, in other days, would signal the start of something, not the end.

It startles me to feel it, and I almost give in to the reflex to resist. But then Harry's hand comes up behind my head and gently presses my face into his neck. I fill my lungs with the scent of him, feel the warmth of his skin against mine, and any instinct to move away is squashed. He strokes my freshly washed curls and murmurs something unintelligible in my ear. I sigh, threading my arms around his waist and pulling him closer to me.

The tip of his nose skates gently across my cheek as he repositions himself so he can look at me. Our faces are so close I can feel his breath against my lips. The hand that isn't holding my head settles on my lower back, and his fingertips curl into the fabric of my sweatshirt. I lift my eyes to meet his and realize I'd forgotten what a deep blue they are, practically sapphire when the light hits them, almost black when his face is in shadow. A lock of hair falls over one of them and I feel the urge to blow it out of his face, so I do, with a tiny puff of breath. It drifts back down exactly where it was before.

He smiles then, a genuine smile, and I feel like a fire has sprung up inside of me. I squeeze him tighter because that seems to be allowed, and I'm afraid to ask for more.

"Can I...?" he asks, staring at my mouth, and I can hear in his voice that he doesn't expect the answer to be yes. But it is, of course it is. I always have a *yes* in me for Harry.

I nod and then his lips are on mine, though neither of us seems to have moved. All the stiffness goes out of my limbs as I let go of the last of my reservations and my arms mold themselves to his body. For a heartbeat, everything is still, and I wonder if we've forgotten how to do this, or if he regrets it.

Then Harry's lips part and the tip of his tongue passes over the seam of my mouth. He kisses me in that familiar way, the one that feels like talking without voices or singing without music. Like swimming without a body, without bones and flesh to slow you down—weightless and painless and free.

I cup his cheeks in my hands and the heat of his skin

scorches my palms. I'm burning up, too, suffocating beneath too many layers. I pull away from Harry, noticing as I do that he doesn't open his eyes when he feels me gone, but waits, knowing I'll be back. The sight of that unquestioning trust squeezes my heart in a pleasantly painful way.

I nuzzle his jaw and whisper, "Come with me."

He opens his eyes as my words sink in and I take his hand. There's a question in them, and I reply with a silent answer of my own, a brief smile that's half permission and half pleading. His fingers tighten around mine as we climb the stairs with careful, measured steps, feigning calm as our hearts pulse in our throats like dogs straining against a leash. I don't want to rush this, and I can sense Harry doesn't, either. What if it's the last time, the *only* time? I won't waste this gift by being impatient.

My room is a disaster, which I would, under normal circumstances, be embarrassed by, but Harry doesn't notice. I'm the only thing he sees as we make our way, still hand in hand, to the bed. He reaches into his back pocket but comes up empty-handed.

"I don't...have anything," he says, his voice heavy with apology. "I stopped carrying..." He shuts his eyes and pulls away with a grimace. *"Fuck."*

"It's okay," I whisper, turning his face toward mine and giving him a soft, lingering kiss. "Don't worry. I have some. The ones I bought with my mom, remember?"

I fetch the box from my drawer. "She said I should never trust a guy with that responsibility. Looks like she was right," I say with a teasing wink.

Harry laughs.

"Probably good advice with other guys," he says, wincing. Proof that he can't stand the idea of me with someone else makes my chest grow tight. *Maybe*...no, that's not what this is about. This is about us, right now, and I'm not going to muck it up by thinking too much about the future.

"But you never had to worry about that with me," he says.

"I know."

"I was always prepared in case something happened. I just... really didn't expect this to happen."

An unspoken question hangs off the end of his sentence: Is *this going to happen?* Without another word, I pull my sweatshirt over my head, taking the T-shirt underneath with it, and then I'm standing in front of him wearing just my bra and leggings.

He's seen me in far less, but he inhales sharply and runs his hands up my sides, sliding them over the curves I used to hate, the small belly no number of laps could ever get rid of. He removes his own shirt and steps out of his jeans and the next thing I know we're climbing naked into my unmade bed. Harry pulls the crumpled sheet over our heads.

We stare at each other, surprised at ourselves and each other. *Is this going to* happen? Harry clears his throat.

"You know, I can't..." He trails off, then tries again. "I'm not ready."

My face falls. "For this?"

"For more than this," he says with hard-won frankness. I can tell by the expression on his face that he thinks he's ruining this with his honesty. Nina, cynic that she is, would say he's using me for his own temporary pleasure, but that's not Harry. He would never give me anything less than everything he has, and where he is today, this is all there is.

"Right now," he adds.

I push the hair out of his eyes with a smile. How good he is, still not denying me hope. But I'm starting to understand the power of individual moments. The joy that can be found when you're not too distracted by the faraway horizon to appreciate the beauty of where you're standing.

"Harry," I say softly. "I spent the last four years of my life preparing for a two-minute race I lost by three seconds. I'm tired of worrying about the future. I just want to be here with you. *Right now.*"

Nodding, he lowers his body onto mine. I love the weight of him, the soft hair on his legs tickling my bare ones, the sharpness of his hip bones digging into mine. *He's thinner,* I think, but there's nothing to be done about it right this second. I feel effervescent, like champagne bubbles rising to the surface of a glass, and grow impatient, but Harry touches me so slowly, determined not to rush.

Gradually, I relax and learn to match his pace, but not before noting that his hands are shaking, gratifying proof of his own desperation. I sigh as he kisses my throat, my collarbone, the space between my breasts, letting myself drown happily in the sensation of knowing someone loves the body that I never could.

As it turns out, the first time is *not* the only time, or the last, which is good because it was awkward and kind of uncomfortable. I thought we knew each other's bodies well, but it turns out there are still things to discover.

We linger in bed all afternoon. Eventually, I glance at the clock and realize how late it is. Seeing Harry sneak out of my bedroom wouldn't shock Nina, but Dad's shift at the restaurant will be ending soon and Mom could be back from study group any second.

"We should get up," I tell Harry, who rolls away from me

with a groan. I rest a hand on his chest. "You probably need to go."

He nods and bends over the edge of the bed in search of his clothes. He dresses slowly, pausing several times to kiss me. I can tell he doesn't want to leave. My throat tightens at the thought of watching him walk out the door, but I know it can't be any other way.

"How come you weren't at practice?" he asks. His voice is rough, like he hasn't used it in a while, but I know he has. The thought makes me smile.

"It's Sunday," I remind him.

"The days kind of run together," he says with a shrug.

"If you thought I'd be at practice, why did you come over?"

Harry shoots me a sheepish grin. "Cowardice?"

I smack him with a pillow. "What were you going to do if I wasn't here, leave a note?"

"It was supposed to be a dry run!" he cries, grabbing a second pillow and returning the blow. "I was going to come back."

I grab his chin and kiss him. "You're not a coward. I think you're the bravest person I know."

He shakes his head. "No, Susie, *you* are the bravest person you know."

The crushing weight of my failure at Trials drops all at once. I can feel it in my shoulders, my arms, my back—it's a physical thing, a never-ending full-body wince. I wipe my eyes.

"Not brave," I say. "Just stubborn."

"They're not mutually exclusive." He releases a deep breath and puts his arm around my bare shoulders. "What's next? Four more years?"

"I...don't know," I lie, but it feels wrong. *Tell him*, a voice in my head insists. *If anyone will understand, he will.* I clutch

Harry's hand in mine so hard it must hurt, but he doesn't shake me off.

Suddenly, he stiffens. I follow his gaze to the wall, and the empty display where my trophies and medals and ribbons once lived. "You took them down," he whispers.

"Harry," I say in a voice so low he puts his head down to hear me better. "I think I'm done."

He nods, processing this. "Are you sure?"

"No," I say, swallowing hard.

He hugs me as I start to weep. It feels so good to be near him; I want to burrow in deeper, get as close as I can get. He rocks me in a soothing rhythm, like you would a child, and yet somehow it feels more intimate than anything we did this afternoon. That was it. The last of my walls. I feel exposed and vulnerable, dreading the moment he walks out the door, because then I have to be alone with it, this terrifying decision that I have made.

I sob against his shoulder until I'm empty and shaking. He dries my face with the edge of the sheet and presses his lips to my forehead.

"It might be interesting," he says with a casualness that seems forced, "to see what your life would be like without swimming. What you might want to do with it."

"Animal shelter," I mutter into his chest. "I saw a post online. They're looking for volunteers."

The force of his laughter vibrates through me. "I knew you'd already have a plan!" he crows. He hugs me tighter. "Never change, Susie. I mean that more than anything I've ever said."

"You think I'm doing the right thing?" I ask, lifting my head so I can see his face.

"I think you won't know until you do it," Harry says.

"Mom and Dad found me a therapist," I tell him. "Someone to talk to about everything that's happened over the past few years. I'm still getting used to it, but...it is making me feel better."

He nods. "That's great. I'm glad you have someone. Talking helps."

"It's what made me realize that I have to do this," I tell him. "I've always been an anxious person, but all the pressure I put on myself made it so much worse. I need to give my shoulder time to heal, and I need to figure out who I am outside of the pool."

"Well, I know that person," he replies, kissing my bad shoulder tenderly. "And I'm excited for you to meet her."

Harry and I say our goodbyes in my room, because I know that if I go downstairs with him, if I walk him out, that I'll follow him to his car, then wait in the street until his taillights disappear around the corner, and that all strikes me as both inevitable and extremely sad.

He kisses me one last time, then leaves, shutting the door firmly behind him. I press my face against it and close my eyes, wondering if he's standing on the other side, fighting his own instinct to come back. It takes longer than it should for the front door to slam and his car to start up. When I look out the window, he's gone.

I sit down on my bed and glance at my swim bag, which is already packed for tomorrow. I take a deep breath, release it, then reach for my phone and set an alarm for four a.m.

CHAPTER THIRTY-FIVE

36 days since US Olympic Team Trials

DURING THE WINTER, I LIVE MY LIFE IN DARKNESS. WITH SUCH short days, the sun is down when I wake up and it's down when I leave evening practice, and I'm in school between, so the only glimpses of daylight I see come through the occasional window.

It's miserable, sometimes. I don't think I realized that until today, when I arrive at the natatorium around five a.m. and the sun is already starting to paint the sky with rosy fingers, reflecting off the green glass surrounding the pool deck, beautiful and bright. Practice doesn't start for another half hour, and mine is the only car in the lot besides Dave's.

In another universe, he wouldn't be here. He would have a swimmer in the Olympics. He'd be halfway across the world. But Jessa failed to make the team, and so did the handful of other GAC swimmers who competed in Trials. Mine isn't the only dream that shattered on the deck of that pool.

The lobby doors are already open. I slip in as quietly as possible, but my footsteps echo in the stillness. School doesn't start for another month, and the place seems sterile and lifeless without the voices of the other swimmers, who are just now rolling over in their beds and shutting off their alarms.

Everything feels different this morning—or maybe it's me who is different. Yesterday with Harry was something I didn't see coming, and I'm still reeling from the surprise and pleasure of it all. All night, I held tight to the glow of being with him again, and pushed back the sadness of knowing it's really, truly over.

But when I woke up, it wasn't the loss of him that crushed me—it was the stark reality of what I'm about to do. I'm still not one hundred percent sure I have the courage to pull it off.

I wonder how school will be this year, now that everything has changed. No Nina, who graduated in June and is off to college in the fall. No Harry, who won't be coming back—he's studying for his GED and is going to enroll in community college once he has it. I probably won't even talk to Tucker in the hallways, now that our common ground is gone.

At least I'll have Amber, but she's got big plans for herself this year, and I don't know how much I'll see her.

And then there's GAC. To me, this place has always been a natatorium that happened to have a school attached and not the other way around. For the past two years, I've spent every lunch period in the commons on the other side of the pool's observation windows. I'll have to find somewhere else to eat now, but the pool won't be easily avoided, centrally located as it is. And most of my teammates still go to school here. Every one of them will be a reminder.

In the locker room, most of the lights are off, but I could navigate the labyrinth of locker bays and benches, stalls and showers blind. Out of habit, I take off my shoes when I reach the pool deck. The tile is cool beneath my feet as I walk along the length of the pool. This place is as familiar to me as the house I've lived in all my life, but with some effort I can see it the way it looked when it was new to me, cavernous and grand.

I sit on the block in front of lane five and let my legs dangle as I switch back and forth between the two perspectives. When I joined GAC, the natatorium was newly built, and it has always looked state of the art to me, but now I can see there are spots of rust on the blocks and paint peeling in places, stains on the grout and fingerprints on the windows. And yet, when I go back to the view from the past, I see a palace crafted with great cost and care for princes and princesses of the pool. Always, at the edge of my vision, *she* is there, haunting every corner of this place. The old me. Who I so badly let down.

My toes touch the surface of the water, troubling it with little ripples. I didn't expect to be alone for long, but I still jump at the sound of Dave clearing his throat nearby.

He strolls over and puts one foot up on the block two lanes over.

"You're early," he says. "And you're not dressed."

I look down at my T-shirt and jeans.

"You know what I mean," he says. "Suit up. You can help me with the lane lines."

"I'm not staying," I say. He flinches slightly, but he doesn't look surprised.

"You're quitting GAC?" he asks coolly. "I thought you might. Easier to blame the club."

"I'm retiring," I tell him.

"No, you're not," he snaps. "You want to make a gesture or have a tantrum, throw your favorite toy on the ground? Go ahead. You won't be the first and you certainly won't be the last. But you're not quitting swimming. Swimming is the only thing you've ever loved."

"No, it isn't," I say quietly, and in my head, I hear Harry telling me I'm brave. Even if he's giving me too much credit, I believe I'm brave enough to do this.

"What, Matthews? How did that work out for you?"

"Great talk, Dave," I say, sliding off the block. The boldness it takes to mouth off to him leaves me light-headed.

"Wait, stop," he says suddenly, stepping in my path. "You shouldn't quit."

"Congratulations. You've convinced me," I say flatly.

"Knock it off with the sarcasm. It's not your style." He looks me dead in the eye. "You've never given up. Not even when you probably should have. And that took you a long way. Further than some swimmers, better swimmers, ever go."

"It doesn't make me happy anymore," I tell him. "It hasn't for a really long time. I was just too stubborn and afraid to quit. But I'm trying to do a better job of taking care of myself, so I can take care of other people, too."

"Swimming isn't supposed to make you happy," he says dismissively. "It's supposed to make you someone people respect and admire. It's supposed to make you a winner."

"People already respect and admire me," I say, thinking of Mom's speech, and Joan, and Beth—and Harry, who always believed in me. "And there are more important things than winning."

"You know, at Trials, I started to believe I was wrong about you," Dave says. "Even though we didn't get what we wanted, you still placed seventh in the country, against some of the best swimmers in the world. You should be proud. I was. But maybe I was right, after all. You don't have what it takes. Not in the pool." He taps his temple. "Up here."

"If you're going to insult me, I have other places to be," I tell him. My interview at the animal shelter is this afternoon. I scheduled it knowing how hard it would be to walk away toward nothing.

But I also have an eleven o'clock appointment with my therapist. I'm nervous as hell—the last thing I want to do is keep revisiting all this misery at the exact moment I'm leaving it behind. But maybe this is the best time to do it, even though it will be hard.

Dave goes on as if I haven't spoken. "A little more luck and you could've made it to the Olympics. It could've been you on that podium with gold around your neck. And in four years, it just might be you. You've got a heart of steel, Susannah. Most people can't take the disappointment you've suffered and still go on but you did. Don't throw it away now on a fit of teenage…" He pauses, searching for the word. *"Pique!"*

"I don't care about that anymore," I say. "It was a beautiful dream, but now it's time to wake up. I built my life around it and let everything else deteriorate. I want to be a healthy person with a full life, and this—" I fling my hand out to indicate the pool, GAC, the whole sport "—makes that impossible. At least, it does for me."

He raises his eyebrows at me. "You think so?" he asks. "I think swimming saved you. Two years ago, you were drowning. And if you'd stopped then, you never would've discovered what you were capable of. Just because something is hard and requires sacrifices doesn't mean it isn't good for you. Just because a dream won't bend to your will when it's convenient doesn't mean it's not worth pursuing. Look how close you came. Nobody could've predicted that, not even me."

"Not even you, huh?"

"You were slow, and now you're fast. A little gratitude would be nice."

"That wasn't you," I say. "That was Beth. You're just the monster under my bed."

Dave shrugs. Unkind words and accusations bounce off him like he's made of rubber. He's too arrogant and conceited to bother feeling insulted. "Don't forget, I hired her, and I did it for you."

I'm not surprised Dave's trying to talk me out of quitting, but I am shocked he would say this. "That's not even true."

"I could see you and I weren't working anymore, so I thought a new coach with a different approach might jostle you out of your complacency long enough to make some improvements," Dave says. "And would you look at that? It did."

I stare at him, openmouthed. "You *fired* her."

"Well, I didn't know that was going to happen at the beginning, but I can't think only of you when I make personnel decisions," Dave says. "I thought I could have someone on my staff who didn't think like me, but it turns out I can't. Where's my credit for trying?"

My hands ball into fists and I dig my fingernails into my palms. "You couldn't have waited another *two weeks*?"

"She was there in the end," he says. "Don't go blaming that loss on me. Beth might've made you fast again, but I made you tough. Tough enough to keep going, even when it felt impossible."

I look away, toward the water. Am I tough? Maybe I was before, but now I don't think so. The hot pain of everything that happened this year has melted the steel in me that Dave claims to admire. But steel can be recast.

"You crushed me," I say, not on my own behalf but that of my younger self. The one I keep seeing in the corners of this place, the one who believed this pool was home. The one he promised to make an Olympian, and then abandoned.

"I created you," Dave says. "But there's still a lot left to do. Go get dressed, and we'll forget this conversation ever happened."

"You think that's all it's going to take? I'm not *thirteen* anymore, Dave. I'm not going to let you tear me down with bullshit backhanded compliments." I laugh, amazed I let him tell me who I was for so long. "I'm done swimming. But even if I wasn't, I'd be done swimming here. Get out of my way."

Dave raises his hands in mock-surrender, stepping aside as I pass him. Even though I know it's the right thing to do, my heart cramps at the thought of walking away from this part of my life. But I'm proud of myself for standing up to him, and getting the last word.

I should've known he wouldn't let me. When I'm almost at the locker room, he calls out, "Maybe you don't like my methods. Maybe you think I'm too demanding, too *mean*. But I'm not the monster under your bed, Susannah. You are."

I rush out of the natatorium with Dave's final words ringing in my ears. I feel like I'm running away in fear instead of striding off into the sunset (sunrise actually) with dignity. I force myself to slow down, to take a deep breath and let it out slowly. Cars are starting to pull into the parking lot, mothers and fathers, like my own parents, who've been making this early-morning drive for years just so their kids could have a shot at the shot I had. The shot I missed.

That's not true, I remind myself. There are other reasons people swim that have nothing to do with the Olympics. Harry came here every day, not to win, but to work out, and maybe make some friends. That's why Amber came—for the camaraderie, the teamwork, the fun. Swimming *is* fun. Somewhere along the line, I forgot that, or at least stopped seeing it.

My teammates shoot me confused looks, but I just smile back.

"You're going the wrong way!" Avik calls as he jogs past. I wave and continue toward the car.

When I open the driver's side door, Nina opens her eyes midsnore. She dozed off waiting for me; she's not used to being up this early. I ran into her on the way to the bathroom this morning as I was heading out. I wasn't going to ask her to come. I thought I should do this alone, but then I remembered that she was with me on my first day of GAC, because it was her first day, too, and I thought I should at least tell her what I was planning to do. She insisted on riding with me.

You might want to talk about it after, was her only explanation for wanting to drive to her old high school with her kid sister long before dawn. My heart swells with tenderness as she rubs her eyes and asks, "Is it done?"

I nod, sliding behind the wheel.

"How'd Dave take it?"

I shrug.

"Did he kidnap the real Susannah and replace her with a mute cyborg?" Nina asks with a yawn. "That sounds like something he'd do."

I smile. "He'll be fine."

Nina laughs. "I'm sure he will. And how about you? How do you feel?"

I take a deep breath and grip the steering wheel, then shift the gear into Drive.

"I feel ready," I tell her, pulling out of the parking spot and angling the car toward home. "For whatever comes next."

EPILOGUE

829 days until US Olympic Team Trials

NCAA Division I Women's Swimming & Diving Championships
Indianapolis, Indiana
Women's 200m Intermediate Medley Finals

The water is breathing. At least, that's how it seems. I've always imagined it as a living thing—benevolent and obedient and faithful. A gentle beast at first, like a pony, but over time something faster. A thoroughbred, maybe. A cheetah sprinting across a flat, grassy plain.

But there's nothing tame about the water. It can't be conquered. If anything, it's a dragon, a wild thing you've got to hold on to by its scales. If you want to ride it, you have to surrender.

I blink and everything around me comes to a standstill, like I've stopped time through sheer will. A light breeze tickles the leaves on the trees outside the natatorium and the sky is a bright, can't-look-directly-at-it blue, no clouds. The people I love are waiting to cheer me on from the stands. In a way, it's like Worlds five years ago. I'm homesick and nervous and ready. More than anything, I'm ready. For whatever comes next.

It's not five years ago, and it's not Worlds. It's not Trials, either. Still, this feels like a homecoming. I paid a heavy price to be here, but here I am, alive to the tenth power. Resurrected.

The world speeds up. The coaches clump together in their bullpen. I catch sight of my own coach and she sees me, too. She smiles at me and nods. We've talked about this race. We have a strategy. All that's left for me to do is execute it flawlessly. The pressure bears down, but it won't crush me. The steel in my heart has found a new home in my spine.

If someone had told me after I quit swimming that three years later I would find myself approaching the block at the NCAA Championships, I would've told them there was no way in hell. I said I was done, and I believed it.

I spent my junior year of high school doing all the things I missed out on while swimming: hanging with friends, volunteering at the animal shelter, working with Dad at the restaurant, studying alongside Mom and helping her prep for family parties, watching TV alone on the couch with a bowl of popcorn on a Thursday night. I even said yes when a boy from my English class asked me to prom.

So when Beth called, I didn't think much of it. We'd been in touch on and off after Trials, and I knew she was in the running for the head coach job at a club in a nearby suburb. I thought she might be looking for advice, although I couldn't fathom why. Instead, she told me she'd been offered the job, that she'd taken it—and that she wanted me to consider coming to swim for her.

I told her no, a knee-jerk reaction, and she didn't press me.

But then I did consider it. I considered it a lot. And the more I imagined getting back in the pool, the more I realized that while I loved my life the way it was, I missed my sport. Intrigued by the possibility of swimming again, but still not convinced, I drove to her facility and told her I was there to show her how slow I'd become.

"You won't want to coach me after you time me," I said. She smiled and said to get in the pool. If I hadn't been in the water when she told me the time on my 200 IM, I would've fallen over. It was much faster than I thought it would be. Our eyes met, and we both knew—I had to come back.

My only condition was that neither of us could discuss the Olympics. I didn't come back for that. I came back in the hopes of getting a scholarship to a good university. For the exercise. To flex the competitive spirit in me that hadn't seen a challenge greater than family game night in a year. But mostly, I came back because I love to swim. And not a moment too soon. I did get that scholarship, at a school with a coach whose training philosophy is similar to Beth's. It's why I'm here now.

Father Bob was right—failure *is* an intersection, but even though I took a detour for a while, I ended up on a better stretch of the same road. Most of the time, I'm happy I did. My career, like all things, has an expiration date. I hope it's far off in the future, but when it comes, at least I'll know I gave it everything I had.

I put my race face on and try not to look like I want to throw up. I bend forward and grab my toes to stretch out my back, then wheel my arms to test my shoulders—no pain. The other swimmers stare at the water, like they've left their bodies altogether, but they've just retreated into the corners of their minds to be alone in the midst of all this chaos.

My mind has the same hidden corner, but I'm too distracted to go there today. Instead, I scan the crowd, looking for a familiar face among the hundreds that have turned out to watch this race.

When my cap snapped back in the ready room, I fought the urge to see it as a bad sign. That was a GAC superstition, and GAC is far behind me now. Besides, I have plenty more, at least five blue-and-gold caps printed with my university's logo and my last name in my bag.

As I rummaged around for a spare, my hand closed around something squishy. When I pulled out the rubber duck, my breath caught in my throat. There was only one person it could be from, but I packed this bag last night and it wasn't in there.

"Flip it over," Jessa said.

I was surprised to see her standing next to me, all casual like we were fifteen years old and this was just another club meet. I knew she was here at Championships, of course; college swimming is a small world, and she's one of UT Austin's rising stars. But we haven't talked in years, and this was the first time I'd seen her in Indianapolis.

I turned the duck over in my hand. The sight of Harry's chicken scratch made my heart speed up, and what he'd written made me want to cry: *Show them outside smoke.*

"Did you put this in here for him?" I asked her, astonished. She never liked Harry. It would've been hard to imagine her doing him a favor back when we were all teammates, and after so many years, when we don't even know each other anymore, it seemed impossible.

"No," Jessa said, slipping into her parka. I didn't believe her, but for some reason I was touched by the boldness of the lie. It was so *Jessa*.

"Okay, but is he *here*?"

Jessa shrugged. Then she smiled and said, "Have a good swim, Susannah."

"You, too," I said, stunned, as she walked away. I hunted wildly in my bag for my phone, but then they called my race.

As we filed out onto the pool deck, I searched my memory for any indication from Harry that he might be coming to the championships. He was never completely gone from my life, but while I was finishing high school we would go for stretches without talking or seeing each other, not for any particular reason, but in the way that people fall in and out of touch. Whenever I did see him, all the old feelings came rushing to the surface. Even though I knew it wasn't our time, I never stopped missing him, and I never stopped loving him.

Then a few months ago, he texted me because he had finished community college and was looking to transfer to a four-year school.

I'm considering universities in California, he said, and I was wondering if you like yours.

I refused to let myself imagine that he might be at the same school as me next year, but we've been talking and texting daily ever since. I know that the year after the Olympics was hard on him, as his depression persisted and he struggled to find a combination of medication and therapy that worked for him, but he's been feeling much better over the last two years. I know he spent Christmas in London with Bruce and Paula, that he's started painting and thinks he's terrible at it but really loves it, that he worked at Wacky Waves with

Tucker over the summer and that he and Bruce are restoring his grandfather's old Mustang.

We've talked for hours on the phone and texted nonstop this spring, but he never told me he was coming to Indianapolis to see me race. I would remember that. And if he *is* here, well…what does that mean?

It's no use looking for him—there are too many people, and it's time to swim. But as I turn back to the block, as if by some sort of miracle, I glance over at the spot in the crowd where my family is sitting and there he is, standing next to Dad, waving his arms. A smile breaks over my face. Across the distance, our eyes meet, and I know what's going to happen next.

I know it when I step up to the block, when I mount it and grab the edge, one foot behind the other. I know it when I pull back like a slingshot, waiting impatiently for *Take your mark* and the frantic beep of the starting signal.

I know it, and I know Harry does, too. That's why he's here.

The crowd falls silent. There's nothing like the moment a race begins. It's the highest height of the roller coaster, the top of the drop, all potential energy and anticipation. That's probably why I've always liked the start best. If you get it right, you could be halfway home.

But even if you don't, there's always the chance you could be outside smoke. Just come out of nowhere and take their breath away.

"Take your mark," the announcer says.

Then the signal sounds.

Here we go.

★ ★ ★ ★ ★

"The credit belongs to the man who is actually in the arena, whose face is marred by dust and sweat and blood; who strives valiantly; who errs, who comes short again and again...who at the best knows in the end the triumph of high achievement, and who at the worst, if he fails, at least fails while daring greatly, so that his place shall never be with those cold and timid souls who neither know victory nor defeat."

—THEODORE ROOSEVELT

ACKNOWLEDGMENTS

My deepest and most heartfelt thanks to everyone who helped me bring this story to life: Joanna Volpe, Jordan Hammesley and all the wonderful New Leaf staff; Natashya Wilson, Bess Brasswell and everyone at Inkyard Press; and my dear friends Gayle Forman, Cambria Rowland, Nikki Pavoggi, Maggie Watts-Petersen, Mary Dubbs, Alex Bracken, Danielle Finnegan, Emily X.R. Pan, Eesha Pandit, Emilie Bandy, Nicole Rodney, T.S. Ferguson, Kendra Levin, Julie Strauss-Gabel, Jed Bennett, Bri Lockhart, Rachel Cone-Gorham, Lara Paquette and Dianna Rowland, each of whom read drafts of this book in its various forms (and under numerous titles) and/or offered me encouragement and advice along the way. Thank you also to everyone who helped me with the details—your contributions and insights have been invaluable. It's been a long and sometimes bumpy ride, so if I've forgotten anyone here, please forgive the memory lapse and know that you have my unending gratitude.

To all my teammates and coaches from my years with the Buffalo Grove Park District In-House Swim League, the Stevenson High School swimming and water polo teams and the Dublin High School swim team—my memories of our time training and competing together inspired and drove this story from its inception. I appreciate everything I learned from and with you, and I loved our time together in the water.

It's impossible to express how incredibly indebted I am to my family, who have always supported me—I am not worthy, but thanks for having my back anyway. And last, to Isaac: dream big, and know that your auntie loves and believes in you.

RESOURCES

This novel is a work of fiction, but there are many teens and adults who confront issues related to mental health in their real, everyday lives, including—but not limited to—depression, anxiety, self-harm and suicidal thoughts. If you or someone you know needs support, there are resources you can consult and people you can reach out to who will listen and help.

CRISIS TEXT LINE

www.CrisisTextLine.org
Text HOME to 741741

The Crisis Text Line provides free 24/7 support for those in crisis from a trained Crisis Counselor via text.

TO WRITE LOVE ON HER ARMS

www.TWLOHA.com

To Write Love on Her Arms is "dedicated to presenting hope and finding help for people struggling with depression, addiction, self-injury, and suicide."

NATIONAL ALLIANCE ON MENTAL ILLNESS
www.NAMI.org

The National Alliance on Mental Illness "provides advocacy, education, support and public awareness" about mental health.

NATIONAL SUICIDE PREVENTION LIFELINE
www.SuicidePreventionLifeline.org
1-800-273-TALK (8255)

"The National Suicide Prevention Lifeline provides free and confidential emotional support to people in suicidal crisis or emotional distress 24 hours a day, 7 days a week."